The Love Resort

Also by Faith Bleasdale

Rubber Gloves or Jimmy Choos?

Pinstripes

Peep Show

Deranged Marriage

Agent Provocateur

To find out more about Faith Bleasdale visit
<u>www.faithbleasdale.com</u>

FAITH BLEASDALE

The Love Resort

BCA

This edition published 2005
by BCA
by arrangement with Hodder and Stoughton
A division of Hodder Headline

CN 137891

Typeset in Plantin Light by
Phoenix Typesetting, Auldgirth, Dumfriesshire

Printed and bound in Great Britain by
Mackays of Chatham plc, Chatham, Kent

In memory of my father who knew everything
there is to know about love.

ACKNOWLEDGEMENTS

Thanks go to my agent Simon Trewin; the idea for this book was born as a result of you taking the mickey out of me. I like to think that your teasing has been incredibly useful. But also thanks for the serious things you do for me. They're quite useful too. Thanks to my editor, Sara Kinsella, who has worked so very, very hard on this book. Also, thanks to all at Hodder for your continuing support.

There are some very special people without whom I wouldn't have survived this year, so my heartfelt thanks go to, Holly, Nonie, Jo C, Lalo, Tamsin, Jo D, Keith, Charlie, Sara and Debbie. And of course, my family. Thanks to Thom, but please stop reading my mind, my mum, who is tougher than she looks and Mary who is braving the cold and holding up so well.

Thanks to my new friends who made the move from rainy London to sunny Singapore much easier than it could have been: thank you for showing me that the cocktails are just as fabulous there, and the shopping even more so.

Finally, but with the biggest fanfare, thanks to Jonathan for being such a wonderful part of my life. You make me laugh, you make me cry, you make me happy, and sometimes you make me despair but I wouldn't change a single thing. Not for all the shoes in Singapore.

I

The Love Resort is an exclusive, holiday resort for couples only,* on one of the most beautiful and romantic Caribbean islands. Magical and enchanting, the resort casts its special love spell on all who visit.

Set in acres of beautiful gardens, blooming with colour, and its own private beach with dove-white sands and sapphire-blue sea, it is the ultimate retreat for you and the one you love.

A luxurious spa, two freshwater swimming pools, a fitness centre and plenty of water sports are available in our all-inclusive package. We promise there will never be a dull moment. Those who simply wish to relax are invited to enjoy a number of love seats from where you can watch the mesmerising sunsets and whisper sweet nothings to your loved one.

Two gourmet restaurants cater for every palate. The beach front offers the finest seafood in a wonderfully romantic and intimate environment. The main restaurant serves food all day, and the buffets are designed to please every appetite.

Whether you are staying in our impressive hotel or in a luxury bungalow, your knowledge of each other will be fulfilled, and the ballroom will serve you with entertainment which will fan those flames of love.

One thing is guaranteed: in The Love Resort, Love blossoms.
Official Love Resort Brochure

'I have taken my romantic novels and brought them to life,
in a place where love conquers all and romance is a way of life.'
Anne-Marie Langdale, Owner, The Love Resort

* Note, in this instance a couple is two people of the opposite sex
who are in a relationship.

'Have you seen this?' Anne-Marie Langdale screeched at a
pitch that might break glass. Ed, her husband, having just
entered the office, contemplated backing out again. Lily Bailey,
her PR manager, physically recoiled. 'Well, well? Is someone
going to fucking well answer me?' Waving a magazine frantically, she stepped menacingly from behind her desk.

Anne-Marie was a contradiction. With her glossy, long
blonde hair that rivalled any in a shampoo advert, and a face
that housed soft, delicate features, it was amazing that the voice
belonged to her. When Ed had first heard her in full cry (some
time after the wedding), he thought he'd imagined it. He soon
came to realise he hadn't. Anne-Marie looked like a heroine
from one of the romantic novels she was so famous for writing,
but didn't sound like one. Her heroines never shouted, and they
definitely never swore, whereas Anne-Marie had a mouth like
a sewer. She was tiny – just over five foot – petite but powerful,
and frightening. She was wearing a floor-length pink chiffon
gown, beneath which her feet were characteristically bare. This
was Anne-Marie's uniform. A uniform that represented who
she wanted to be, but not who she was.

'What is it, darling?' Ed asked, in a deep commanding voice,
the result of thousands of pounds' worth of elocution lessons.
Ed hailed from Sussex and had possessed a fairly accentless
voice, but Anne-Marie had wanted to change it to the way she
imagined the heroes of her novels would speak. Now he spoke
effortlessly as his wife wanted, and couldn't remember his old
voice, let alone revert to it.

'That crappy cheap magazine. The shits. The bastards. The c***s.' She waved the magazine again before throwing it on the floor in disgust.

'Let me see it.' Ed threw a glance at Lily, who was rooted to the spot behind her own desk. He picked up the magazine, then led Anne-Marie to the sofa in the corner of the office and managed to get her to sit down. He then went to Lily's desk and opened the magazine. It was the *Traveller*, one of the UK's most respected travel magazines. They exchanged another look, took a deep breath, and began to read.

> The Love Resort is a bizarre place. Décor-wise, it looks and feels romantic, in a relatively tasteful way. Which surprised me as Anne-Marie Langdale herself is a paragon to bad taste. On the surface she has managed to capture the essence of romance and transfer it into a tangible, saleable asset. However, the people who stay at the resort often look as if they don't belong. It's full of couples (most of whom are past their prime), in garish colours, who spoil the illusion of the resort. I believe that Ms Langdale's idea was to fill the place with people who resemble characters from her own romance novels, but instead, ordinary (albeit rich) couples are allowed to step into her world for two weeks at a time.

'It compliments the resort.' Ed could see that Lily was struggling to say something positive.

'You fucking idiot. It says I've got bad taste, which is just fucking untrue. Then it says that the visitors aren't in keeping with the theme. And they're sodding well right about that. I wanted young, beautiful people in my resort, not hideous old people. Understand? Do you understand?' Her eyes bulged, almost popping out of her head.

'Anne-Marie, we do understand, honestly, darling, we do,' Ed soothed. He sighed and looked around him. Their office was a two-roomed bungalow in the grounds of the resort, while the administration offices were in the main complex. Anne-Marie felt that her office ought to be set apart, reinforcing her position. Her husband and her PR manager worked with her, but the office was out of bounds to anyone else unless they were summoned. It was large and open plan, with three desks, a sofa, a small meeting table and a separate filing room. The walls were white; the ceilings fitted with colonial-type fans, which emitted a constant low buzz. The office was sparsely furnished, the result of various feng shui experts, expensive interior designers and Anne-Marie's personal psychic.

'Well then, if you understand you'll do something about it. No wonder I can't write. No wonder I'm suffering from writer's block. It's hideous, it's all fucking hideous. You two are meant to be helping me.' She rounded on them, her face murderous. 'You'd better fix this and fast. I'm going to lie down.' She picked up the skirt of her gown and swept out of the room without a backward glance.

Anne-Marie lay in her pink circular bed with a cold compress on her head. She tried to count herself calm, as her therapist had taught her, but every time she got to the number nine, she wanted to hit something. It wasn't supposed to be like this.

Twenty years ago, she'd written her first romantic novel. It was something she'd always wanted to do, and the pleasure she got from immersing herself in romance was immeasurable. She found herself a publisher and had never looked back. In fact, now she was so far forward that the pleasure, the sheer happiness she used to feel about her work was out of her reach.

Her private line rang and she reached over and snatched up the pink handset.

'Hello.' Her voice was coated with treacle. Only a handful of people had this number; only the most important.

'Anne-Marie, darling, it's Abigail,' Abigail Bell, Anne-Marie's publisher and best friend announced, her voice reassuringly deep, with a husky edge that could be attributed to a twenty-year, thirty-a-day habit.

'Oh, thank goodness it's you. I'm utterly desolate.' Anne-Marie's voice cracked.

'But you're in the Caribbean; you're in your gorgeous, gorgeous resort. I thought you'd always be happy there.'

'But it's full of ugly people. Remember when we talked about it, when I planned it? I told you that the beautiful people would fill the place and I'd be inspired.'

'Are they really ugly?' Abigail asked.

'Far too ugly to go in my novels, and that's the problem. I can't write when I'm surrounded by such ugliness. Abigail, some of these people are . . .'

'Are what, darling? Are what?'

'Oh, I don't know if I can bear it.'

'Come on, darling, you can tell me.'

'Some of them, quite a lot of them, are fat.' Anne-Marie dissolved into tears.

'Anne-Marie, darling, you know that the book is due now.'

'I can't, I just can't . . .' Her sobs were increasing in volume.

'Then I shall just have to come out and help you,' Abigail stated. 'Now, which is the best flight, do you think?'

'Oh, thank you.' Anne-Marie's despair began to subside.

Anne-Marie felt better after hanging up the telephone. At least she would have her best friend by her side for support. Abigail understood her; she was the only one who did. Ed didn't – he didn't know the first thing about the pressure she was under, the overwhelming stress, or the expectations that she had to live up to. Oh, he ran the business efficiently and profitably, but he wasn't in tune with her emotional needs.

Then there was Lily. As well as PR manager to the resort, Lily was supposed to be Anne-Marie's personal publicist (for anything other than her books), and she didn't understand her either. Anne-Marie had wanted to sack her after she'd been there for two months, but Ed said that the contract they'd given her secured her job for two years, and so she'd have to be paid in full for doing nothing. When Anne-Marie demanded to know why she'd got such a contract, he'd physically cowered as he pointed out that Anne-Marie had set her heart on Lily and ordered him to give her whatever she wanted. Lily came highly recommended; she used to work for a film star and Anne-Marie liked the glamour that this suggested. She'd been blinded by it. But she blamed Ed; he should have stopped her.

She was almost alone, she realised. But not for long. First she would come up with an idea to get the young people into her resort. The beautiful people who would inspire her once more. People who could be in her new book; a cast of characters that would cure her writer's block. And, of course, she would have Abigail.

Anne-Marie had met Abigail Bell and her husband, Philip, after she had written her first book. They ran a dynamic young publishing company that specialised in romance. They snapped up her first book, *Only Where the Sun Shines*, for a pittance, and it was an instant hit. Since then, she had become the international queen of romantic fiction and Bell Publishing's top money-spinner. From the beginning Anne-Marie had insisted that Abigail act as her agent as well as her publisher; she was the only woman she could trust. In return, Abigail had guided Anne-Marie throughout her entire career, proving to her that she had put her trust in the right person.

After Anne-Marie had completed her fourth book and established her popularity, Abigail had told her that it was time to push herself forward into the spotlight. She laughed as she remembered how scared she had been. At that time she wasn't the woman she was now; not even recognisably. Anne-Marie shuddered as she remembered how she used to be. She'd worn her mousy hair short, and had sported glasses that were too big for her tiny face. Her clothes were dowdy and cheap, and her features sullen. She looked as if she should be writing horror novels, or at least tragedies, not romance. However, Anne-Marie had never cared about the way she looked. Not the way she had learnt to now.

Abigail had taken Anne-Marie for lunch in a small, dark restaurant, and told her that they had a problem.

'The thing is, darling, that your fans are increasing by the day and they want to meet you.'

'Well, that's good, isn't it?' Anne-Marie had asked nervously.

'Darling, it's wonderful. However, to these people you *are* romance. Your books take them out of their dull worlds and into places they can only dream of, with people they can only dream of. That's why you are gold. However, before we can launch you, at readings, signings and various conferences, we need to be sure that you don't let them down.'

'Why would I?'

'This is delicate, but the upshot is that you need to start prac-tising what you preach. You write about women who are beautiful – and you are beautiful.'

'Do you think so?' Anne-Marie was doubtful; she had never been called beautiful by anyone in her whole life. She was twenty-eight going on forty, she knew that, but what no one understood was that she had all the beauty she needed in her books. She didn't need anything else.

'Yes, without the glasses, plus a little hair work, make-up and some nice clothes. What I'm saying is that you need to look like a heroine from your books, you need to give that to your fans, because, you see, darling, you represent hope to them.'

'So I need a makeover?' Anne-Marie had never really con-sidered her appearance. She was a writer, sitting at her desk in the living room of her flat, wearing her tracksuit, or her pyjamas sometimes. She lived a solitary life.

'I am going to introduce you to a stylist who will work wonders on you. There is one more thing.'

'What?' Anne-Marie was unsure if she should be happy about the conversation or not. She wanted to be a success, she was a success, but did she want to become someone she wasn't?

'You need to get yourself a man.'

'A man?' Her eyes had widened. Anne-Marie had once dated a piano tuner who wore brown sandals with grey socks, but he was the only one. They'd had sex, twice, but not like the sex in her books. You couldn't have the passion that she wrote about with a man who wore brown sandals over grey socks, after all. Her life was lived vicariously through her books. She was every heroine she wrote about; her lovers were her heroes. The conversation with Abigail scared her. She knew that things were changing and change could be dangerous; treacherous even.

'Yes. I'll find you one. Someone who will play the hero to your heroine. Anne-Marie, it's time for you to start living the life that you were born to live.'

Suddenly and surprisingly, Anne-Marie found herself smiling. 'You think that this was the life I was meant for? Love and beauty and romance?' Her eyes widened. She believed in it, she wrote about it, she longed for it, but she didn't think she would ever have it.

'I am one hundred per cent sure of it,' Abigail had replied.

Dear, dear Abigail . . . On that note, Anne-Marie thought about getting up and writing. Her new-found optimism almost demanded it, but instead she decided to arrange a massage. And perhaps a facial. Then she'd write.

Anne-Marie sent the masseur away. The resort had a top spa but Anne-Marie preferred the privacy of being worked on in her own house, which was on the edge of the resort. She had personally designed it, although she'd left the resort to a team of architects. Set on stilts, it afforded the most wonderful view, and she had a terrace on each floor to take full advantage of it. From there she could see the whole resort; the sandy beach, the glistening sea, the luxury bungalows, the brightly coloured gardens; she could see her world. A living room, a kitchen, a bathroom and a den were on the ground floor (the den was really for Ed). Upstairs there was one enormous bedroom, two bathrooms, and two dressing rooms. She didn't need more rooms; she had a hotel for guests, after all. Not that she had many personal guests.

She looked at the clock and saw that it was time to dress for dinner. She wondered where Ed was, but suspected that he would still be in the office, trying to come up with ways of cheering her up. He was such a walkover, never had been able to stand up to her. Sometimes she wished he would tell her to shut up, and then physically take her in his arms and kiss her, but he wouldn't. And honestly, she didn't really like him kissing her. She actually didn't like him an awful lot.

As she climbed into the shower she thought about the staff. When she had been hiring, she and Ed had worked closely with various department managers so she had been able to control what the employees looked like. The activities boys, all physically buff; the waiters, all terribly handsome; the entertainment boys, all utterly divine. The women she hired (although not so many) were all pretty in an innocent way. No one with over-long nails or large chests got through her process. She wanted the place filled with maidens. The one thing they all had in common was that they were young. Young and beautiful. Toned and taut. Rippling . . .

She ensured that she saw photos of all potential staff, apart from those who worked behind the scenes: the kitchen staff and the chambermaids. Ed was in charge of the actual interviewing, and he had delegated much of that to the managers of each area, but Anne-Marie kept tabs on them all. She knew how they looked but she didn't deal directly with them if she could help it. She smiled at them when she saw them around the resort, but they were all aware that they were not to approach her, or try to engage her. They could speak to her only when and if she spoke to them. She often chose not to speak to them.

She had mental affairs with some of 'her' boys. She deserved that, although she would never act on it. She was in her forties, rich beyond her needs and still well presented. She had so many to choose from, she shuddered as she imagined it. She felt herself come alive as she pictured them in her head, although that was where they stayed. She was married, after all. For better for worse. Till death do us part.

The Love Resort had been her idea. She wanted to surround herself with the love and the romance she wrote so eloquently about. If she managed to get it to appeal to young lovers then it would be perfect. Suddenly an idea formed in her head. Things were about to get exciting. Abigail was coming, and she, Anne-Marie, would get her resort exactly as she wanted it. Then she would write about it; the best book of her life. The old people's visits would be phased out. The only reason she hadn't banned them already was because Ed wouldn't let her turn paying customers away. But soon the beautiful people would come and then she could do as she pleased. Her genius was simply astounding.

The queen of romance was back on her throne, and she thought she might even start writing the following day.

'Lock the door,' Ed ordered, as soon as Anne-Marie had gone.

'Yes, sir,' Lily replied coyly. She walked slowly over to the door and turned the key. Ed gazed at her appreciatively. She was just so damn sexy. In her thigh-skimming skirt, her high heels, and the sheer blouse that was so inviting, she was everything a woman should be. Everything his wife wasn't.

'Over here,' he commanded, and she obeyed.

'What if she comes back?' Lily approached her lover.

'With that mood, she'll be gone for hours.' He lifted her on to her desk, and removed her clothes. They made frantic love, with an urgency that reflected their limited time together.

★

'Jesus, that was amazing.' Lily buttoned up her blouse.

'It always is,' Ed replied, grinning.

'Ed, I really love you, you know that, don't you?'

'I do, and I love you.' He reached over and hugged her tightly.

'I wish it was just us. All the time.' Lily's eyes filled with tears.

'It will be, I promise. Be patient.' He kissed her tears away.

'Why did you marry her?' Lily asked suddenly.

'You know why.' Ed had told her the story many times, although it felt to him more as if he was making excuses for his decision. Which, he believed, hadn't really been his; there had been no decision for him to make. It had been a total ambush. He was a weak man who had married his wife because he was flattered, because she told him to, because he didn't have any balls.

'You were flattered, she was famous, and sweet, and you were swept up in it all – yes I know, I know, but it doesn't make sense.' Ed could see that Lily was getting agitated, which she always did when they talked about his marriage.

'Well, the truth is, darling, I was. But I was also set up.' She obviously found it hard to understand. He couldn't blame her because most of the time he didn't understand it either.

'So, it wasn't love at first sight?'

'Lily, the moment you walked into this office for your job interview, it was love at first sight. And I had never been in love before, which is the truth.'

He stared at her, absorbing her beauty. He couldn't believe his luck. Why this beautiful, plucky, twenty-nine-year-old American would be interested in him was beyond him. Fourteen years of marriage to Anne-Marie had knocked what little self-confidence he still had out of him. Lily, with her overt sexuality, her genuine interest in him and her compassion, had begun to restore it from the moment that she first seduced him.

Anne-Marie and Ed had been dining with some of their guests. It was a chore, but once a week a raffle was held and the prize was dinner with the star and her husband. The guests loved it, and paid the hundred-dollar ticket price without complaint. The dinner had been boring, and afterwards Anne-Marie had swept off in a foul mood to bed, leaving Ed to do his nightly check on the happiness of their guests. Lily had been sitting at the bar and she'd asked him to join her. They'd spoken a little about the evening's entertainment (twenty greatest love songs with Juliana), before she'd asked him to join her back at her bungalow.

'Why?' he'd asked when she'd shut the door and begun tearing at his clothes.

'You are gorgeous, clever, sweet and kind. Everything I want in a man.' As she'd kissed him in a way that Anne-Marie never had, he'd decided not to argue.

Ed stared at Lily as she worked. He couldn't keep his eyes off her. He thought back to when he was introduced to Anne-Marie. She was sweet when he met her. Dressed all in pink, she seemed girlish, with long silky blonde hair, which he later discovered was a wig. She was shy at first as well, vulnerable, and she giggled, like a girl. He was attracted to her. He wasn't in love with her; he'd never been in love with her. He knew that now he was in love with Lily.

He had stopped feeling bitter about his marriage and now he just felt sad. Anne-Marie loved only romance, and they had never had that. What they had was something they had created. Ed had been fixed up: hair, teeth, body and clothes all worked on. Anne-Marie had managed to turn him into one of her heroes and he had done nothing to stop her. Which is something he'd felt ashamed of ever since; something he was desperate to put right. Thinking about it made him strengthen his resolve.

'I'm going to leave her.' He had told Lily this before, but this time he was more determined.

'But can we really walk away?'

'We can, but not just yet. We'd be penniless.'

'I don't care.'

'But I do. I will not run off with you and be unable to give you the life you deserve.' He was determined to be a man about it, to prove to Lily that he wasn't the coward that he felt he was. He had to ensure that he could take care of her. He needed to take care of her.

'Then we'll wait for the right time.'

'We'll figure it out, I promise. I don't love her, I love you.'

2

About The Owner

Anne-Marie Langdale is a world-famous novelist and widely acknowledged queen of romance. She has published fifteen titles, all of which were international bestsellers.* The Love Resort is her way of bringing her books to life and to you.

Born in Oxfordshire, Anne-Marie had a wonderful traditional English upbringing. She was tipped for fame at an early age, her genius for writing discovered during her school days.

Beautiful, popular, outgoing, compassionate are just a few words consistently used to describe this great literary talent.

Official Love Resort Brochure

* If you wish to purchase any of Anne-Marie Langdale's books they are available in all good bookshops or at The Love Resort gift shop.

'You're late,' Anne-Marie snapped, although her tone was devoid of its customary sharpness.

'Sorry, darling, I went for a swim. It's awfully hot today.' Ed looked around him at the empty white room and noted to himself, not for the first time, that their house looked so unlived in.

'It is.' Anne-Marie barely noticed in her air-conditioned home.

'Are you OK? You had a rest,' he asked tentatively. He really didn't want confrontation tonight.

'Oh, yes, I'm perfectly fine. Ed, can you ask Lily to join us for a light supper?'

Ed's heart started pounding. What if she'd found out about them? She'd take them both to supper and skewer them. Then she'd probably eat them. Oh God, she couldn't know.

'Ed? You've turned a funny colour.'

'Sorry, sorry. Why do you want Lily to join us? I rather fancied spending time alone with my wife.'

'Oh, Ed, you're so sweet,' she replied insincerely. 'No, this is business. We will dine here tonight, away from the frightful guests, and I've got an idea that might help us.'

'I'll give her a call.'

'Tell her that I want her here at eight. Now, you get showered and changed and I'll go and organise drinks.'

Ed called Lily and relayed the message. She sounded scared, but he tried to reassure her without Anne-Marie hearing anything. He then went upstairs, through the pink bedroom, to his pink dressing room, where he discarded his clothes, before entering his own bathroom, which was thankfully devoid of pink, and getting into his shower.

Lily put the phone down and felt an involuntary shiver. Ed had said it was business, but Anne-Marie never invited her to the house to eat. What if she'd found out? She'd kill her. She'd probably invited her to supper to kill her. The worst thing was that because Anne-Marie was her boss, Lily had no choice but to go to her death. She showered and changed into a dress; Anne-Marie believed in dressing for dinner. After applying her make-up Lily checked in the mirror – pretty good; at least when she was murdered she would be looking fantastic.

'Hello, Lily, take a seat.'

Anne-Marie showed Lily to the sofa and handed her a glass of champagne. Lily took it with thanks. She was terrified. Anne-Marie being nice was scarier than her being nasty.

'Evening, Lily.' Ed approached, freshly showered.

A wave of desire passed over her and she had to hold herself back. 'Ed.'

They both looked at the floor.

'We'll eat shortly. Oh, I wanted to tell you that my dear friend and publisher, Abigail, will be arriving next week. She wants to see the resort for herself and is going to help us to overcome our difficulties.'

'That's wonderful news,' Lily responded, looking at Ed as his face froze in what looked like horror.

'I want the best bungalow made available for her.' As in the office, Anne-Marie was issuing orders.

'I'm not sure but I think that it might be booked,' Ed mumbled.

'Well, do what you can. I want her to be comfortable. The two of us will be shut away up here most of the days working, so don't worry about the office being overcrowded.'

Ed nodded and Lily wanted to jump for joy. Anne-Marie's publisher arriving would mean that she, Lily, and Ed spent their days alone together. How perfect. All thoughts of being killed were replaced by imagining what she and Ed would get up to.

'I'll check out the bookings tomorrow.'

'Shall we sit?' As Anne-Marie swept to the table, they followed her silently; Lily was still not exactly sure what it was that her employer wanted from her.

'Lily, I do hope you like oysters. So romantic, don't you think?'

'I do.' She wished that this was her and Ed, alone with the champagne and the oysters, and then they'd get naked and go to the Jacuzzi and then . . .

'Lily? Lily, did you hear me?'

She looked up and shook her head. 'Gee, sorry, Anne-Marie, these oysters are too good.' She laughed, and Ed noisily joined in.

'I said that I wish to run a competition,' Anne-Marie announced triumphantly.

'Really? What kind?' Lily tried to focus, telling herself not to look at Ed.

'A new love competition. You see, it will be open to anyone under the age of thirty who is in the first year of a relationship.'

'What?' Ed asked.

'I know, it's so exciting. Sorry, I'll calm down and try to explain slowly. We are going to launch what I'm calling "the New Love package". It's to encourage younger people who are in newish relationships. They don't have to be under thirty officially, but our competition winners will be selected on that basis. We need to be more aggressive in our quest to find the right people for our resort.'

'Anne-Marie, this competition, when will we run it?' Lily drank more champagne and sucked down another oyster. She was beginning to feel tipsy, and wondered if Ed would get away later so they could be together.

'Now. *Exclusive Holidays* is my choice of publication for the launch, and as the biggest competitor of the *Traveller* it's perfect. It'll teach them not to mess with me. Also, it's read by educated, attractive young people. We offer young couples the chance to win our new package and then *Exclusive Holidays* does an article on their time here, and then all lovely young people will want to come. Lily, you might have to pull some strings to get it in quickly. I want the competition winners here as soon as possible.'

'It might take time,' Ed said.

'I know, darling, but I'm sure Lily can pull it off.'

Lily was well aware that it wasn't a strong belief in her abilities that prompted this; it was nothing more than an order.

'How much are we going to charge for the package?' Ed sounded concerned. 'You can work that out. I just want the young people here.' Anne-Marie's eyes darkened, but then she smiled. 'So, here's how this competition works. We get a spread in *Exclusive Holidays*, describing the resort, and in return we offer two weeks, all-inclusive, to three couples, but they have to have been together for less than a year, obviously. I want new passion and romance, not the old worn-out kind we seem to get now. I don't care about the competition question – you do that, Lily – but what I do want is a photo of the couples with the entries and a brief profile. I'm going to judge this competition myself and the winners will be the best-looking couples.'

'I'll get on to it first thing,' Lily offered, trying to hold herself together. She was feeling incredibly horny.

'Are we paying for their flights?'

'Yes, economy. If you're so concerned about saving money, Ed, you can pick them up from the airport yourself.' Anne-Marie laughed nastily. 'And on that note, I'm going to bed. Ed, you can check the resort; make sure the ugly guests are happy. And tell the staff I shall be lunching in the restaurant tomorrow. My public deserves to see me occasionally, I suppose.' She shook her head and swept away.

Lily watched her go, then grabbed Ed and dragged him outside. As soon as they got to the bushes by the house, hidden from view, she undid his belt, pulled his pants down, then hitched up her skirt as she pushed him to the ground . . .

'My God,' Ed said, as they re-dressed. Lily giggled. 'Come on, I'll walk you back to your bungalow.'

As Ed led Lily to her bedroom, they were silent. They began to undress, more slowly this time, each looking at the other as they did so. Just as Lily was unfastening her skirt, the telephone rang. She snatched it up, noticing the look of fear on Ed's face and hating that aspect of their relationship.

'Lily Bailey.' She tried to smile reassuringly at Ed, who looked increasingly uncomfortable. 'Harriet?' Lily said. 'Of course, how are you . . . ?'

★

Lily hung up; Ed was lying back on the bed, his shirt open. She moved towards him and kissed him, barely able to control her glee.

'Are you going to tell me who that was?' Ed asked.

'Baby, you are not going to believe this.'

3

Visit The Love Resort – It's All About Love

Anne-Marie Langdale had a vision. The vision was of a place
that can only be described as heaven on earth, a place that
epitomises Love. As Anne-Marie describes in her own words:⋆

> If Love were a place, it would be here
> If Love was a flower, it would grow here
> If Love was the stars, they would glow here
> But Love is a feeling, so warm and true
> And as Love is a feeling, it is felt here.

Official Love Resort Brochure

⋆This is an extract from an exclusive poem by Anne-Marie
Langdale, given as a gift with every booking.

Todd Cortes sat in the boardroom, looked at the legal docu-
ment in front of him and sighed. What on earth had he done?

He was a movie star. He was a heart-throb. He was a good
actor. He had built his career on 'pretty boy' parts, but now after
proving he could take on serious roles, he was in a strong
position. However, his personal life wasn't. Todd was gay. He'd
known he was gay for as long as he could remember and despite
modern society's increasingly *laissez-faire* attitudes, Hollywood
wouldn't let him be gay. He had always been honest with the
Studios he'd worked for, and in return they had told him,
honestly, that he had to pretend to be straight. Hence a number

of fake girlfriends (normally using women that needed publicity), and a real private life so highly secret the CIA would be proud of it.

But that had all changed. He was working for a Studio who had offered him the chance to direct his next film. It was his ultimate aim; he loved acting but had been itching to get behind the camera for a while. After two big smashes for the Studio, they had given him their offer. And then they'd given him their price.

He'd had a close call – almost too close – and the result had been that the studio publicity department had ordered Todd to date Katie Ray, an actress with the biggest ego on the planet. She was a terrible actress, a horrible person, a typical diva, who, Todd knew, had used sex to get her where she was. She was everything he despised about Hollywood, although, with his lies, he was becoming so too.

Katie had been generating bad publicity due to her attitude, and the Studio still had her under contract for more films. They wanted the public to like her, to ensure that the box office reflected that, and the publicity department decided that the only way to do this was to get her to date Todd. She would also appear in the film he was to direct. Everyone loved Todd, so therefore if Todd loved Katie, everyone would love Katie. And they would also be convinced that Todd was straight. Simple. Katie agreed; she would do anything for fame. But now the situation was out of control. And Todd didn't know what to do. He also knew, deep down, that he had no choice.

Todd looked at his watch. Why was she always late? He wondered how many marriages were discussed in a meeting room. Probably more than he thought. Todd, as usual, did as he was told. He didn't believe he had a choice. His career meant the world to him, thus he had sold his soul to the Studio. That wasn't the worst of it, he mused as he took his seat, as everyone started fawning around him. The worst thing, the very worst thing, was that he was a total fraud and he was going to be living an even bigger lie.

'I'm *sooo* sorry I'm late, Todd,' Katie said, as she flung open the door and made her entrance. She went straight up to him, kissing him on the lips before plonking herself down in the chair next to him, purposely flashing as much leg as she could, and her knickers into the bargain. Todd rolled his eyes.

'At least you're here,' Harriet, their appointed publicist, replied dryly. 'As we don't have much time, I'll get straight to the point. The wedding is soon. The planner is working on the details now, and will be seeing me tomorrow to discuss it. Then we'll pick a date. The press will be given false stories, we need to keep them off the scent, and then, at the last minute, correct details will be leaked.'

'Is that necessary?' Todd paled. The publicist was following her orders, he knew that, but the way she was talking about them, it left him feeling as if he were nothing more than a commodity. Which, he admitted to himself, was exactly what he was to the studio bosses.

'It is. We need coverage. Then there's the honeymoon.'

'No one said anything about a honeymoon.' Todd trembled.

'But what a wonderful idea,' Katie added, licking her lips.

'They decided at the last minute. Otherwise it looks suspicious. So, here's what you're going to do. We did some research; we wanted something that would give you the romantic image we're trying to project. So, you'll spend two weeks—'

'Two weeks?' Todd's eyes were wide with horror.

'Yes, two weeks. At The Love Resort.'

The silence was all-consuming.

Todd didn't know what to think. The agreement he'd signed mentioned a marriage but not a honeymoon. He weighed up the chances of objecting but he looked around the table at the happiness shining on the faces of the moneymen, the people who would really benefit from this wedding, and knew that he wouldn't be able to get out of it now. So, he, Katie and The Love Resort it would be then.

A fake wedding, a fake honeymoon, and a fake bridegroom. He was losing his pride, his honour, and he was deceiving people who paid to see him in films. He didn't feel great about himself, but he told himself that it was temporary. As soon as he directed his film, made it a success, then he'd face the world with his truth and be able to stop living a lie. The problem was that the idea of coming out to the world terrified him almost as much as it terrified the Studio. He was going to have to add 'coward' to his ever-growing list of negative traits.

He snuck a look at his wife-to-be, who had furrowed her brow (how with all the Botox she was rumoured to have had, he had no idea), and seemed to be trying to look thoughtful. He resisted the urge to laugh; he wasn't sure if Katie even knew how to think.

'The Love Resort sounds real tacky,' Katie said. 'Why can't we stay on a deserted island. Of course, a luxury deserted island. You know, somewhere where we're alone. Apart from the staff.'

'The resort is owned by Anne-Marie Langdale, the famous novelist,' Harriet explained, ignoring Katie's comments. 'It's exclusive, and it's romantic. You guys will prove how genuine your love is by staying at The Love Resort. Perfect. It's for couples only; it'll probably be full of honeymooners. You'll be in luxury accommodation and we will have you flown over there by private jet.'

'Really? Private jet?' Katie crossed her legs, showing another flash of her underwear. The men in the room were all turning red. Todd looked away.

'Yes, Katie, and I've been assured that you will have your own private swimming pool and Jacuzzi, and your own cook, so that although you will be expected to be seen around the resort sometimes, most of the time you will have all the privacy that you crave. Well, as long as the publicity is done.'

'Oh, well, maybe I'll consider it.'

'No, Katie, you won't consider it, because it's already been decided.'

'So, here are the plans.' Harriet stood up in the large room. Twenty of the top studio executives stared at her. She turned to Todd and Katie. Katie was flicking her overhighlighted hair, Todd looked and felt as if he was about to be beheaded; he refused to meet Harriet's eyes. She cleared her throat. 'The wedding will take place as soon as possible, fitting in with all schedules. It'll be held at Bernie's house, which he has kindly lent for the occasion.'

'My pleasure.' Bernie Chester was the head of the Studio and one of the most powerful men in Hollywood.

'So, Bernie is also giving Katie away. We'll invite four hundred people, the closest friends of everyone involved, and everything is set. We've told the press they're going to Vegas this week. Next week, we'll leak that they're going to marry in Malibu, and so on until someone will leak the truth. We invite the press to gather outside the venue and we promise them a photo call, which will keep the fans happy at the same time.'

'We could always release pictures to the press,' Todd suggested, feeling sick now the reality was hitting him.

'Sure, Todd, but if they see you guys marrying for themselves, it will be better. We have to convince the world – you know what the speculation is like. So then you will stay the night in a hotel, before flying off to The Love Resort the following day. The press will no doubt follow you to the airport and when you're at the resort we're going to have someone come over at some point to interview you.'

'Why? It's our honeymoon,' Katie asked.

'Someone will fly over for one day. You two are about to become Hollywood's hottest married couple. Your public needs to know about your honeymoon. I'm going to choose the best publication – maybe *Entertainment* or *Movie World*.

Anyway, they will fly over, interview you, take photos and that's it. Oh, apart from the fact that you have to sing the resort's praises – that's part of the deal.'

'Harriet, I think you've done a fine job,' Bernie said.

'We'll also release publicity photos of you with Anne-Marie Langdale. Imagine the captions: "Hollywood's hottest newly-weds with the queen of romance".'

Everyone broke into riotous applause.

4

Your Holiday

If you make the wise decision to holiday at The Love Resort then your expectations will be exceeded.

Not just luxury accommodation, attentive service, the best amenities and fantastic food will be made available to you. A holiday at the Love Resort gives you more. Much more!

There is a magic here that has to be seen to be believed.* There is a wonderful experience awaiting you, which you would be foolish to miss.

Official Love Resort Brochure

* In this case there is no actual magic for you to see. It's meant in a figurative sense and the Love Resort is not liable if you don't 'see' any magic.

Lily was able to arrange the competition for exactly when Anne-Marie wanted it. The editor of Exclusive Holidays saw the competition as a huge coup and was instantly willing to shuffle some features around to accommodate it. It was a huge relief to Lily, who had been enduring increasingly threatening looks from her boss. Lily was suffering from nightmares about Anne-Marie, a knife and a garrotte. She wrote the copy, she came up with the wording for 'the New Love package', and she set the question. This was all done within a week of Anne-Marie coming up with the idea. Lily had worked on nothing else. And although she was still unsure if the competition would result in a flurry of more youthful bookings, she was determined to do her job well, and to try to keep her difficult boss happy. Despite the way Anne-Marie treated her, she still felt that she owed her. After all, she was stealing her husband. Not a natural home-wrecker, Lily couldn't stop the guilt any more than she could stop her feelings for Ed. For the first time in her life, her emotions were in control of her.

'Well, it's a good start,' Anne-Marie conceded, when Lily showed her all that had been arranged.

'We could have the winners here within two months.'

'I want them sooner.' Anne-Marie glared at Lily.

'Well, then we will have to add into the competition that those applying must be free to come at the time we want them,' Lily responded calmly. She was struggling, but determined to do anything in her power to keep her boss happy.

'Fine, add that. How about Abigail?'

'What about her?'

'Lily, do you never listen to what I say? I wanted her to have the best bungalow.'

'Ed said he was dealing with that.'

'Well, where is Ed?'

'Tennis lesson.'

'Go and tell him that I want him here as soon as he's finished. Really, Lily, I thought you'd be far more efficient than you are.'

Lily walked away, smarting. She had worked for difficult people before, but never had she been treated this badly. If it weren't for Ed, she would have walked, but she couldn't. Not until he did.

After Ed had been delivered to Anne-Marie and was being interrogated as to his intentions for Abigail, Lily sat at her desk, putting the finishing touches to the latest press release. Lost in thought, she almost jumped when the fax machine sprang into action. She picked the message up, read it and smiled. Was this a fair swap for Ed? Anne-Marie would probably think it was more than fair. She was sure that it would make her working life easier; she silently thanked the Studio for giving her this gift.

'Katie Ray and Todd Cortes are getting married,' Lily announced.

Anne-Marie looked up intrigued. 'The Hollywood stars?'

'You may have read about it. They've been dating for a few months and are just about to announce their engagement.'

'Lily, do you really think I have time for gossip?' Anne-Marie snapped.

Lily counted to five, and smiled tightly. 'Of course not. But I can get them to honeymoon here.' Lily was beginning to get excited; this would really put The Love Resort on the map with the young, rich and famous. Maybe Anne-Marie would get what she wanted after all.

'How?' Anne-Marie asked suspiciously.

'I used to work for the Studio. Anyway, if we give them a free honeymoon, luxury all the way, and spring for a private jet, then we can have them.'

Anne-Marie's face was a picture. 'They only happen to be the hottest couple on the planet. Oh my God, it'll be perfect. My book will write itself. When, when will they come?' She jumped up and jigged around with childlike excitement.

'They're getting married soon; we're getting the dates in the next couple of days.' Lily had never seen Anne-Marie this way; she guessed that Ed hadn't either, as he wore an amused grin.

'So, we can have them and the competition winners at the same time?'

'If you think that's a good idea.'

'The publicity will be unsurpassable. I want them all at the same time. Hang on. I've just thought of it.'

'What?'

'The huge success I am going to be as a result of this. Think of it: we'll be so in demand with beautiful people.'

'We are already in demand,' Ed pointed out.

'Ed, don't you ever listen? These will be the sort of people we want.'

'It'll cost.'

'It'll be worth it,' Anne-Marie stated. 'My new book will not only be full of beautiful people but the inspiration will be Todd and Katie. Can't you just see it?' Anne-Marie hopped from one foot to another, then started circling the office. 'They will be my main characters, the competition winners my supporting cast. Oh, it's so blissfully perfect. The publicity for my book can be based around this, and both the book and the resort can be assured of huge success.' She finished her speech with a curtsy, as Lily and Ed looked on, open-mouthed. Lily was unsure if she was expected to applaud or not.

'I'll do what I can,' she stuttered, as she recovered. She wasn't sure if it was a genius idea or a completely insane one for Anne-Marie to base her book around these strangers. However, she knew that it was best not to argue with her boss.

'Of course you will, dear, that's what I pay you for. Now, Ed, we need to get ready to collect Abigail.'

'Abigail, over here.' Anne-Marie waved frantically as her publisher appeared through customs. Abigail rushed over, and the two women embraced. Ed hung back; Abigail looked just as he remembered her: tall, scary, and without the hint of a conscience. Otherwise why would she have snared him into her Anne-Marie trap? God, how he hated her. This woman had a lot to answer for.

'Oh, hi, Ed,' she said, kissing the air next to his cheek and thrusting her Louis Vuitton luggage at him. He smiled wanly. It was no surprise that she treated him as if he was staff; after all, she had recruited him. She had used his sister to get him and Anne-Marie together and his flattered ego to ensure they fell in love, before finally the monster that had been hidden from him was unleashed. He had no doubt that Abigail knew exactly what she was doing to him. As a result, he held her largely responsible for ruining his life.

'You must be exhausted, let's get you home so you can rest.' Anne-Marie sounded like a schoolgirl as she linked her arm through Abigail's and they set off. Ed sighed and trailed behind them. He almost laughed out loud at the sight of them: Anne-Marie in her long flowing pale green dress and satin slippers, and Abigail in her power suit and high-heeled shoes. How she had managed to travel for ten hours like that, he had no idea. The thought of the heat and her inappropriate outfit made him feel slightly better; she would regret it as soon as they left the air-conditioned terminal. He looked around the airport at the holiday-makers in shorts, T-shirts, summer skirts, and flip-flops, and shook his head as he hurried after the two bizarre women, and out into the hot Caribbean air.

They talked non-stop in the car, Anne-Marie with her most annoying little-girl voice, and Abigail with her mouth full of gravel. Ed was relieved when the porter took the luggage and them to the bungalow. He went straight to the office to see Lily and reclaim some of his sanity. What little he had left.

'She's here?' Lily looked up at him and smiled tenderly.

'Oh, yes, the witches are once again together.'

'Ed, you're so naughty.'

'And, with her here, I'm about to be naughtier. Tonight, I'll sneak down to yours before dinner – she won't notice. Then after dinner I'll do the same.'

'Twice in one night?' Lily arched one of her eyebrows.

'Let's see if we can make it three times.'

'We might as well go for four in that case.'

Ed strode over and kissed her. She was definitely the woman for him.

'So, you see my problem,' Anne-Marie said as she and Abigail sat on the terrace outside Abigail's bungalow, sipping martinis and soaking up the sun.

Anne-Marie hitched her long dress up and put her bare feet

up on a footstool. Abigail had discarded her jacket, but looked uncomfortable in her heavy skirt and blouse. Anne-Marie pretended not to notice; she needed to talk to her; it couldn't wait.

'Oh, darling, I do. This place was going to be your inspiration, but instead it's killing your creativity. Maybe you should sell it.' Abigail wiped her brow with her sleeve.

Anne-Marie looked horrified. 'But I love it here. It's so much nicer than England. The weather is fabulous every day. My house, although small, is darling. I have food prepared for me whenever I want it, and I have my own spa. Apart from that, the beauty is unsurpassable.' She looked at the view and felt it hit her as it always did. It was, indeed, breathtakingly beautiful.

'You're not wrong there.' Abigail lit a cigarette.

'But it's the people. You see, Ed did the figures – you know he runs the business side of things – well, he charges people about ten thousand dollars for two weeks here.'

'What?' Abigail choked on her martini.

'He says that it's fair. They get all this, it's all-inclusive and they also get me. Of course, it can cost more.'

'Anne-Marie, I hate to point out the obvious, but that's your problem, right there.'

'What do you mean?'

'Philip and I could maybe afford to stay here, but when we were in our twenties, or even our thirties, we couldn't have done. You're pricing the youngsters out of the market.'

'But what about young rich famous people?'

'Well, I don't know, but there must be some reason they're not staying.'

'Yes, because it's becoming well known that it's full of old, fat, unstylish people. Oh, Abigail, I'm so disappointed.' Anne-Marie felt as if she was about to crumble.

'I understand. So, what are we to do?' Abigail violently stubbed her cigarette out.

'Well, I've already done it. I've run a competition.' Anne-Marie cheered up as she told Abigail all about it. 'And also, this is a miracle, but you'll never guess what I've pulled off.' Anne-Marie's face filled with childlike excitement.

'Well, don't keep me in suspense, I can't bear it,' Abigail said, without a flicker of emotion.

'Darling, I've said it before, you're a genius. How on earth did you swing it?' Abigail looked genuinely interested after Anne-Marie finished telling her about Todd and Katie.

'Oh, I have my ways,' she replied mysteriously. 'Anyway, I'd better get going. I'm sure you'd like to shower and change.' Anne-Marie looked at Abigail dripping with sweat, and tried not to grimace. 'I thought we'd have dinner at the house tonight. I'll get someone to escort you up. I've decided to send Ed away – he can dine with the staff or with Lily – and we'll be alone together to have a delicious gossip. Does eight sound OK?'

'Yes, I'll be ready and waiting.'

'That young man you sent to bring me up here – André?' Abigail said as they dined on Anne-Marie's terrace.

'Yes?'

'He's very attractive.'

'Oh, I know. All the staff are. I'll take you on a tour tomorrow and you'll see.'

'Anne-Marie, if the staff are so beautiful, and the resort certainly is, can't you base your book around that, and ignore the guests?'

'No, impossible. You see, they're everywhere and just as I imagine André walking out of the crystal-clear sea, his hair sparkling like a crown with droplets of water, his chest shimmering in the sun, as he makes his way slowly up the beach . . . this fat grey-haired woman in a gold lamé swimming costume makes an appearance and it's all ruined.'

'Well, let's hope that the competition winners and Todd and Katie solve the problem.' Abigail's voice was sharp and Anne-Marie was slightly puzzled.

'Oh, I am sure that they will. I'm utterly convinced of it.'

'Philip sends his love.'

'It was such a shame he couldn't come with you.' Anne-Marie was glad that Abigail's husband and business partner wasn't there. She had always found him a bit creepy, not like dear Abigail.

'Well, you know when you work together it's hard to take holidays at the same time. I'm sure it's the same with you and Ed. Anyway, Philip's really looking forward to hearing about the resort from me and he can't wait for your next book.'

'Of course he can't.' Anne-Marie's eyes glistened. 'It's going to be my best book ever.'

'Sure it is. When you do think you'll be writing it?'

Anne-Marie looked at Abigail. Was that impatience in her voice or had she imagined it? No, she was just being paranoid with everything that was going on.

'Oh, very, very soon, and there'll be no stopping me, you'll see.'

'When should we leave?' Ed asked, as he and Lily lay in bed.

'Where would we go?'

'To England, or America if you prefer – I don't mind as long as we're together.'

'That would be nice. What would we do?'

'I'd find work as an accountant, and you'd get a job in publicity. Of course, we wouldn't have as much money as I'd like . . .'

'But we'd have each other.' They giggled like love-sick teenagers. Lily made Ed feel so young.

'We wouldn't be that hard up.'

'Can we leave her?' Lily asked uncertainly.

'Yes. Yes, we can.' Ed scowled, and then smiled. Anne-Marie had given him a lot, materially, but he'd sacrificed everything for her. He had given up his career to mastermind hers. He'd looked after the business side of the resort and it would be down to him that it would make a healthy profit this year. But she had never once said thank you. And it was clear that she cared more about Abigail than she did him. Of course he could leave her, and he would.

'I told the Kitchen that we were having a working dinner here,' Ed said as he climbed out of bed and began to dress.

'Well, we have worked,' Lily replied coquettishly.

'We certainly did. Come on, up you get.'

'Do I have to?' she asked.

He went to the bed and kissed her tenderly. 'Yes. Now I shall go and fix us some drinks and ensure we're looking all business-like by the time the food arrives.'

After they'd eaten, Lily led Ed back to bed.

'You're insatiable.'

'Are you complaining?'

'No. God, no.' He didn't want to tell her about his sex life with Anne-Marie – it didn't seem right – but he couldn't help thinking about it. After the first two years of marriage, she had told him that she didn't want to sleep with him any more. She said that she needed to conserve all her passion for her books and if she had sex with him, her writing suffered. He'd been surprised and then upset, but now he was relieved. But he didn't want Lily to have to hear about it; she didn't need to.

'Ed, was it ever like this with . . . ?' Lily asked, as if reading his mind.

'Never, darling, never. What we have is something special. Let's not tarnish it, eh?'

5

To win a two-week break at The Love Resort, you must answer this question. Which famous novelist owns The Love Resort? You must also complete the tie-breaker in less than fifty words: Love Conquers All because . . . Please send your answers, together with a photograph of you and your partner, and a brief profile, to PO Box 333, London W14.

'The competition entries have just arrived by courier,' Lily announced breathlessly, as Anne-Marie let her into her house. It was just after five in the evening, and Anne-Marie had been on tenterhooks all day. Lily, caught up in the excitement and under strict orders, had sprinted up to the house.

'Fabulous. How many do we have?'

'A thousand.'

'Is that all?'

'It's a good response, particularly as it was really short notice.' Lily tried not to feel annoyed.

'I suppose.' Anne-Marie looked thoughtful, and then she smiled. 'This calls for a celebration. Lily, come in and have some champagne with Abigail and myself, and help us choose our winners.'

Lily froze in shock.

'Come on, come in.' Anne-Marie grabbed her arm and pulled.

'Hi, Lily,' Abigail barked. Lily smiled weakly. She found

Abigail even scarier than her boss. With her deep voice, her curt manner and her seeming inability to smile, she was terrifying.

'Abigail, darling, would you do the honours?' Anne-Marie asked, as she handed Abigail a bottle. She then asked Lily to collect some glasses. The three women sat on the floor, with the competition entries at their feet as they sipped champagne and prepared to choose the winners.

'Here's what we'll do. First, let's get rid of any who are too old. Anyone over thirty can go.' Anne-Marie looked at her pile. 'Of course, I bloody well couldn't specify an age, due to some sort of ridiculous political correctness. But the younger the better is the rule. Although obviously over twenty-one.'

All three of them set to work.

'OK, I've discarded quite a lot,' Lily said as her one pile became two.

'Amazing how many people are in new relationships after forty.' Abigail handed her pile over.

'Terrible. It's so, so wrong. No one in my novels starts relationships past the age of twenty-five. Right, well, that's narrowed it down a bit,' Anne-Marie said. 'Lily, pour more drinks and we'll continue.'

Lily glanced at the piles of rejections and did as she was told.

'What now?' she asked. She was more than a little uncomfortable with the situation. She was with her boss, the wife of her lover, and the world's scariest woman. It was far from ideal, although looking through the entries was actually quite fun. Especially as Anne-Marie always served the best champagne, and it was certainly flowing.

'Right, now I want to discard any couple who is unattractive.' Anne-Marie paused and regarded the other two women. 'I'm sure you can tell, but if in doubt, ask me.' She began trawling through the photographs. 'Yuk, look at this couple,' waving a photograph. 'I can't believe that they could be in love. Ugly people and love don't work. No, not at all.' She took a long drink.

Lily felt she ought to be shocked by her boss's outburst but she wasn't really surprised. Instead she picked up the bottle and refilled the glasses again.

'In my books I have rules that I follow, don't I, Abigail?' Anne-Marie was warming to her theme.

Lily looked at Abigail, who nodded.

'Her characters are always good-looking unless they are the baddies,' Abigail stated.

'Yes, because baddies can be ugly but they never find love,' Anne-Marie added.

'And women don't get drunk, and they never swear,' Abigail said, taking another drink.

Lily didn't know how she was supposed to react to this information so she refilled the glasses again.

'No, they never fucking swear,' Anne-Marie said without irony. 'And they rarely wear trousers and always look their best for their men.' Anne-Marie pushed her hair, which had come loose from its neat plait, off her face.

'Men are always tall, impeccably dressed and strong,' Abigail continued. 'And they can drink, but not to the point of alcoholism, and they rarely swear. Or if they do they say "blast", and words like that. Old-fashioned heroes, that's what they are.'

Lily finally spoke. 'Well, that's just great.'

'That's not all,' Abigail informed her.

'It isn't?'

'No, her books never contain one-night stands, any kinky sex, or graphic sex, for that matter. Men always call when they say they will; women always laugh in the right places. Isn't that right, Anne-Marie?'

'Abigail knows. She knows my books as well as I do.'

'That's great. Another drink, anyone?' Lily emptied the bottle.

'Right, well, I'm done.' Abigail downed what was left in her glass and presented her pile.

'Me too.' Lily, already tipsy, followed suit.

'What do we have left?' Anne-Marie looked at her empty glass. 'Lily, be a dear and fetch another bottle.'

Lily stood up, wondering how much she'd drunk already, and went to get the champagne.

'We still have quite a few candidates. Right, Lily, let's see what you have.'

'OK.' Lily put a serious expression on her face. She hated to admit it but she was almost enjoying herself. 'I have twenty couples. All young, good-looking and with the right profiles.'

'Hmm. Abigail?'

'I might have been more brutal. I have only ten.' Lily could believe that.

'Well, I've got nineteen. That's nearly fifty left, and we only need three. Gosh, this is harder than I thought.' Anne-Marie took another drink. 'Any suggestions?'

'I know, how about hair colour?' Lily suggested. Was she drunk? She wasn't sure.

'Fantastic idea. If we have couples with the same coloured hair then great, but if not then let's go with women. Put them into piles, redheads, brunettes and blondes. Anything else discard. I'm not having anyone with bright green hair at my resort.'

As Lily worked and saw her two companions doing the same, she thought that they were getting somewhere.

'There are quite a few cute couples,' Lily said.

'We need something special, for the book,' Abigail reminded them.

'Yes, we want that bit extra,' agreed Anne-Marie. 'I know, we'll all give them marks out of ten and the highest score wins.'

'Ok, good plan.' Lily held up the first couple.

'Five,' Abigail awarded.

'Six,' Anne-Marie said.

'I think I'd give seven,' Lily finished, writing the score down.

After an hour and another bottle of champagne, they were down to their three couples.

'Oh my God, we've done it!' Lily exclaimed, the drink having numbed her earlier terror at the situation.

'This is fantabulous,' Anne-Marie slurred.

'The cast of your book,' Abigail announced, picking up the first winners. 'First we have Tim Hall and Thea Lawson.' She held the photo up. 'Tim is a twenty-four-year-old writer, and Thea is a twenty-three-year-old actress.' Abigail's voice was unsteady.

They were both blond. Tim's hair flopped over his face, his blue eyes twinkled mischievously, and his smile was devastatingly sexy. Thea had shoulder-length blonde hair, grey eyes, and lips that looked sexy in a film star way.

'Tim and Thea, our first winners.' Anne-Marie cheered, and raised her glass. 'Lily, the brunettes?'

'In the brunette category I would like to present, Lee Jeffrey and Carla Clarke. Both twenty-one, newly graduated – Lee, law, Carla, English lit. And here they are!' Lily held the photo up. Lee was traditionally handsome with very dark brown slightly curly hair, dark eyes and strong features. Carla was tall and slim with lighter brown hair, long and straight, large Bambi eyes and a shy smile.

'And finally,' Anne-Marie said, 'the redhead category.' This had been an easier choice because there weren't many and they wouldn't have chosen a man with red hair anyway. 'I give you, Jimmy Dorsea and Emily Watts. Jimmy is twenty-six and owns his own business; Emily is twenty-two and works as a barmaid.'

It was obvious that Emily was the real reason for this choice. The young girl with corkscrew curls and country complexion stood out. A country maiden and her handsome squire. Jimmy had short, dark blond hair, and was tall and well-built. He was undeniably good-looking but Emily was sensational.

'There we have it, our competition winners!' Lily announced as she led a round of applause.

She looked at them; together they would make such a handsome group; it was clear that Anne-Marie had got the cast she'd been after. She hoped they would live up to her high expectations in real life. Lily was caught up with it all, despite herself. Tim and Thea would be the most romantic together, she decided. They would constantly be holding hands and gazing at each other. Lee and Carla would be more of a sporty, active couple, but still very in love. Emily and Jimmy would be the most passionate. She envisaged their late night walks on the beach where they would be unable to resist each other.

Anne-Marie happily downed yet another glass of champagne. 'My story is almost ready to begin. Todd and Katie will be the main characters but these six will be the supporting cast. New love – it's so utterly, utterly, wonderful. Oh, I'd better get some more champagne.' She stumbled as she stood but rebalanced herself and went to the kitchen.

'They look gorgeous,' Abigail said. 'Let's hope that she gets on with the book now.' Lily noticed her eyes darken.

'They sure are good-looking,' she concurred.

The door opened and Ed appeared.

'What's going on?'

'Oh, Ed, darling husband,' said Anne-Marie, reappearing with another bottle, 'we have just chosen our competition winners.'

'And?'

'Come and have a look. They're gorgeous, lovely, young, and wonderful.'

Ed moved in closer and looked at the winners. 'What were the tie-breakers like?' he asked.

'What tie-breakers?' Anne-Marie replied, before they all fell about laughing.

Ed's presence had a sobering effect on Lily. She saw him

raise an eyebrow at her, and she shrugged in response. She noticed him take in the empty champagne bottles and she felt sorry for him as confusion crossed his face. Lily felt awful; they were acting like giggly school girls, his wife, his mistress and his nemesis.

'Come on then, let's have a look, and I'll read the tie-breakers.' He picked up the first one. '"Love conquers all because love can stop the unhappy storm." Oh my God, that's awful.'

'Who was that?' Lily asked, wanting to reach over and touch him.

'Carla and Lee. Right, next. "Love conquers all because love is the sun, the moon and the stars, it makes the world go round, it makes us whole." That is Tim and Thea.'

'Ed, have a drink.' He accepted.

'OK, finally Emily and Jimmy. "Love conquers all because it turns the rain into the sun, it lives inside you and it never lets you feel cold." Lily began to laugh and Abigail and Anne-Marie joined in.

'What the fuck is it with love and the weather?' Abigail asked.

6

Special Occasions

Let The Love Resort help you to celebrate!

A holiday at The Love Resort is more than a holiday. But we also offer special packages for those special occasions.*

Engagement Package

Where better to propose to your loved one than at The Love Resort? This package comes with champagne, a special sunset boat trip and a very intimate post-proposal meal.

Wedding Package

Why not get married at The Love Resort? The perfect setting, a special romantic service, video souvenir of your day, a top photographer and a meal and cake makes your important day the best day of your life.

Anniversary Package

Celebrate your wedding anniversary at The Love Resort with a special meal, champagne and a poem written just for you by Anne-Marie Langdale.

Official Love Resort Brochure

* Normal Love Resort rules apply to these packages.

*

'It's a zoo out there,' David, Todd's brother and best man, said, twitching the curtain.

'But they won't see anything,' Todd pointed out, his stomach twisted with fear.

'They'll get a glimpse of you when you pose for press photographs and they'll probably still be waiting when you leave to go to the hotel.'

'You think they'll still be here?' Todd was green. He was upset about the crowds – loyal fans who he was deceiving – but more than that, he was terrified now the reality had hit him. He didn't want to get married. He especially didn't want to get married to Katie Ray.

'Todd, do you know what you're getting yourself into?' David asked, as if reading his mind.

'I don't have a choice.' Todd and David had had this conversation so many times before, it was almost scripted.

'You do.'

'I'm marrying her.' Todd knew that David was trying to protect him, as his older brother had always done, but this time he couldn't.

'I know, but I just don't want you to.'

'Neither do I. David, you know how this stuff works. God, how I suffer for my art.'

'You suffer too much, little brother. I think God is telling you to come out of the closet and stand your ground.'

Todd smiled at him. He knew he was right. He should stand up for what he believed in. He was doing a disservice to gay people everywhere by playing the game and it shouldn't be like that.

'She's not that bad,' Todd mused.

'She's worse,' David replied. 'Remember dinner?'

Todd did. They had all gone out together for their much-publicised rehearsal dinner. It wasn't the first time David had met Katie, but, Todd recalled, it was the first time she'd been her over-the-top self with him. She had fawned over him, kept going on about how they were going to be family soon. She'd even called him 'brother'. Todd, glad to have her draped over anyone else but himself, had found it hard to keep a straight face. But David hadn't found it amusing and was convinced that Katie was treating the wedding as if it were real. Nothing Todd could say could persuade him otherwise.

'She's not,' Todd argued unconvincingly.

'Todd, this is your last chance.'

Todd sighed. The urgency in David's voice was getting to him, making him feel panicked. He wasn't of sound mind, and he was sure that there was something in the wedding vows that precluded people like him from marrying. Or was that wills? A knock on the door interrupted his thoughts; David answered it.

'Oh my God,' David laughed and, despite himself, Todd joined in as a vision of pink taffeta entered the room.

'Shut up,' Harriet stormed, shuffling uncomfortably.

'What has she done to you?' David shrieked, doubled over.

'I have come to see if you're ready.' Harriet tried to arrange her dress so she could sit down. One of Todd's conditions, showing that he did have a sense of humour, was that Harriet would have to be one of Katie's bridesmaids. Harriet had tried to refuse but in the end she'd had to concede. It wasn't much but at least it felt like some kind of revenge.

'Has she dressed all the bridesmaids like that?' Todd asked, mouth twitching.

'Yes. All ten,' Harriet scowled. 'Now, are you ready?'

'Sure, yes, all ready to go.' Todd smiled at her, a smile that wasn't returned. He saw out of the corner of his eye that David's shoulders were shaking. Harriet had arranged the wedding, so it seemed only fair that she got to be part of it. She nodded, got up and left.

'That was mean,' David pointed out, succumbing to laughter.

'It's made my day a bit more bearable, though,' Todd replied.

David did up Todd's cufflinks and patted his shoulder reassuringly. Todd felt tears pricking his eyes. David tried one last time to talk him out of the marriage, but to no avail. Todd was reluctantly resolute.

The garden that had been chosen for the wedding ceremony had been changed beyond all recognition. The demands that were made by Katie had been met by the wedding planner down to the last detail. There were a huge number of pink trellises to match the roses she was going to carry. Arches had been erected at specific points, so Katie could stop and be looked at. There were twenty human statues whose job was to sprinkle her with pink rose petals when she walked down the long aisle and then to sprinkle the married couple again when they returned. Pink was Katie's chosen colour, as had been made clear.

For the reception a marquee had been erected. It was the biggest marquee available; although smaller than Katie had originally wanted. Inside it was decorated with cherubim, more pink roses, heart-shaped ice sculptures and golden leaf. It was everything Katie had asked for. Todd hadn't tried to argue; he didn't care. Not that Katie had picked up on that.

'It's time, Todd.' Todd stood up, legs shaking. David took his arm. 'You can back out. You can stop it all now,' he said, eyes wide.

Todd looked at him. He could run away, get out of there. He could go and start afresh, doing something, or nothing. He had the money. He could walk away now. But despite the feeling of dread that was eating up his insides, he couldn't.

'Let's go.' He moved forward. He saw disappointment cross David's face as he moved forward too.

★

It seemed to take ages to make his way up the aisle, or whatever it was called. He smiled at strangers as he passed; although some of his work colleagues were there, he barely knew anyone that well. There were other actors, directors, producers, Katie's friends, her giant entourage, and various people who worked at the Studio. Hollywood royalty. Everyone important. It was all so fake.

The version of the 'Wedding March' was longer than usual because it took Katie several minutes to reach Todd, who stood under an array of pink roses, waiting for her. As she reached him, Bernie pulled back her veil and she smiled at him. He had to admit she looked good. Her dress was the finest silk, she was like a movie star of the 1950s. He hadn't credited her with enough taste for that. Her bridesmaids looked like frilly monstrosities, but she was beautiful. He had an urge to touch the silk, to feel how soft it was, but he held himself back. He looked at her shoes, thinking how pretty they were, before the registrar interrupted him and began the ceremony.

Owing to the size of the audience, the registrar had a microphone, which stunned Todd for a moment, and he exchanged a snigger with David. When it was time for them to repeat their vows, he held the microphone in front of them – 'Like a cheap karaoke show,' David whispered.

Todd was an actor and he acted his socks off. He repeated his vows as if he meant them, and he even kissed her the way he kissed all his leading ladies. Afterwards, when they had signed the register and made their way down the long pink walkway, he smiled constantly as the rose petals fell on his head.

The newlyweds went straight to pose for the press and wave at the fans. As they cheered and the flashbulbs went off, Katie posed like a true professional. Todd posed like a fraud.

The reception seemed to drag on. At first they had to endure the welcoming line, which seemed to take for ever. Then an hour of chatting and mingling, followed by a seven-course dinner. The speeches were so false that Todd couldn't bear to recall any of them. He longed to get away, but he couldn't. He and Katie were booked into the honeymoon suite of the Beverly Wilshire, and then they were flying to The Love Resort. Until they returned home, and he and Katie had separate rooms in the same house, they would be together all the time. The thought terrified him. He'd seen the predatory way she looked at him. He felt her hand where he really didn't want it during dinner and her toes creeping up his legs in a way that did nothing for him. His wife was determined, and he wondered if it would be safe for him to sleep while she was in the same room. He feared not.

The crowds were still gathered at nine o'clock, when Katie and Todd were driven away. Despite barely getting to see them through the tinted limousine windows, they all cheered and clapped. It made him more depressed. Katie took his hand.

'Hello, husband,' she whispered seductively.

As Todd stared at her open-mouthed, he was literally lost for words.

7

Menu

We would not expect you to book a holiday without being fully informed. Below is a typical Love Resort dinner menu* which we hope will tickle your fancy!

STARTERS

Special salmon carpaccio with darling dill dressing

Precious prawns with sexy seafood dressing

Adoring aubergine and perfect parmesan plate

MAIN COURSE

Flirty fish of the day

Love lamb shank

Tender tomato and pasta bake (V)

All above are served with partnership potatoes and friendship fresh vegetables.

DESSERTS

Sensuous summer pudding

Frisky fresh fruit with wicked whipped cream

Together for ever fritters

Official Love Resort Brochure

*Note: if you stay at The Love Resort we do not guarantee you will receive this menu.

'This is what I thought,' Lily said, handing Anne-Marie her publicity proposals as Ed looked on adoringly.

Anne-Marie almost smiled as she began to read. She had a new lease of life, Lily felt. Abigail coming had obviously cheered her up no end and she seemed happy for the first time since Lily had known her. This was making Lily feel increasingly guilty. It had been a few days since Anne-Marie had shouted at her, and being on this unfamiliar territory was unnerving her.

She had never planned to fall in love with a married man. Especially not a man who happened to be married to her boss. But it had happened. There was nothing she could do about it. As soon as she saw him she had felt something. It was weird. He was older than her, and conventionally good-looking, which she was never usually drawn to. Although she tried to ignore the attraction, to fight it, to banish it, it grew stronger until she had to give in to it. She was head over heels, there was no denying it. Lily Bailey, who had worked for some of the hottest men in Hollywood, who had dated quite a few, was in love with an older, married man, and although she had never been happier, she had also never been more confused.

Ed coughed and nodded at her, and Lily realised she'd been staring at her boss, open-mouthed. The thing was that Anne-Marie was behaving as she had when Lily had first met her. She was pleased. She was being nice. She was scaring the hell out of her.

'Lily, dear, this all looks wonderful.'

Lily couldn't remember the last time her boss had compli-
mented her, if, indeed, she ever had. 'Thank you,' she stammered.

'You do realise that we've turned away paying guests?' Ed
cut in gruffly.

'Oh, Ed, I wish you'd think of something other than money.
The publicity this will generate will cover all the expense a
thousand times over. Now, can we go through the schedule once
more?'

The three sat around the small table in the office, where
papers were scattered among the bottles of mineral water.

'Todd and Katie will be arriving late at night. To deflect any
gawping, we've arranged for a special couples' talent competition
to be held. Lily, you're in charge of that.'

Lily grimaced to herself. A couples' talent night would be like
visiting hell.

'In fact, Lily, you shall be the judge.'

Lily nodded. *Worse* than visiting hell.

'What about me?' Ed asked.

'Darling, we shall be greeting our most important guests.
They'll expect it. We'll show them personally to the honeymoon bungalow, and the only other people with us will be
Marcus, who is to be their butler for the week, Erik, their chef,
and Mary, their personal maid.'

'Darling, no one has their own maid and chef on this resort,'
Ed protested.

'This is Katie and Todd Cortes. Don't you understand, Ed,
they're the most famous couple in the world . . . the universe . . .'
Her voice was haloed in hysteria. 'We will give them their own
staff, we will do whatever it fucking well takes to make them
happy because they will fucking well make this resort the most
fucking desirable fucking place in the fucking world.' She
stopped, looking as if she had shocked herself, before flicking

her hair and plastering the scary smile back on her face.

'Sorry, darling.' Ed returned the smile.

Lily felt relieved; her boss hadn't been taken over by an alien. All was well.

'Where was I?' Anne-Marie asked sweetly.

'You said we were going to greet them with their staff.'

'Yes, of course. Now, we shall settle them in and explain how things will work for their stay. They are on honeymoon and will largely want their privacy, but there is going to be a magazine interview, as you know, and they will be photographed in various places in the resort, including the restaurant, pool, love seats, gardens of romance and the beach. And they must eat in one of the restaurants at least once.'

'That is a fabulous idea,' Ed agreed, glancing knowingly at Lily. Lily knew that Anne-Marie was taking all the glory but that didn't bother her. After all, she was stealing her husband; it seemed only fair.

'The publicity will be invaluable. I think that we should both be present when the magazine people are there. It'll be good for the profile of the resort if we're there as well as Todd and Katie.'

'Splendid idea,' Ed boomed.

'And you can ensure that they don't make any digs about the resort.' Anne-Marie shuddered.

'Oh, they can't. They've signed an agreement only to print what Katie and Todd say, along with a glowing reference to the resort. We procured that as part of the whole deal,' Lily explained.

'Good. Right. So moving on . . . The day after they arrive our competition winners will be here. Ed, what accommodation did you decide on?'

'The hotel. I've reserved three sea-view rooms for them, all close together.'

'That's fine.' Anne-Marie consulted the schedule that Lily

had given her. 'They arrive at five in the afternoon. Lily and you will be going to the airport to greet them. Bring them back and get them settled in. It doesn't matter who does it.'

Lily tuned out; she knew all this. After all, she'd devised it.

'So, once they're all in, we're just going to play it by ear?' Ed asked.

'Yes, obviously I need to keep an eye on them, for research purposes. I mean, to see how the New Love package works. I shall also be keeping a close eye on Todd and Katie. I expect you both to help me. Oh, and I want it known that any guest not respecting their privacy will be removed from the resort.'

'That's a bit harsh, isn't it?'

'No. They are not going to reveal the honeymoon destination for fear of journalists infiltrating the resort, but our guests will soon realise what incredible company they are in. Now, the competition winners will be interviewed for *Exclusive Holidays*, with photos, but the genius is that we're arranging it so we will be in charge.' This was being passed off as her genius. 'And I think that's all for now. I need to go and see Abigail.'

'Abigail, are you listening to me?'

'Um?'

'I said, perhaps the Hollywood star and the model actually get married on the island after a whirlwind romance.'

'That's a lovely idea, darling. Anne-Marie, why don't you jot down an outline for me?'

They were sitting on the terrace, on sun-loungers, Anne-Marie with her long pink dress hitched up; Abigail, wearing a vest top and pair of shorts, her holiday uniform.

'Abigail, why on earth would I do that? I don't do outlines. No, as soon as they all get here I shall simply start writing. In fact, I can't wait to get started.' She shook her head; Abigail was clearly distracted – maybe the sun was getting to her. Anne-Marie had never seen Abigail with any colour, but she was slightly pink. It had to be the sun, otherwise why would she ask for something as preposterous as an outline?

'You could start now.'

'Did I not tell you? We've got the full works at the spa this afternoon. I thought it would be fun. And I've ordered lunch for us both up at the house. So, I'll probably start tomorrow.'

'Lovely.' Abigail started to get up.

'Oh, and I thought we could have dinner tonight at the restaurant – you know, show our faces. Ed insists on it.'

'Super,' Abigail responded.

'And while we're having massages I can tell you all about our latest plans. Abigail, are you sure you're all right? You've got a funny look on your face.'

Anne-Marie dressed for dinner, aware that the lilac gown she had chosen set her eyes (or her coloured contact lenses) off brilliantly. She chose the pink diamond necklace (an anniversary present to herself ten years after first being published), then applied her make-up. She could hear Ed in his dressing room; she had told him she wanted him in a suit. There was no real reason for all this effort, but she was dining in public and liked to ensure that her party looked their best. She had arranged for herself, Ed, Abigail and Lily to dine with the rest of the managers. It was a rare occurrence, but one that Ed warranted necessary – something to do with morale. Whatever, she found it terribly boring.

Satisfied with her appearance, she walked downstairs, where she poured herself a glass of champagne from the bottle in the ice bucket and wandered on to her terrace. The view always took her breath away. The orange and pink sky heralded the beginning of another evening, the sea lapped beneath her. She sipped her champagne. It was as if God had made this just for her.

She sensed Ed's presence beside her with annoyance. This

was her moment, her view; she wished he wouldn't ruin it for her; he always seemed to ruin it for her.

'Anne-Marie, Abigail just phoned. She's got a headache so she won't be able to join us for dinner.'

'Oh, the poor darling. She looked a bit off earlier. Is there anything I can do?'

'No, she's ordering a light supper in and having an early night. She said she'd probably go straight to bed.'

'Fine. Then let's go and face the ugly people.'

'I do wish you wouldn't call your guests that,' Ed chastised.

'I do wish they didn't need to be called that,' she snapped back.

8

Rules And Conditions Of The Love Resort

Couples must be over twenty-one.

You must have been in a relationship, together, for over three months.

A couple must be two people of the opposite sex.

'Relations' must be conducted in private.

Anyone found breaking these rules will be asked to leave The Love Resort.
  The Love Resort Booking Form

'David?'
  'Yes, what time is it?'
  'Early. Are you asleep?'
  'No, Todd, I *was* asleep. I got hammered with some of your friends after you left last night.'
  'At least someone had a good time,' Todd said sulkily.
  'I have no idea if I had a good time. I can't quite remember.'
  'Shit, hope you didn't do anything stupid.'
  'What, like getting married? Anyway, how was the wedding night?'
  'I haven't slept a wink. She keeps touching me.'
  'Where?'
  'It doesn't matter where. She's a groper. Anyway, I moved to

the sofa as soon as she fell asleep, and managed to get a bit of sleep, but she scares me.'

'I don't blame you for that. She scares me too.'

'Can't you say anything to help?'

'Not really. Not the way my head and stomach feel right now. Anyway, aren't you supposed to be on a plane?'

'I am on a plane. She's in the bathroom redoing her make-up. When am I coming back?'

'You know that, it's two weeks.'

'I might not still be alive by then.'

'Try to be. Bye.'

Katie took her seat opposite Todd. 'How are you?' she asked, her voice full of concern.

'Tired. I just wish we'd get there.'

'It's not long now,' Katie reassured him as she picked up the booklet that they'd been given. Todd, having already read it, watched her flick through. It contained information about The Love Resort, along with details of their accommodation. Attached was a schedule.

'We must be the only people who need a typed schedule for our honeymoon,' she said sadly.

Todd nodded. Like with his scripts, he'd committed it to memory. All their publicity commitments had been planned for the first week, leaving the second week totally clear. Two weeks seemed like an awfully long time; Todd wished that the schedule was fuller. He also wished for once that Katie had insisted on bringing her ever-expanding entourage with them. He had a feeling that they would have too much time alone. Far too much time.

'Have you read all this?' she asked.

Todd held up a selection of paper sculptures: ducks, a plane and a flower. She giggled and he laughed.

'Thank God for origami,' he said.

'It's my favourite herb,' she replied.

'Welcome to The Love Resort.' Anne-Marie flung her arms around Katie and then Todd, much to their surprise. 'I am the owner, Anne-Marie Langdale, and I am here to personally welcome you to your honeymoon.'

'Why, thank you,' Katie said sweetly.

'And this is my husband, Edward,' Anne-Marie elaborated, pulling him forward.

'It's nice to meet you,' Todd added. 'I love your novels.' Everyone looked surprised, apart from Anne-Marie. Todd went red; Ed was looking at him in a funny way.

'And you. Welcome, and congratulations on your wedding,' Ed said, as per Anne-Marie's instructions.

Ed organised everyone into the limousine, and poured champagne to toast their arrival. He had to admit to feeling excited. Katie Ray was a gorgeous film star; her husband, Todd, one of the best male actors of the time, and Ed, ordinary Ed, was sitting in the back of a twelve-seat stretch limo, drinking champagne with them. He never thought that he'd be there.

Anne-Marie gushed for the entire journey, giving Ed a chance to study the newlyweds. They were so gorgeous together and Katie looked radiant. He felt a little sad, as he'd never had that with Anne-Marie, but then he banished that thought, because he had Lily now. He just hoped the movie stars' marriage would work out better than his had.

They arrived at the resort and were driven to their luxury accommodation. Anne-Marie gave them a tour.

'It's lovely, really lovely,' Todd said.

'Now I want to introduce you to your helpers for the duration of your stay. Erik is your personal chef, Marcus your butler and Mary your maid. They are all on call for you twenty-four hours a day for your entire stay.'

'Isn't that a bit much for them?' Todd asked.

'No, of course not. I mean, when you sleep they sleep. And, of course, you will want plenty of privacy. You have a special telephone in your bungalow which is directly connected to their pagers. You press, they come. Very easy. Now, Erik, Marcus, Mary, here, please.' She snapped her fingers and three faces appeared from behind a wall, the way Anne-Marie had choreographed the whole thing.

Katie stepped forward to greet her staff, Todd standing slightly behind her.

'Hello.' Katie held her hand out to Erik, who took it but looked unsure what to do with it, while Marcus held his hand out to Todd. Todd looked at him in surprise as he shook hands. His arm began to tingle. He was sure he had seen something in his eyes, and it wasn't just that he was starstruck. He barely heard Katie asking irritating questions and listing her food intolerances as he stared at him. If his butler wasn't the best-looking gay man in the world then Todd would have sex with Katie.

'This is so romantic,' Katie said, as she and Todd were finally alone. He looked at her. Was she squinting at him, or was it a wink?

'I'm really tired, Katie; it's late. I need to sleep.'

'Oh, you poor darling, of course you do. Shall we order something first?'

'I wouldn't mind a brandy. There's a stocked bar on the terrace.'

'I know, let me get you one, and then maybe a bath?' She raised an eyebrow suggestively.

'No, I think I'll just have a quick shower.'

She was inching towards him in *that way* again. He backed himself into one of the two bathrooms. As he closed the door he saw her shrug and then go to fix them drinks. He locked the door, undressed and stood under the shower, enjoying the warm water and the luxury of being alone. He could see what she was doing; he just didn't understand it. She knew he was gay, so why was she acting otherwise? Was she so paranoid about their cover being blown? God, he hoped that was it, although he doubted it. It was as if she was trying to be the perfect wife. This would be great if it wasn't a fact that he didn't want a wife. He tried to think of the positive aspects. He'd met Anne-Marie, who was fascinating, if not a bit weird, and it was true, he did love her novels. And the resort might be a bit over the top, but the stilt bungalow they were in was lovely. The terrace housed a large bar, two sun-loungers, their own pool, Jacuzzi and a table and chairs. It was private, surrounded by trees and foliage, but it afforded a wonderful view of the sea. The bedroom was large, with a bed the size of a tennis court, which was a great comfort to him. The living area was cosy and homely, and there was a fridge filled to the brim with Cristal, Katie's favourite champagne, as per her request. (He hoped that she'd drink enough of it to pass out rather than make a pass at him.) The bathrooms were also more than adequate – dark marble surfaces, shiny gold taps and the softest towels.

After his shower, Todd changed into full pyjamas in the bathroom. Although he knew he'd be far too hot, he couldn't risk any degree of nudity. He walked tentatively into the bedroom and saw Katie through the slightly open door, in the living room. She was draped across the sofa, wearing a negligee. Almost too scared to breathe, he climbed into bed and shut his eyes tightly. He was so tired, but fought sleep, in case she appeared. However, as images of Marcus flooded his head, he was soon dreaming.

'Abigail, are you there?' Anne-Marie trilled as she opened the front door to her publisher's bungalow.

'Hold on,' Abigail shouted back.

Anne-Marie tapped her foot as she waited. 'Oh, gosh, darling, sorry, were you asleep?' she asked, as Abigail walked out and shut the bedroom door behind her.

'I must have dropped off. You know, too much wine with dinner.'

'Oh, well, share a glass of champagne with me. I want to tell you about our guests.' Anne-Marie waved a bottle in front of her face; she could have sworn she saw Abigail sigh.

'Of course, let's go on to the terrace. Tell me all.' Abigail opened the champagne, and poured two glasses.

Anne-Marie decided she must have imagined it.

'They are so beautiful and glamorous, and such perfect manners. I cannot tell you how wonderful they are going to be – I mean when they're translated into my main characters. He's tall, dark and handsome, with twinkly eyes and a smile that would melt stone. She's beautiful in a cultivated way. I thought that the story would be the glamorous model that falls in love with the man who wants to live a simple life away from the cameras and the fame. They are opposites. She loves the limelight; he wouldn't know how to deal with it.'

'I thought he was going to be an actor?'

'No, too much like the real him. No, I thought I would make him a sort of eccentric hermit, but very rich, of course. Family money.'

'Darling, it all sounds wonderful, but shouldn't you be writing it down?'

'Oh, I will, all in good time. Now the model is a bit hard at first but she softens with love. I mean, she won't be a bitch or anything, you'll see her vulnerability from the word go.'

'It sounds super,' Abigail replied, as she drained her glass.

'They're here and in their bungalow,' Ed said.

'Anne-Marie?' Lily needed to be sure.

'She's gone to see Abigail.'

'Should give us at least an hour.'

'Then let's not waste it.'

Afterwards she lay in his arms, stroking his hair tenderly.

'How was the couple's talent competition?' he asked.

'Horrible. So many couples, so little talent.'

'As usual. So how did you judge?'

'Well, it's a bit naughty, but the Butlers – you know, that really overweight couple? Well, they did a duet, as Sonny and Cher. I was almost dying with laughter so I thought they deserved to win.' They both snickered.

'Well, soon we will be away from here and you'll never have to judge another competition.'

'You know, in a weird, warped kind of way I might miss this place.'

Ed laughed. 'Yeah, but not enough to make us want to stay.'

'Jesus, no.' At that moment she would give everything up in a second for him. Soon she would feel this happy all the time, and she couldn't believe her luck.

9

How To Get To Us

Direct flights depart from the UK and USA twice a week with two major airlines (see next page for times and prices).

Transfers will be arranged with your booking. The Love Resort is only a twenty-minute drive from the airport, affording you the chance to admire the island* as you begin your holiday.

The Love Resort Booking Form

* If you arrive at night, you may not have enough visibility to admire the island.

'Passports, confirmation letter, insurance, mosquito cream, suntan lotion, after-sun lotion, plasters. I think that's everything,' Emily Watts said, as she handed the overstuffed bag to Jimmy Dorsea. The suitcases were already in the car and they were about to set off for the airport. They had to be there at eleven and although Jimmy estimated it would take, at most, four hours from their home in North Devon to Gatwick at that time in the morning, Emily had insisted on allowing five. 'Just in case,' she said. He hadn't argued, mainly because there was little point in arguing with Emily, but he was also too excited. Like a child, he was going on his first major holiday with the woman he loved and he'd never been out of Europe before. He impulsively kissed her cheek.

'What was that for?'

'Because even at this time in the morning you look beautiful,' he replied truthfully.

'Oh, you.' But she kissed him back and, at that moment, he felt happier than he ever had.

They had been together for eight months. Jimmy was a mechanic; he owned his own garage and was happy with his life. Actually, with Emily he was ecstatic. He had met her at the pub that her parents owned, where she worked. He'd stood in front of the bar, she'd turned to serve him, and her eyes had sparkled as she'd pushed one of her curls off her face. When she'd smiled at him he'd almost buckled. He believed it was love at first sight.

'Jimmy, we have got everything, haven't we?' She sounded worried.

'Em, by the weight of your suitcase, we've got everything you own.' He laughed, kindly.

'Don't exaggerate, you know that simply isn't true,' she grinned.

He adored her. She was beautiful, confident and she knew what she wanted. He couldn't believe that someone like her would go for someone like him, but she had. It hadn't happened overnight. He'd visited the pub on numerous occasions, each time with the intention of asking her out; each time losing his nerve. Then one day she'd asked him on a date. He couldn't believe it.

Their relationship hadn't always been easy. She could be demanding, sulky and sometimes a bit mean, but that was because she was so incredible. Incredible people were difficult, it was a fact. And love wasn't easy; all his mates told him that. Jimmy knew that he was one lucky man, he was certain of it. He also knew he was the envy of most of the men in Bideford.

It had been his idea to enter the competition, because Emily had been hassling him to take her away and the prices of the two-week holidays she chose almost caused him to collapse. So, when he'd seen the competition he'd entered it, and when they had won, he'd been both surprised and relieved.

Emily went off to check that she hadn't forgotten anything, encouraging Jimmy to do the same. Instead, he waited for her, vowing to make the most of their holiday, to stop worrying about his garage, which he'd never left for more than a week before, and he would use the time to prove to her how much he loved her. He thought about the engagement ring he'd bought. It'd cost him, but he was determined to make his marriage proposal perfect. She deserved that.

'I can't believe how exciting this is,' Emily said, for the hundredth time.

'I know. Just think, this time tomorrow we'll be lying in the sun, maybe with a cocktail.'

'Or two. I intend to take advantage of the all-inclusive.'

'Um, it's going to be brilliant. Em?' He squeezed her hand.

'Yes?'

'I really love you.'

'Oh, Jimmy, I love you too.' She squeezed his hand back.

Thea leant in. She then poked him with her index finger but nothing happened. She moved closer, looking dubious. After a few seconds, she went to the bathroom and came back with the toothbrush mug filled with water. She poured it over his head. Nothing.

Thea sighed. She had ordered a taxi to take them to the airport and she'd set every alarm clock they owned. The problem was that Tim didn't seem to want to wake up.

She thought back to the previous day, when she'd tried to keep a close eye on him, but he said he had to go and pick up his money from the post office, and stupidly she let him go alone. He arrived home hours later. Pickled. She had done her best, but Tim liked a drink, and he was probably only getting into the holiday spirit, she told herself, as she prodded him again.

They'd known each other their whole lives and had lived together for three years. They couldn't be any closer; Tim really was all she had. But lately they'd hit a bit of a bad patch. Her work as an extra was stressing her out; her dream to be a proper actress seemed to be moving further away. Tim had been trying to write a novel since he'd graduated three years ago, but as he found it harder and harder, he'd been drinking a bit too much. The holiday would sort both of them out, and when he returned he'd be inspired to start writing. She was sure of it. It was just what he needed.

Thea shouted in his ear.

'What's all the bloody noise about and why can't I open my eyes?' Tim asked, suddenly sitting up. 'Oh, there they go, that's better.' He ran a hand through his hair. 'Why's my hair wet? You didn't pee on me, did you?'

'Tim, we're going on holiday today.'

'Oh, good. Have I packed?' A smile spread across his face.

'You're all packed,' Thea replied. 'So if you get yourself into the shower, I'll make coffee and then we can go.'

'Oh, great.' He perked up. 'Where are we going again?' Thea groaned but she melted, when he grinned, adding, 'Only joking. Caribbean here we come!' He rushed to the shower, kissing her on his way.

Thea made coffee and once again said a silent prayer of thanks that she'd won the competition. She'd bought *Exclusive Holidays* on a whim; after a particularly bad day at work she'd picked it up along with a family-size bar of chocolate. At first, looking at the holiday destinations had made her feel bitter, which she knew they would, but then the pictures of the white sands and tranquil seas had calmed her. Finally they inspired her. So when she saw the competition for a free holiday at The Love Resort, her chocolate buzz helped to convince her it was a good idea and she entered. And, lo and behold, she'd won.

Thea began to round up their luggage as she heard Tim

singing loudly and tunelessly in the shower. Yes, this holiday was exactly what they both needed. They would return and everything would be all right once again.

'What on earth are you doing?'

'I was just filling my hipflask.' Tim looked guilty; Thea snatched the silver flask from him. She'd given it to him for his eighteenth birthday; had it engraved, 'To T lots of love T.' Not terribly imaginative, but she was young.

'Sorry. I don't mean to be such a nag.'

'I know, but you have to stop worrying so much. I'm good, T.'

'You are?' She wanted to laugh at the earnest expression on his face.

'Yes. I love you.'

'I love you too.'

Carla lay awake in her sister Claire's bed, too excited to sleep. She was upset that Lee had to sleep on the sofa but Claire only had one room and they had shared the bed. It didn't matter, they were about to spend two weeks totally together. Two weeks with Lee would be paradise.

She thought back to when she'd met him. She'd started university full of excitement. That first week she'd made friends with various people from her corridor and from her course, but when her neighbour introduced her to a group of lads who were in the same hall as them, that was when her university life had truly begun. Lee was, of course, one of those lads.

She decided to get up, have a shower, and make breakfast for Lee. She put on her jeans, feeling all the excitement that holidays invoke.

'Are you awake?' she asked, waving a cup of coffee under Lee's nose.

'Yes. This sofa is pretty uncomfortable.'

'Oh, sorry.'

'Carla, I'm not complaining. It was nice to be able to stay at all. Is that coffee for me, babes?' She handed it to him, and he kissed her cheek.

'Have you got everything?' she asked as they piled their luggage up by the front door.

'Sure, all I need is my girlfriend and I'm good to go.'

'As we're early, how about another coffee?'

'I'll make it. White, two sugars.'

'How sweet you never have to ask.'

'Well, Carla, if they put us through a *Mr and Mrs* type test we'll pass with flying colours.'

'Oh, yeah? You're that confident?'

'Yes. Favourite colour, blue; eyes, hazel; you squeeze the toothpaste, annoyingly I might add, from the middle; and you have an unnatural attachment to dead plants.'

'OK, well, your favourite colour is green; your eyes are dark brown; you barely use toothpaste and your worst habit is, um, no, you're perfect.'

'Thank you, you're not so bad yourself.'

'Thank you.'

'This holiday is going to be fantastic.'

'Oh, it will be.'

A woman and a photographer stood by the check-in desk, looking conspicuous, and holding up a sign saying '*Exclusive Holidays*'.

'There we are,' Emily said, pointing the woman out to Jimmy and then stalking up to her.

'Hello, I'm Emily and that's Jimmy.'

'I'm Gemma and this is Paul.' Gemma stuck out her hand and Emily grabbed it, shaking it enthusiastically. Jimmy nodded shyly. The photographer smiled and started taking photos.

'Hello, are we first?' Emily asked, startled by the flash.

'Yup. What a lovely West Country accent you've got.'

'North Devon,' Jimmy explained timidly.

'Well, welcome. Congratulations. I hope you don't mind if we wait for the others, it's just that you'll get bored if I go through everything three times.'

'Course not,' Emily said, taking Jimmy's hand and smiling up at him. Two more people approached; Jimmy couldn't help but stare.

'You must be Thea and Tim. I'm Gemma and this is Paul.' Once again, Paul took a photo by way of greeting.

'Hello,' Thea said, before Tim grabbed her and gave her a snog. Everyone looked surprised.

'Sorry, can't help myself,' Tim explained, kissing Gemma's cheek.

Jimmy shuffled from foot to foot. This couple seemed so glamorous compared to him. Especially as Tim was explaining that Thea was an actress and he was a writer. He saw that Emily looked impressed, and felt out of his depth.

'Jimmy has his own car restoration business, and I help out in my parents' business,' Emily told them, as Jimmy continued to study the wheel of the luggage trolley. He was sure that if he had a spanner on him he could make it go straight.

After a few moments of silence, Lee and Carla arrived. Introductions were made and then Gemma called for their attention. Jimmy thought the way that Lee strutted up to the group showed him to be pretty confident, although Carla seemed a bit shyer. Both Tim and Lee were far more confident than he was, and that worried him.

'First we need a group photo. Paul?'

'Righto. Now, men in a row with your women in front of you.' Paul helped them arrange themselves, and then he rearranged them before taking the photos.

'Fantastic,' Gemma enthused. 'Now I am going to check you all in together. Then you will go through to the departure lounge and wait for your flight. Please don't miss it; there won't be another free flight available to you if you do. The flight takes off at one p.m., which gives you just under two hours. It lasts for just under ten hours and you will be met at the other end by a representative from The Love Resort. If you can all give me your passports and follow me . . . ? Any questions?' she asked in a singsong voice. They all shook their heads.

They stood behind her while she organised everything. She sorted out seat allocation and the luggage, while they all smiled awkwardly at each other.

Jimmy held on tightly to Emily's hand. He felt a bit intimidated. A writer, an actress, a soon-to-be lawyer and an English graduate. Despite Emily's elevation of his own job, he still felt inadequate. Still, he told himself, they seemed friendly enough.

'Great, you're all ready to go. You've all got seats with your partners and I suggest it would be a good idea for you to try to stay together in a group. I know this is a romantic holiday you're embarking on, but it wouldn't hurt to bond a bit,' Gemma suggested, and led them to passport control. 'I have to leave you here. There are your passports and tickets and I hope you have a wonderful holiday.'

'We will,' Emily replied. They all said their goodbyes to her, then Tim led them enthusiastically onward.

Tim managed to get everyone through passport and customs in record time. He was like a military leader. Finally he led them to the nearest bar.

'I suggest that we use this as our sort of base camp. Then if the girlies want to go shopping or whatever, they always know where to find us.'

'I always know where to find you,' Thea muttered.

'What was that darling?'

'Nothing. I need to go and buy some books.' She mumbled in defeat.

'I'll come with you. I want something trashy for the plane,' Carla said.

'Oh, me too,' Emily concurred.

'I'll have a glass of red wine and a whisky chaser,' Tim requested from the barman.

'I'll have a pint,' Lee said.

'Isn't it a bit early?' Jimmy asked, and he saw Thea smile and Emily look angry.

'Jimmy,' Tim leant in close, 'two things. One, we are now on holiday, and on holiday it's never too early, and secondly, I am a bit nervous about flying.'

'I'll have a pint then,' Jimmy said quickly, and Emily smiled approvingly at him.

'So you're an English lit grad?' Thea asked as they stood in WH Smith, looking at books.

'Yes, but don't be horrified that I'm buying Jilly Cooper for my holiday reading.'

'I'm not. Can I borrow it after you?' Thea decided that she liked Carla, and picked up a thriller.

'Sure. What about you, Emily? What are you after?'

'I don't know, something fun.' She sounded unsure.

'Oh, maybe we should all buy a book by Anne-Marie Langdale – you know, the woman who owns this resort. Horrible cheesy romance, but it would be a giggle,' Thea suggested.

They each picked up a novel, vying to choose the worst title.

'I have to win. This one's called *A Romance Made in Devon*,' Emily squealed excitedly.

'How appropriate, although she's probably never been to Devon,' Carla said.

'Probably not and she'll make us all out to be simpletons, like people do.'

'Really? Why?' Thea asked.

'Something about the countryside and our accents, I think. I mean, I'm not that well educated but I'm not stupid.'

'It's nothing to do with education. I just graduated but I don't have an ounce of common sense. Anyway, I think your accent's sexy,' Carla added.

'You do?'

'Yes.'

'I agree, and if I learn it then it will help me with my career,' Thea added, wanting to sound friendly, although there was something about Emily that she was unsure of. Thea chastised herself; she always judged too quickly.

'Fine, I'll teach you,' Emily offered, excited.

'Same again,' Tim ordered. 'All round,' he added, shooting a look at Jimmy.

'So, tell me again. What happened that made you so scared?' Jimmy asked, accepting his second pint hesitantly. He liked a drink but he'd never had even one in the morning before.

'There was that film about the crash and everyone had to try to get out on those blow-up-doll-like things, and of course only about two people did. Then there was that film about those people who crashed and had to eat each other. Oh, and you're always hearing about drunk pilots and stuff like that, and they only tell you to put your head between your legs so that if it crashes you die quicker,' Tim finished.

Jimmy drank half of his pint very quickly.

'I think you're just scaring yourself. There are hardly any plane crashes these days,' Lee said reasonably.

Still, Jimmy ordered a whisky chaser, feeling his nerves increase.

'Hardly any, but not none. Now, what happens if the plane I happen to be on is the rare occurrence? It could be. I'm doomed. And so are you, by the way.' He downed his latest drinks.

'But they check them mechanically – they do check them,

don't they?' Jimmy asked. He'd never been on a long flight before and it had not occurred to him to be scared of flying until Tim started.

'Of course they do. They're really thorough these days,' Lee reasoned.

'But we haven't even touched on terrorism. I think we need another round,' Tim added.

'Those sunglasses really suit you,' Emily said as Carla posed for them.

'Yes, but I can't afford them,' she replied, looking at the price tag. 'I'll just have to stick to the ones that came free with a magazine, which I've had for years.'

'You see, quality needn't be expensive.' Thea smiled, but she was worried about Tim. About how the other girls would go back to their wonderfully sober boyfriends and Tim would need to be carried on to the plane. Even though she was supposed to be on holiday, she couldn't relax.

'Shall we go and look at shoes we can't afford next?' Emily suggested.

They nodded and set off.

'But security is better now than it's ever been,' Lee said, and then hiccuped.

'Did they make us take off our shoes?' Tim asked. 'No, and my shoes look like they could have bombs in them.'

'But they don't?' Jimmy was horrified.

'No, of course not, but they didn't check. I'm sorry, but I'm disappointed in the way they didn't check my shoes.'

'Or mine,' Jimmy agreed.

'Guys, let's have another drink and talk about football,' Lee suggested.

Jimmy was in no state to argue any more.

*

'I think we'd better go,' Thea said, looking at the time. They made their way to the bar, chattering about themselves and the holiday.

'Ladies,' Lee said, grabbing for Carla and almost knocking her out.

'Oh, no,' Carla said. 'How did you all get in such a state? We've only been gone an hour.'

'Jimmy, are you drunk?' Emily asked. Jimmy shook his head.

'Tim,' Thea snapped.

'Oh, darling, don't be cross with me.' He lunged towards her and tried to kiss her, but she dodged out of the way.

'Our flight is boarding and unless you guys pull yourselves together this is going to be the shortest holiday in the history of the world,' Thea told them.

She managed to organise everyone. The women took the bags, the boys were to walk behind their girlfriends and not speak. If they were going to fall over, or anything stupid like that, they were just to lean on their girlfriends' shoulders and the others would help. In the event, they weren't quite as drunk as they first seemed, and Tim walked as if he'd been drinking water. They boarded and took their seats.

'When do we get to order drinks?' Tim asked. Thea scowled at him.

'Can I rest my head on your shoulder?' Lee asked. Carla nodded.

'I just wish they'd checked my shoes,' Jimmy repeated, and Emily gave him a confused look.

10

Welcome Letter

Dear Guests,

Congratulations on a wonderful choice of holiday. The owner, management and all the staff wish to extend a very warm welcome to you.

A welcome meeting will be awaiting you to outline The Love Resort and the opportunities that are available for you.

You will find all the information you need in this guest handbook, and the friendly staff are always on hand to answer any of your questions.

Enjoy your stay!

Anne-Marie Langdale

Guest Handbook

'So, what do you want to do today?' Katie asked, as she and Todd breakfasted on their terrace on the first day of their honeymoon.

'Sit in the sun?' He couldn't stop the sarcasm in his voice, and he felt guilty. She was only trying to be friendly – too friendly, admittedly, but there was no reason for him to be mean. He smiled, trying to convey his apology.

'Great, great.' He noticed that she looked hurt for a moment; it wasn't often that Katie showed any vulnerability and it made him feel awful.

'I'm going to collapse by the pool.' He smiled again, but it felt like a mammoth effort. He was tired, having at first been too scared to sleep, then too tired to stay awake, resulting in him being tormented all night by nightmares where she was the predator and he was her helpless prey.

'Great,' she smiled as she took a sip of orange juice and pushed her half-eaten breakfast away. 'I'll get all this cleared up and go change.'

From inside he could hear her call Marcus to clear the dishes away, then she called Mary to request she come and do some urgent laundry, then she called Erik and asked him to come and discuss lunch. Perhaps she had her new entourage after all, Todd thought.

He poured himself another coffee and sighed. He picked up the newspaper, which had been left outside the door, and started to read. Despite everything, he felt sorry for Katie. She was so sure that it was wrong to do anything for herself now that she was famous, and he didn't think that was necessarily her fault. He shook his head as he drank his coffee. He was going soft. David would be furious.

'It's OK, I'm done,' Todd said to Marcus, aware that he was blushing slightly. All of a sudden he had gone from composed film star to insecure teenager.

'Was everything all right?' he asked, pointing to Katie's half-full plate.

'Sure, she doesn't really eat,' he explained, feeling tongue-tied and awkward.

Marcus threw him his best smile, displaying the whitest teeth that Todd had ever seen, and started loading up the tray.

'Oh, Marcus, darling,' Katie said as she emerged, dropping her sarong like a stripper and sauntering towards them, 'what a glorious day.'

Both Todd and Marcus looked at her, eyes wide with amusement.

'Ma'am.' He bowed, but Todd could see his eyes were still laughing.

'Marcus, do you think you could help me? I need some headache pills, and I don't seem to have any.'

'You have a headache, Katie?' Todd asked.

'No, but I might. It's the sun, you see; it might give me a headache.' She emphasised the word 'might'.

'Any preference?'

'No. Maybe Advil or something like that. I'm not fussy.' As she said this she looked straight at Todd. Todd guessed that she was trying to impress him by acting all low maintenance, but he would never believe that of her.

'And shall I just bring them?' he asked.

'What do you mean?'

'Well, this is your honeymoon.'

'Oh, I understand. Yes, you can just bring them. If we want privacy we'll close the door and hang the "Do not disturb" sign on it,' she laughed.

Todd shuddered at the idea, and Marcus, shooting Todd one last smile, left.

As soon as he'd gone, Mary arrived. Todd greeted her warmly, glad that there was a steady stream of people.

'Oh, Mary, darling, I wonder if you could help me with my laundry?' Katie asked, in her nicest voice.

Todd, who had heard the way she spoke to her own staff, or anyone she didn't consider important found her behaviour amusing. She was being nice to them, and Todd couldn't help but feel that it was because of him. It didn't sound, or feel genuine.

'Of course, ma'am.'

'Oh, Mary, stop all that ma'am business and call me Katie. Would you like an autographed picture?'

'Um, yes, please,' Mary replied, looking confused. Todd chuckled to himself.

'Come with me, and let's see what needs doing.' Katie started towards the door and Mary followed behind her.

Todd set himself up on a sun-lounger by the pool and picked up the script of the movie he was due to direct. It wasn't only homework, but also a reminder of why he was there, why he had to stay and why he had to make the marriage look like it was working. He covered himself in the highest factor sun lotion, rubbing it in with the paranoia of someone whose youthful appearance mattered, and he lay back. He knew he was vain and ambitious, he didn't make excuses for that. He wasn't a bad person and, anyway, he was paying the price. It was a high price.

'Todd, shall I do your back?' Katie trilled, sitting herself down next to him and making him jump.

'No, I'm staying on my front for now.' He balked at the thought of her touching him.

'Well, could you do mine?' she asked, fluttering her eyelashes and acting coy. He made a face and took the bottle of suntan lotion from her. As soon as he had rubbed it into her back, he handed it to her and lay down again.

'Thank you . . . such lovely hands, so wonderfully soft,' she said in a husky voice. Then she began to make a number of noises that Todd could only assume were meant to turn him on. Horrified, he buried his head in his script.

The script was good, and Todd found it as absorbing as when he first read it. He began visualising it, imagining how he would direct it. He felt an electric buzz running through his veins, and he knew that he was right.

'Sir, madam.' Erik, the rotund chef, appeared in front of them, sweat dripping off his brow, and pale as if he never saw any sun, which, stuck in the kitchen nearly all day every day, he didn't.

'Erik,' Todd greeting him, 'those pancakes at breakfast were the best I ever tasted.'

'Thank you, sir.' The effect of the compliment was visible on his cheek. 'You wish to discuss lunch?'

'Oh, yes, Erik, but Todd's working, so how about we go inside?' suggested Katie.

'Thanks,' Todd said in surprise.

'Before I go, I do have a message from Mrs Langdale. She wondered if you would like to have lunch with her and her publisher today.'

'Sure, that'd be great. But can we have it here?' Todd answered.

'Of course, sir.'

As Erik and Katie disappeared, he turned his attention back to his script. She was trying so hard he had to give her that. For a moment he felt sorry for her again. So she was known as the biggest pain in the arse in Hollywood. She was also known for being the biggest slut when it came to sleeping her way into film roles, but she was in the false marriage too, she was just handling it differently; she was deluding herself that it was actually real. As soon as they'd been declared man and wife, Katie had launched her mission to make her husband straight. Todd had been alarmed, then very scared. He knew that he'd never succumb to her wild idea that she would suddenly make him heterosexual but he thought that maybe they could have some sort of friendship. He felt she deserved that. At the very least he had to earn her trust. Because for his movie to work, she had to be good in it, and it would take a great director, or a magician, or a miracle worker to get that out of her. He silently chastised himself; again, it all came back to his career.

Before they started fake dating, he'd watched her first three films. She was awful. She was so wooden just watching gave him splinters. There was nothing believable about her performance. To be fair, the scripts of the films were terrible and so was the directing, but still, she was undeniably bad. He would get a good performance out of her, not because he believed for one minute that she could act, but because he had to. And a good director could get a good performance out of anyone, he truly believed that.

Todd was still thinking about the film when Anne-Marie descended on him. He stood up, smiling at her. He had forgotten about lunch. He was introduced to Anne-Marie's publisher, and as Katie came out in her pink sarong, he rushed inside to put some shorts and a T-shirt on.

'So, Abigail, what did you think?' Anne-Marie asked as they sat on the terrace of her house.

'I think that they are the best-looking couple I have ever seen.'

'Me too. Her skin is so smooth, her eyes sparkled like diamonds – and did you see how silky her hair is? And Todd, well, he's just so gorgeous. Lovely broad shoulders and lean, smooth chest – and the way his boyish dark hair falls into his eyes . . .' Anne-Marie sighed. 'I couldn't have asked for a more perfect-looking couple in my book.'

'So you're ready to start writing?'

'Well, of course I have the story and I have the main characters, but I need to wait for my supporting cast, who are arriving this afternoon.'

'So maybe tomorrow?' Abigail's voice was sharp.

Hurt flashed across Anne-Marie's eyes. Her publisher wasn't being mean; she couldn't be. She banished the unbearable thought. 'Oh, Abigail, darling, your concern for my career is so lovely, so kind, and I do appreciate your support.'

'Of course I'm concerned; I'm your publisher and your friend,' she smiled sweetly.

'Oh, you are my best friend. Soon, Abigail, soon, it will all start and I know that this one will be written in record time because it's all here.' She tapped her head.

No, she must have imagined it. Abigail was only looking out for her friend, that was all, and Anne-Marie mustn't let paranoia creep into her mind again.

Todd was having a lie-down after lunch, having abandoned his script for a while. He heard Katie talking to Mary, her voice fairly loud. He smiled as he listened intently to their conversation.

'Oh, you have done such a terrific job,' Katie said. Todd wondered if she had sunstroke.

'The laundry you gave me will be back tonight. I should bring it?'

'Yes, please. As I said to the others, if there is a "Do not disturb" sign on, then leave the clothes by the door, but otherwise I want you to feel this is your home too.' He didn't think that she'd drunk much with lunch, but maybe she had.

'Right.' Todd pictured Mary looking uncomfortable and a little confused by Katie's gushing.

'Oh, this is such an adorable place, don't you think?'

'Yes.' Mary's voice was unsure.

'And my husband and I are very happy here. Oh, isn't he adorable?'

'Yes, yes!'

Todd laughed out loud. So Mary had the hots for him too! His laughter drowned out the rest of the conversation.

'I came to check that you have enough champagne,' Marcus said.

Todd, back on the sun-lounger, looked up at Marcus. 'Not sure, the way she drinks it,' he replied.

'Well, I'll do a stock-take and replenish any that need it. Is there anything else that I can do for you?'

'No, thanks.'

Todd looked at him and practically swooned. He was tall,

with beautiful dark skin, and shaven black hair. His arm muscles were evident beneath the polo shirt, and his legs, clad in white shorts, were long and muscular. He turned to go and Todd realised he needed to do something.

'Marcus?'

'Yes, sir?'

'Firstly, please call me Todd, not sir. Where are you from?'

'I've lived in the Caribbean for as long as I can remember.' Todd listened as Marcus explained that his father was Jamaican and his mother American. They had met while working in the tourism industry, which was why Marcus had chosen to follow them.

'Lucky you.'

'It's nice.' He seemed unsure.

'It is that. Marcus, my wife is inside doing God knows what. I don't suppose you could help me with the suntan lotion?' He handed the bottle to Marcus and longed to feel his touch. While Marcus applied it, hands shaking, Todd felt every sense in his body come to life. Then he felt guilty. He shouldn't have put Marcus in that position. But when he turned to thank him, they shared a look of understanding. It was an intense look, a look in which Todd was conveying the truth to Marcus. He knew he shouldn't, but he couldn't help himself.

'This is better than expected. Not only do we have Abigail keeping her busy, but now the film stars. When the competition winners arrive shortly we'll have all the time in the world together,' Ed said as he rebuttoned his trousers.

'We do have work to do,' Lily pointed out.

'Spoil sport. We'll be good and get our work done; but still, we should be able to spend more time together than usual.'

'Do you feel guilty?' Lily asked.

'Yes, if I'm honest I do. God knows why. She's treated me like dirt for so long. Anyway, you can comfort yourself with the knowledge that she doesn't love me and definitely won't miss me.'

'Apart from maybe in a professional capacity.'

'Exactly. It'd be more like losing a member of staff than a husband.'

'You know, despite the fact that she's so awful, I can't help feeling sorry for her.'

'And that is why I love you, Lily – you're so sweet.' He laughed. 'Come on, let's go get Anne-Marie's gorgeous winners.'

'The plane has landed,' Lily told Ed. 'They'll be through any time now.'

'Do we need to hold up the card?'

'We'd better.' Lily smiled. Ed winked as he held the card aloft. Normally this job would be done by a number of members of staff at the resort, but because of the importance Anne-Marie had put on the competition winners, Lily and Ed were acting as reps. They had taken one of the resort's mini-buses and a driver, and arrived at the airport in plenty of time.

'They'll be tired.'

'Yes, well, once we've shown them to their rooms they have an hour before Anne-Marie's welcome meeting.'

'The rumour mill about Todd and Katie has started.'

'What's being said?' Lily asked.

'Nothing much. It's just that the staff know they're here so, as per Anne-Marie's wishes, the chances are that the rest of the resort will know before long.'

'Well, your wife thinks they're the best things ever. I had to listen to her going on for hours and hours about them and how wonderful they were. I think even Abigail's getting a bit fed up with her.'

'What makes you say that?' Ed brightened at the news.

'Oh, she made this face; I don't think she thought I saw her.'

'You are kidding?' He couldn't imagine Abigail making a face at his wife. She was the person who had turned her into the monster. Abigail was Anne-Marie's Frankenstein.

'I'm not. Oh, look, I think that's them.' Lily moved forward to greet their visitors. 'My name is Lily Bailey. I'm in charge of public relations for the resort. This is Ed Smith.'

'I'm Anne-Marie Langdale's husband, and we'd like to welcome you all to The Love Resort.'

'Thank you,' Emily said. Everyone introduced themselves.

'Right, if you've got everything, let's get going. I'm sure you all want to get to your rooms and rest.' Lily started marching the group to the mini-bus like an overenthusiastic school teacher, which amused Ed no end.

Ed let Lily explain about the resort's history and its facilities during the short drive. He listened as she gave the couples some background on the island but not too much; guests were not encouraged to spend too much time out of the resort except on organised trips. Organised by them, of course.

'So, as you can see, the island is very tropical,' Lily said. As she spoke, Ed took time to study their new guests.

Emily was almost bouncing up and down with excitement as Jimmy held her hand tightly. She was truly gorgeous, and her smile was almost infectious. Jimmy was alternating between looking out of the window and looking at Emily. Ed smiled too. He was in love; he understood.

'When we get to the resort, and you're settled in your rooms, you'll find there are full details of all the main attractions.'

Ed looked at Tim, who lay across the back seat of the mini-bus with his legs draped over his girlfriend. Ed thought that Thea looked like she was listening intently, perhaps as if she expected to be quizzed later. He couldn't be sure but Tim looked as if he was sleeping. But then it had been a long journey.

'And, of course, the facilities at the resort ensure that there's more than enough for you to do there, if you don't want to leave,' Lily announced.

'Great,' Lee said, nodding his head. He had his arm draped over Carla's shoulder and she had her head tilted, nestled in his chest.

Ed had to concede, Anne-Marie had got her good-looking cast, and they seemed exactly as she was expecting.

'My goodness, this is fantastic,' Jimmy exclaimed when they were left in their room.

'Oh, Jimmy, it's everything I dreamt it would be. It's perfect, so perfect.' Emily jumped up and down on the teak king-size four-poster bed, before they explored their room like children. They ran to the terrace, which had two sun-loungers covered in soft beige material, overlooking the sea. Then they went to the large bathroom, where the cool marble tiles glistened. Finally Jimmy stood behind Emily as she opened the closet, which was big enough to house their volume of luggage several times over.

She pulled out the soft fluffy robe. 'I am going to live in this,' she squealed, slipping it on, then taking it off again.

'It's fantastic,' Jimmy repeated, putting the television on and beginning to flick through the cable channels. He could barely believe that it was all real.

'Oh no, you don't. We won't have time for watching telly while we're here.' Emily approached him seductively and he couldn't stop grinning as he kissed his gorgeous girlfriend.

'What do you mean there's no minibar?' Tim stormed, before slamming down the handset.

'What's going on?' Thea emerged from the bathroom with shampoo in her hair from her aborted shower.

'I just telephoned them to ask them about the minibar. I

thought they must have forgotten to put one in but they said that they don't have them in the rooms.'

'Is that all? I heard you shouting and thought you were being mugged.' Thea looked around at her luxurious surroundings. Every cupboard door was open, as were the drawers, as if Tim expected them to put a bar in there. She sighed. When she'd first walked in, the room was everything she expected. On the wooden desk, a bowl of inviting fruit welcomed them. The crisp white bed linen was crying out to be slept under. The mosquito net over the bed added to its romance; like something out of a film. But Tim had managed to find fault.

'Thea, this is a posh resort and there is no minibar.'

'Tim, it's all-inclusive. You go to the bar and get what you want.'

'That's what she said.'

'Who's she?'

'The woman on the end of the phone. Well, in that case I shall do as you both tell me.'

Thea watched in horror as Tim stalked past her and out of the room.

'Bloody hell, there's about a hundred channels on this TV,' Lee said, beaming at Carla.

'Well, I'm not sure you've come all this way to watch TV,' Carla replied in what she hoped was her seductive voice. She was sitting on the bed, trying to get him to look at her. But the TV had won. What was it with men?

'Of course not, I've come here to get a wicked tan as well,' he replied with a wink.

She tried another tack. 'I have never seen a bed as big as this.'

'Yeah, it's great.' He didn't look up from the television. 'But you know that journey has really taken it out of me. I'm knackered.' He lay back on the bed. She debated pouncing on him but then she decided that she probably didn't smell so good after the journey.

'I'm going to take a shower.' She threw him a last loving look before going to the bathroom. Poor darling looked wiped out, and she knew that a good night's sleep would have him back to normal. For now, without Lee, she had to content herself with the free toiletries provided. She looked at them, presented in a pink heart-shaped basket, all with The Love Resort brand labels, and she felt excited. This was all so new to her. It was going to be nothing short of wonderful.

'So what do you think?' Anne-Marie asked.

'Of what?' Ed replied. He and Lily had just got back to the office.

'Our competition winners, of course. You've met them. I still haven't seen them.' Anne-Marie was desperate to meet them, but she wanted to orchestrate it. Their first meeting had to be perfect, so she needed to be patient.

'Oh, Anne-Marie, they are delightful,' Lily quickly put in. 'More attractive than in the photos, and they all look so in love.'

'They do? They do?'

'Oh, undoubtedly. I think you picked well,' Lily finished.

'Of course I did,' Anne-Marie replied. 'Now, I want you to ensure they are all in the welcome room on time, and then I shall make my entrance.'

'Can you get that, Tim?' Thea shouted. Then she remembered. Tim had gone on the hunt for drink. She stepped out of the bathroom and picked up the receiver.

'Hi, Thea?' an American voice enquired.

'Yes.'

'It's Lily. Just to tell you that you need to be in the welcome room in forty-five minutes.'

'Fine.' Thea looked at herself. She was wearing a towel, and her hair was still soggy. She hung up and quickly pulled on some clothes, and tied her hair up. She knew that her most time-consuming act would be persuading Tim to leave the bar, and she needed most of the forty-five minutes for that.

'Who was that?' Emily purred as she slid out of bed, putting on her fluffy robe.

'Lily. We've got the welcome thing to go to.'

'Great. We get to meet the famous romance writer. I was going to ask her to sign a book; do you think that's OK?' Emily sounded shy; hesitant.

'Of course it's OK. You'll have to go home with a signed book or everyone will think we're nuts.' Jimmy fell in love with her all over again at that moment. The vulnerable side to her melted his heart.

He went over and kissed her. 'I'd better go and shower then.'

'I think I'll join you,' she replied.

'So, this is a holiday but we have to go to a meeting. I just don't get it,' Lee objected.

'What's not to get? We get a horrible cocktail and a few details about the resort, we meet the famous author and we also find out what our publicity commitments are.'

'Wow, you seem to have it all organised in your mind. I just don't see why we have to go to a meeting on holiday.'

'So, if they called it the welcome party you'd feel better?'

'Christ, Carla, I think you just might be a genius.' He reached over and grabbed her in a bear hug. 'I suppose I'd better get washed and changed.'

'Hurry up, and we can get a quick beer before this thing.'

Lee's eyes lit up. 'Perfect. It's all-inclusive, after all.'

It wasn't hard to find Tim. He was sitting at the second bar she tried, engaged in a loud conversation with an American, who kept patting him on the back and ordering whisky for them both.

'Tim.' Thea approached him cautiously, like stalking prey. She worried that he would escape if she startled him.

'Thea, my darling.' He placed a wet kiss on her cheek, which she immediately rubbed with her hand. 'This is . . . damn, I can't remember your name.' He gestured at his drinking partner. Thea cringed at the over-the-top public school accent he'd adopted.

'I hate to break up the party, but we have to go to this meeting, Tim.' She watched as Tim looked at his half-full whisky, then at Thea, then at his new friend. Thea held her breath. It could go one of two ways. He would come quietly or he wouldn't come at all. Tim repeated his looking ritual once more. Then, to Thea's relief, he downed his drink and stood up.

'It has been a pleasure and I am sure that we will do it again.'

Thea rolled her eyes, said her goodbyes and steered Tim towards the welcome room.

The six of them greeted each other like old friends. Then the awkwardness of strangers set in.

'The rooms are lovely,' Carla said.

'Really splendid,' Emily concurred. 'And it's so hot.'

'The bar's great,' Tim said.

Thea cringed. She was going to have to tell him to cut down on the drinking. The holiday was supposed to be an opportunity for them both to re-charge, not for Tim to spend two weeks drunk.

'This holiday is going to be so cool,' Lee said.

Before anyone could respond the door opened.

They turned and stared. Leading the pack of three was the tiniest, pinkest woman they had ever seen.

'Oh, my darlings, welcome, welcome.' Anne-Marie went up

to each of them, hugging them to her and clapping her hands. Hot on her heels were Ed and Lily.

Immediately, Thea knew that this had all been a hideous mistake. This woman wasn't normal, although she should have known that anyone who owned something called The Love Resort wouldn't be. She noticed Tim staring at Anne-Marie Langdale with his mouth open; she poked him and gestured. Was this romance? A pink fluffy woman who didn't seem to be wearing shoes? She fought the urge to laugh and deliberately avoided looking at the others.

'Now before we start, I thought we should all toast your arrival.' Anne-Marie clapped her hands and they all turned to see a guy walk in with a bottle of champagne, followed by a woman with a tray of glasses. As they each had a drink, Anne-Marie launched into a formal talk about the resort. Thea tried desperately to follow what she was saying, but she found it increasingly hard to concentrate.

'I trust your journey was all right?' Anne Marie said when she'd finished her talk.

'It was fantastic,' Tim replied. 'And can I just say it's an honour to meet you.'

'Why, thank you, Timothy.'

Thea rolled her eyes. She noticed her travelling companions were watching the exchange with interest.

'No, Anne-Marie, thank *you*. And as I am a writer myself I'm hoping for the chance to get some pointers from you.'

Thea didn't know whether to laugh or cry.

'Abigail, Abigail, are you there?' Anne-Marie's voice trilled as she opened the door.

'Hang on.'

Anne-Marie stopped and stood just inside the door. She was sure that Abigail had shouted at her, or snapped at least.

Then Abigail emerged, looking the worse for wear.

'I had a headache, I was sleeping,' she snapped again.

'Oh, darling, I am sorry. Can I get you some pills?' Anne-Marie refused to acknowledge the bad mood, although she felt really hurt by it.

'No.'

'Abigail . . . ?' Confusion crossed Anne-Marie's face. Why was her friend being so mean?

'I'm sorry, darling, I just had a row with Philip on the phone and then I went to sleep. Sorry, I didn't mean to snap.'

Anne-Marie almost jumped for joy with relief. 'What was the row about?'

'Darling, I really don't want to say.'

'But I'm your friend, you must tell me.' She was jigging about.

'It was about your book.'

'My book?' Her excitement at not being in Abigail's bad books evaporated; Anne-Marie felt as if she might cry.

'Yes. Don't worry, darling, I told him that you would be delivering soon. You know what he's like; we've got catalogues to print up, publicity and marketing schedules to do and he thinks that the book's way overdue.'

'Oh, and you stuck up for me. You are such a doll. The competition winners are here, and I've met them – they're lovely, adorable, just what we need. Now they're here I promise to start writing the book tomorrow and you can tell your husband that.' Anne-Marie wished she could get her hands on Philip. What a bastard for putting Abigail through such an ordeal.

'I will and I'm sure he'll be delighted. What can I do for you?' she rubbed her head.

'Dinner, tonight? I'll pick you up about eight.'

'Perfect. But listen, you didn't need to come here, just tele-phone me.'

'But that would have woken you up anyway,' Anne-Marie

reasoned sweetly, and swept out. Abigail obviously was having a tough time, poor darling. The sun didn't seem to be agreeing with her, and now her beastly husband . . . Anne-Marie vowed to do something to make it up to her. She would write the book. She just needed some help.

'Anne-Marie, calm down. I don't understand what the problem is.' Ed was in the living room with his wife, who was pacing, and muttering and swearing. Lily had been summoned.

'I'll tell you when Lily gets here.'

Ed went to pour drinks. He had no idea what had made his newly calm wife so agitated. He hoped she hadn't found out about his relationship.

'Lily, come in.' Ed returned with the drinks to find Anne-Marie leading Lily in.

'Lily.'

'Ed.' Lily looked nervous; Ed was sure that she was thinking the same as he was. The trouble with subterfuge was that you were constantly thinking you'd been discovered.

'Right, well, I don't have much time. The thing is that I am under an enormous, enormous amount of pressure with my new book and with the resort and everything—'

'I thought all was fine now we have Todd and Katie and the competition winners here.'

'If you let me finish, Edward, it's OK, as you say, but I still need some help. You know that I need to deliver this book, and soon.' Ed watched his wife begin pacing again.

'Whatever I can do to help . . .' Lily offered. She looked relieved.

'Good. Because, you see, I need to get inside these relationships. Properly inside them, in order to write my book.'

'Anne-Marie, I thought you were just basing your characters on these people, not actually writing about them.' Ed was worried about the implications of her thoughts.

'I am, Ed, I am. But still I need to know as much as I can about them to base my characters on them. I don't expect you to understand. But I do expect you two to be my eyes and ears for the next two weeks.'

'What do you mean?'

'I mean, Lily, dear, that I have devised a plan. You and Ed are going to spy.'

11

Perfect Privacy

It's not often that you get a chance to be together and forget
about the outside world. Well, that is exactly what this holiday
is offering you. You will be given the gift of privacy, so you can
be as intimate as you want. Nothing else matters here apart
from your love. And to this end, we will ensure that your
privacy is respected at all times during your stay here.*
 Guest Handbook

* If for some reason your privacy is violated whilst you are staying
here, please report this to the Management who will sort out any
problems.

Todd looked at her. Again he felt sorry for her; she was trying
hard. She was wearing a beautiful satin wrap dress, an unusual
shade of green, which seemed to match her eyes. Todd admired
her style but was unable to tell her. He didn't want her to think
that this was a sign he was about to get back into the closet; part
of who he was was a man who appreciated pretty clothes. He
didn't expect her to understand.

They were sitting on their terrace, sipping champagne.
Tonight, they were having a romantic dinner for two, all organised by Anne-Marie. Todd couldn't argue against it; he even had
to thank Anne-Marie for her thoughtfulness. He and Katie had
been alone all day, although he'd had his head buried in a script
for most of it, and he'd managed to resist all attempts by her to

drag him into conversation. It was proving hard; she was more resilient than he'd imagined. He resolved that this evening, he would try to be nice to her, but at the same time he would try to ensure that she knew that he wanted only to be friends.

They sat at the beautifully laid table, candlelight bouncing off the water on their pool, the warmth of the Caribbean evening touching them, and as Todd realised how breathtaking it really was, the fact that he was a fraud once again threatened to drown him in guilt.

Marcus arrived with another waiter. 'Good evening, sir, ma'am. Erik has prepared a feast for you tonight.' Todd thought he heard Marcus's voice shake slightly as he explained the menu and also asked them to choose the wine, and he wanted to jump for joy. He had seen it; it wasn't his imagination. He had seen the interest, the attraction. Todd was under no illusions that it was love, but he recognised lust when he saw it and he'd just been given a major dose. God, he wanted to kick himself. He was on his honeymoon and was flirting with his butler. It wasn't right, it was out of order. It was unfair on Katie.

'Todd, I just want you to know how incredibly happy I am,' Katie said.

'Oh, so am I,' Todd replied distractedly, as he continued fighting with himself.

Lily couldn't believe that she was doing it. As soon as the staff had left, she'd taken her position, as per Anne-Marie's instructions, outside the film stars' bungalow. As it was a stilt bungalow built into a hillside she had had to scramble up the back, unseen, before finding the best vantage point. They were both on the terrace, so she positioned herself behind a thick bush beside their swimming pool. She crouched down, clutching the binoculars that Anne-Marie had insisted on hanging around her neck. She didn't really need them – she was close enough to hear and to see everything. As it was getting dark, she also had a torch, in order to see to make notes. Lily felt awful; invasive. But Anne-Marie wasn't going to take no for an answer. She wondered fleetingly how Ed was getting on. She was pretty sure he didn't have to hide in a bush. If only she could have stood up to her boss. Forget morals, she was spying on famous people on their honeymoon. She was no lawyer but she was sure she was breaking about one hundred laws.

At first sight, the honeymooners looked every bit the romantic couple. Boy, Lily thought, they were both so attractive, as they sat across from each other. Katie's face was illuminated by the candles and she looked every inch the movie star; Todd was so handsome, his hair flopping across his forehead, his shirt showing off the outline of his taut body. She shook her head; Anne-Marie had already turned her into a proper voyeur. Although, it was understandable. Todd was one of the best-looking men in the world.

As they ate, she noticed that Katie was doing all the work. She was flirting for Hollywood, and Todd seemed quiet and a bit distant. Lily began to panic as she realised that this wasn't what Anne-Marie was after. Then she cursed; she'd have to lie. From her point of view, Todd was edging away from Katie, who was edging towards him. She wondered if they'd had a fight, which was the only explanation she could think of. She was a bit sorry that she'd missed that.

'I'm really sorry, but I am beat. It must be the sun; I have to hit the sack,' Todd said. Lily saw him look at the dessertspoon that Katie was wielding in his direction. She was practically on his lap. Lily shuffled slightly closer.

'Oh.' Katie sounded so disappointed. Lily was certain there'd been an argument and Katie was obviously at fault. Otherwise Todd, she was sure, would have leaped across the table and ripped her dress off by now. Actually Lily might tell Anne-Marie that that was what had happened.

Todd stood up. He said good night and he walked away. Lily

could barely breathe. Katie sat, head hung. She discarded the dessert she was trying to coax Todd to eat and she sat at the table alone. Lily felt terribly sad as she watched Katie start to cry.

Ed wondered what Lily was up to, annoyed that this latest scheme of his wife's was keeping them apart. His mission was to keep an eye on the competition winners, all of them if they were together, or if not, to use his discretion as to which couple to follow. He sighed. It was madness. He and Lily had both been issued with notebooks and ordered to make notes of guests' behaviour, conversations, mannerisms and anything else that could be useful, ready to brief Anne-Marie the following day. Ed had a feeling that he and Lily were actually being given the task of writing her damn book for her. His wife was, of course, dining with her publisher, without a thought for them.

He had procured the table next to the competition winners. They had all left the welcome meeting together and gone to the bar, where Tim took charge of ordering drinks, with Lee encouraging him. It had been Jimmy's idea to go to dinner, and they'd decided to dine as a group. He was unsure if Anne-Marie would find this a plus for her story or not (although, of course, it was only the first night), but he continued making notes as he ordered a light dinner as cover. At least having them all together made his mission easier. If they were off in different directions, how would he know who to follow? And he would put money on his choosing the wrong couple. In his wife's eyes, anyway. He shook his head and told himself not to think about it.

'Who thought that Anne-Marie looked really scary?' Tim asked as he poured wine for everyone.

'Oh, yeah, Tim, I noticed your horrified expression when she walked in,' Lee said.

'I know! I had to nudge him. Bloody hell, Tim, let's hope she didn't notice,' Thea added. 'Mind you, all that sucking up you did meant that you're her favourite now,' she teased.

'But she's a romance writer, that's how they're supposed to look,' Emily protested.

'No, Emily, she looked like something out of a horror film,' Tim laughed. 'But having her on my side is not a bad move.'

Ed crossed out all recent notes.

'I wonder what tomorrow will have in store. The first proper day of our holiday,' Carla mused.

'I need sleep. And a tan, of course, although we've got heaps of time,' Thea pointed out.

'We could go diving, Carla,' Lee suggested.

'I can't dive. But one of those organised boat trips might be fun.'

'Diving sounds scary – the idea of drowning, or getting your air cut off,' Tim said.

'I've known you less than twenty-four hours but I know you watch too many disaster movies,' Lee stated.

'It's true, I do,' Tim admitted.

Ed was finding it all a bit dull. This spying was hardly James Bond action, was it?

'Dinner was delicious but I'm beat,' Carla said as they finished dessert.

'Fancy a moonlight walk on the beach?' Tim asked. Ed covertly looked at Thea, whose face had lit up.

'That'd be fun.' She leant over to touch Tim's face. Ed sighed with relief. Finally he had something romantic.

'That was a nice idea. Lee, wasn't that a nice idea?' Carla asked.

'Sure, babes. But I thought we'd have an early night.' He raised his eyebrows and Carla giggled.

'What about us?' Emily asked. Jimmy was red-faced.

'I have plans for us.' Jimmy didn't sound suggestive, like Lee. Ed scribbled furiously.

After dinner, Ed decided to follow Tim and Thea, as the others had gone back to their rooms. When he'd agreed to do

Anne-Marie's bidding (after all, he knew it was fruitless to argue), he had said that he wasn't going to hide in wardrobes or anything like that. His wife had scowled but eventually agreed that that might be going too far.

He stood behind a beach hut where he was out of sight and watched them, although he could no longer hear them. Tim was holding their shoes; Thea had her arm linked into his. At one point they stopped and faced each other, he brushed hair out of her eyes. Ed could hear the echo of laughter, which he told himself to remember, as they went to the water's edge, and it looked as if Tim was going in before Thea pulled him back. They stayed out for half an hour before turning round and making their way back. Ed almost held his breath as they got close to him.

'Tim, I really enjoyed the walk,' Thea said, genuinely thrilled.

'Good. It seemed like the thing to do.' Tim sounded bashful.

'You don't need to explain. It was lovely, that's all. But I'm exhausted; do you want to go to bed?'

'Yeah, I do want to go to bed.' He kissed her cheek and they made their way to their room.

When they were out of sight, Ed went home.

Carla thought she must have jet lag. She'd never had it before so she couldn't be sure, but she was wide awake although she was so tired she wanted to cry.

After dinner they'd come back to the room, showered and gone to bed, both too tired for conversation. Not that Lee was a huge conversationalist at the best of times, but tonight she was too tired to think, let alone speak. Next to her, he was snoring away. It was so unfair. She propped herself up on her elbow and stared at him. He was so perfect; apart from the electric drill noise that he emitted.

Jimmy was awake, having slept for only a couple of hours. Then his eyes had sprung wide open and refused to close again. He couldn't stop smiling as he remembered the way Emily looked when he'd led her back to the room to find a bottle of champagne and two glasses on their terrace. They'd watched the beautiful Caribbean night sky together and talked, really talked. He had thought about proposing, but he'd bottled it. He couldn't quite decide if it was perfect enough. Or maybe he'd chickened out. Did all men feel like this when on the verge of such a major decision? He wished he had someone to ask. He was sure that Lee and Tim weren't the best people.

After they'd finished the champagne, they'd both been giggly and a little tipsy, as they'd made love before falling asleep. He wasn't surprised that he couldn't sleep. Perhaps, like a child, he was just too excited. There was so much to look forward to.

'Anne-Marie, it's late, really late,' Ed pointed out.

'I don't care. I gave you both a job to do and I want to hear all about it. I stayed up especially, and you know how important my sleep is to me. Call her.'

Ed did as he was told, and a weary-sounding Lily informed him that she would be there as soon as possible.

'I haven't had time to write it up,' Ed said, hoping she didn't want to see his notebook.

'Give me a verbal report and then in the morning, I'll have the written one.'

Lily arrived, looking slightly dishevelled, which Ed thought made her look even sexier, if that was possible.

Anne-Marie ordered them to sit on the sofa; she placed herself across from them in an armchair. Ed wondered if this was anything like being in MI5.

'Lily, tell me about the evening.' Anne-Marie's eyes lit up, and she licked her lips, greedy for details, as Lily began recounting the tale.

After Ed had given his version of events, he stood up. 'Anne-Marie, I'm going to walk Lily back and then do my nightly check.' This should buy him at least an hour with her. His wife looked at him, but she was clearly distracted.

'OK, good work. Can you ensure that you've typed everything up by tomorrow morning?'

Ed nodded. He wondered if his wife was losing it, although it was hard to tell with her.

'So, how was your first evening as a spy?' Ed asked, as he shut the door behind them.

'You know, surprising. That stuff I said . . .'

'Was embellished?' Ed raised an eyebrow.

'Total crap. Todd and Katie barely said two words to each other and although she tried her best, he didn't go near her.'

'How strange for newlyweds.'

'That's what I thought.'

'Maybe you should be a writer; all that stuff about gazing into each other's eyes, jumping across the table, very imaginative.' Ed laughed; he imagined Lily's work going straight into Anne-Marie's book.

'Well, I guessed that she'd probably kill me if I told her the truth.'

'Of course, it would have been your fault. Well, at least my subjects behaved the way she wanted. Well, pretty much. Lee wasn't exactly romantic, more lecherous really.'

'Oh, really? Well, you made him so like a true Romeo.'

'Umm, maybe you weren't the only one stretching the truth slightly.' He winked at her, and patted her on the bottom.

12

Every week, a special barbecue is held for the guests.* Enjoy
a beautiful Caribbean evening with delectable food and, of
course, your loved one. A live steel band provides the entertainment, playing love songs to get you in the mood for love!
We look forward to seeing you there.
  Guest Handbook

* The barbecue is held every Sunday evening outside the main
restaurant. It is part of your all-inclusive package. If it rains then it
will be moved to the ballroom.

'I'm glad you're all here.' Anne-Marie looked at Ed, Lily and
Abigail as they sat in the office. 'I feel that we are heading in the
right direction.'

'With the book?' Abigail asked.

'Yes, yes! It's all going splendidly, but I need to outline
tonight's plan.' Ed groaned involuntarily. 'What was that Ed?'

'Nothing, darling, just a touch of indigestion, that's all,' he
grimaced, worried about what his wife had in store for him.

'Tonight, I have arranged for Lily and myself to dine with
Todd and Katie on the premise of discussing the publicity
arrangements.'

Ed held back another groan. That meant another night with
him watching the competition winners. And another night
without Lily.

'Of course, if we're dining with them, we can't really take notes. I know, I'll use my Dictaphone.'

'Are you sure?' Lily's eyes were wide.

'Yes, darling, don't you think that it might be too risky?' Ed suggested. He knew that spying on them was wrong, but taping them – whatever next?

'Oh, don't be silly. No one will find out,' Abigail stated.

'Thank you, Abigail, you're right as always,' Anne-Marie smiled.

Ed couldn't believe how far they were going for the as yet unwritten book.

'So that brings me to you two,' Anne-Marie continued.

'Us?' Ed shuddered as he looked at Abigail.

'Yes. Now you two will have to go to the romantic barbecue tonight and watch our competition winners.'

'You want me to go?' Abigail sounded as horrified as Ed felt.

'Of course, darling, I can't possibly expect Ed to be able to gather information on them all. Not at an event like that. I mean, we were lucky they dined together last night, in a way, although that didn't show too much romance, but tonight they might not be in a group. You two will have to ensure that you spend time watching each of the couples, then report back. Now, do you want Dictaphones?'

'No thanks. I'd rather collect information and make notes,' Ed said quickly. At least he wouldn't have to spend all evening with Abigail; they could split up.

'So what time do I have to be there?' Abigail asked, annoyed, which gave Ed a small amount of satisfaction.

'At seven. Ed will come and collect you. This is all going to be worth it.'

'For the book,' Abigail finished.

'So you're sure they're all going?'

'Yes, Anne-Marie, I went round and spoke to them myself.'

Lily smiled as her boss handed her a drink. She sat on the sofa in Anne-Marie's house. It seemed a lamp was shining in her eyes, she felt as if she was being interrogated. Perhaps she was getting too paranoid.

'Good, and what were they doing today?' Anne-Marie's eyes narrowed. Lily took out her notebook.

'Well, Emily and Jimmy had lunch at the Coral Restaurant – they missed breakfast – and then they spent the afternoon in their room. That's where I spoke to them. They were sunbathing on the terrace.'

'Um, so they spent the day gazing into each other's eyes.'

'I guess so.' Lily raised an eyebrow. They were doing what normal people did on holiday, as far as she was concerned. 'Anyway, I saw Lee and Carla on the beach. They too missed breakfast, and they spent all the rest of the day doing water sports. They're both quite sporty, actually. Carla said that she was trying to exhaust herself because she had trouble sleeping last night.'

'Right. So they engaged in romantic water sports – um, yes, I think I can use that.' Lily had no idea how – it sounded obscene, more like something you'd find in a porn novel than a romantic one.

'Tim and Thea slept nearly all day, according to Thea. I found them at the burger bar. Thea was a bit annoyed at wasting a day, Tim told her that they had ages left so not to be so silly. They said they were going to take a walk round the resort, to explore, before getting changed for tonight.'

'More romantic strolls. How lovely. How appropriate.'

'That's about all for now.'

'Good work, Lily. Of course I know you gave me the shortened version, so you can fill in the details in your typed report.'

'Oh, hi, Lily,' Ed said, as he entered the room. Lily wanted to swoon. He was so handsome.

'Ed, how are you?'

'Just about to go and get Abigail.' His look told Lily all she needed to know.

'Right, now don't forget, I really need some romantic dialogue,' Anne-Marie launched in. 'Remind Abigail of that, although she'll probably already know. Now off you go, you don't want to be late.'

'Abigail.'

'Ed.'

'We'd better get going.' Ed knew there was no option but to see this through. 'At first I thought that perhaps we should split up, but then I thought that we'd look more conspicuous on our own. So I think we should stick together, ensuring we have equal time with each couple.'

'Your wife has you well trained.' The disdain was evident in her voice, and Ed wanted to put her straight, but he held his tongue.

'Well, anything for the book, Abigail,' he said sarcastically. She shot him a dirty look. Tonight was going to be anything but fun.

They reached the terrace where the barbecue was beginning to liven up. A long table was laid out, ready for the sumptuous feast that the chefs were preparing. The steel drum band was setting up, and staff were running around all over the place. A few couples had arrived and were drinking and eyeing the food greedily.

'Christ, Anne-Marie was right about one thing, there's a lot of fat couples here.'

'Abigail, keep your voice down. We don't want the guests to hear you.'

'No, of course not. But no wonder she doesn't feel inspired to write.'

'Right, shall I get you a drink?'

'I think you'd better. Before your guests mistake me for part of the feast.' Ed tried to give her a withering look but he couldn't. Even after all these years she terrified him. He went to get two drinks, spotting Thea and Tim by the bar.

'Hi, glad you made it.' He felt stupid.

'Well, we didn't have far to come,' Tim replied, picking up two drinks and draining one before starting on the other.

'Well, I hope to see you later,' Ed said pleasantly. He returned to Abigail and handed her a glass of wine. 'Our first couple are here.' He gestured to them.

'Right then, we'd better get to work.' Abigail looked less than thrilled but they made their way to the drinks table, draining their glasses as cover.

'Tim, perhaps we should move away from the drinks table,' Thea suggested. 'Hello,' she said.

Ed and Abigail spun round, and Ed noticed Abigail turn red.

'Oh, hi again. Just getting a drink.' Ed took Abigail's arm and moved her away slightly. 'We don't want to be too obvious,' he whispered.

'Tim, did you hear me? I said we should move away. Perhaps get nearer to the food. When it's ready we want to be at the front of the queue.'

'We do? Oh, in that case, let me just get a couple more drinks. Actually, this is silly. I'll just take the bottle.' Tim picked up a newly opened bottle of wine, and clutched it to his chest.

Abigail and Ed didn't move. He started arranging glasses and edging nearer.

'You can't do that,' Thea hissed.

'Why ever not?' Tim asked.

'Ed,' Abigail said. He put his fingers to his lips; he missed what Thea replied.

'Who do you think you are? My wife?' Tim asked loudly.

'No, Tim, I'm your girlfriend,' she stated. They moved away.

'Why did you interrupt that?' Ed asked.

'Because, Ed, in case you hadn't noticed, we're supposed to be collecting material for your wife's book and that wasn't material.'

'Oh, yes. I guess listening to other people's conversations is a bit addictive.'

'Yes, but let's hope, for both our sakes, that the conversation gets a little more romantic.'

Emily and Jimmy sat down at a table with their food. Ed and Abigail stood fairly near, holding full plates in an attempt to blend in.

'You can't possibly eat all that,' Emily said.

'I'm going to give it a bloody good go.' Jimmy rubbed his stomach.

'Well, don't blame me if you get indigestion.'

'Oh, bloody hell,' Abigail said. 'What the hell is this?'

'Shush,' Ed hissed. 'Listen, they're normal couples, we can't expect them to spout lines of dialogue that can go straight into the novel.'

'We can't?'

'Do you and Philip speak like that to each other?'

'We barely speak, unless it's about business.'

Ed was a little surprised by the revelation. 'Right . . . well, my point is that we can't expect them to be romantic all the time. My wife does, but then she doesn't always live in the real world.'

'You can say that again.'

Once more, Ed was stunned. He turned his attention back to the couple.

'Well, this food is almost as delicious as you,' Jimmy said.

Ed and Abigail smiled at each other.

'Oh, Jimmy, you softy. Blimey, did you have to have that much garlic?'

'So, I'm thinking that we're not going to get much out of tonight.'

'Abigail, can I ask you something?'

'Yes.'

'Can you write?'

'What?'

'Well, it's just that you know how Anne-Marie is, and although this spying lark has provided us with material we can use, she wants more. So to keep her happy, we sort of . . .'

'Embellished?'

'That's a good way of putting it.'

'Oh, isn't that the last couple over there? Let's see what they have to say.'

Lee and Carla stood by a gazebo; they looked as if they were surveying the scene.

'Well, babes, are you sure you want to go to this?' Lee asked.

Ed and Abigail had snuck behind the gazebo.

'It might be fun. The food smells divine.'

'So do you.'

'Thank you. Would you rather have a quiet dinner somewhere?'

'Well, that band sounds awful.'

'Who'd have thought that "My Heart Will Go On" could sound like that?' They laughed.

Ed had to agree. The poor band had to play arrangements that murdered the most popular love songs on a weekly basis.

'And there's no bloody talent here.'

'Lee,' Carla admonished.

Ed raised his eyebrow at Abigail. When the coast was clear they emerged.

'Right, so how about I go back and start making shit up?' Abigail suggested.

'I think that's a brilliant idea,' Ed replied.

Lily and Anne-Marie sat on the terrace with Todd.

'I'm sure she'll be here in a minute, she's just getting ready,' Todd said.

Lily kept quiet. They'd been waiting for half an hour and her stomach was threatening to rumble.

'Oh, Todd darling, don't worry. When you're famous, time means nothing.' Anne-Marie smiled broadly.

'Tell me, Anne-Marie, where do you get your inspiration from?' Todd asked.

'Everywhere. Love is all around.'

Lily tried hard not to laugh.

'It is. You know your last book, *For the Love of a Great Man*?'

'You read my last book?'

'Oh, I've read all your books.' Todd and Anne-Marie smiled at each other. 'In the last one, I thought that your hero, Brett, was the perfect man.'

Lily gawped.

'What do you mean?' Anne-Marie asked.

'I mean, that when I play a hero, I will use your character as my inspiration,' Todd gushed.

'Oh dear Todd, you are so lovely.'

Katie emerged just as Lily thought she couldn't take any more of the mutual appreciation.

'You look breathtaking,' Todd said, as his wife sat down. Lily had to agree. No wonder she was so late. Wearing a long pink dress, she almost resembled Anne-Marie, although she didn't have any ruffles. She was a tasteful version of her.

'Thank you, darling.' She kissed Todd. Lily looked away; Katie was eating him up.

Todd pulled back. 'Katie, we have company.'

'Oh, I'm sorry,' she giggled. 'I just can't resist him.'

'Shall we eat?' Lily suggested.

13

Let Your Relationship Flourish

Day-to-day mundane matters can get in the way of romance. Bills, car trouble, house problems, your work life taking up too much time can all affect your relationship. Well, one thing we guarantee is that there are no mundane matters at The Love Resort. There is nothing but romance to get in your way!

Recapture the romance your relationship used to enjoy, or simply enhance it. Your relationship cannot fail to improve here.* The only thing that matters here is Love.
Official Love Resort Brochure

* If for some reason your relationship is not improved by your stay in The Love Resort, the owners of The Love Resort are not liable in any way.

'Oh, Lily, of course I don't expect you to sit in the bushes all day. You've got work to do.' Anne-Marie smiled. 'We can't keep an eye on them all the time. I've got your information, and with last night, which was wonderful, and the interview, I might even have enough. But, if we need more, we need more. We'll address it then.'

'Of course, Anne-Marie.' Lily sighed. The woman was insane. Lily had woken early to get the Todd and Katie tape typed up. The whole situation was absurd, and Lily wasn't sure how long she'd be able to go along with it. She also didn't believe that Anne-Marie would leave it at that. She knew they didn't have a book's worth of material, or anywhere near that yet.

'Also, we don't need to watch the competition winners today as tonight we have the welcome dinner arranged. That will give us an excellent opportunity to observe. I'll use my Dictaphone again. And Todd and Katie are going out on a private yacht today. They're doing a tour of the islands and won't be back until late. I thought about it, but there's nowhere to stow you away.'

Lily was lost for words as she busied herself shuffling papers.

'Did you sleep well?' Lee asked as he sat up.

Carla was pouring herself a cup of coffee. She turned round. Lee's hair was stuck to his head and his eyes looked as if they were reluctant to open.

'I think I might have done but I remember being awake quite a lot. This jet lag is a right pain. I'll probably only start sleeping properly when it's time to go home.'

'Oh. I slept like a log.'

'Must have been all that wine you were knocking back.'

'Hey, I didn't drink that much.' Lee stretched and yawned. He looked so sleepy and sexy.

'I'm starving, how about you shower and then take me to breakfast?'

'OK. Give me half an hour, and a cup of that coffee.' He got out of bed, kissed her and took the coffee cup from her, before disappearing into the bathroom.

Carla went to the wardrobe and opened it. Her clothes were all hung up neatly; Lee hadn't unpacked yet. She decided to dress and then unpack for him. Enjoying playing the role of 'wifey', she picked out a pair of shorts and a T-shirt and lay them on the bed, along with some old trainers. Lee wasn't a sandal kind of guy, something she was pleased about.

'What's all this?' he asked as he emerged from the shower.

'I told you I was starving; I'm trying to hurry things up.'

'Cool, babes.' Lee dressed as Carla waited for him out on the terrace. She looked at the sea view, still barely able to believe that she was there. The smell of the heat, the sea and the gardens all mixed together was intoxicating. She was ready to begin a new phase of her life; a new phase with Lee. They'd graduated, they were taking their first holiday together and they were in a luxury resort. Everything was perfect.

'My God, look at this!' Lee exclaimed as they surveyed the breakfast buffet in front of them.

'I have never seen such a feast,' Carla replied, delighted. 'If I'd known it was this good I'd have got up yesterday.'

'I tell you what, I'll go and order eggs and you get juice. Then we'll meet by the bacon in five minutes.' He winked and squeezed her bottom.

'Deal.' She felt like a child in a toy shop. Carla loved breakfast, always had, it was her favourite meal of the day and here she had a breakfast fit for a king. She piled a plate full of pastries, and took it back to their table where a silver pot of coffee sat waiting for them. She then went to her rendezvous with Lee and the bacon.

'I think I've just committed a deadly sin,' Carla announced as she sat back in her chair.

'What?'

'Gluttony. I've stuffed myself silly.'

'Well, in that case we need to repent. I know we're on holiday but how about we go to the gym?' Lee was big on exercise, but Carla was still aching from windsurfing the previous day.

'Um, lying in the sun, or going to the gym. What about swimming? I'll do lengths.'

'I guess that's OK. Shall we go?'

'Yes, if I can still walk.'

Carla took his hand as they made their way to the pool. The first pool they passed had a game of volleyball in it, music blaring from a sound system. Carla screwed up her nose, and marched straight past. Lee was staring, open-mouthed.

'What are you staring at?'

'This place, it's weird.'

'It is a bit, but I read in the information that there's another pool. Let's hope it's a bit more normal than this one.'

The second pool was smaller and quieter. It was almost abandoned. Lee went to collect some towels and Carla went to select the sun-loungers. She was spoilt for choice. They arranged the towels and covered themselves in sun cream. Lee had peeled his T-shirt off; Carla was in her tiniest bikini.

'Looking good,' Lee said, raising his eyebrows at her.

'Thanks. Race you.' Carla dived into the pool with Lee hot on her heels.

Carla felt as if she'd been in the pool for ever, and she was sure that she'd only burnt a fraction of the calories that she'd consumed, but then she wasn't normally neurotic about her more-than-healthy appetite. She climbed out of the pool and shook herself over Lee.

'Ughh, Carla, you bitch.'

'Sorry, it was an accident.' She laughed as Lee tried to look angry, and she lay down on the sun-lounger. This was the life.

Carla put her book down after fanning herself with it. They'd swum, Lee had fallen asleep and Carla had read a quarter of her novel. Now she was hungry.

'What time is it?' she asked.

'God, it's four.'

'I'm hungry.'

'We've missed lunch.'

'I know, but there's the beach bar, which serves burgers and things all day.'

'My God, you really did read all the information, didn't you?'

'Jet lag.' Carla laughed, and wrapped her sarong around her.

'Well, I think that it's good to be early,' Emily said as they lay by the pool after breakfast. 'Especially as we wasted most of yesterday.'

'You woke me at half past six,' Jimmy pointed out.

'But that meant that we were able to have breakfast, go to the gift shop and get the pick of the sunbeds.'

'Em, we're on holiday.'

'I know, but I wanted to send my postcards so they arrive before we get back. I should have thought of it yesterday.' To illustrate her point, Emily began writing.

'But we haven't got much to tell them yet.'

'Jimmy, we've got enough. It's sunny, romantic, beautiful. That's all you put on postcards, anyway.'

'I guess. I just don't really see the point in them.'

'You wouldn't. But I know my parents and friends want to hear all about the luxurious holiday we're enjoying.' Jimmy shrugged indulgently. She wanted to boast a bit, but so what? The holiday was going to be amazing and if Emily wanted to send postcards, then she should be allowed to. He was learning a lot about his girlfriend this holiday.

At breakfast she had been wearing her 'breakfast outfit'. The white terry tracksuit bottoms and skinny pink T-shirt (which Jimmy thought was more a gym outfit, but what did he know?) was apparently the best attire for breakfast as her day outfit (tiny sexy bikini and sarong) wasn't suitable.

'Em, how many outfits a day do you actually need?' Jimmy had tried not to sound like he was teasing.

'Well, there's the breakfast, the day, which is really for the pool, but if we were going to go out I'd have to change. I'm not sure if I need to change for lunch, and of course for the evening I'd change.'

Jimmy reached over and kissed her. She was so damn adorable with her outfits for every occasion. It amused him and touched his heart equally.

'This is so lovely,' Emily said a few minutes later, putting down her pen, 'although it seems we're the only ones here from the competition.'

'They're probably still in bed.'

'Oh, well. Never mind.'

'Jimmy, have you got your sunscreen on?' Emily asked.

'I actually applied it after breakfast. It said to do it an hour before going in the sun.'

'I know, I did buy it. Anyway, if you feel you're going to burn, make sure you tell me.'

Jimmy pulled his baseball cap down over his forehead. It was hotter than he'd ever experienced. He thought about removing his T-shirt but he felt a bit self-conscious, although all the other men were bare-chested.

'Take your T-shirt off,' Emily ordered, as if reading his mind.

He opened his mouth to argue, but instead did as he was told. He picked up his thriller and started reading. Jimmy didn't read much – hardly ever – but he decided he should on holiday. He didn't seem to be able to concentrate on the words, though; were there too many distractions: Emily, looking so incredibly sexy in her green bikini, with a bandana tied around her curls; the noise coming from the pool, where a large group of people were talking loudly, probably to make themselves heard over the music blaring out of the sound system. Jimmy went back to concentrating on his gorgeous girlfriend.

Thea woke with a start. Then she realised that the reason she was awake was because Tim was singing. She opened her eyes and looked around. He was in the shower, which she had to admit was a good sign. She looked at her watch; it was half past twelve. They'd missed breakfast again.

'Tim?' She pushed open the bathroom door and went to the sink.

'Hi, Thea, I'm just finishing, but if you want to join me . . . ?'

'No, thanks. I'll wait.' She couldn't figure out why she felt grouchy.

When Thea emerged, clean and feeling much better, Tim was dressed. He was wearing a bright red Hawaiian shirt and a pair of navy shorts; full of holiday spirit.

'Lunch?'

'I'm starving. I suggest we run for it.' Thea frantically threw on a pair of shorts and a T-shirt. Tim laughed, took hold of her hand and dragged her out of the room. They made it to the restaurant, which was fairly empty. Thea sat at a table, slightly out of breath, while Tim insisted on fetching lunch for them both from the buffet.

'I want to wait on you. Let me take care of you,' he beamed, and Thea laughed.

He was definitely in the holiday spirit. She began to think she'd been right all along. He was miserable at home, struggling for inspiration, and constricted. Here he was already like a different person – well, during the day he was. She tried not to think about how much wine he'd managed to consume the previous night, although he had been well-behaved.

'So, what do you fancy doing for what's left of today?' she asked, as they tucked in.

'I don't know. I read that they organise lots of activities here.'

'Tim, are we really the activities types?'

'Um, good point. Well, you remember the last time we went on holiday together?'

'Yes, we were about eight years old.'

'I know and we went to that place in Wales with the beach and everything.'

'Where are you going with this? It's not exactly like Wales here.'

'No, but remember how much I loved the beach then? Maybe we can spend the afternoon on the beach.'

'Of course we can, but I still don't get the connection with Wales.'

'Oh, I'm sure there isn't any. I just thought about it, that's all.'

They collected two towels and were able to nab the last two sun-loungers on the beach.

'Race you to the sea,' Tim said, getting up and running.

'That's cheating,' Thea replied, grabbing hold of his shorts and pulling him back. They collapsed in a heap on the sand, giggling like teenagers.

'This is fabulous, Thea,' Tim said. His face was so close to hers . . . she stopped. No, she must be imagining it. She stood up, shaking her head. She'd been with Tim since she woke and she was absolutely, one hundred per cent certain that he had not had anything to drink.

They dove into the waves, which didn't look big but were fairly strong, and they swam a little way out until Thea got scared and made Tim go back to shore.

'I don't think there are sharks, Thea,' Tim said as they collapsed on their beds.

'You don't know for sure. And also the current can change at any point and we could have been swept away, as far as Australia.'

'You've got some imagination. If I was going to be swept away, I'd like to be swept away with you.'

'You say the sweetest things.'

'Hi, guys,' Lee said, as Emily and Jimmy approached.

'What are you up to?' Emily asked.

'We just grabbed a burger, and now I can't move. Sit down.'

'We were just on our way back to the room,' Jimmy said.

'But not for anything important.' Emily sat down; Jimmy followed suit.

'Have you had a good day?' Lee enquired.

'Yes, lovely. We sat by the pool for most of it.'

'We were by the pool. Oh, did you sit by the noisy pool?' Carla asked.

'I guess, as it was definitely noisy,' Jimmy replied.

'Is there another pool?' Emily looked slightly upset.

'Yes, if you go past that pool it's behind the gym. It's much quieter.'

'But actually the pool we were at was quite amusing,' Emily stated defensively.

'Yeah, it looked fun, and our pool doesn't have a bar. Maybe we'll hang out there tomorrow, Carla.'

Carla nodded in agreement. It didn't matter, they'd had a nice quiet day together. She smiled at Jimmy. He was such a sweetie, although he came across as being a bit serious. Perhaps he was just shy.

'You've got a nice colour to you,' she told him.

'Thanks.' Jimmy sounded surprised, but he looked at his arms to check.

'I just get more freckles,' Emily moaned.

'I think they're really cute,' Lee said, before Carla shot him a look, and Emily blushed.

'They're gorgeous,' Jimmy stated, kissing his girlfriend. Carla shook her head. Lee was a flirt – harmless, but still she didn't really like it, and Jimmy obviously felt protective of his girlfriend.

'Thank you.' Emily blushed again.

'Mind you, babes, you're going golden brown,' Lee placated Carla and she grinned at him.

'Hey, Tim,' she shouted, and waved him over.

'Hello. Is this a party?'

'Not really. We bumped into Lee and Carla on the way back to our room,' Emily explained.

'Thea is having an afternoon nap, she's really suffering from jet lag. Who fancies a quick beer?'

They all agreed. They were on holiday, after all.

'This is the life. Perhaps we should buy one.'

'Buy one what?' Todd looked at Katie, who was almost bursting out of her bikini, which was pink. She always seemed to be wearing pink.

'A yacht.'

'What?' Todd looked incredulous. Anne-Marie, a woman he'd admired before he'd met her, was actually becoming the second bane of his life. The first being his wife. Anne-Marie had organised for them to have a private cruise; she thought that she was doing him a favour. It was his fault for gushing about her novels. He hoped that neither Anne-Marie nor Lily guessed the real reason for his devotion to her hero. He wasn't sure that the famous author would be pleased with the news that he imagined himself as the heroine.

'We can afford one.'

'Katie . . .' He wasn't sure if he had the energy to argue with her.

'Look, I know, I know, where would we keep it? But there must be an exclusive island where we could park it.' Todd decided to remain quiet. If Katie kept on with her fantasy life, and he ignored her, then perhaps she'd eventually get the message. Although he was beginning to think that his wife was one determined woman.

'And don't you think I'd look really cute in a sailor's outfit?'

'What?' Todd spluttered. Did she think that by turning herself into one of the Village People he'd suddenly fall for her?

'I know, it'd be adorable. I could get a little outfit and a hat. I wonder how much yachts cost.'

'Do you think it's lunchtime yet?' Todd asked, desperate to

change the subject before he ended up the proud owner of a yacht and a sailor wife.

'Oh, darling, let me go and check.'

Todd had to admit the idea of owning a yacht appealed to him. The lunch table, set up on the upper deck was stunning. As they ate fresh seafood, looking out on the dazzling blue sea, he felt something special. If only he could share it with someone special. He couldn't help but picture Marcus sitting opposite him. Now, he really would look cute in a sailor's outfit.

'Todd, Todd, are you listening?' Katie's voice interrupted his thoughts.

'Sorry. I was miles away.'

'I was just saying that we could perhaps do this again before the end of our honeymoon. More champagne?'

Todd nodded, and Katie filled up his glass. He noticed that she'd been drinking fairly quickly. Perhaps that was his fault.

'Yeah, we could do this again. I really love the sea.' He should try to make more of an effort.

'It's breathtaking. We can see for miles and miles.' Katie had a dreamy look in her eye and Todd, once again, felt threatened.

After lunch they went to lie on the lower deck.

'This sun is too hot for me. I'm going inside,' he announced after a few minutes in the punishing afternoon sun. He was worried about premature ageing.

'Fine. I'm staying here, I need to work on my tan.' She sat up, licked her lips and in one swift movement released her breasts from her bikini top. Todd had never moved so fast in his life.

He lay on the sofa inside, grateful to the air conditioning. As he was on his own he pulled out the script. He had decided, to be fair to Katie, that he wouldn't spend so much time on it. But with her sunning herself, he was free to indulge. He pulled out a notebook and started work . . .

*

'Mr Cortes, sir.' Todd looked up to see the yacht's butler looking down on him.

'Hi.'

'It's time to get ready for cocktails.'

'Lovely.' He swung his legs off the sofa. 'Where's Katie?'

'Mrs Cortes is still sunbathing. Shall I go and get her?'

'No, I'll go. Thanks.'

Todd made his way to where she lay, surprised that three hours had passed just like that. He stopped just short of her. She was lying down, her eyes were closed and she was pink. Almost as pink as her bikini bottoms.

'Katie!' he shouted.

She sat up suddenly. 'What's wrong?'

'Katie, I think you fell asleep. You're a bit red.' It was the understatement of the century, like describing himself as a bit gay. Katie looked at herself. Todd looked at her. Her entire front was pink, or red, he wasn't sure, but her breasts were almost glowing.

'Ahhhhh,' she screamed, and stood up.

'Here, put this on.' Todd threw her a towel. Although it covered her body, it left her pink face exposed.

'How could you let this happen to me?' she shouted, glaring at him.

Todd was relieved. This was the first time she'd ever shouted at him. It felt like a good thing.

'I fell asleep myself. I assumed you'd have put on enough sunscreen.' He cringed as he realised his chosen words weren't going to help.

'I did put on sunscreen, but this fucking water makes the sun hotter, and why didn't anyone tell me that? Now I look like a fucking lobster and we've got a photo shoot to do. And it hurts.' She started bawling loudly, but Todd couldn't tell if it was genuine or not.

'OK, here's what to do. You go and get into a cold bath, which should take the stinging away. I'll ask the skipper to get us home and we'll get calamine lotion and you'll be fine by the morning.'

'You really think so?'

'Yes.'

'How do you know so much about it?'

'I just do.'

'Fine, but if I peel, I'm going to kill you.' She stomped off and Todd finally allowed himself a smile.

His penance for letting her sleep (although he could have argued that it was the amount she drank at lunch, or her own stupidity, he didn't), was that he had to carry everything to the bungalow whilst ensuring that she wasn't seen by anyone. It took them a long time, and a lot of hiding in the bushes before they actually got back in.

'I'm calling Mary,' Katie snapped. Todd tried to look ashamed as he nodded. Katie picked up the phone. 'Oh, Mary, thank God. Can you get here straight away? It's an emergency. Bring stuff for sunburn. Oh, please hurry.'

Todd tried not to laugh. Within seconds, he opened the door to Mary, who was armed.

'Hi, Mary.'

'Where is she? What happened?' Mary entered the room like a whirlwind, Todd thought, then she spotted Katie and rushed to her.

'Oh, thank goodness,' Katie said meekly. Todd decided to stand back.

'Oh dear, Miss Katie. This looks bad but I can help. Todd, we need some cold wet towels.' Mary touched Katie's skin. 'Yes, it's still too hot. Go, go.'

Todd looked with surprise at Mary issuing orders to him. Only yesterday she was refusing to call him by his first name. However, he did as he was told.

'You can fix this, can't you? It's so important that I don't look red,' Katie cried as Todd returned with the towels.

'Of course I can. Now first we make the skin cooler. Then we smother it with aloe vera. You need to reapply it every half-hour. I shall stay with you and do it myself.' Todd was surprised once again that Mary sounded so assertive.

'Oh, Mary, thank you so much.' And again, he thought he'd never heard her treat her staff with such gratitude before.

Todd tried to keep out of the way, as Katie was being treated for what you would have imagined were ninety-degree burns rather than too much sun. However, he made himself useful, fetching them drinks and organising dinner for the three of them.

When Marcus delivered it, he seemed surprised to see Mary there, eating with them, and Todd took the opportunity of being alone with him to explain.

'She got sunburn on the yacht. Mary's taking care of it.'

'I see.'

'I don't see what's wrong with Mary eating with us, but your boss might not agree. I'd really appreciate it if you kept this to yourself,' Todd asked kindly.

'Anything for you.'

Todd was stunned. He was sure that Marcus had winked at him before walking off.

14

Special Love Resort Cocktail

While you are staying with us, we strongly recommend you try The Lover, The Love Resort cocktail especially created for you. The recipe was devised by a world-famous mixologist, and we believe it encompasses romance and combines it with a delicious, refreshing drink. If you enjoy this cocktail then you may purchase the recipe exclusively from the gift shop and take home some of the romance that you enjoyed while you were here.*

    Guest Handbook

* The cocktail is exclusive to The Love Resort, and although you have permission to reproduce it in your own home you may not sell the recipe on to anyone else.

Thea had given up. She woke up from her nap at six; Tim was nowhere to be seen. She'd dressed quickly and, like the previous night, she'd made her way to the bar. There she had been greeted by the rest of the competition winners, all drinking with Tim. She wasn't annoyed – well, she was a bit – but she'd had a drink and reminded them that they ought to get changed for the dinner with Anne-Marie. Tim told them to get changed quickly and by seven they were all back in the bar. It was clear that Tim was trying to get everyone wasted. Thea had given in to the 'if you can't beat them join them' theory and she was drunker than she had remembered being in a long time.

The bar was rather like a hut with a straw roof by the side of one of the swimming pools. They were all perched high up on bar stools, leaning on the wooden bar for support. Tim looked handsome, Thea reflected, in his striped shirt and his good pair of trousers. It made a change for him not to be wearing jeans. He had even got some smart shoes on; as if he'd made the effort. She was proud of him; of being with him. But then she was also drunk.

'You know, we've got to have this dinner,' Jimmy said.

Thea could hear the panic in his voice. 'Are you all right?' she asked.

'I feel drunk.' Jimmy looked at his shoes and then looked at Emily, who seemed oblivious to him. Thea smiled at him sympathetically. Emily was clearly drunker than he was; she seemed unable to focus on anything.

'Food will sober you up, have another one,' Tim said.

'I'm not sure I can, I feel a bit pissed,' Carla announced.

'I'll have one,' Lee said.

'Can you imagine her face when we all turn up wasted? It'll turn as pink as that thing she was wearing,' Thea giggled. She was feeling naughty and rebellious. She slipped off her sandals and wiggled her toes in the warm air. As the evening wrapped itself around her, she felt happier than she had in ages. She had to let go of things, relax more, enjoy herself. She giggled; she was really enjoying herself. She remembered back to when she always had fun.

'Let's propose a toast,' Tim announced dramatically. 'Here's to Anne-Marie the pink, and the bloody good idea of all-inclusive.'

'So, is everything ready?' Anne-Marie asked Ed as they left their house for dinner.

'Yes, darling, I phoned and checked. Abigail is being escorted down as requested and Lily will join us. Tonight you get to know your competition winners.'

'And aren't they lovely? I think they are the best winners we could have had.'

'Um, yes.' Ed had to hand it to his wife: she was totally consumed with these people in a way she'd never been with her paying guests. She had never made him spy on them.

Anne-Marie, Lily, Ed and Abigail stood in the private dining area.

'I thought you said that you told them to be here at eight sharp,' Anne-Marie seethed.

Ed knew that she had planned to make her customary entrance. She expected them all to be waiting for her. She was the celebrity and they were meant to worship her. But instead, they had thrown the doors open to an empty room and it was quarter past eight. Ed braced himself for trouble.

'I did tell them,' Lily replied defensively.

'Well, you obviously didn't stress it enough. Oh God, I don't know why I bother paying you ridiculous amounts of money for your limited talents. I should just do everything myself.'

Abigail cringed; Ed bit his tongue; Lily coloured. Ed was used to such outbursts but poor Lily was always hurt by them. Anne-Marie scowled at them both and ordered him to go and find the competition winners.

'Now, I shall go and wait in one of the rooms next door. When they arrive, you may notify me.' She turned to go. 'Oh, Abigail, darling, I am so sorry for you to have to witness this.'

Abigail remained silent, but Ed noticed her looking at him with what he thought might have been sympathy.

Ed approached the bar. He thought about trying their rooms but on the way he heard a loud and unusually raucous noise and followed that. He spotted them immediately; the couples had undergone a dramatic transformation. Tim was behind the bar, pouring drinks into a cocktail mixer, much to the dismay of the barmen. Lee sat on a barstool near him, enthusiastically pointing at the bottles for Tim to use. The others, scattered around the bar, were making a racket and they were obviously drunk. And, Ed noticed, they were also receiving looks from the rest of the guests – and not approving ones. He made a sympathetic grimace at the guests in a lame attempt to placate them, then turned to the youngsters.

'Guys, guys, you're supposed to be at dinner.'

'Really? And who might you be?' Tim demanded, holding up his cocktail shaker victoriously and letting some of the blue liquid seep down the side.

'It's Ed, you idiot.'

'Oh, fuck,' Lee said, sliding off his stool and stumbling as he tried to stand up.

'We might not be quite ready for dinner. You see, we might be drunk,' Tim added, attempting to leapfrog over the bar but landing spread-eagled on top of it.

'Are we very late?' Jimmy asked.

'Over half an hour. You really should come.' As he said this, Ed wondered if that was right. Anne-Marie would freak out when she saw them, and for some reason this made him want to laugh, despite the trouble ahead – as he or Lily would certainly be blamed. Employing his best school-teacher impression, he managed to round them up, and lead them away.

Abigail and Lily stood open-mouthed as Ed led the couples in. They were all swaying or, at the very least, unsteady on their feet. Apart from Jimmy, who looked petrified.

'Um, we should get Anne-Marie,' Ed suggested, looking at them. He didn't know whether to laugh or cry.

'Right.' Lily made to go. 'Oh shit, I can't do it.'

'I'll go,' Abigail offered.

Ed looked surprised. 'Are you going to warn her?'

'I think I'd better, don't you?' Abigail winked at him, and Ed wondered if events could get any more bizarre.

'Perhaps if we sit them around the table, then it might not be so noticeable,' Ed suggested, and they set about doing just that.

'So, shall we have a drink?' Tim asked, plonking himself down on a chair and rubbing his hands together.

'We should wait for Anne-Marie,' Lily told him.

'Bugger Anne-Marie,' Tim shouted, as the woman herself made her second grand entrance.

Anne-Marie cringed, and then told herself to keep calm. So, he'd had the cheek to say bugger her, shown her total disrespect, but she had no option but to let it go. Holiday high jinks, that was all it was, she kept telling herself, after Abigail's warning.

'Good evening. Now, as we're late, I think we should get on with dinner.' She took her place at the head of the table and looked around her.

This wasn't right. This wasn't supposed to happen. Her gorgeous people were too drunk. No one got this drunk in her novels. They sipped on champagne or cocktails, but they didn't get like this. 'Will everyone be drinking water?' she asked, with a threatening edge.

'Why on earth would everyone be doing that?' Tim asked, looking really confused.

'I was thinking that perhaps water with our meals would be perfect,' Anne-Marie pushed.

'Well, I for one would really like some red wine,' Lee said.

'How about we order some wine and some water?' Abigail suggested.

'Fine,' Anne-Marie replied, intoning it was anything but. How had this happened? Apart from Jimmy, her gorgeous young people all looked sweaty, flushed and dishevelled. They were characters in her book – she was about to start writing it, in fact. But tonight they were unsuitable as anything. She took a deep breath. This would not be allowed to happen again.

Wine was brought in, with the first courses hot on its heels. When Ed had ordered the wine, she'd asked for the food to be hurried up, hoping it might sober the little buggers up.

'Shall I give you some advice?' Tim asked.

'Me?' Anne-Marie was shocked. Not only did they look awful but they *were* awful. Where did this leave her book?

'Yes, of course you.' Tim waggled a fork at her.

'What sort of advice?' Abigail asked.

Anne-Marie shot a hurt look at her publisher; she sounded as if she was encouraging him. She shook her head; she must be imagining things.

'Well, it's about this place, really. You see, it's very nice, which I am sure you know, but the problem is the bar. The barmen seem to think that they should only serve drinks that they know about and, to be honest, for a five-star resort, I don't think it's good enough,' Tim explained.

'I don't quite understand,' Anne-Marie replied, anger boiling up. She counted herself calm. It was their third night, they were young, and they'd had a bit too much to drink. Perhaps it was something to do with jet lag.

'What he's trying to say,' Lee continued, 'is that the barmen only serve the drinks they know, and it's not very imaginative.'

The competition winners fell about laughing; their host had no idea why. Nothing remotely funny had been said.

'So what drinks are you suggesting?' Anne-Marie pushed the words out through gritted teeth. She wouldn't let them get to her. By tomorrow they would be her perfect competition winners again. Somehow, she would make sure of it. Or Ed and Lily would, anyway.

'Oh, I really liked the Blow-Job,' Emily said.

'The what?' She felt a nerve in her neck pulsing.

'It's called the Blow-Job, or the BJ for short, and it's bloody amazing,' Tim explained. 'I'll give you the recipe. Just between you and me, Anne-Marie, I am a bit of a cocktail connoisseur,' Tim smiled.

'What . . . ?'

'I really liked the Cunnilingus,' Carla added.

'That's what all the girls say,' Tim replied, laughing so hard that he choked.

'What was that one I liked?' Jimmy asked timidly. 'You know, the last one you made?'

'That was the Anal Sex. Illegal in some countries, but highly enjoyable.' Tim laughed so hard that this time he fell off his chair.

'Oh shit, sorry,' Thea said, trying to pick him up.

Ed, Lily and Abigail had visible tears in their eyes; Anne-Marie had nothing but anger in hers. She stood up; she had to put a stop to it now, before her novel was completely ruined.

'I will not have my resort tainted but this filfth. You . . . you won a competition to be here, and you are my guests. I have extended lovely hospitality towards you and this is how you repay me. You have been here a matter of days and you have offended me, shown me no respect and I will not have it.'

'Oh God, I am sorry,' Emily hiccuped and then began to cry.

'Look what you did,' Lee started, pointing a finger at Anne-Marie.

'I did? What I did? I am not staying here any longer. You'd better buck your ideas up pronto or there will be trouble.' Anne-Marie had steam coming out of her ears as she turned to leave. She would go, and when she saw them next they would be back to the way she wanted, needed them to be.

Anne-Marie paced her room. What had happened? *How* had this happened? Her perfect couples were drunken, rude, sewer-mouthed, and not at all perfect. She wondered why no one had come after her. She knew that Lily and Ed would probably be trying to get the drunks fed and into bed, but Abigail saw how distressed she was, and she should have rushed to be by her side. She was indisputably pissed off at the fucking freeloaders; she would not let them ruin her resort or her novel. No, she would not. They were her characters, and they would behave the way she demanded. She had to ensure it, otherwise her book was doomed.

'Em, don't cry,' Jimmy slurred. He felt awful, and a little worried. What if they were in trouble? He was also upset that Lee had stuck up for Emily when he should have done. He blamed it on the drink.

'Yeah, she's just an uptight bitch,' Thea said.

Jimmy looked at her with surprise, she sounded so angry.

'Well, perhaps we should apologise,' Carla suggested, looking at the others.

Jimmy was relieved someone else was voicing his thoughts.

'No, what we should do is give her an Anal Sex. That'll sort her out.' Tim fell off his chair a second time and everyone, Abigail, Ed and Lily included, finally let their laughter flow.

15

Your All-Inclusive Holiday

Now you have arrived, you can put your money away. If you choose, you need not spend another cent or penny at The Love Resort.*

The resort offers you as much as you want to eat and drink, extensive activities, entertainment and spa treatments.

Please see listed in this handbook everything that is available to you and indulge, indulge, indulge!

Guest Handbook

* All-inclusive does not include purchases from the gift shop, phone calls, some spa treatments and The Love Resort raffle, and food and drink are limited to what is available on the menus.

'I will not have it,' Anne-Marie screeched.

Lily, Ed and Abigail had all been summoned.

'Listen, darling, they were probably overexcited. I'm sure that today they'll be perfectly well-behaved,' Abigail reasoned.

After Anne-Marie stormed out, the six winners had kept them in stitches with their ridiculous cocktails and their ideas for the resort. Ed, Lily and Abigail had all stayed with them, being entertained. No one thought about Anne-Marie at all.

'Abigail, with all due respect, even taking that into account, not only did they get drunk and upset the bar staff by trying to do their jobs, but as soon as they left the horrific dinner, they all ended up in the pool, fully clothed, and no one is supposed to go in the pool after seven p.m. I made that clear at the welcome meeting.'

'They're young,' Ed said. 'That's what young people do.' There was an accusatory hint in his voice.

'Not the young people I expected, not the young people I wanted. And I have to report that one of them, I don't know who, broke the padlock on the bar last night and stole bottles.'

'It's all-inclusive; you can't steal something that's all-inclusive.'

'Well, then, Ed, in that case it's vandalism. All-inclusive does not mean breaking locks.' Her voice had reached its highest pitch.

'Do you want me to talk to them?' Lily asked. She had no idea what was going to happen next. It was becoming clear that the looks that Anne-Marie wanted were there, but not the pliable personalities. They could put it down to the drink, but she was sure that something was off. For example, she could have sworn she saw Lee winking at her and checking her out last night. One thing that she was sure of was that spying was going to be increased, perhaps for different reasons this time.

'Well, I don't see what choice I have,' Anne-Marie sneered. 'I need them in line. What will Todd and Katie think?'

'Well, they probably won't know about it.'

'What makes you say that?'

'They have their private bungalow, they don't really venture out.'

'That's not the point. They are supposed to be dining in public at some point and if they come across this behaviour, then they'll think that the resort is trashy.'

'Let's give it another day or so. Last night could have been a one-off, after all.'

'Let's make sure it is. Otherwise I am holding you responsible.' Anne-Marie pointed at Ed and Lily. Lily wasn't surprised.

'Perhaps if we keep a closer eye on them . . .' Ed suggested.

'Well, yes, that's exactly what I expect you to do. And also, I expect you to find a way to make them behave as I want them to.' The anger in her eyes showed that she was far from joking. 'Today, you make sure you know where they are. If they put a foot wrong then I want to know about it. Todd and Katie will have to wait. And tonight we shall all be watching them. Is that clear?'

'Yes, darling,' Ed replied.

Lily nodded. How they were supposed to control these people she had no idea, but she also knew she had no choice but to try.

'My head,' Thea moaned as she opened her eyes.

'It's a lovely head,' Tim replied, snuggling up to her. All at once she felt warm and safe. He made her feel safe, she realised. Despite everything. Despite him being unsafe at times.

'What happened last night?' Thea made to sit up. 'Holy shit.' The room was filled with bottles of various kinds.

'Ah, well, they wouldn't give me a minibar so I decided to make my own. You helped.' Tim looked proud of himself.

'I did?' Oh God, not only was she a drunk now, but she was committing crimes. And she was supposed to be getting Tim to cut down on drinking, not encouraging him to drink more.

'Yes, you helped carry some of them back, although you wouldn't help me break the lock.'

'You broke the lock?'

'Yes, of the outside bar. You know, they locked it up, which I thought was a bit of a cheek as this resort is supposed to be all-inclusive and nowhere in the boring welcome meeting did she say that there was a time limit on drinking. Anyway, I managed to get in, luckily.'

'Tim, we'll be thrown out,' Thea said, panicking. So maybe she shouldn't have entered the competition. She just saw an opportunity for a holiday, and she thought it would sort them both out – lack of funds precluding her getting a holiday any other way. And she was exhausted, disheartened with her career and feeling really down. But Tim and all-inclusive were not really the best combination. She should have known that.

'Don't be silly. I'm sure everyone does it. Now, shall we take ourselves to breakfast and then to the swimming pool?'

'Tim, why are you speaking like that?'

'Oh, because the place is full of Americans and they love it. Don't you remember last night?'

'What else?'

'We met this American couple, and I managed to persuade them, in my most charming way, to help carry the bottles. They were a bit reluctant until I told them that it was British royal custom.'

'Oh my God. Oh my God. I think I'm going to be sick.'

Thea decided a shower would make her feel better. It just wasn't fair. Tim was fine; he even looked good, not like her. As she walked into the marbled bathroom, she saw a glimpse of herself in the ornate mirror and quickly ran into the shower. As she stood under the gold shower head, she made a wish to feel human again.

'Hurry up, Thea; we'll miss all the good food. You know how fat those other guests are – they'll eat everything in sight. Including us, if we're not careful.'

'I'm coming.' Thea stepped out of the shower, in her fluffy bathrobe and stopped.

'What?' Tim asked.

'I've never seen that before.' Tim was wearing yet another Hawaiian shirt, bright red, orange and green, covered in palm trees, with a pair of navy-blue shorts and some deck shoes.

'That, my darling, is because I've never worn it before. Now, I thought I'd lay your clothes out for you.'

'How sweet.' She kissed his cheek. He'd pulled out the same things she was wearing yesterday. Her old grey bikini, which used to be black when she was about sixteen, if she recalled right, and her only sarong, turquoise and yellow.

'My God, do we clash or what?' she giggled, slipping on her pink flip-flops. 'I think we might even give those Americans a run for their money.'

'I need some breakfast,' Lee said, crawling out of bed and straight into the bathroom.

'It smells like a brewery in here.' Carla wrinkled her nose.

'Um, that would be me.'

'I was pretty gone too.'

'I know but I think you smell it more on men.'

'In that case I'm going to become a lesbian.'

'Can I join in?' Lee asked, as his laughter was drowned out by the shower.

Carla lay in the four-poster bed, sinking into the soft, white bed linen, and tried to remember the previous night. Her hair was knotted when she woke up, and she thought she remembered them going in the pool at some stage. Had Lee paid her any attention? That she had no idea about. She thought she remembered him flirting with other women. But Lee was a big flirt; she'd always known that about him, so she couldn't complain. Could she?

He emerged from the bathroom and began to get dressed. He pulled on a pair of shorts and rummaged in his suitcase for a T-shirt, while Carla went to the bathroom.

After showering, she chose her only other bikini: a small pale blue one, which she hoped wasn't too revealing. But as she looked at her flat stomach, her long legs and her tiny chest, she knew that there wasn't much to reveal. Not like Emily, with her curves. She felt envious; especially as she was sure Lee had been paying her a bit too much attention. He'd flirted with Thea, she was sure, and also even with Lily a bit, but Emily most of all. She pulled on a white T-shirt dress and her blue flip-flops, and went on to the balcony, where he was sitting. Perhaps if she tried harder then he wouldn't need to pay attention to other women.

'So, gorgeous boy, are you going to take me to breakfast or what?'

Lee stood up and pinched her bottom. 'I might have to take you to or what looking like that.'

'So, you think I should wear the gold bikini after breakfast?' Emily asked.

'Yes.' Jimmy struggled with the word. He had never known such a hangover.

'Last night was such fun, wasn't it?' she continued.

'I'm not sure. I think we might be in real trouble.' He frowned. He hated to be sensible but he wasn't used to such childish behaviour. After they left the dinner, they'd gone to the bar, drank more, although Jimmy stopped quite quickly. He always knew when to stop, when he was crossing the line. He just hoped that Emily, who was happier than he'd ever seen her, hadn't noticed. Then Tim, who was clearly the ringleader, made everyone jump in the pool. Jimmy objected but Emily looked at him with such disgust that he'd followed them. Lee, who Jimmy at first thought was a nice bloke, kept looking at Emily's nipples, visible through her wet top, and Jimmy had felt fury building up, but he couldn't act because Emily would have killed him. Jimmy began to feel that perhaps it was all a mistake; that perhaps he was the only one there with romance as his first priority. This thought depressed him; he sounded so boring.

'Right, Jimmy, get dressed, I want breakfast.'

Jimmy looked at her in her breakfast outfit and wanted to eat her there and then. He stood up and went to the wardrobe.

He noticed Emily sigh, and hoped it was the hangover. She sat down at the wooden writing table and searched her jewellery case. As he dressed he watched her pull out a few pairs of earrings, hold them up to her ears before finally deciding. He pulled on a pair of khaki shorts and a polo shirt, then waited by the door for her to apply her lip-gloss. Finally she rushed over to him and kissed him.

'Love you, Em.'

'I love you too,' she replied.

The main pool was fairly busy as Thea and Carla, having bumped into each other at breakfast, picked out six sun-loungers, which they arranged together. Emily and Jimmy had arrived just as they were leaving and had asked them to save them some too.

'My God, look at these people!' Thea exclaimed as she surveyed the pool. A game of pool volleyball was underway.

'How do they know which is the ball?' Carla asked as the sea of shiny bald heads bobbed up and down, and other, un-identifiable, bits flapped around. She screwed her nose up.

'Is there anyone here with hair?' Thea asked.

'Just us.'

'Oh my God, imagine if that's what Anne-Marie does to people. They come with hair, they leave with none and that could happen to us.'

'Ugh. After last night, I'm not sure I'd blame her for scalping us.' Carla settled down on her sun-lounger and pulled out a book.

By the time everyone else had joined them, beach volleyball had turned into a swimming race. The bald men huffed and puffed as their wives cheered them on from the side of the pool. A large stereo had started playing Celine Dion.

'Have I gone to hell?' Tim asked.

'I think so,' Lee concurred.

'This is a strange place,' Jimmy added.

'Well, it's called The Love Resort,' Tim pointed out. 'And look at its owner.'

No one could argue with that.

*

Lily had drawn the short straw. When they'd seen the competition winners setting up their sunbeds together after breakfast, Anne-Marie had decided that Lily would have to spend the day by the pool. Undercover. Oh, and her undercover role was as an entertainment assistant. In true Anne-Marie style Lily had been made to wear a yellow pleated skirt, which barely covered her bum, and a white polo shirt. She also wore a whistle and had to pretend to be helping out with the activities, while keeping an eye on the three couples.

She wasn't sure, because she had been too scared to ask Anne-Marie, if she was supposed to be taking notes for her book or just making sure they were not causing trouble. Or both. She decided to cover all bases.

Thea was lying on her stomach, reading a book. Lily couldn't make out what it was. But she did notice how one of her legs dangled over the edge of the sun bed and rested on Tim's. Tim seemed to be asleep, eyes closed, lying on his back. They looked like a normal couple. There was silence, apart from Celine Dion's voice ringing out over the entire area. So far so good.

Lily had to speak to some guests who wanted to know the rules for the Lilo races, so by the time she returned to her mission, Jimmy was nowhere to be seen. Emily was asleep, as were the others. Lily fielded a few more activities-related questions as she watched.

'No, I'm sorry but I don't recall which day the banana eating competition is. You should call Guest Services,' she suggested, trying to look past the couple who were standing in front of her, and at Lee, who was in the pool with Carla. They were laughing and joking; she excused herself to get a closer look.

'Hi, Lily,' Lee shouted out. She was sure she caught him looking up her skirt.

*

'Where have you been?' Emily demanded as Jimmy returned. Lily thought she sounded annoyed. She began rounding up used towels so she could get closer.

'Yes, sir, of course I'll get you a clean towel.' She gritted her teeth.

'You were dozing so I thought I'd go and arrange something,' Jimmy said.

'What?' Emily demanded.

'Well, I've hired a boat for the afternoon, for the two of us,' Jimmy mumbled.

Lily nodded her head in approval. Anne-Marie would be pleased with this. Jimmy and Emily were going to spend the afternoon on a romantic boat trip for two. There was hope for her characters after all.

'What?' Emily shouted as she sat upright. Lily nearly jumped out of her skin. She noticed the others all looking away, and she felt tempted to do the same.

'I thought it would be nice.' Jimmy looked at his feet. He had turned a very bright shade of pink. It wasn't the sun, Lily thought, although why Emily was reacting like this she had no idea. If Ed whisked her away on a boat she'd be over the moon.

'Jimmy, why didn't you ask me?' Emily sounded furious.

'Em, I've booked it.' Jimmy's voice was quiet and Lily had to strain to hear him. Her heart went out to him. He was a nice guy, Jimmy. He was the least offensive at Anne-Marie's dinner and he obviously doted on Emily. That girl was too good-looking for her own good, Lily thought. Poor Jimmy.

'Fine, I guess I don't have a choice. What time are we leaving?'

'After lunch.' Jimmy was still staring at his feet, Emily was pouting and the others were all finding their reading material extremely interesting.

Lily decided to call her boss. She would tell her that Emily and Jimmy were going for a romantic cruise (in the hope that this would please her), and then she'd watch the others and try to work out how to make them sound like die-hard romantics.

'Drinks time,' Tim announced, as he stood up. Lee joined him immediately.

'Not me,' Thea said. 'I've still got a rotten hangover.'

The guys both swam across the pool to the bar.

'So . . .' Carla said.

Lily was back from her phone call and torn as to who she should spy on. She decided to see what Thea and Carla had to say, although so far, not very much.

'So,' Thea said, 'what are you going to do now you've finished university?'

'I don't know,' Carla admitted. She looked embarrassed and thoughtful.

'No idea?'

'No. God, that sounds awful.'

'Not really. I always knew I wanted to act and I took that as my degree. There was never a decision to make, despite the fact the bright lights haven't hit me yet.'

'You guys are so glamorous. You an actress, your boyfriend a writer.'

'What?'

'Tim, he's a writer.'

'Oh, yeah.' Thea stopped.

'What has he written? I did ask him but he sort of changed the subject.'

'Tim's a frustrated writer. Which I take to mean one who doesn't write. He says that the book is just around the corner, but I don't know.' She stopped suddenly.

Lily nodded to herself. That explained a lot. They thought that they had a successful writer and actress among their winners, but it looked as if perhaps the truth had been stretched. Lily couldn't help but hear warning bells turning into sirens.

'Anyway, I guess whatever you do; you'll want to be near Lee.'

'He's going to be in London.'

This was better. Carla talked about following her love to London, and Thea talked of Tim's flourishing writing career. Lily nodded to herself. She was getting quite good at this.

'We live in London.'

'Good. At least I'll know someone! You know, I might try to study some more. A postgrad course, maybe journalism.'

'Really? That sounds pretty interesting.'

'Shit, Thea, you know I've never thought about it before, but I love English and I'm interested in writing, so journalism would be perfect. I can't believe it's only just occurred to me.'

'So you've never discussed it with Lee?'

'He hasn't got a clue.'

Lily thought that Carla looked distressed as the conversation filtered out. She decided to make her way to the bar to see what Tim and Lee had to say. She wasn't sure she was ready for them. She stepped behind the bar, told the barman to ignore her and hoped that no one asked her to serve them. She didn't know her way around the bottles.

Lee and Tim sat on the bar stools.

'So, you and your bird, how long have you been together?' Lee asked. Lily crouched down and pretended she was looking for something on the shelf nearest them; hoping they wouldn't see her.

'Who?' Tim replied.

'Thea.' Lee sounded confused.

'Oh yes, her. Well, about for ever. We've always known each other anyway. What about you and Carla?' he asked.

Lily's knee started to hurt, but she couldn't get up yet.

'Less than a year. I thought you would have been too; you know the competition rules,' Lee replied.

'Oh yes, well, we've known each other for ever, but we've

only been biblical for a short while, if you see what I mean,' Tim laughed.

'I do, man.' Lee charged his glass.

Lily rolled her eyes.

'You two seem quite different,' Tim said.

'What do you mean?'

'Well, I don't know really. I mean, she's a bit more serious or sensible or something – you know, a bit like Jimmy.'

'What do you think of him and Emily?' Lee asked.

'They seem different too. I think she has a bit of a thing for you.'

'Really?'

Oh dear God, Lily thought. This is what she was afraid of. If this was true and anything happened, Anne-Marie would skin them all alive. Including her.

'She looks at you in a certain way. Although what would I know? I'm always drunk.' Tim laughed again.

'Well, man, I am pretty irresistible,' Lee said, but then he laughed.

Lily hoped he was joking. The trouble with spying was that it made every comment seem so much worse than it probably was. She decided to go and find Ed. He'd put everything into perspective for her.

The trip seemed to last for ever. Jimmy had been unable to get anything out of Emily. She had come along, she'd gone snorkelling, and she'd listened as the guide pointed out places of interest, but she refused to be engaged in conversation with him whenever they were left alone. He felt in his backpack for the ring, comforted by its presence, nervously working himself up for the moment when he'd propose. He knew that she'd forgive him when he'd done that – that she would understand why he'd brought her out here. He hoped she would, anyway. He had to convince her that he loved her with all his heart, because he did, and although she could be difficult sometimes, he couldn't imagine life without her. He believed he understood her. Her confidence was a mask for her insecurity, therefore she was difficult, she was reflecting this. So, if he gave her the commitment she needed, then she would no longer feel insecure and they would have a great life together.

Suddenly Jimmy felt himself turn green. As he rushed to the side of the boat, he saw Emily running up to him.

'What's wrong?'

'Seasick,' he muttered as he vomited. When he'd finished throwing up, Jimmy lay down inside, green and wretched. Emily came and told him that she'd asked the captain to take them back as quickly as possible, and then she went to sunbathe.

He lay on his back, on his own. He'd messed everything up good and proper.

'So, what do you want to do today?' Katie asked Todd, hopefully.

'I'm sorry, but I have to work. I'll be by the pool with my script, though, so you are welcome to join me.' The invitation was awkward. They were still barely talking after the previous night. When Mary had finally left, after applying lotion to Katie for what seemed like hours, Todd had tried to apologise again. She'd cut him off and gone to bed, complaining of a 'sun' headache. This was the first time on their honeymoon that she'd been distant from him, and he knew he should like it, but for some reason it made him feel even guiltier. He couldn't win.

'Oh, I might later on; I've got some stuff to organise with Mary.'

He began to get his things as Mary walked in.

'You look so much better, ma'am.'

Todd had to agree. The red was beginning to look more of a brown and nothing was peeling. Which he was grateful for as that would have earned him a death sentence.

'Mary, call me Katie. How many times do I have to ask you to call me Katie?'

Todd smiled to himself and went to change.

'So, is everything clear then?' Katie asked Mary. As Todd got changed he couldn't help but overhear their conversation. He was about to leave, but he opened the door and stopped.

'Yes, ma'am.'

'Katie. Please. Can I get you something to drink before you start?'

'A glass of water, please.'

'Oh, sit down while I get it for you,' Katie smiled.

'I can—'

'Nonsense, Mary, let me do something nice for you, after all you do for me.'

He saw Mary sat bolt upright on the cream suede sofa, her uniform riding up around her knees. Her hands were folded on her lap. Todd couldn't bring himself to leave. He had never seen Katie like this before.

'Is it all right?' Katie asked.

'It's very nice,' Mary replied.

'Oh, good.' She was visibly relieved. 'So, Mary, do you live on the island?'

'Yes, all my life.'

'And do you like it?'

'I do.'

'I bet. It must be lovely to live somewhere so beautiful. I live in LA, which to be honest is really fake. And ugly and filled with pollution. I used to live in the countryside in America. It was beautiful there.'

'It was?'

Katie nodded. Still Todd hung back. He'd never heard this about Katie, and certainly not from her.

'Do you have family?' Katie asked.

'A husband and three children.'

'And do you love them very much?'

'I do.'

'Oh, Mary, I long to love like you.'

'Eh?' She shuffled around a bit and tried to pull her uniform down slightly. Todd noticed that Katie was oblivious to her discomfort.

'To have a man to love and who loves you. To have children who need you, who depend on you. My family back home, in the country, they didn't really love me. They do now, but only because I send them money. Can you imagine having to buy love?' Todd felt terrible for her.

'No?' Mary looked shocked as a tear rolled down Katie's cheek. 'You know you have a fine husband.'

Todd felt his blood run cold; now he felt terrible for himself.

'I do, but, well, this is meant to be a secret, but as we're such good friends I can tell you. He doesn't love me.'

'He doesn't?'

'No. He loves men.' Katie collapsed in tears as Mary took her in her arms and comforted her.

Todd froze. Did Katie not know that he was still here? She had just told their maid his big secret. The one that no one was supposed to know outside the studio. Fuck. He couldn't believe it, and he didn't know what to do. Unable to face the scene in the living room he escaped through the other door and angrily took his script to the pool. He was angry with Katie for blurting out their secret; he was angry with himself because her tears spoke volumes.

'You're working again,' Marcus said.

'Never ends,' Todd replied, sitting up. He looked at Marcus flirtatiously.

'Can I clear the breakfast things?'

'Sure.' Todd frantically searched his brain for something to say. 'How long have you worked here?' Not great, but a start.

'Just over a year. My parents have a small hotel in Barbados, so I thought I'd take a different place to learn the ropes.'

'That's great!' Todd chastised himself for being such an idiot. 'Are you planning on running it one day?'

'That's the plan. I've got ideas; I'd like to make it more upmarket. That's why I came here, although this isn't what I had in mind, to be honest.'

'Thank God.' Todd laughed, and began to relax. This was nothing to do with Katie, it was to do with him. If she had someone to confide in then why couldn't he?

'So are you enjoying your honeymoon?' Marcus's intention was clear.

'Not really.' Todd looked him straight in the eye. If Katie was going to be indiscreet, what was there to stop him?

'Can you get out?' Marcus asked. Todd was taken aback by his forwardness, but also turned on by it.

'Not tonight. I agreed to have dinner with Katie.' He needed to tread carefully. He couldn't blow this; he'd come too far to risk everything for one night of lust and, despite her betrayal of him, this still wasn't fair on Katie. He was disappointed, bitterly disappointed.

'There's a place in town. I can get someone to drive you. Tomorrow?'

'I can't . . .'

'I'll send a car. It will be waiting at the front at nine. No one will know.' He stared at Marcus, who looked and sounded determined. Todd felt his heart speed up.

'But . . .'

'It's up to you. The car will be there.'

As he watched Marcus leave, he knew that he couldn't be so reckless. Could he? Katie had been pretty reckless. Perhaps two could play at that game after all.

16

The Love Resort Evening Entertainment

The entertainment schedule below is run on a weekly basis and is the same every week, unless advertised otherwise.

Monday – *Couples' Karaoke*

Tuesday – *Romantic Disco*

Wednesday – *Couples' Talent Competition*

Thursday – *Taste of the Caribbean, Limbo Night!*

Friday – *Love Songs with Juliana*

Saturday – *Live Romantic Piano Renditions by Candlelight*

Sunday – *Romantic Barbeque*

'I have called you all here because I want them fucking well sent home.' Anne-Marie paced the office, while Ed, Lily and Abigail sat listening.

'We can't send them home,' Ed said. 'Think of the publicity.'

'What about the other guests, Ed? What about Todd and Katie, hmm?'

'But, Anne-Marie, what about your book?' Abigail put in.

'Well, that's not going to get written. Oh no, not at all while I have to suffer in the face of those awful people. It's as if they all entered the competition to spite me, to hurt me, to ruin me.' She was thunderous.

After their impeccable behaviour (according to Lily) during the previous day, Anne-Marie had felt more hopeful. How lovely that Jimmy and Emily were taking a beautiful romantic cruise together. How wonderful that Carla told Thea that she would follow Lee to the ends of the earth. How romantic that Thea had confided in Carla that Tim wrote her love letters and poems daily. How heart-warming that Lee had told Tim that he didn't notice any woman other than Carla. How utterly charming that Tim had told Lee that Thea was his soul mate. For a while she had thought that her book was back on track.

But they'd blown it. When Anne-Marie had attended the evening entertainment to watch them, she'd thought that it would be to enhance the days' events and get more material. Not to ruin her night, and cause her book what might be irrevocable damage.

They'd arrived at the romantic disco just after nine. The first thing Anne-Marie noticed was that there were five of them, not six. Jimmy was missing. She discovered that Jimmy had a bad case of seasickness and was in bed. So much for a romantic hero. They didn't get seasick. Then Tim, of course, went to the bar and started lining up drinks. The other guests couldn't fail to notice how he ordered four different drinks at a time, and then tried to get the others to do the same. The amount of alcohol he consumed in one night was more than most of the guests consumed in their whole stay. He was clearly taking advantage of her hospitality and she was mad as hell. She had been talked out of telling him off about breaking into the bar by Ed, who said that they needed to keep things sweet for the publicity, but she was itching to get her hands on him, jumped-up drunken bastard that he was.

Her paying guests watched the group with growing unease, and then when Tim started singing along to the disco, he had the cheek to try to make them all join in. Some of them did, others looked horrified. A few guests even walked out in protest. Anne-Marie was furious. The competition winners were cheapening her resort. When they were supposed to be making it classier!

'It's karaoke night on Mondays,' Anne-Marie had protested in vain. Abigail was nowhere to be seen, Ed and Lily had gone to talk to all the other guests to pacify them, leaving her all alone with 'those people'.

Lee asked Emily to dance and kept giving everyone the thumbs-up as they swayed along to Whitney Houston. He even had his hand on her bottom! Carla looked as if she would cry, until Tim grabbed her for a dance and then promptly fell on top of her. Anne-Marie didn't know what to do; she wanted to kill them all.

She called a premature halt to the entertainment at eleven, sending the DJ away before she went angrily home. Then when she woke she discovered that Tim had found the karaoke machine and held his own karaoke night. The bare-faced cheek. And Ed and Lily hadn't stopped him. They said they were unable to, because quite a few of the other guests joined in, but Anne-Marie didn't believe that. They kept the barmen there until four, and they probably upset the other guests. After all, she'd had two complaints already that morning! She could no longer cope with them. It had only been four days and they were already ruining her life.

Her nerves were shot to pieces. The book that she was trying so desperately hard to write was being ridiculed by these people. Abigail wouldn't be able to protect her for ever and she had promised her a book. She couldn't bear the thought of upsetting dear Abigail. But did these young hooligans care? Of course they did not.

One guest had been woken by Emily throwing her shoes at Lee, who'd ducked and they'd hit the guest's window instead. Then Carla had been found crying hysterically by another guest, who had escorted her to Lily, who had to put her to bed. Lee was asking anyone who would listen to him, 'What the fuck is it with women?' and Tim had been singing 'Hound Dog' at full blast on a loop for half an hour. She was amazed that only two couples had complained. She guessed the others were far too polite. She wouldn't entertain Ed's suggestion that some of the guests had enjoyed themselves, she just wouldn't.

'I want them on a plane home,' she screamed. 'Today.'

'Anne-Marie, we have the interviews of the competition winners tomorrow; we need them here for that. Otherwise how will we explain it to the magazine?'

'And what if they go home and tell everyone, or a newspaper or something, that you threw them out? They'll twist it and make us look bad,' Ed added.

'So what do you suggest?' her eyes were blazing.

'I suggest, darling, that you get tomorrow over with and then you give them a talking to,' Abigail said calmly.

'Oh, Abigail, where would I be without you? Will it really be all right?'

'Of course, darling. Now Lily can deal with the guests who complained and maybe you should go for a lie-down,' Abigail suggested.

'I will, and don't forget to keep an eye on things. God, Ed, Lily, you should never have let this happen.' She swished out of the room.

'That was some row we had last night,' Lee said as he woke up.

'I don't really know what to say.' Carla really didn't; she didn't remember much apart from sobbing her heart out.

'It was my fault, you're right; I behaved like a total wanker.'

'Is that what I said?' She couldn't exactly remember. However, she was certain that Lee's attention to Emily was the cause of the row. He'd spent nearly the whole evening with her.

It rankled. It made her want to kill the other girl. Especially when they'd danced so closely together. Now it all flooded back. She was jealous but she was also humiliated because she was sure that everyone saw her crying.

'Oh yes, but with a few hundred "fuckings" thrown in. I think I'm going to the gym and then to see if I can get a game of tennis,' Lee said.

'Fine.' She didn't have the strength to argue. She watched him go, and knew that she was in real trouble. Frustrated, she decided to spend the day on their private balcony, reading, recovering from yet another hangover and reflecting on where she was going wrong. She couldn't help but blame Emily. Just because her boyfriend wasn't there, she had to commandeer Lee's attention. And he hadn't been sorry. Not as sorry as he should have been. His apologies were perfunctory, but she could see his mind was elsewhere. She knew instinctively that it was Emily he was thinking about. She felt her stomach churn. She was close to losing him and she was scared.

'Are you all right?' Jimmy asked as Emily woke.

'Why shouldn't I be?'

'Well, you were very angry with me for staying in bed last night and you lost your shoes.' He had been unable to get any sense out of her when she'd got in. She had been acting like a madwoman.

'Did I?'

'Yes.'

'Oh, I was just drunk – you know what Tim's like. Sorry.'

Jimmy opened his mouth, then closed it again. He knew better than to push her.

Emily and Jimmy barely spoke through breakfast. Jimmy didn't understand it. He'd tried so hard to ask her about the evening last night. It was awful for him having to be away from her and maybe that's why she was angry. She was upset with

him for leaving her with two other couples, and he could see
why. He was grateful that he felt better today, so he could make
it up to her. He'd make sure he was by her side for the rest of
the trip, and then she'd be back to her old self in no time.

'Em, what do you want to do today?' he asked.

'Have you seen any of the others?'

'No, no sign. Maybe if we go and sit by the pool, they'll join
us.'

'OK, darling, that's what we'll do.' Emily seemed to brighten;
she even managed to give him a kiss.

'Tim, you can't drink that,' Thea screeched as she woke up and
saw Tim drinking red wine from a bottle.

'Why, is there something wrong with it?'

'No, Tim, there's something wrong with *you*. It's nine a.m.'
Thea woke in a foul mood, which she attributed to yet another
hangover, and the fact that Tim had managed to disrupt the
resort again last night. Through her hangover haze she could
remember Anne-Marie's fury. She'd tried and failed to stop
Tim. Then Carla had been in a right state, calling Emily a
whore, and sobbing. And she wasn't sure but she thought that
she heard Emily calling Lee a bastard and throwing her shoes
at him. She rubbed her head. It had been a mad night.

'Oh, I suppose it's a bit early.' He failed to look contrite.

'Tim, you stopped drinking at four. Well, I thought you did,
but maybe you didn't.'

'I did.'

'That's it. I've had enough.' She flung herself out of bed,
pulled on a pair of shorts and a T-shirt and, picking up her bag,
she opened the door.

'Where are you going?' He sounded panicked.

'Out,' she shouted.

'Thea, Thea, don't leave me,' he begged, as she walked away.

She took a path that led her round the resort. She was fuming and needed to walk off the anger. She was tempted to go to Anne-Marie and ask if she could send her home, but then Anne-Marie would eat her up. Her disapproval of them had been clear last night. Under the influence, they'd found it amusing. Now, though, she felt ashamed. They were on a free holiday, thanks to Anne-Marie. The least they could do was to show her some respect. But she really felt that this holiday was a terrible mistake, that the competition was a mistake, that she wanted – no, needed – to go home. Tim was out of control, and she didn't know what to do about it.

She felt herself begin to sweat, she was walking fast and the heat was getting to her. Her flip-flops began to rub at her toes, so she slowed down. She strolled, more calmly past the flower garden, past the perfectly manicured lawn. She could smell the scent of freshly cut grass mingled with the heat and the faint floral smell. She felt even calmer as her surroundings began to work their magic on her.

Thea returned to the room feeling fine. Her walk had helped to clear her head. She had to carry on, no matter how hard it was, and just hope that she could reassert some sort of control over Tim.

She let herself into the room and noticed that the drink was gone. Tim was on the terrace, eyes closed as if he was asleep. She was sure he'd just hidden the booze somewhere, but she didn't like to ask, and when he finally woke up he didn't mention it. She didn't see him have a drink for the rest of the day; she was impressed with the effort he was making. He appeared to be genuinely contrite. Perhaps things would be all right after all.

Jimmy, after a silent day, was actually glad to see the others as they walked into the restaurant.

'Come and join us,' Thea said pleasantly. Tim was next to her.

'Hi, guys,' Emily said enthusiastically, as she sat down.

'How are you?' Carla asked Jimmy; Jimmy noticed that she ignored Emily.

'Fine. Feel a bit stupid.'

'There's nothing stupid about seasickness. Every time I go to France on the ferry I suffer from it.' Jimmy smiled at Carla, but then he wasn't sure if he should. After all, Carla was acting as if Emily didn't exist. He was confused, especially as the mood was fairly subdued. He felt as if everyone knew something that he didn't.

'I wonder what tonight has in store for us,' Tim said.

'Shall we order? I'm starving,' Lee said quickly.

'Sure,' Carla said, picking up the menu.

The atmosphere really was strained; even Tim was quieter than usual, Jimmy decided.

'What exactly went on last night?' he asked good-naturedly.

Carla and Thea looked at each other, then looked away; no one would meet his eyes. Jimmy began to feel panicked.

'By the way, before we get carried away, we've had a warning,' Thea said, ignoring Jimmy's question. 'I bumped into Ed earlier and he advised us, in that friendly way of his, to keep a low profile.'

'What sort of warning?' Jimmy asked, immediately feeling scared, especially as no one would tell him what they did last night. He assumed that they didn't remember; he hoped that was all it was.

'Best behaviour. Firstly, we were too drunk at Anne-Marie's dinner. Last night, Anne-Marie was unimpressed with our behaviour – not you, Jimmy, obviously. Tomorrow we have our interviews and if we screw up tonight, my guess is that they'll send us home.'

'They wouldn't,' Emily gasped.

'That would be awful,' Carla agreed. Jimmy saw fear in both of their faces.

'I think we should have a quiet night tonight, in that case,' Lee suggested.

'I agree,' Thea said.

'Perhaps we should stay in tonight,' Jimmy offered, desperate to ensure there was no more trouble. He needed to find the perfect opportunity to propose to Emily after his previous attempts had gone so wrong. He couldn't leave the resort until he'd done that.

'OK, here's what I suggest,' Tim said. 'I suggest that after dinner we all go back to our rooms, with our loved ones.'

Everyone looked at him suspiciously, especially Thea.

'Where's the catch?'

'No catch. I want to spend the evening with my girlfriend, that's all.' Tim leant over and kissed Thea tenderly on the forehead.

Jimmy smiled. It was all going to be all right.

Ed felt relieved. He was sitting near them, and they hadn't seemed to notice him. He could hear what they were saying and he was glad that he could go back to Anne-Marie with good news. They'd had two evenings of overindulgence but they were back to being as sensible as they were when they first arrived. His spying mission would be a success. His wife wouldn't have reason to shout, swear or physically harm him. It was a good night.

After Lily's efforts yesterday, he hoped that this would be the end of it. Although he doubted it. His wife was increasingly obsessed. At first it was a case of studying them for her book; now her orders were to ensure that they didn't cause trouble. Well, thankfully, they were on best behaviour that night.

'We need to talk,' Thea said, as Tim sat on the edge of the bed, fiddling with the remote control, and she climbed on top of the pillows.

'I'm sorry,' he replied automatically without looking round.

'Tim, what's happening?' she asked.

'I'm just trying to have a good time.' He looked at her. 'What's so wrong with that? I can't believe we're on holiday at a resort that actually seems to object to fun.'

'I know, but we've caused trouble and, Tim, you have to admit you're the ringleader.' Thea stared at him, feeling wretched and worried and full of love.

'I'm sorry, Thea, really, and I'll behave myself from now on.'

'You will?'

'Scouts' honour.'

'Tim, I know you were never a scout.'

'OK, I promise, Thea.'

'Good.' She sank back on her pillow mountain.

'Why don't you come here and we'll snuggle up and watch this film?'

Thea moved into the crook of his arm and smiled up at him. He could be so cute when he wanted to be.

'Lee, we need to talk,' Carla started. She was sitting in a chair facing the television, which Lee was glued to. As usual. She decided to be bold. 'About last night.'

Lee sighed. 'I guess I owe you an explanation.'

'Just tell me why you spent all your time with her.' Despite trying to be brave, she was fighting tears.

'I felt sorry for her. You know, without Jimmy there. But I realise now that it was insensitive of me and I am sorry.'

'Is that it? You just felt sorry for her?' She desperately wanted to believe him; although Carla wasn't stupid and deep down she knew that there was more to it. But she decided to accept things. She couldn't help but think that it was Emily's fault. She had been wearing a tiny, revealing dress, which, seeing as she wasn't with Jimmy, Carla thought was a bit slutty of her. Then she'd definitely been making eyes at Lee, Carla had noticed that. She couldn't bear not to have a man fawning over her, so as hers was absent, she'd taken someone else's. Carla really disliked Emily and vowed that she would keep Lee out of her way from now on.

'I promise, and I'm really sorry for humiliating you.'

'It's OK,' Carla said quickly. She would make it work, of that she was determined, as she concentrated on the programme that Lee had finally selected.

'No, babes, it's not. I swear that it won't happen again. From now on, you're the only girl I dance with.' He leant over and engulfed her in a bear hug and she giggled into his shoulder.

'Em, we need to talk,' Jimmy said. He stood with his hands in his chino pockets by the end of the bed, on which Emily was lying, reading a magazine.

'What about?' She didn't look up.

'You seem really unhappy, and I don't know why.' He felt totally lost, as she finally looked up at him.

'It's just a bad hangover, but I'm sorry, I shouldn't take it out on you.'

'I shouldn't have left you last night.'

'You were ill.'

He felt frustrated with himself. Why on earth was he apologising for being ill? Why did he feel that it was his fault?

'I know but the atmosphere today, the warning, and no one will tell me what happened . . .'

'Oh, Jimmy, I'm sorry, it's just a bit embarrassing. You see, because you weren't there Lee asked me to dance and Carla got a bit upset. I mean, it was a mixture of drink and everything.'

'Lee fancies you?' Jimmy felt that he'd hit the nail on the head.

'No, of course not. He just felt sorry for me. But Carla took it badly and started crying. That's all, really. I guess they had words.'

'So what about your shoes?' He wasn't sure that he was getting the whole story.

'Well, I told you I was drunk and I just got frustrated because Carla wouldn't believe that it was innocent. I think I threw them but I can't be sure.' She looked down at the bed. 'What must you think of me?' A tear rolled down her cheek.

'I think that you're gorgeous.' He went to her and took hold of her hand. Poor Emily. She'd been on her own, and Lee, who Jimmy didn't trust, had obviously taken advantage of her. He couldn't blame Carla for being upset, but then she should have spoken to her own boyfriend, not blamed Emily. Women always blamed other women, he knew that from TV. He was glad that they were on their own now because otherwise he would have wanted to punch Lee. Not that he'd ever punched anyone in his life. From now on, it would be a romantic holiday for him and his future fiancée.

'Jimmy, you're the best. I love you.'

'Hey, how about we sit outside and watch the stars?' He smiled his little-boy smile.

'That sounds lovely.' She held him close as he led her to the terrace.

Todd had woken early with a burst of energy and set to work, leaving Katie asleep. His mind wasn't as focused on the script as it had been the previous day; he was focused only on Marcus's offer. The carrot had been dangled and although he told himself that he wouldn't go, that he couldn't go, it was making him want to even more. Katie's betrayal provided him with his only justification. Was it enough?

His thoughts were interrupted by the clip-clop sounds of Katie's expensive shoes.

'Morning,' she said, smiling.

'Hey.' He returned the smile.

'Have you had breakfast?' She looked at him and then at

herself. He followed her gaze. Today she was wearing the tiniest hot-pink bikini yet with a pair of Jimmy Choo sandals; Todd thought the shoes were gorgeous, but he couldn't share his thoughts with her.

'No. Shall I order it now?' She nodded and he went to the phone.

'Mary says I should keep out of the sun today,' Katie said, as she sipped her coffee.

'Well, is there something we can do inside?' Todd cringed as he realised what he'd said.

'Oh, Todd, there's plenty we can do inside,' Katie laughed. 'But what do you want to do?' She licked her lips provocatively.

Todd coloured. He had dug himself into yet another hole. How long could he use work as an excuse?'

'Uh, do you play backgammon?' he asked, mainly out of desperation.

'No.' Katie narrowed her eyes.

'Chess?'

'Do I look like a chess player?'

'Not dressed like that.' Again he cringed. He'd put his foot, his leg, his whole body in his mouth. 'What games do you play?' He felt like crying. Why was his mouth betraying him? He was trying to be nice, without being too nice, and the results he knew, as Katie started doing that thing she did with her eyelashes, was that he was unwittingly encouraging her.

'Strip poker?' she suggested, giggling.

Todd was literally lost for words.

In the end, he persuaded her that it would be fun for her to learn more about the character she was set to play in the film. He managed to flatter her into thinking it was a great idea. Todd decided that he could use work as an excuse for the whole honeymoon and he might need to. He was getting tired of it. Tired of watching her pout at him, flick her hair, shove her breasts in his face. Most men would give anything to be where

he was, and in his situation. Most straight men, that is. He
needed to come up with a plan. He needed some space. Katie
the predator was both scaring and suffocating him.

'What exactly do you mean, you have to go out?' Katie asked,
the sweetness slipping out of her voice with each word.

'Katie, please, I need to go, OK? As long as everyone thinks
we're together, we're in the clear. Believe me, no one will know.
I promise.' He was begging her, desperate to get out. He battled
with his conscience, he battled with reason, but now all he
wanted to do was to see Marcus.

'Where are you going?'

'Out. Look, order room service, tell them that I'm in bed sick,
or something. I won't be late.' This last statement was a lie; he
hoped to be very late. He felt guilty. Katie looked hurt, but
he couldn't help that. She had married him for her career, she
knew all about him, she had to accept things, the way he'd
had to.

'Fine.' Katie stormed off.

Lily was on the way to the bungalow for her second night's
spying on the film stars when she literally ran into Katie.

'Hello,' Lily said, surprised to see her out.

'Oh, hi.' Katie looked embarrassed, Lily noted. 'I just took a
walk on the beach before dinner. It's nice there. Anyway, I'd
better get back.'

'Where's Todd?' Lily asked, concealing her binoculars.

'Oh, he's back at the villa. He's got a bit of a headache.
Anyway, see you later.'

Lily watched her leave, and left a certain amount of time
before she followed. Glad that she didn't have to watch the
competition winners, she scrambled up the bank, the same way
she'd done the first time she'd been charged with watching the
honeymooners, and climbed over the back. However, this time,

it was more important, as Anne-Marie said that her book now hinged on the reports that Lily gave her about Todd and Katie – at least until they found a way of making the competition winners behave.

Lily made her way to the bushes, but there was no sign of either of them outside. Sighing, she moved closer, trying to ensure she was out of sight. Finally, she positioned herself by the patio doors, behind a tree in a pot. She knelt down and then looked inside. The sight that greeted her wasn't what she expected.

'Oh, Mary, thank you so much,' Katie said, as Lily saw them both sitting on the sofa with champagne glasses in their hands. She moved the tree a bit nearer to the open door, so she could hear more clearly.

'It's OK. You seem to cry too much for a honeymooner.'

'But it's not real.'

'No, but most things aren't what they seem.' Mary took Katie's hand; Katie gripped it tightly. Lily wondered what the hell they were talking about. What wasn't real?

'You think?'

'Yes. Out there you talk about these couples, so normal and in love, but you don't know. Behind the scenes no one is who they seem. You mark my words.'

'How on earth did you get so wise?'

'Ah, you flatter me, ma'am.'

Lily wanted to jump out and ask them to explain themselves, but she knew that she couldn't. Had Katie and Todd had another row?

'No, Mary, no, and please, call me Katie. Anyway, do you know what I've done for him?'

'No, Katie, but I think you've done a lot.' Lily watched Mary drain her glass and offer it to Katie to be refilled. Was she hallucinating?

'I have, Mary, I have done a lot. I even had my pubic hair shaped and dyed as the American flag.'

'You did what?' Mary nearly choked; if Lily had had a drink, she would have done too.

'Yes, well, I know that Todd's very patriotic. And I always wear pink.'

Lily adjusted herself, trying to be silent. Her legs were going to sleep but she couldn't leave. What she was hearing wouldn't be much use to Anne-Marie, but she was gripped. There was no sign of Todd, and no one had mentioned his whereabouts, not while she'd been listening, anyway. Where the hell could he be?

'Mary, have you ever been to Los Angeles?' Katie asked, as she poured more drinks.

'I've never left the Island,' Mary replied.

'Maybe you should come and stay with me?'

'What about my husband and my children?' Lily thought Mary looked as shocked as she was by the offer.

'Bring them. Mary, I think you're like family to me, like the mother I never had. I mean I did have one but she wasn't very nice. And she wasn't wise like you. So, you could all come. Oh please say you will.'

'I will! I will!' Mary bounced up and down on the sofa as Katie went to refill the glasses.

'Oh dear, I think we've finished another bottle of Cristal.' Lily looked and saw two empty bottles on the floor.

'I don't know what this stuff is, but it's darn good,' Mary said, before resuming her bouncing.

Lily really had seen everything now.

The car that drew up had blacked-out windows, but Todd felt safe as Marcus had informed him of the licence plate. He was relieved that he obviously understood his need for privacy and secrecy. As he sat in the back and the car began to wind its way around the bumpy island roads, he felt alive for the first time in ages. For the first time since he'd been told to start 'dating'

Katie. This is what he'd been warned about. That he'd die inside, lose himself, if he continued to be someone he wasn't. And he felt dangerously close to doing just that.

They pulled up outside a hotel, a small, plain place. He automatically felt nervous; as if he was doing something wrong. But he wasn't – this wasn't wrong. He went to get out of the car, but the driver stopped him and handed him a key.

'I'll be waiting to take you back when you're ready,' he said, before he drove off.

Todd told himself that it only seemed seedy because of the need for extreme secrecy, as he made his way to room twenty-four. The place was quiet and deserted, apart from a tired-looking concierge who purposely didn't acknowledge him. He unlocked the door and stopped. Sitting on a small armchair facing the door was Marcus. And he was completely naked.

'It must be hard for you living here,' Todd said, as he stroked the hair on Marcus's chest.

'It's not so bad. Only when I fall for a famous film star, then it's hard.'

'Because we have to keep it secret?'

'Because we do, and you have a wife, and you are staying where I work. That just about makes it as hard as it can be.'

'But we can do this again?'

'I don't think so.'

'Why? What was wrong?'

'Oh, nothing was wrong, but what if your wife called for me? I don't have this time off. I took a risk. It could cost me my job and my reputation.'

'So, if we want to be together again we have to find a way of meeting at the resort.' Todd panicked suddenly. It wasn't as if he believed he'd found the love of his life, but he had begun to find himself again, and that was important to him.

The same car dropped him home. He was shown how to get into the resort from a back way, so no one would see him. He breathed a sigh of relief as he made his way into the bungalow, then stopped. Mary was on the sofa, her head back, her mouth open and emitting a quiet snore. And with her head in her lap was his wife, emitting a louder one.

17

Time For Each Other

The Love Resort offers you and your loved one the chance to spend quality time together. Your privacy will be respected, giving you the golden opportunity for romance. Our rooms are designed to make you feel relaxed, so you can enjoy each other when you want to be alone.★

Remember, although there are activities for you, you must also make time for each other. Enjoy each other; indulge the person you love in this peaceful and tranquil setting.

Guest Handbook

★ We do not offer room service as part of a normal package, but if you wish to have a meal in your rooms, this can be arranged with a twenty-four-hour notification. We cannot guarantee it, but we will do our best to accommodate you.

'Not one complaint. They went to bed after dinner. Nothing else to report.'

'Their own beds?' Anne-Marie tapped her manicured nails on the table nervously.

'Yes, their own beds.'

Even Ed had been surprised by their restraint. After dinner he'd followed to ensure that the competition winners were in their own rooms and they were. He'd gone back to tell his wife, but she'd been asleep, so he'd gone to Lily's bungalow to await her return.

'Really, Ed, really?' Anne-Marie looked delighted.

'I promise. They were perfectly behaved,' he continued.

As they left the house to go to the office, he wondered how Lily was. Last night she'd returned and told him about the strange events. They had been baffled as they tried to work it out. But they couldn't dwell on it; they'd had to fabricate a romantic report for Anne-Marie, which had taken them hours. Ed was sure that the truth would have killed her.

At the office, Lily was already at her desk.

'Good morning,' Lily said to Anne-Marie and Ed.

'Ah, tell me, how was last night?' Anne-Marie asked, before she had even sat down.

'The report's on your desk. Again, another perfect romantic evening. Those two should be role models for marriage.'

Ed wondered how Lily could keep a straight face. He was struggling.

'Thank you, dear. As Ed told me, our reprobate winners were also well-behaved. I hope that it's a turning point.'

'Perhaps we can make sure that it is.' Ed didn't like to take anything for granted, but he was feeling optimistic.

'Right. Good. The interviews. I've prepared a list of questions for you. I see you scheduled Jimmy and Emily first, Thea and Tim second and Lee and Carla last. Then we have the group interview. After that, you take them on to the photographer. Have you briefed him?'

'Yes, as discussed. Emily and Jimmy on the sandy beach, him carrying her into the water. Thea and Tim on a love seat, with the orchid garden in the background. Carla and Lee on a catamaran, holding each other and laughing.'

'Perfect.'

Perfectly hideous, Ed thought. He bit his lip.

'Is there anything else I can do?' Lily asked as Ed buried himself in work.

'Just make sure that the questions get asked and answered

properly. I wouldn't put anything past those idiots. However, when you come back to me with their answers, I am going to edit them anyway.'

'Are you sure that's a good idea?'

'Oh, what, so I should let Tim say the best thing about this resort is how easy the bar is to break into? Let alone what the others might come out with. You think I should let them do this?' Her voice had risen an octave.

'Of course not.' Lily gulped. 'I was just thinking—'

'Lily, dear, listen to me.' Anne-Marie bared her teeth. 'You do the fucking job I fucking overpay you to do, and leave me to do the hard work. As usual. And if you ever, ever question me again, I'll send your scrawny arse all the way back to America, where you will never, I repeat, never, get a fucking job again after the reference I plan to write for you. Is that clear?'

Lily nodded. Ed saw she was close to tears. His wife could be such a bitch. But at least her outburst reminded him not to feel so guilty. He tried to smile reassuringly at Lily. He didn't trust himself to speak; he was afraid that if he did, he would definitely give the game away.

'Right Lily, are we ready to go?' Anne-Marie handed her a Dictaphone.

'Of course.' Lily pulled herself together.

'So, darling, is there anything pressing for today?' Ed asked politely.

'Not really. I am still worried about those winners. I know they behaved themselves last night, but, Ed, as far as I'm concerned, they're on probation. One more complaint about them and I'm throwing them out.'

'I agree, darling,' he concurred. 'But we have to ensure that they are not in a position to come back to us and give the resort bad publicity.'

'Of course. Ed, you know my book is ruined.'

'Can't anything be salvaged from it?'

'Well, of course the lovely Katie and Todd are still my main characters. And I think now that it's about a group getting stranded on an island. But, the supporting cast, well, I don't know. They're not right. Not right at all.' For once, instead of shouting, she sounded downcast. She was hoping the interviews would save her book, but she was still unsure.

'How about you use their looks and invent their personalities?'

'What do you mean?' It sounded like more work than she intended. So far she had enough material from Lily for a good few chapters and she could even use some about the competition winners – not much, but some. She was hoping that she'd have more, and the book would write itself. Now that looked increasingly unlikely.

'OK. Tim, good-looking, blond is the wit of the group, leave out the drinking. Thea, who looks a bit on edge all the time, in reality is the female version of Tim. They are the couple who make everyone laugh while being hopelessly in love with each other. Carla is slightly vulnerable, insecure, while Lee is always trying to protect her. Jimmy is the traditional tall and handsome man, and Emily is a young, innocent, who's in love for the first time.'

Anne-Marie looked at Ed in surprise. 'Edward, darling, I think you might have something. Why didn't I think of that? Oh my goodness, I may have just saved my novel. I must go and tell Abigail.' Feeling positive, once again, she swept out of the office.

'Aabbiigaail,' Anne-Marie trilled. She found her publisher on the terrace, with André, her butler, clearing away the breakfast dishes. Anne-Marie leant in to air-kiss her friend. 'I hope he's not disturbing you.'

'No, darling, not at all. Thank you, André,' she smiled at him; he nodded and left.

'Well, that all sounds great,' Abigail said when Anne-Marie finished telling her her new plans.

'The winners didn't turn out to be the way I thought, or hoped, but I am so terribly adaptable.'

'Which is why you're such a star.'

'Oh, thank you. Now what should I do about them, because apart from their looks I really don't need them any more?'

'Anne-Marie, you can't send them away, darling. They would go to the papers and you'd look like an ogre.'

'But what if I told my side – you know, how they turned up drunk at the dinner I gave for them and talked about anal sex? I mean, how insulting to have that bandied around at your dinner table?'

'Oh, I agree, but you understand what the media is like; they would unfairly take the couples' side. Six young people against the famous, talented and wealthy Anne-Marie Langdale. I'm sorry, darling, but you know it's true.'

'So I should let them stay.' Anne-Marie pouted. She didn't want them around any more. Not after they'd got the interviews done and she had enough information for her book. Not only did she have no further use for them, but she was also worried about what they might do next. Her book, and her nerves, were fragile enough without them sapping her inspiration further.

'I don't see what else you can do.'

'Well, tomorrow we have the big American magazine here to interview Todd and Katie. Thank goodness they turned out to be everything I expected.'

'So, you're going to start writing now?' Abigail looked hopeful.

'Soon, darling, soon. You know you can't rush the creative process.'

Thea was up early and she left Tim sleeping as she went to take a walk on the beach. It was such a treat to be able to stroll in the sun, watching the sea, just feeling free. That's what she felt. The setting was so beautiful, as the waves lapped around her feet, and the sun spread its warmth. She enjoyed the sensation of the soft sand between her toes.

Last night had been uneventful. After their chat, Tim had opened a bottle of wine that seemed to come from his wardrobe, and they'd watched the film. Thea had fallen asleep halfway through it, and for the first time in ages, she'd slept soundly.

Although last night had been quiet, she'd been grateful for it. There was no way they were in trouble, for once, and she hoped from now on, the rest of the holiday would provide her with much-needed relaxation. No more worrying, she told herself. It wasn't doing her any good. She wanted not to worry for the rest of their stay.

'Do you want to come to breakfast?' Jimmy asked.

He was close to despair. Last night, after they'd watched the stars for a while, Emily had led him inside and started undressing. She initiated making love with an intensity that proved that she loved him. She had been so tender and loving; he had been happier than ever. But this morning, she was distant again. He thought that maybe she was upset because he hadn't proposed to her yet. He had hinted at marriage before they left Devon and she had hinted that she liked the idea. Maybe it was because she had expected a proposal from him; he should probably have asked her under the stars last night. He cursed himself for being such an idiot. He kept missing opportunities. When they were engaged, he knew that everything would be back to normal; they would be stronger than ever. He needed to do it soon.

'Sure.' Emily replied unenthusiastically.

Jimmy smiled at her, willing her to smile in return, which she did, although he found it unconvincing.

'Hey, we've got the interview with Lily today, which should be fun.'

'Yeah, and then we'll be in the magazine.' Emily perked up.

Jimmy kissed her. Not only would they be in the magazine, but they'd be using the article to announce their engagement. Maybe he was better at this romance lark than he thought.

Carla felt humiliated, although she thought she'd managed to make a joke out of things. Last night, after the film, she'd got into bed, wearing her sexiest nightgown: black, see-through and very revealing. She was sure that Lee would be all over her in no time. But instead he'd turned away, barely glancing at her. He soon started snoring so she was sure that he didn't hear her crying herself to sleep.

They'd cleared the air, so why had he shunned her? Lee prided himself on being a red-blooded man – well, last night proved otherwise. It was her, obviously. He didn't want her. What could she do to rectify things?

She looked at him sleeping and decided to get up. She'd make coffee and then they'd go to breakfast. Today she would ensure that they were back on track. No, more than that, she would ensure that their relationship flourished, like it said in the brochure.

'Oh my God, what happened to me?' Mary screamed.

Todd stood in front of her with a cup of coffee; Katie was in her lap. Todd tried not to laugh at the horrified look on Mary's face.

'I guess my wife happened to you,' Todd reassured the terrified woman. Last night, he'd seen Katie in a slightly different light. He'd left her and she'd turned to Mary once again. Bereft of her entourage, she was vulnerable and he hadn't taken that into account. He felt guilty and vowed to make it up to her. And poor Mary probably had no idea that the champagne they were drinking cost over two hundred dollars a bottle, probably her monthly wages. He shook his head.

'Katie, Katie, wake,' Mary lifted her head gently.

'Mary, you stayed with me, you really stayed with me.' Katie sat up and flung her arms around her. Then she looked at Todd.

'Hey. Sorry for leaving you alone last night.'

'We had a good girls' chat, didn't we?' Katie smiled.

Todd could only imagine what they'd talked about.

'I am worried that they will sack me,' Mary said.

'Why on earth would they do that?' Katie asked, slightly hysterically.

'I am meant to be staying in my quarters.'

'But you are on call to us twenty-four hours a day, so, therefore, we called you,' Todd pointed out.

'You will tell them?' Mary asked.

'Of course, if anyone asks us. And, Mary, I think Katie and I can manage fine without you today. Take some rest.'

'Katie?' Mary looked at her uncertainly.

'You take the day off, and, Mary, think about coming to visit me in America. I really meant it.' Katie hugged Mary again and kissed her warmly on the cheek. Todd hid a smile; his wife was full of surprises.

Todd called Marcus to organise breakfast. Against all reason, he was desperate to see him again.

'Hi,' Katie said as she sat down opposite Todd.

'I really am sorry about last night.'

'Todd, we're grown-ups; you are allowed to go out.'

'I know, but, well, it wasn't fair on you.'

'I was with Mary. You know she's so wise and so caring, and she has so little. Don't you think that's amazing?'

'I do.'

'I want to do something for her, Todd, can you help me?'

'What do you mean?'

'She listened to me talking about myself all night and all she did was comfort me. There was nothing in it for her apart from some champagne, and she'd never heard of Cristal. She was nice for the sake of it. I mean, she's never seen a film with us in; in fact, the last film she saw was *Gone with the Wind*. So she didn't want anything from me. Todd, that's never happened to me before.'

He looked at her with surprise. 'What never? Not even before you were famous?'

'No, Todd, not even then.'

Todd hated himself for thinking it, but was this another of her tactics? It was definitely the kind of thing she would do; although if she was acting she was giving the performance of her life. Could she really have changed in a few days? He wasn't sure, but there was definitely something going on.

Todd reached over and squeezed her hand. She glanced up at him in surprise, and he saw that there was humanity in her eyes. He tried to convey that he understood with his. They were interrupted by Marcus, putting a tray down loudly on the table.

'Sorry.' He sounded anything but.

'Morning,' Todd said, taking his hand away.

'Smells lovely,' Katie added, looking at them suspiciously.

'Katie, would you mind dishing up breakfast? I forgot to ask Marcus to do something.' He followed the butler out.

'Marcus, wait.' Todd caught up with him just before he reached the main resort.

'What do you want?' Marcus scowled.

'I was just comforting her. Why did you look at me as if I'd done something wrong?'

'I was jealous, I guess,' Marcus replied.

'Don't be. She's a bit mixed up and lonely. I was just being nice.'

'Nothing more than that?'

'No.' Todd needed Marcus to believe him.

'Look, Todd, when I got back last night there were questions and it wasn't easy to deflect them.'

'Is there somewhere here we can meet? Tonight?' Todd knew he had to see Marcus again; reason had deserted him.

'Tonight is no good, my managers will be watching me. Maybe tomorrow.'

'Please?'

'I'll find somewhere for tomorrow and I'll let you know.'

Todd went back to his villa and his wife, feeling full of anticipation. It was so long since he'd been able to be himself and he thanked The Love Resort for that.

18

'So, Jimmy, how did you and Emily meet?' Lily asked.

The interview was taking place in the quiet garden, which had been cleared for the purpose. They sat at a small wooden table, a parasol keeping the relentless sun off their faces, and three glasses of water sat before them. In the middle of the table, as a reminder, sat Lily's Dictaphone.

'We met at my father's pub. I was serving behind the bar and Jimmy was a regular. We'd seen each other, but Jimmy was quite shy, really, so I served him a pint and then he mumbled something. So I asked him to repeat it and he asked me on a date!' Emily replied.

Jimmy nodded, although Lily thought he was a bit confused. In fact, thinking about these two, she guessed that Emily had asked him out. She couldn't imagine Jimmy having the nerve to make such a bold move. Still, she was there to interview them, not to judge.

'How lovely.' Lily wondered what Anne-Marie would do with that answer or, more to the point, what she'd make Lily do with it. She was sure that flowers, and maybe even a Shakespeare sonnet, would be added to the story. 'And what first attracted you to each other? Jimmy?'

'She's the most beautiful girl I've ever seen. I didn't know her at first, so I have to say that it was her looks that I was drawn to.' Jimmy was blushing.

Lily thought he was such a sweetheart. She wasn't sure that Emily deserved him, especially after her behaviour the other night. Imagine flirting with Neanderthal man Lee, when you had gorgeous, kind Jimmy.

'That's lovely,' she said, instead of voicing her thoughts.

'Actually, it wasn't just that!' Jimmy shouted.

Lily was startled at the outburst.

As, it seemed was Emily. 'Really? Go on.' Lily saw Jimmy was as red as a lobster, and Emily was looking at him as if he were quite mad. Lily smiled, inviting confidence. This was getting interesting.

'I saw her serving this drink behind the bar, it was the first time I'd ever seen her and she laughed and all of a sudden everything stopped, and her smile lit up the entire pub and it lit me up from the inside out.' Jimmy looked at his shoes.

'Wow,' Lily said. She couldn't believe that he'd come out with that. Anne-Marie's editing skills would not be required there.

'Really?' Emily asked, in the softest voice she'd ever used.

Lily studied her. She seemed touched, and a bit embarrassed. Whether she was embarrassed by Jimmy's words or by her own behaviour, Lily couldn't say.

'Emily?' Lily prompted.

'And I thought that he was a really interesting person,' Emily replied.

'What do you mean by that?' Lily pushed. She wanted more for Jimmy as much as she wanted it for the interview.

'Well, he had his own business and he's quite young, so I thought that was good,' Emily replied.

Lily was almost lost for words. She took a sip of water while she thought of a response.

She felt sorry for Jimmy. Emily obviously did too; she smiled apologetically at Jimmy but he didn't seem to be looking her way. Lily couldn't blame him.

'What made you apply for the competition?' Lily asked, willing Emily to stop being such a bitch.

'Well, we wanted to go somewhere in the Caribbean, and we saw the resort in the magazine, and well, really we thought that we had to come here. I mean, it's so romantic and exclusive, so we decided to try to win the competition and we said that if we didn't win, we'd come here anyway.' Emily smiled; Lily wanted to hit her.

'Is that right, Jimmy?' Lily asked, feeling desperately that it wasn't. Jimmy nodded, but he looked sad. Lily wanted to hug him and tell him that he could do better. Although if she did that, Anne-Marie would probably kill her.

'And how is the holiday living up to your expectations?' Lily asked, putting on a fake smile.

'Oh, the resort is so perfect, and so up-market. It's really – what's the word? – really elegant. And the other guests are also so amazing. I really feel at home here,' Emily replied.

Lily willed Jimmy to speak. To tell Emily that she was a shallow harlot and he was going to find someone else who was more deserving of him. Although Jimmy could sometimes seem a bit serious, Lily thought he was warm-hearted and had a lot going for him. If he learnt how to control his blushing, and sorted out his dress sense, he'd be a great catch. And she would put money on the fact that he was a much fuller person when Emily wasn't around.

'Lily, can I interject here?' Jimmy said.

Lily looked at him hopefully. 'Sure.' She braced herself.

'As I said before, Emily is the most beautiful girl in the world. I love her with all my heart. Em, I do. And this holiday, this setting is perfect.'

'I'm glad you think so,' Lily answered, a little scared about what might be about to happen.

'No, you don't understand.' He was almost shouting as he stood up. Then to Emily and Lily's surprise, he cleared his throat, dropped to one knee and held out a box.

'Emily, you are the best thing that's ever happened to me and you are my one true love. Will you do me the great honour of being my wife?' He was red, and flushed, but also evidently proud of himself.

Was he insane? Lily was expecting him to tell Emily to get lost and dig gold somewhere else, but this . . . ? Anne-Marie would be delighted, but Emily looked anything but. Lily fought the urge to rugby tackle Jimmy to the ground. Instead she watched as Emily took the box from him.

'May I?' She opened it. Jimmy knelt immobile as Emily looked at the ring. Lily leant in to get a closer look as well. It was pretty: a square-cut diamond set in gold with two smaller diamonds either side. Jimmy had taste in jewellery, if not in women.

'Emily?' Lily prompted, thinking that Jimmy would either fall over, or have very bruised knees if she didn't answer him soon. She also couldn't believe that she was examining the ring so thoroughly before answering. Actually she could; Emily was a horrible girl. Poor Jimmy looked on the verge of tears.

'Yes!' she exclaimed at last, and Jimmy let out a very relieved smile, while Emily looked like she'd been sentenced to death.

'How wonderful that we are going to have these as our official engagement photographs,' Jimmy said, as they walked back up the beach. Emily nodded; Jimmy took her hand. He was the happiest man in the world. Now he knew what people meant when they said that. At times in the interview he felt that she was being cold, but only because he hadn't proposed. Her reaction when he did told him everything. She'd looked at the ring for ages, which told him that he'd picked well. She was emotional, as if she was fighting back tears, which is why it had taken her a while to answer him. But answer him she had, and now they were getting married. He couldn't believe it.

'Why have you taken your ring off?' Jimmy asked, noticing her put it straight back in the box when the photographer had finished, and feeling hurt. As they made their way to the photographer he'd been on cloud nine. Now he'd sunk to cloud one or two. Something was wrong on what should have been a joyous occasion and he didn't know what it was, but it scared him. When the photographer was taking the photos, Emily had had trouble looking at Jimmy. When the photographer had asked them to kiss, she'd given him a peck and was reluctant when they were asked to re-do it with more passion. She seemed distant, almost repulsed by him. She was behaving very strangely.

Emily was his first serious girlfriend and he adored her. It wasn't just her looks, but she made him laugh and she was fun, always planning things. Learning to surf, eating out, and not just English food – she had opened a new world for him and he realised that without her he was really quite dull.

'It's a bit big, and I'm worried about losing it,' she lied.

'But you said earlier it was a perfect fit.' Jimmy had been

telling himself all holiday that he needed to act like a man. Hence the proposal. But what if that wasn't enough? What more could he do?

'Well, it is, but not quite perfect. Oh, Jimmy, I was trying to spare you. I need a tiny alteration and really that's not your fault. I would never forgive myself if I lost it. Now, we need to wait for the others at the bar, so why don't I just go and put this in the safe and meet you there?'

Jimmy watched his fiancée go and he wondered why, despite the fact that the woman he loved had agreed to marry him, he was feeling so unhappy all of a sudden.

'So, Tim, how would describe your perfect romantic date with Thea?' Lily asked, looking at the blond couple. They had arrived hand in hand, looking every inch the perfect pair. They were so damn good-looking, Lily reflected, as if they were made for each other. However, the interview wasn't proving easy. Tim looked amused every time she spoke and Thea appeared petrified. Lily couldn't figure these two out. Mind you, after Jimmy and Emily . . .

'Well, it would begin with champagne, of course,' Tim smiled. 'Then I would take her for dinner, in a restaurant like the one you have here. Fine food, fine wine and such a perfect setting. Then we would take a romantic stroll, ideally on the beach here, and we would end the evening by sitting in one of your wonderful love seats and talking about our love.' He beamed widely.

'Really? That does sound wonderful.' Lily wanted to tell him that he sounded like Anne-Marie, but she held her tongue. He was obviously insane.

'Tim is very romantic,' Thea added pointedly, looking at Lily.

'I can see that. So, what in your opinion is the best thing about The Love Resort?'

'For me, personally, it's being with the one I love, so very, very much, in an idyllic place. Our love can't fail to flourish here, no one's could.'

Well, Lily thought, Tim was a writer. Perhaps he could be a romantic novelist, although Lily had a sneaking suspicion he was quoting the *Guest Handbook* to her. She stifled a giggle. This was just too perfect and too awful at the same time.

'Thea, what do you think?' She tried to assume a reassuring face, as Thea looked lost.

'I think the setting is wonderful, beautiful, and that's really great. Really.'

Thea was evidently tired. Lily wondered what was going on. It was obvious from his behaviour that Tim was a bit of a handful, so perhaps that was it. Perhaps she was worn out from trying to keep up with him.

'Thea, would you say this holiday has improved your relationship?' Lily asked. Thea's expression was horrified. Lily smiled encouragingly, wondering what it was with this pair.

'It has brought us closer together. I think that Tim's right. A relationship benefits from this resort.' Lily didn't believe her; but then she was pretty certain that Thea didn't believe herself.

'Lily, you see, I'm a writer.' Tim leant in close. 'A tortured soul. I need beauty around me to exist. Without it I would die.' He swept his arms around to emphasise his point. Lily couldn't believe what she was hearing; and by the look on her face nor could Thea. 'I see myself as a bit like Anne-Marie in that way. So, that's why I have the most beautiful girlfriend in the world and also why I appreciate this setting so much. A man surrounded by this kind of beauty cannot help but be inspired.' With that he leant over, grabbed Thea and kissed her hard on the mouth. It was unclear who was the most shocked, Lily herself or Thea. Lily couldn't wait to tell Anne-Marie. This interview was turning out to be incredibly interesting.

★

'Tim, why did you say all that shit?' Thea hissed as they sat, legs entwined on the love seat. Having got over the shock, she was angry with him. She felt that he was making a fool out of her.

'You told me that I was ruining the holiday for you, so I tried to put things right. Why can I never win with you?'

'Because you go too far.'

'SMILE,' the photographer shouted. They smiled.

'What do you mean?' Tim asked through his smile.

'With the drink, with the romance, with everything. You can't just be a normal boyfriend; you have to be something out of one of her novels.'

'Thea, have I made you very angry?' Tim asked.

Thea detected the fear in his voice and it cut her up as it always did. But why did he have to say what he did? It was so over the top; Lily's face had showed that. But on the other hand, she knew that was who he was. He wasn't a simple character, which was why his novel was taking so long. That, and because he drank a bit. He was a writer, a creative, tortured soul, and Thea was the only one who understood him. Wasn't she? As the camera flashed again, Tim looked like a deer caught in the headlights.

'Oh, Tim, anger has nothing to do with it.' As a hole opened up in her and a great sadness washed over her, Thea realised she had no energy for anger. She wasn't sure if she had the energy for anything any more.

'So, Lee, how do you find the entertainment at the resort?'

Lily poured another glass of water. Lee and Carla had looked a bit distant when they arrived for their interview and as her efforts at small talk had failed, Lily decided to get straight on with it. She tried not to sound harsh, but she didn't like Lee. He kept giving her looks, as if he had X-ray vision. She hoped he didn't.

'Oh, it's very good.' Lee looked at Lily then at Carla.

'Carla?' Lily liked Carla. Well, she felt sorry for her. The other night, when she'd been sobbing her heart out, she'd been pretty incoherent but what was clear was that she really loved Lee. Lily decided that both Carla and Jimmy needed to get lessons in who not to fall in love with, although it seemed for both of them it was too late.

'Well, it's fun and romantic, all rolled into one really.' Romantic? At a guess, Lee was the most unromantic man in the resort. He was certainly the antithesis of Tim.

'If you had to sum up your time here so far, what would you say?'

Lily studied the two blank faces in front of her and wondered what on earth was going on. They were as clueless as if she'd asked them how to build a nuclear bomb. Lee was mono-syllabic, although generally he was only talkative when he had more of an audience. Carla's features swung from pretty and smiling, to murderous. Lily sat back and waited for someone to speak.

'I would say that it has been fun, and very sunny. And the food is delicious, so all good,' Lee said.

'And romantic,' Carla hissed, again in a way that told Lily that it was anything but. Carla obviously hadn't forgiven him for the other night and Lily was glad. She didn't know how she put up with him, although by the looks of it she wasn't doing. Had she not known better, Lily would conclude that The Love Resort was ruining relationships. She willed someone to speak.

'Of course, romantic,' he added. 'I feel privileged to be here with Carla, I definitely do. She's a top bird and I really, really love her.' He smiled triumphantly. Lily decided not to push. Carla looked as if she wanted to hit him. Lily wondered if she should just make the interview up. After all, it would be easier than trying to get anything out of these two. Just as she was about to wrap it up, Carla cleared her throat.

'Lee and I haven't been out of university long and so we really built our love on a student foundation. It's very different. We go to bars and clubs, but not really to restaurants. This feels very grown-up – which is, of course, wonderful for us. Lee is about to go to law school and I'm going to train as a journalist.' She beamed triumphantly; Lee was obviously totally confused. 'So, we are about to enter the grown-up world and this romantic interlude has certainly given us a taste for that.'

'Lovely,' Lily said, finally seeing some passion in Carla, and thankful that she had something she could use. 'Finally, tell me how you feel your relationship has benefited from being here. Lee?'

'We've grown closer. Much closer.'

'Fantastic. Carla?'

'I think we've seen ourselves for who we are and the foundations of our relationship, the ones we built before we came here, have been strengthened, and enhanced by the magic of The Love Resort.' Carla looked at Lee with determination in her eyes. What she was saying was true. Lily wondered if there was hope for these two after all.

'Wow, Carla, you have a great way with words. Good luck with the journalism,' Lily said.

'Look Carla, I'm really sorry,' Lee said, as he tried to catch her up. Carla had given him the silent treatment throughout the photographs and still was doing, as they made their way to meet the others.

At first she'd been too angry to speak, now she wanted to scream at him.

'I can't believe you. I asked you to make a bit more effort, that's all, so we could enjoy the holiday, but you just made a fool out of me again. Those answers you gave were so lame.' Carla glared at him. He wasn't even trying. After the other night, after dancing with Emily, he'd promised her that things would be better, that he'd be the boyfriend she wanted him to be. Well, that hadn't really lasted. Carla couldn't remember having ever been so angry with him.

'Carla, stop a minute.' He put his hands on her shoulders. 'I can't do the romantic thing. You've always known that. So, why are you surprised by my behaviour? I am sorry, but I can't be who I'm not.'

Carla looked at him. She felt winded. She did know him, and she loved him for who he was, and he was right, she shouldn't have expected him to behave like a romantic; she knew he wasn't. What was she doing? Her anger deflated.

'I'm sorry. Look, Lee, we've still got a fair way to go on this holiday, so how about we try to enjoy ourselves and I'll be more relaxed?' She smiled at him warmly. She had to take his feelings into account; she had to make this holiday work.

'Deal, babes,' he agreed, and slung an arm around her shoulder as they walked off.

'Hi, guys, did you have your photos taken yet?' Thea asked as they arrived at the bar where Jimmy and Emily were sitting.

'Yes, on the beach,' Emily replied.

'We had to sit in one of the love seats. It was a bit cheesy,' Thea explained.

'It was tackiness personified,' Tim elaborated, and then ordered drinks.

'We got engaged,' Jimmy blurted out. He didn't know why, but he wanted the others to know. He wanted to see how Emily reacted to what they'd say and he wanted his relationship back. He felt childish but part of him wanted them to know that she was his. Unless she told him otherwise.

'My God, you did?' Tim patted Jimmy on the back.

'Wow, congratulations,' Thea offered.

'Thank you, but, Jimmy, I did ask you to keep it quiet. You see,' Emily said, turning to look at him, 'I wanted my parents to be the first to know.'

'Never mind,' Tim said. 'I don't have a clue who your parents are, so I'm not going to let it slip. Right, this calls for a celebration. Barman, champagne over here, please.'

Jimmy tried to keep himself calm. She wouldn't wear the ring and she didn't want anyone to know. He tried to tell himself that it was perfectly reasonable for her to want her folks to be the first to know, but he didn't quite believe it. He didn't know what to believe right now, apart from the fact that he was beginning to feel like an utter fool.

He had always been a bit blind when it came to Emily, but his eyes were being slowly, reluctantly opened. She wasn't acting like someone who had just got engaged, she was acting like someone who didn't want to be engaged. But before they left they'd talked about marriage. In fact, Jimmy recalled, it was Emily who brought the subject up. She said that the resort would be a perfect setting for a proposal. Which is why he'd bought the ring. As he thought about this he felt sad. He hadn't even come up with that idea himself. It had been hers. They'd often talked about plans for the future. Emily had pointed out houses she liked, and venues for weddings. She'd even told him how many children she wanted (three). He felt sick with fear, and something else he couldn't identify. She was behaving badly, and he had no idea what to do.

Lee and Carla arrived, looking thunderous.

'We need to do the photographs first,' the photographer told them as Tim tried to get them to have a drink. 'Now can you all go and stand by the fence?' They obediently made their way to the rose-covered fence and lined up.

'No, that's no good. You look like an army. Right. Men at the back, women in front. In front of your own boyfriend, of course,' the photographer instructed.

'Or in someone's case, their fiancée,' Tim quipped.

'What?' Carla asked, looking at Thea.

'Oh God, not us, no, Jimmy and Emily.'

'What?' Lee asked, as Emily turned red. Carla and Jimmy both looked at the floor.

'Can you all look at the camera?' The photographer snapped, and as he took the photograph they all did, but only Tim smiled.

'Thank God that is over,' Thea said, going back to the seat where they'd started out. 'I am so sweaty.' She grabbed Tim's shirt and used it to pat her face.

'You're getting a nice colour, though. Oh, of course, congratulations, Jimmy, Emily, that's so wonderful.' Carla's eyes sparkled. Now Emily was engaged, hopefully she would leave Lee alone, although looking at them, she doubted it.

'Thank you,' Jimmy said, raising his glass.

'To Emily and Jimmy,' Tim toasted.

'To the most beautiful girl in the world, thank you,' Jimmy added.

'Jimmy, you are so sweet,' Carla said, glaring at Emily.

'So, is this fake champagne?' Tim added, laughing.

Emily and Lee said nothing.

'So, it's all finished?' Anne-Marie asked as she, Ed and Lily sat in the office.

'Yes. I'll type up the interviews soon, but here's a quick round-up.' Lily could barely contain her excitement. 'Jimmy proposed to Emily.' She was triumphant. No matter that her money said the marriage would never go ahead, it was still a coup.

'He proposed while you were interviewing them?'

'Yes, and she said yes.'

'How wonderful for our publicity. They were the only couple I liked, after all.'

'Also, Tim surprised us. He was very articulate.'

'What did he say?' Anne-Marie was unconvinced.

'That he needed beauty to exist, and he thought he was a bit like you. He said this place was inspiring to him.' Lily resisted the urge to giggle about the comparison between Tim and Anne-Marie. They both liked a drink, they were both blond . . . no, that was as far as she could go with that.

'Do you think I misjudged him? I mean, he sounds so utterly sensible, a kindred spirit. Do you think I should give him another chance?' Anne-Marie was almost hopping with excitement.

'Perhaps,' Lily lied. They were anything but what Anne-Marie thought they'd be, of that she was almost convinced. 'Oh, Carla was quite articulate and romantic; Lee was a bit monosyllabic.'

'As long as he didn't mention the lack of talent.'

'He certainly did not.'

'Good. When you've finished, and we've reviewed the answers, I might invite them to dinner again; let them redeem themselves. Maybe I judged them too quickly.'

'So, we're not sending them home?' Ed asked.

'Don't be silly. However, they did disrupt the resort, so I still want to keep an eye on them. Especially as we have the big magazine people flying in tomorrow to do the interview with Todd and Katie. So, tonight, Lily, you have to help Ed watch the competition winners and leave Todd and Katie.'

'OK, boss.' Lily was relieved. She was running out of ideas of how Todd seduced Katie, and how Katie responded. She would never make a writer.

'Now, I shall go to the house. I need quiet to think about my novel.'

'See you later,' Lily said knowingly. Thinking about it was all Anne-Marie ever did.

'And don't disturb poor Abigail; she's got another of her heads.'

Lily and Ed obediently shook their heads.

I don't feel that we've been alone enough lately,' Ed said, when his wife had gone.

'Well, we are now. Lock the door.' Lily began undoing her blouse.

'When these guys are gone, I think we should just leave,' Ed said, as he turned to her. 'The last few days have been so busy, and I've missed you.'

'Are you sure?' Lily felt her excitement mounting. She couldn't wait and neither her guilt nor anything else could stop her now.

'In a couple of weeks we'll be together.'

'That soon?'

'It's not soon enough, my darling.'

'Everything is fine, Harriet,' Todd said. He reasoned that there weren't many men who had calls from their publicist on their honeymoon to check their itinerary.

'Are you sure?' He knew she wasn't concerned for their welfare, just for the Studio.

'Yes, it's fine.' Todd looked at Katie and smiled. It was fine. Sort of.

'So are you going to be OK to do the pictures and interview tomorrow? You have all the information?'

'Of course.'

'Good. Listen, the press is going mad over here, guessing where you are, and they might find you. Be careful, all right? I mean, too many people know where you are for us to be sure of your privacy.'

Todd thought of Marcus. 'We are being careful,' he replied.

'Good.' She hung up.

'That was Harriet.'

'I guessed that,' said Katie. 'Is everything OK?'

'Yeah, she just wanted to check in with us about the magazine people.'

'Did she say anything else?'

'No, apart from our marriage has rocked America. Apparently the press is on the hunt for us.'

'They don't know we're here yet?'

'No, but they might find out.' He paused. 'Harriet said we should be careful.'

'Todd, I'm not the one that needs to know that.' She looked at him pointedly, as if to tell him that she knew exactly what he'd been up to.

'I know,' he answered, dejectedly. He made a decision. When the magazine people left tomorrow, he would tell Marcus he couldn't see him again. Too much was at risk. His pleasure was something that he could ill afford, and it wasn't fair on Katie.

He thought about her more and more as a person, and he even believed they could perhaps be friends. But he had to persuade her that they weren't going to be together romantically, and he needed to earn her friendship, her trust. Which meant that Marcus, and anyone else for now, was history.

19

Make Yourself At Home!

At The Love Resort, your happiness is the only thing that matters to us. The resort becomes your home for the entire length of your stay and therefore we want you to feel that you can treat it as such.

We are here to serve you; the resort is here to be used for your pleasure. So relax, have fun, and if you need anything, Guest Services are at your disposal twenty-four hours a day.

Remember, our home is your home!

Guest Handbook

'We've done our duty, by the interview, praising the resort and all that, so I think it's only fair that as we did nothing last night, we have some fun tonight, especially as we have something to celebrate,' Tim announced, as he got the barman to open another bottle of sparkling wine.

Thea tried to forget everything that she'd been thinking. She took a long swig of her drink and decided that there was no harm in trying to have fun. She deserved it. This wasn't the time to confront Tim; she decided to make an effort. They would have time to sort everything out when they got home. But she didn't want to think about that yet.

'Emily, can we talk?' Jimmy said when they were in their room, getting changed for dinner. He wanted to tell her that he knew they had a big problem; if he was being honest with himself he'd known it before he'd proposed, but he'd carried on regardless. At first he thought that it would solve all their problems, but then he knew he was doing it because he was jealous of Lee. He wanted Lee to know that she was his, and to stop looking at her in *that* way.

'Jimmy, let's just enjoy tonight. I think it's best.' Jimmy thought about saying something, but instead he went to shower. They would just have a good time; he'd worry about everything else later. He had to keep remembering that he was still on holiday and he would have a good time with his fiancée if it killed him. After all, why would she have agreed to marry him if she didn't love him? Perhaps he was being paranoid.

'What do you think about Emily and Jimmy?' Carla asked Lee when they were getting dressed.

'She didn't look thrilled,' he replied absently, as he concentrated really hard on choosing a T-shirt.

Neither did you, Carla wanted to say, but she held her tongue. What was it with him and the country harlot? She decided to leave it. She knew that she had every right to be furious with Lee, and she was. But she would have plenty of time to confront him later. For now, she needed to turn his attention back to her. She stood in her bra and knickers in front of the wardrobe, trying to decide what to wear.

'Hey, Carla, I think you're the best. You know that, don't you?'

She looked surprised at his unprovoked compliment. 'Thank you,' she replied but went back to the task in hand with the same sense of resolve.

'Can you believe he asked her to marry him?' Tim asked.

'She's gorgeous. Although I think he's too good for her,' Thea replied.

'Yeah, he's decent and she's a princess. High maintenance, mark my words.'

'Wow, Tim, you never fail to surprise me. How do you know about high-maintenance women?'

'I read your *Cosmopolitan*. Anyway, Thea, I'm glad you're not like that.'

'Oh, great, Tim, you're glad I'm easy.'

'No, not easy. But not a demanding woman like Emily. Poor Jimmy will have a stroke or a heart attack if he marries her.'

'Do you think you're being a bit harsh?'

'She's quite good fun and I like her, but I wouldn't want to marry her.'

'Well, that's one thing I can be glad about. Come on, let's get to dinner.'

They met in the Coral Restaurant, and arranged a table on the terrace, overlooking the sea. Tim held court, basically because no one else seemed able to speak. Thea tried to think of something to say – Tim hated silence; it scared him – but the atmosphere was oppressive.

Emily picked at her food, while her low-cut green dress was drawing Lee's eyes to her chest. Thea wanted to reach out and comfort Carla. She was so pretty; why was her boyfriend looking at Emily? She felt like taking a swing at him. Thea knew that the day had been trying, but events were now scaring her.

'I know, we could play cleavage ball,' Tim announced, before quickly flicking a pea at Thea's cleavage. 'Bullseye,' he shouted, getting up from his chair, as Thea, giggling, wrestled it from her bra.

'Tim,' she chastised good-naturedly.

'Well, if you girls will wear those low-cut things, what do you expect?' Suddenly the atmosphere diffused and everyone laughed. Thea was grateful to Tim, and kissed his cheek.

After dinner they decided to go to the entertainment bar. For once, Anne-Marie wasn't there to keep an eye on them, and Lily and Ed didn't seem to be around either. The entertainment for that evening was a limbo show, and then couples' limbo dancing. Tim, of course, led them, but Lee was hot on his heels as they drank more and more. They started with the resort cocktails, but soon moved on to shooters.

'Six tequilas,' Tim ordered.

'Followed by six Lover cocktails,' Lee shouted.

'Oh God, I'm drunk,' Jimmy slurred.

Thea was hot on his heels. Seeing the overweight couples trying to squeeze themselves under the bar was almost too much for her to bear. 'Oh my God, if that woman gets under that bar, I'll eat my hat.'

'You don't have a hat,' Carla pointed out, as they saw the woman collapse on the floor.

'They'll need a crane to get her up again,' Tim predicted.

'That's mean, Tim.'

'But true.'

They all fell about laughing, until Tim decided that they should participate.

'I can't do that,' Lee protested.

'Oh, don't be so boring. We'll go first.' Tim grabbed Thea's hand and led her to the floor. They were quite good, until he fell over and pulled her on top of him. They both collapsed laughing, as the audience cheered them.

'Sorry, Thea,' he gasped breathlessly.

'Don't be. I don't think we're cut out for this. Oh God, Jimmy and Emily are up, look.'

Thea looked but she cringed as she did so. Poor Jimmy tried his best but was awful, which just made Emily angry. Thea and Tim laughed but it was clear that Emily wasn't happy; Jimmy looked defeated.

'Couldn't you have tried harder?' Emily hissed.

'No, I couldn't. It's just a stupid game,' Jimmy hissed back, surprising both Emily and Thea. Thea resisted the urge to cheer.

Carla and Lee went last, but it was clear he wasn't interested;

he was less than half-hearted about the whole thing. Thea felt angry for Carla, who looked really embarrassed by the whole situation. She went over to her.

'It's just a dumb thing.'

'A bit like my boyfriend,' Carla replied.

Finally, they all agreed limbo dancing was stupid, and they went to the 'Enchanting Evening' bar, where the jukebox played and they were the only ones in there.

'Those other guests were so competitive,' Thea shrieked when they sat down. 'And the prize was one of Anne-Marie's bloody dresses, not even money or anything useful.'

'But the dress was signed,' Carla giggled.

'I guess you could auction it on eBay,' Jimmy mused.

'Shit, why didn't we think of that? I might have tried harder,' Tim finished.

Only Lee and Emily remained silent.

Tim's impressions of the couples, especially as he stuffed the sofa cushions up his shirt to emphasise the point, kept them amused for ages, and the drinks kept flowing.

'You didn't make any effort at all,' said an American voice.

They looked up to see a couple walk into the bar. The woman was wearing a dress not dissimilar to Anne-Marie's, floaty and pink, and the man was wearing a pair of slacks with a smart shirt tucked in.

'Fresh blood,' Tim said before going over to where they sat.

'Hello, may I introduce myself? My name is Timothy; I am from Great Britain,' he enunciated.

'Hi. Patricia.' The American woman held out her arm. Tim took her hand and kissed it. Her husband looked surprised.

'Charmed, I'm sure.'

'Oh my God, he's priceless,' Carla whispered to Thea, giggling.

'He bloody well is,' she replied, shaking her head.

'My husband is called Anthony,' the woman continued.

'Nice to meet you, old chap. I say, why don't you come and join us?'

'We're fine,' Anthony growled.

'We would love to,' Patricia answered, glaring at him. They stood up and went to join the others.

'I would like to introduce you to Patricia and Anthony. This is Thea, my beloved, that's Jimmy, Emily, Lee and Carla.' Tim sat down and summoned the barman over.

'Where are you from?' Thea asked politely.

'California, where the sun always shines,' Patricia replied.

'If you can ever see it,' her husband snapped.

As the drinks arrived, the atmosphere dropped. Lee kept looking at Emily. Jimmy was staring at his drink. Thea engaged Carla in conversation, and Tim started working his 'British' charm on Patricia.

'Of course, being British is wonderful.'

'I just love your accent.'

'Oh, thank you. Well, I am rather well educated. Eton, just like the princes.'

'Do you know them?' Her eyes were like saucers.

'Oh, my dear, no, I was at school a while before them, but I have met the queen on quite a few occasions.' Thea choked on her drink.

'You have? What's she like?'

'Really rather tiny, actually. But I never miss one of her garden parties.'

Anthony looked at Tim as if he was going to kill him, but instead he stood up. 'I've had enough of this resort for one night, or for a lifetime. I'm going to bed.' He looked daggers at Tim and at his wife.

'Well, you go on. I'm staying here with these charming English people.'

Anthony scowled at her and left.

'Thea, let's go choose some songs,' Carla said. They went to the jukebox.

'What the fuck is he doing?' Thea asked.

'Who? Tim?'

'Yes, all that rubbish about knowing the queen, and that accent. It's not even close to Hugh Grant's.'

'He's funny, though.' Carla looked confused.

'Fucking hysterical. Anyway, we've got a choice between Mariah Carey and Elton John.'

'Elton. Someone should take the song choices here in hand.'

'Are you going to tell Anne-Marie?'

'No, but I might send her a postcard.'

When they returned to the table, more drinks had arrived. Jimmy hadn't touched his; Emily was downing hers, as was Lee. The awkwardness in the atmosphere was evident, but Patricia and Tim were in a world of their own.

'If you ever visit England, I will personally introduce you to the queen.'

'You could do that?'

'Oh, yes, quite sure. She'd love you.'

Thea looked at him and snapped. 'Tim, I need to go to bed,' she declared. Patricia looked mortified.

'I'll follow you later,' Patricia looked relieved.

'But I don't want to go alone,' she replied. He whispered something to Patricia and stood up.

'Listen, Thea,' he said as soon as they were outside, 'I'm not ready to go to bed yet and I'm not really happy with you insisting on babysitting me.'

'Oh, really? But you're happy enough at home when I make sure the rent and the bills are paid, and when I feed you and work my sodding socks off to ensure you don't have to.' She felt unusually satisfied for speaking her mind.

'I never ask you to do anything for me; you're the one that insists on it all the time. Thea, you are always suffocating me,' Tim shouted.

Thea recoiled in shock, turned on her heels and stormed off in tears. She found herself, ironically, on the love seat they'd been photographed on earlier. Then she sobbed her heart out.

'Where's Thea gone?' Carla asked suspiciously.

'To bed. She's tired. I'm not. Simple.' Tim's good nature seemed to have left him. He was angry.

'Is she all right?' Carla asked.

'She's fine. Will you leave it?' Tim snapped.

Jimmy and Carla exchanged a glance.

'I'm glad you didn't have to go,' Patricia said.

'And leave your fine company?' He was all smiles again. 'Not when we were just getting acquainted.'

Carla's eyes were wide as she noticed that Tim's hand was on Patricia's leg. She felt sick and looked at Jimmy. She then saw Patricia curling her hair around her fingers, and pouting provocatively.

'Perhaps it's time to call it a night,' Jimmy said quickly. Without a word, Lee and Emily stood up and followed them out.

'You go, I'm staying,' Tim said, barely glancing at them.

'That was weird,' Lee said, shocked.

'What on earth is he doing?' Carla asked.

'As if anyone would want her when they had Thea,' Lee continued, and Emily took a sharp intake of breath.

'Oh, look, Thea's over there,' Carla said, pointing to a love seat. She moved towards her, Jimmy hot on her heels.

'You know that we could be in big trouble,' Lily said as she and Ed made their way towards the bar.

'I know.'

'I hope they've been behaving themselves.'

'You know, Lily, I don't care if they haven't. Anne-Marie has had us doing her dirty work for her for far too long. If they've caused trouble tonight, then good.'

'But we'll get the blame.'

'She can't hurt us. She can shout or scream but she can't change the way I feel about you.'

'Still, it was a bit bad that we fell asleep. Shall we go and check that everything's OK?'

'Sure, if we must.' Ed took Lily's hand and led her towards the entertainment hall. Despite all his bravado, he knew that they would have to tell Anne-Marie something about how the competition winners had spent the evening.

'Shit, isn't that Lee and Emily?' Lily asked. Ed nodded. They crept closer, but also stayed out of sight.

'Wait,' Lee was saying, as Emily started to go after the others.

'Why, so you can tell me who else you fancy?'

Ed and Lily looked at each other in the darkness. Ed felt a sinking feeling; this wasn't what they were hoping for.

'Emily, don't. I don't fancy Thea.'

'It didn't sound like it.'

'Oh, listen, I was making a valid comment. There's only one girl for me.'

'Carla?' Emily almost screamed.

'You know full well it isn't her.'

'Holy shit,' Lily whispered.

'I've wanted to do that from the moment I saw you,' Lee said, after he'd kissed her.

'Me too.'

'But this is wrong.'

'I know. But it feels right.'

'Oh, shit, what now?'

'Please don't make me go back to Jimmy.'

'Well, what else can we do?'

'Let's go to the hammock and spend a bit more time together. Please.'

'OK, but then we have to go back to our rooms.'

'I know.' They kissed again, before walking off.

'Where are you going?' Ed asked Lily, as the sound of Lee and Emily's footsteps faded.

'To the hammock to drag them back to their rooms. If Anne-Marie finds out, she'll kill them. And us.'

'Lily, let's leave them to it.'

'But Anne-Marie . . . ?'

'Forget about her. Look, let's think about us and let those kids do what they want. Never interfere in love.'

'More like lust, if you ask me.'

'That either.' He winked. He didn't have the energy to chase them round the resort and he didn't care what his wife thought. 'Come on, let's go back to yours.'

'Thea.' Carla and Jimmy stood in front of her.

'He's a fucking shit,' Thea said, wiping her eyes.

'He's drunk,' Carla replied. 'I'm sure that's all it is.' But she wasn't so sure. Thea looked distraught and she had no idea how to deal with it.

'He's always drunk.'

'Can we do anything? Jimmy asked, but Thea shook her head.

'Will you walk me back to my room?' she asked tearfully. They nodded.

Expecting Lee and Emily to be behind them, Carla turned round. She looked at Jimmy, as the penny seemed to drop.

'Let's go,' Jimmy said, and took Thea's arm. Carla followed in silence.

'I feel like such an idiot,' Thea said, as they reached her door.

'Don't. You're not the idiot here,' Jimmy said.

'Not by a long shot,' Carla added sadly.

★

'Should we go back to the bar and look for them?' Jimmy suggested, once Thea was safely in her room. Carla nodded.

They walked into the bar, and then stopped.

'Shit,' Jimmy said.

'Oh my God,' Carla agreed.

The barman was dancing around screaming at Tim and the American woman, who were lying on the floor kissing. 'I need to close up,' he said, over and over.

'Tim, mate, you've got to leave,' Jimmy said tentatively, interrupting them.

'What? Oh, hello, Jimmy. What did you say?'

'The barman needs to leave,' Carla repeated sternly.

'Oh, bloody hell, does no one know how to have a good time in this place?' Tim said.

'You do,' Patricia replied.

Tim stood and pulled her up by her hand. 'Give me two bottles of wine and I'll go.' The barman, looking totally out of his depth, did so. 'Come on. Let's go and make our own fun.'

Carla and Jimmy watched, horrified, as they left together. For a fleeting second they'd forgotten about their own partners.

He turned to Carla. 'It's all going wrong,' he said.

'Seems so.' She had tears in her eyes.

'Shall we look for them?' Jimmy felt so lost.

'I hate to say it, but it's obvious that they're together.'

'And they've made utter fools out of us.'

20

You've Left The Stress At Home

At The Love Resort we believe that stress is left at the door. All you need to do is relax, enjoy yourselves and fall in love all over again. To help you with this, our spa treatments have been designed with this in mind.

Visit the spa with your loved one and enjoy the couples' packages on offer.* Whether you wish to have a Mr and Mrs Manicure, a Partners' Pedicure, a romantic relaxing massage for two (conducted side by side, enabling you to hold hands throughout), His and Hers head rubs, or our sensual seaweed wrap for two, all will be available to you and you won't fail to feel rejuvenated and relaxed afterwards.

Official Love Resort Brochure

* A full list of spa treatments and a booking form are available at reception.

The phone rang. Ed leant over and snatched it up, at the same time looking at the clock and seeing that it was only six in the morning. As he listened, he realised that perhaps Lily was right, and they should have put a stop to it.

'Who the hell was that?' Anne-Marie, wearing a pink eye mask, demanded.

'That was Security.'

'Why are they calling this early? Do they not know I need my sleep?'

'Anne-Marie, there's a huge problem.' Ed was already out of bed, and feeling responsible.

'You'd better tell me.' Anne-Marie pulled her mask off and sat up.

Ed explained while they dressed hurriedly, then made their way out. Anne-Marie strode purposefully; Ed held on to her arm. It was unusual for them to have any physical contact but she was so angry he felt he needed to support her. Probably because he knew that he could have prevented the latest débâcle.

They came upon a crowd of about ten couples, all standing and staring. Anne-Marie screeched and pushed her way through. Then she screamed. Ed covered his ears. Anne-Marie's scream seemed to have woken the sleeping pair, who sat up and looked mortified. Anne-Marie turned to the audience, switching on her sickly sweet smile.

'I do apologise for this,' she said. 'I will make it up to you.'

With that she grabbed Lee, pulled him out of the hammock, threw Emily's clothes at her and ordered Ed to bring the two competition winners into the office, before stalking off. The guests who were watching hadn't moved – seemed unable to move – and they stayed rooted to the spot, as she walked away.

Ed had to listen to weak apologies and Emily's familiar tears as he marched Lee and Emily up to the office.

'You have to believe I'm sorry,' Emily cried.

'Save it for my wife.'

Ed and Anne-Marie stood in the office. Lee and Emily faced them.

'Would you like to explain yourselves?' Anne-Marie asked frostily. Lee opened his mouth to speak, but before he could, Emily burst into tears.

'Well, those tears are very touching, Emily. But I am still waiting for an explanation.' Anne-Marie glared at Emily, who stopped crying. 'I know,' Anne-Marie continued. 'Let's start with you, Lee.'

Lee stared at Anne-Marie, but didn't speak.

'Well, as you both seem to be maintaining your silence, perhaps I should tell you?' Anne-Marie's eyes flared with anger.

'Well, you see—' Lee started.

'Shut up. By the time Ed and I got down to the hammock, you'd attracted quite a crowd. At the resort, there are a few people who like to breakfast early, but after seeing you two, I'm sure they lost their appetites.

'Ed, have you called Lily?' Anne-Marie shrilled.

Ed nodded.

Summoned to the office Lily had no time to shower before she threw on her clothes and made her way there. She knew that Lee and Emily had been caught and couldn't help but feel a little guilty about it.

En route, she heard a shout, a squeal and a bang. She rushed to the bungalow it had come from.

Tim was lying on the terrace outside, half-naked. A male guest was towering over him his arm drawn back ready to punch, and a female guest, also half-naked, was trying to restrain him.

'Mr and Mrs Greyton, what's happened?' Lily gasped, coming up the steps.

'Well, I just happened to get up this morning to find my wife's side of the bed empty,' Anthony Greyton said angrily. 'So, I pulled on my clothes and went to find her. Well, I can tell you, I didn't have far to go. I just came out on to the terrace to see them, there, on the sun-lounger, asleep together.'

'Oh my God!' Lily was genuinely horrified.

'So, I picked my wife off, and hit this British upstart.'

'Anthony, he's related to royalty,' Patricia cried.

'I don't care if he's heir to the throne. He's a shit and I should kill him.'

Lily looked at each of them. Tim was rubbing his eye, which was beginning to show a bruise. Mrs Greyton was still not fully dressed, which was a little unnerving, and the couple next door had come out of their bungalow to see what was going on. Lily, thinking quickly, ushered the miscreants inside. She managed to get them to put their clothes on and, reassuring Mr Greyton that the matter would be dealt with, she marched Tim up to the office.

'What's he doing here?' Anne-Marie demanded, when Lily pushed him in.

'Ed, Anne-Marie, can I talk to you outside?'

The three of them stood outside the office, each telling their story.

Anne-Marie almost had steam coming out of her ears.

'So, Timothy, what do you have to say for yourself?'

'Well, I can see how it might look quite bad.' Ed fought the urge to find Tim amusing; after all, Thea wouldn't.

'Yes, quite bad,' Anne-Marie concurred. 'In fact, I'm finding it hard to think of how your behaviour could be worse.'

'Well, you see—'

'Shut up!' Tim jumped. 'I just don't know what to do with you,' Anne-Marie said, and began pacing.

'The magazine,' Lily reminded her, and Anne-Marie looked even angrier.

'They'll be here in just under two hours. By that time, I need to know that you and your abandoned partners are out of the way.'

'What magazine?' Tim asked.

'Shut up. I cannot risk them being anywhere near the resort while I have such an important day,' Anne-Marie fretted.

'I can take them,' Ed offered.

'Take them where?' Lily asked.

'OK, here's what we do. Lily, go and organise a mini-bus and a driver. Then get someone to pacify all the guests who witnessed any of this and, of course, Mr and Mrs Greyton. I will take these three, with their partners, out of the resort for the day. It will be the most uncomfortable day of your lives, of course.'

'Oh, Ed, thank you.' For once, Anne-Marie's tone was of genuine gratitude.

'You're welcome. I'll bring them back at six when everyone will be gone. Lily, see how much damage limitation you can do before the magazine people arrive and, if need be, appoint someone else to take over when you and Anne-Marie are tied up.'

'Of course, Ed,' Lily agreed.

'As my husband said, it will be the most uncomfortable day for you, cooped up in a mini-bus with your real partners. I'm sure that will be a good start to your punishment.' Anne-Marie widened her eyes.

'Punishment? We're not children,' Tim said.

'Well, you have all behaved like children. What will Thea, your girlfriend, say Tim?' Anne-Marie demanded, as she descended, stabbing a finger at him.

'Oh, Thea isn't my girlfriend,' Tim replied.

Carla woke to a banging noise. She thought it was in her head, then she realised it was the door. Slowly she got up and opened it. Ed and Lee stood outside – Ed with a kind and sympathetic expression and Lee looking sheepish.

'You've got half an hour,' Ed said, pushing Lee through the door.

'Are you going to tell me what's going on?' Carla asked calmly. She had been so out of it last night that she'd passed out and hadn't noticed that Lee was absent from her bed until he'd appeared at the door. Her tears had acted as a major sleeping pill.

'It's Emily.'

'Really?' The sarcasm dripped from her voice.

'Yes, we got caught.' Lee at least had the decency to be embarrassed.

'Why her?' Carla demanded. She had so much she wanted to say, and so many questions she wanted to ask, but that was the first one.

'I don't know. For some reason she's different.' Lee sat on the bed and sighed. 'When I first met her, I fancied her, right, but then I fancied Thea too, because she's a looker.'

'Charming.'

'Do you want to hear this or not?'

Carla looked at him. Did she? No. But she knew that she needed to.

'At first, I disliked the way she treated Jimmy, and the way she was this demanding princess, but I told her that near the beginning of the holiday and she had looked crestfallen. Since then, the attraction grew. Now I can't get her out of my head.'

'How lovely.'

'And there's something else,' Lee said.

'What?'

'Tim and Thea aren't a real couple either.'

His words were almost enough to shock her into silence. But then she remembered what being a fake couple on this holiday meant.

'So, I take it that our holiday is in jeopardy now – not that it's been a ball anyway?' She started pacing. 'Well, are you going to say anything at all?'

'Carla, you're a mate. I know what I did was wrong, but technically I don't think it was.' He cringed as he finished, as if anticipating her response.

'Technically speaking, of course, you are single. However, let's just get past the bullshit, shall we? Emily isn't single. In fact you might just have managed to be responsible for the shortest engagement of all time. And then there's me. Well, I'm just a mate, sure I am, but that doesn't mean that you have the right to disrespect me at all times. You have humiliated me with your comments, and now with your actions. They think we're a couple and unless we come clean, then they think you cheated on me. Which doesn't matter as much as the fact that you have fucking well let me down. You've used me for the last three years. Oh fuck it, what the hell was I thinking?'

'What?' Lee was backing against the wall as she advanced, eyes blazing.

'I devoted so much time to you, to loving you. I didn't ever think of myself, I thought only of you. This holiday, everything. But you know what, Lee? That wasn't your fault – oh, no, it was mine. But I've had my epiphany now. I've seen the error of my ways.' She stood close to him; she could feel his breath quickening. 'I have been a major fool, but you know what? You've been an even bigger one. Because you knew how I felt and you let me. You knew I'd do anything for you and you let me. You say I'm a friend, but I'm not, because you probably treat a piece of shit better than you've treated me.'

'Carla, I didn't know,' he'd protested.

'You did. You just chose not to.' She knew that was true. Lee, the first man she'd slept with. When she met him at university, at one of the student bars, she had been instantly smitten. She gave him her virginity, but when he said that night was a one-off, she had devoted her whole time there to changing his mind. This holiday, the whole reason she'd entered the stupid competition, was for that end. The Love Resort was supposed to make him see how he was really in love with her, not someone else.

Oh God, she knew that he wasn't the one to blame here. It was her. Her stupidity. Her devotion to a man who it was clear only wanted her as a friend. She had seen it yesterday at the magazine interview, but she'd pushed it back, and now the truth was staring her in the face and it wasn't Lee she hated. It was herself.

As she started to cry quietly, he apologised and admitted that yes, he did know she was in love with him, and then he apologised some more. Then he told her about the bus trip.

Jimmy had vowed not to cry. He was hurting more than he ever thought possible, he was confused and angry, but he wasn't going to give her the satisfaction of seeing him cry. Less than twenty-four hours ago he thought he was going to marry her and now he wanted to kill her.

He woke up to a hangover and no Emily. He was just going to go to search for her, but then the door opened and she stood there. He looked at her for what seemed like an eternity, the questions in his eyes refusing to be voiced. She mumbled something about a shower and had gone into the bathroom.

Then, for the first time in his life, something had snapped in him as he finally found his balls.

'Do you think you're going to tell me where you've been all night?' he'd shouted as he opened the shower door. His face was ablaze with anger.

'Jimmy . . .'

'You are an inconsiderate little bitch. We got engaged yesterday, you agreed to marry me, and then you do this. What, Emily? What is it? I know it's something to do with Lee. I know you think I'm stupid but I'm damn well not. You disappeared, leaving me and Carla alone. What did you think you were doing? Trying your best to hurt us? Trying to rip our hearts out, and leave us feeling humiliated? Well congratulations, you succeeded.'

After everything he'd done for her, she had made a right fool out of him. Mind you, he was ashamed at how he'd let her. He'd been blinded by her; he should have seen it coming, all the warning signs were there. He'd put so much effort into trying to make her happy that he'd failed to see he couldn't. He desperately needed to put things into perspective, but it was all too horrible.

He felt disgusted; he couldn't even identify most of the emotions he was feeling. The frustration and the anger made him want to burst. Emily had been critical of him almost since they first arrived at the resort, but did he stand up to her? No, he just tried harder to please her. He felt like a major idiot. He'd entered the competition because she had demanded a five-star holiday and he couldn't afford one. He'd have been happier with two weeks in Italy but, no, it had to be somewhere she could boast about. When he'd won, he'd been so shocked, but her reaction hadn't been exactly as he'd hoped. She accused him of being cheap because he didn't pay for the holiday. Jesus, he should have told her where to go then.

They say love is blind but could he really have been that stupid? He was almost as angry with himself for his stupidity as he was with Emily.

'Well?' he demanded.

'Jimmy, I am sorry. I didn't want it to happen, and really, I don't know why I let it, but I couldn't help myself.'

'You've been flirting with him from the beginning.'

'No, that's not true. He flirted with me, but then he flirted with Thea as well, and we just grew attracted to each other. It kind of took me by surprise.'

'Well, that makes two of us.'

'Jimmy, look, I feel awful, and I know I've been a real bitch, but you have to believe our relationship wasn't right.'

'So why did you agree to marry me?'

'I thought that that was what I wanted, before this holiday, before Lee.'

'But yesterday you said you'd be my wife.'

'Jimmy, you asked me in front of Lily, who was interviewing us. I couldn't turn you down. You put me in an impossible situation. Look, I knew then that we weren't working but I wanted to wait until we got home, I thought it would be easier for you.'

'Oh, yeah, it'd be a picnic to have you break my heart at home.'

'Jimmy, don't.'

'Why? Why did you do it?'

'I love him,' she explained softly, uncertainly.

'I hope you do,' Jimmy said. 'I hope you love him because then one day he can rip your fucking heart out the way you did mine.'

Thea tried to think of the last time that she had actually been this angry with Tim. As in, really, really angry. She couldn't remember.

He wasn't contrite when he walked in. Why would he be, he was Tim. She could smell the alcohol on him, either from the previous night or this morning. He actually smiled at her; smiled.

'Morning. Gosh, what a mad night.' There was no sorrow at all in his voice.

'Tim, do you realise what you did?'

'Well, yes, of course I realise. Quite funny, when you think about it.'

'You know something, it really isn't. Because I've been lying here all night thinking about it and I haven't laughed once.'

'Oh . . .'

She had always found it difficult to be angry with Tim, but she snapped and suddenly it was the easiest thing in the world.

'Tim, you have nearly got us thrown out of here so many times and we've been here less than a week, and I have asked, nicely, that you behave, but you can't. I've watched you drinking constantly and obviously you have a problem and I want to help you, I really do, but you are totally oblivious to it all. And then you don't come back. Where were you last night?'

'Oh dear, you haven't heard, have you?'

'Tim, just tell me.'

'Well, I think I was very drunk because I ended up with that American woman, Patricia or whatever her name was. I, er, well, I, er, don't know what exactly happened but I woke up on her terrace this morning.'

'You passed out on her terrace?'

'With her.'

'With her?'

'I wasn't naked – well, only half. She was, though.'

'Naked?'

'Her husband found us.' He pulled back his hair and showed Thea the bruise that sat angrily on the side of his face. Thea stared at it, blinked and then slapped him as hard as she could.

'Ow, Thea, that hurt. Why are you doing this?'

'Why am I . . . ? Tim, you were caught with another woman last night. A married woman. And to all intents and purposes on this holiday we are a couple. So, do you see why I'm doing this?'

Thea blamed herself. It was a stupid idea, coming on holiday with Tim, her life-long best friend, posing as her boyfriend. In fact, it was totally insane. She thought it would be easy; for so long everyone had thought of them as a couple, but they weren't. She needed a rest, and Tim needed to sort his life out. But coming here was obviously the worst idea that she'd ever had.

'Thea, you know I told you this holiday was a bad idea.' He had; he'd been reluctant to pose as a couple, but she'd talked him round. She had to take some responsibility.

'For once I wish I'd listened to you.' Thea put her head in her hands and cried.

21

Memo: To All Love Resort Guests

Please note that today the wonderful magazine *Movie World*
will be coming to the resort to interview our VIP guests, Todd
and Katie Cortes. The interview will be held in the resort and
photographs will also be taken.

   We apologise for any inconvenience this causes, and will
keep disruption to your facilities to a minimum. And we assure
you that Todd and Katie will be making a public appearance
one evening. Stay tuned for news of when!

Katie tiptoed into the living room and saw him asleep on the
sofa.

'Todd,' she snapped.

He opened his eyes. 'I must have fallen asleep here.' He sat
up. Katie looked thunderous.

'Well, luckily it was me that woke you, not a member of the
press.'

Todd watched her go. He felt like a shit, but he was
consumed with his own desperation. Seeing Marcus after the
night before last had been painful. He desperately wanted to
touch him. But after being reminded about the risks, he felt
depressed as the reality of his situation hit home. The pretence.
The reason for it. The fact that he couldn't risk seeing Marcus.
It was all a huge mess. And now Katie was angry, and for once
he thought that she had a right to be.

The phone rang, and Katie snatched it up in the bedroom.

Todd got up and vowed to make it up to her – as much as he could without giving in to any of her crazy ideas about them. He groaned. His 'honeymoon' was crashing down on him.

'We have hair and make-up coming in half an hour,' Katie told him, as he walked into the bedroom.

'I'll shower quickly.' He turned to walk to the bathroom. 'Katie,' he said; suddenly stopping.

'What?' she asked.

'I am sorry.'

'What for?' She was waiting for an answer, but he just shrugged. Where would he start?

'Hello, darlings,' Anne-Marie said, as Katie opened the door to her and ushered her in. She kissed Katie and Todd on their cheeks and then clicked her fingers. Four people, two men and two women, appeared behind her.

'Hi,' Katie said.

'Now, here are your hair, make-up and stylists. They have been sent by *Movie World*, so I have it on very good authority that they're the best.'

'Darling, we're the best,' one of them said. 'As if this princess needs our help. Why, everyone knows that you are the best-dressed woman in the whole world.'

Todd groaned inwardly. He realised that the few days they'd spent away from Hollywood seemed like an eternity. But now Hollywood had come to them, and he didn't like it at all.

'Thank you.' Katie beamed.

'Right, now, I shall leave you but you know where I am. The journalist and photographer are being given a tour. Someone will come and get you when you're ready. Oh, this is so exciting, so wonderful.' Anne-Marie clapped her small hands together and left.

Todd was on the terrace, drinking coffee; looking over the notes Harriet had faxed him about the day ahead and keeping out of the way. He was surprised, although he shouldn't have been. She was back. As soon as the stylists had walked in, Katie Ray had returned. With a vengeance.

'You fucking idiot, everyone knows that if you do that, hair burns,' her voice streamed out, filling his peace with anger.

'Oh, be gentle with the princess, or what will I have left to dress?' another voice followed.

Todd could just visualise the scene. It was Katie Ray at her best. Those four people dancing to her tune, taking her criticism, wanting to cry but keeping quiet. The Katie that he was beginning to warm to was gone. Perhaps she'd just been a figment of his imagination. A mirage. Or had he done this? God, was everything his fault?

'Katie?' a voice said timidly. Katie spun round. It was Mary.

'Yes?' she asked unkindly.

'I came to see if I can do anything.'

'Well, actually you can,' Katie said, her voice devoid of any warmth. 'This place is a pigsty; I've got a mountain of laundry and, of course, then the ironing. I have no idea how you could let it get in such a state.'

On hearing this exchange, Todd went inside to where Mary stood staring, with a shocked look on her face. 'I'm sorry.'

Katie looked at her new entourage. 'Of course she's sorry, she needs this job,' she laughed unkindly. 'Mary, just get it done.'

'Mary, hold on.' Todd followed her out. He saw her freeze, furiously wiping away any tears that were springing from her eyes.

'I'm fine.'

Todd put his arms around her. 'I know that's not true. But listen, you have to believe that she was herself with you, and this is someone who isn't real. And although the unreal person is a monster, I won't let her hurt you.'

'She has hurt me, sir. Because I tried to care for her and now she treats me like a nothing.'

'Mary, she treats everyone like that. It's not right, I know, but when she was alone and vulnerable, she needed you. Now she has her fixers she doesn't. Believe me, she will be back to needing you tomorrow.'

'Maybe I won't be here then,' she sulked.

'Mary, you know that you will.' He smiled and hugged her, and she dried her tears.

The make-up artist appeared.

'We're ready for you, Mr Cortes.'

'Oh, for God's sake, call me Todd. And remember,' he said, mimicking Katie, 'violet is definitely not my colour.' He winked at Mary, who managed to laugh.

After engaging in damage limitation, which didn't extend to Mr and Mrs Greyton, who were on their way to the airport, Lily was with Anne-Marie in the office.

'How are things?' Lily asked.

'Well, the shoot is almost ready to go. The journalist and photographer are still deciding on location, the stylists should be finishing soon, and we shall go and join them to ensure that nothing goes wrong.'

'Sure. Well, the guests seem OK. They took your offer of a dinner with them very gratefully and I've arranged it for a few days from now. Sorry, I know you're tired, but I think it'll do the trick.'

'You're right.' Anne-Marie had lost her fight, and was, for the first time, pleased to have Lily by her side.

'So, all we need to talk about now, and we can wait for Ed, is what you're going to do with the competition winners.'

'I've thought about this. I want them on a plane home. As soon as possible.'

'And if they try to give us adverse publicity?'

'I thought we could get some legal agreement drawn up. After all, Tim has confessed that Thea and he aren't a real couple, and the others have cheated, so can't we use that as a threat?'

'Good idea. I'll call the lawyers. I'm pretty sure the couples won't object to signing. Now, I'll get one of the secretaries to look into flights.'

'Thanks, Lily, thanks.'

'Right, so we're ready to go. I know it's awful, but we do have the article in *Exclusive Holidays*, and today is going to be a huge success.' She smiled.

'Have you seen Abigail today?'

'No, but then we've been preoccupied. Do you want me to call her?'

'No, there's no time, I'll call on her later.'

Anne-Marie, Lily, Todd and Katie stood at the Honey Gazebo with the features editor of *Movie World*, who was hopping from foot to foot with excitement, and the photographer, who was looking through his camera at them all. Behind them, the crew hung back in case they were needed.

'This is so exciting,' the journalist cooed, 'so exciting.'

'Sure is,' Lily concurred.

'Oh, we're delighted, absolutely delighted,' Anne-Marie enthused.

'Now, I'm sure our publicist has told you what you can and cannot talk about,' Katie stated.

'To explain, I am acting on your behalf today, as your publicist, and I have briefed them on every point, but I shall be present to ensure that there is no diverting from what was agreed,' Lily said.

'Good. So what are we waiting for?' Katie demanded.

Todd sighed.

'Anything wrong, Todd?' Lily asked, concerned.

'No, nothing,' he replied quickly. 'Just a bit tired.'

'Of course you are, it's your honeymoon,' she chortled.

And everyone laughed, apart from Todd and Katie.

*

Interviewer: 'So, we've seen pictures of your gorgeous wedding and now we have been given the privilege to see how your honeymoon is going. Can you tell us why you picked The Love Resort?'

Katie: 'Well, as you can see, it's such a wonderful setting. Just look around you. It's romantic, stunning, relaxing, and for Todd and me, the perfect place for us to celebrate our love.'

Katie smiled. Anne-Marie clapped her hands. Todd kept his grin fixed in place.

'It's going well, isn't it?' Anne-Marie said, as they took a break for Katie to have four people fuss over her as she demanded.

'Very,' Lily agreed.

'You're a fucking imbecile; do you even know anything about hair?' Katie screamed.

'You hurt my princess one more time and I ensure you never work in this town again,' the stylist chastised.

'My God,' Lily went to stand by Todd, 'should I step in here?'

'No, she loves shouting at people. Funnily enough, it's always the hairdresser,' he explained.

'So, what would your publicist do right now?'

'She'd roll her eyes and let them get on with it,' Todd replied.

'I can do that,' Lily replied with a wink.

Interviewer: 'What so far has been the highlight of your married life, Todd?'

Katie: 'Well, of course the wedding day was wonderful, utterly magical, but the honeymoon has been so very special. Everyone has ensured that we have had the most fantastic time, but also respected our privacy.'

Interviewer: 'Do you want to add anything, Todd?'

Todd: 'Katie's really said it all, hasn't she? I'm such a lucky man.'

The three of them beamed at each other and Anne-Marie clapped her hands again.

'Right, we're going to start the photographs because the light is perfect,' the photographer interrupted. He then began barking orders at his assistants, who had appeared from nowhere. Every now and then, guests would stop and gawp at what was going on, before Anne-Marie kindly asked them to leave. They all did as they were told.

Todd managed to get a cigarette from someone, while Katie was being fussed around yet again. The day was turning out to be one of the most insufferable of his life. Almost worse than the wedding day. He flicked his ash into the Love Garden and looked at the scene. Lily was pacifying Katie, who was having yet another tantrum. This time because the flowers that they were asking her to pose against didn't match her nail polish. She wanted green flowers instead. Everyone was trying to come up with suggestions, and the hairdresser was chewing gum and fixing Katie's hair yet again. Someone was trying to use the nail polish on the flowers, and the photographer was telling everyone to hurry up, while the interviewer tried to keep him under control. Todd wondered what they called a collection of divas. He put his cigarette out as he was called for the photos.

'Todd, lift Katie up. Ah, perfect.'

'Todd, can you frolic in the sea? Someone, roll his trouser legs up for him. Great, great.' Todd nearly fell over as someone dived at his trousers.

'Katie, bend down to pick up a shell. Todd put your hands around her waist and look over her shoulder. Lovely.'

'Hold hands and walk down the beach. Gaze into each other's eyes. A bit more, Todd – smile. Katie, you look gorgeous, gorgeous.'

'Now, I want you to kiss. No, not on the cheek, Todd. I want a proper movie kiss. Take her in your arms, and kiss her, long and hard. Again, longer this time. Ah, yes, I think that's it.'

Todd broke off from the kiss, and looked at the sand. It was like all his other movie kisses: he was acting and he didn't feel a thing. But it hit him again, his constant companion, guilt. He was fooling all these people and he didn't feel very proud doing it.

'That was great,' Katie said.

Todd nodded, half-heartedly. 'Have we finished now?' he asked.

'Yes, and I think after a shower, I'd like a quiet dinner.'

'Sure.' He was thinking about Marcus, about how he was supposed to see him tonight, about how he couldn't. About how he really wanted to. About how awful he was and didn't deserve this great life he'd got. Then he stopped. It was too dangerous and it was also far too late.

The *Movie World* people left and Katie was charm itself when she said her goodbyes. Todd really didn't understand her, although sometimes he thought he did. She was vulnerable, insecure, which in turn led her to believe people when they told her how wonderful she was. He guessed she'd never been happy, or liked for who she was, which would explain how she didn't know who she was. He was sure that was it, and if it was then he felt sorry for her. She had shown a softer side, although it hadn't lasted, and he couldn't help but think that when she was at her worst she didn't deserve anything but contempt.

Well, he'd have dinner with her and he would try to make an effort with her. The least he could do was try to be her friend.

22

The Love Resort caters for your every whim during your stay but we also strongly advise that you take some time out to go on the island tour.*

The island itself can be driven around in one hour and twenty minutes. As well as offering the breathtaking beauty that you would expect, there are also many wonderful things to see and do.

Visit the waterfalls – they have to be seen to be believed.

Shop in a traditional Caribbean market.

Visit the tropical gardens with the world-famous aviary and see the unusual island foliage.

Finally, on your way back, have a drink at the island's oldest bar.

All this and more means that the Island Tour is a must-do.
Guest Handbook

* To book the island tour, which is not part of the all-inclusive package, call Guest Services. You can choose from group tours or individual tours, depending on your personal preference.

Ed was trapped in a mini-bus with six unhappy people. The atmosphere wasn't pretty, although the excursion he was taking them on was. He had very quickly decided to play the part of tour guide; otherwise he felt the silence would have killed him. However, he considered he should have been grateful that they hadn't killed each other.

He had escorted them to their rooms as discussed – Emily, then Lee and finally Tim. He wished he could have been a fly on the wall, but chastised himself for his voyeurism. He waited patiently in the lobby connecting all the rooms for half an hour, and when no one appeared he went to collect them. Three angry faces and three sheepish ones followed him on to the mini-bus. No one had spoken, apart from him.

'We are just passing the small food market, one of the most famous on the island for local produce,' Ed said, in his newly adopted cheery tour-guide voice. He glanced round. Why he had volunteered to take this lot out, he didn't know, but he was beginning to feel depressed by their depression. The revelation that Thea and Tim weren't a couple had shocked everyone. It had made his wife angry beyond belief. It was only because the *Movie World* people were arriving that she'd let them go. And Thea and Tim looked so perfect together; he thought that they genuinely loved each other. But what did he know?

'So, our first stop today will be the magnificent waterfall and we will reach there in approximately ten minutes.' Ed glanced back, but no one was looking at him. Not that he was surprised; they weren't even looking at each other. He thought that maybe there would be a huge row at some stage, but again perhaps they would just stay quiet. He had no idea what Anne-Marie would be planning on doing with them, but he was expecting to be going out again the following day. To the airport. One thing was sure: the resort would be a very different place without them.

'Right. Well, we're here at the waterfall and we've scheduled thirty minutes for you to look around. But no one will leave my side, or I'll probably have to kill you.' Ed grimaced. The beauty of the waterfall was totally wasted on them all.

'This waterfall is one of the island's premier attractions. Over seven million people visit it every year. The water is said to have healing properties. I know we don't have long, but would you like to go for a dip?' Ed looked at the six blank faces, who finally managed to shake their heads. 'Right then, let's just walk around it. Follow me . . .'

'Right, well, I think we've seen enough here. Let's go back on the mini-bus and get to our next destination where we shall stop for lunch.'

It was just getting dark as the mini-bus pulled back into the resort. Ed looked at his six passengers and six weary, unhappy faces looked back at him. He felt sorry for them, especially the cuckolded ones, but then, he didn't have time for sentiment. In order to get through the upcoming days until he and Lily were going to leave, he needed to keep Anne-Marie sweet and un-suspecting. Their lapse last night had taught him that. He had his future to secure.

'What now?' Tim asked as the bus came to a standstill.

'We're going to the room where we hold the welcome meet-ings. Wait there and I'll get Anne-Marie and Lily.' Without any further discussion, he led them to the room and then went to phone the others.

Ed stood outside the door, waiting for them. He needed a few minutes away from the competition winners. Finally he noticed, as he put his ear to the closed door, the silence had been broken.

'So, I guess we have you three selfish bastards to thank for this hideous situation,' Thea fumed. She glared at Tim, then Lee and finally Emily. Although her anger was directed at Tim initially, she was now furious with the other two. Carla and she had become friends, and she genuinely liked her. Jimmy had always shown such gentlemanly concern, especially last night when she was upset. She had never quite liked Emily, and now she knew why. Thief.

'Actually, I might be to blame but at least I didn't lie about our relationship to get here,' Emily spat back.

'Oh fuck.' Thea turned to Tim, who now was the sole

recipient of her fury once more. She rubbed her head. Of course, everyone knew that she and Tim weren't a couple, although it probably wouldn't have taken a genius to figure it out.

'Well, it kind of slipped out.'

'It slipped out, when?'

'When Anne-Marie was telling us off. So, actually, if you look at it that way, I'm not as bad as them, because I didn't cheat.' He smiled, then ducked as if expecting to be hit.

'You told everyone that we weren't really a couple? You fucking dickhead. What did she say?'

'Well, she said she might sue.'

'Oh, Tim, you're priceless. You break into a bar, you steal drink, you sleep with another man's wife on his terrace, and then you tell Anne-Marie that we lied and cheated to get here. Are you trying to ruin my life totally or what?'

'He's not the only one who lied about being in a relationship,' Emily said.

'But you just said—' Thea stopped in her tracks.

'No, not me and Jimmy, the other two.'

'Carla?' Thea looked at her, everything suddenly making sense.

'I wanted a holiday. He was my best friend. I thought that there was something more – until he proved himself to be an utter bastard who couldn't care less about my feelings.'

'That's not fair. You got me here on false pretences – don't pretend you didn't. You were determined to get me to fall in love with you, which would never happen, and you thought this would be the perfect place to do it. I told you that I didn't want to pretend to be your boyfriend but you said it was just for a free holiday. Christ, you're mad.'

'God, Carla, I thought you were amazing for putting up with him before, but now I know, all I can say is that you had a lucky escape, babes,' Thea stated.

'I have to say I agree with you,' Carla managed a weak smile.

'You bitches don't know what you're talking about; he's too good for either of you.' Emily's voice cracked.

Carla and Thea looked at each other, and stood shoulder to shoulder as Carla spoke.

'The only person here who is too good for anyone is Jimmy. Emily, you deserve Lee. I hope he treats you like shit, because then you'll know how Jimmy feels.'

'Thanks, but I can speak for myself,' Jimmy said, standing up. 'They are right, though. I don't think lying to get here is a big deal. I only did it because she went on and on and on about having a five-star holiday just so she could boast to her friends about it. Christ, Emily, how I didn't realise that you're so shallow I shall never know. Even when we were being interviewed and Lily asked her what she saw in me she said it was because I had my own business. The warning bells were ringing then, but I was stupid enough to think I loved you. And I proposed. Jesus, can you believe I asked her to marry me? If there was a stupid award here, I'd be bloody well getting it. Lee, I guess at the moment I'm too angry and hurt to see it, but I should probably be shaking your hand and buying you a drink. Thanks for taking her off my hands.' Jimmy was shaking. It was the longest speech he'd ever made.

'Now hang on,' Emily shouted. 'I didn't ask you to propose and I feel bad about what happened. Jimmy, you and I were in a relationship which was wrong. You have to see that, you have to.' Her voice was desperate.

'I don't have to see anything. I don't give a shit what you say,' Jimmy shouted back.

'Good for you,' Thea agreed.

'Yes, I agree,' Tim encouraged.

'You shut up, you're the fucking limit,' Thea shouted.

'Oh, let's start that again, shall we, Little Miss Perfect?' Tim replied.

'What do you mean by that?'

'Always on my case: "Tim, you drink too much. Tim, you should do some work. Tim, the house is a mess." Well, Thea, the pressure you put me under would lead any man to drink.'

'I have always looked out for you, taken care of you, for years, ever since I've known you.'

'Well, maybe if you hadn't, I would have been able to take care of myself.'

'How could you?'

'Quite fucking easily.'

'Maybe we should calm down,' Lee suggested.

'Really, Lee, really, should we? Why, so you bunch of scumbags can get away with it?' Carla demanded.

'Don't speak to him like that,' Emily shouted.

'You bitch, how fucking dare you?'

'Carla, isn't it time you admitted that you were the one in the wrong? Lee never gave you any hint of encouragement.'

'Oh, he told you that, did he? Did he tell you how he slept with me before I entered the competition, how he got drunk and came home and crawled into my bed? I'd call that encouragement. And then the next day I went to the doctor for the morning-after pill and that was when I found this stupid competition.'

'Well, no, but you said he was drunk.'

'He was drunk last night when he shagged you in public.'

'It wasn't like that.'

'Oh, really?'

Emily went to stand in between Carla and Lee. 'No, he really loves me and you can't understand that.'

'Oh, I think I can.' Carla's eyes were blazing as she pushed Emily.

'Don't touch her,' Lee said, grabbing hold of Carla's arm.

'You get off her,' Jimmy intervened, pushing Lee out of the way.

'Leave him alone,' Emily shouted.

'You leave him alone,' Carla shouted back.

Thea stood, as everything seemed to happen in slow motion. Who threw the first punch she couldn't say. But Lee fell to the floor and Emily went to hit Jimmy and Carla jumped on top of her, knocking her over.

As Anne-Marie, Ed and Lily entered the room, Tim was standing on a chair.

'Fight, fight, fight, fight, fight. . .' he was chanting.

'Get them off each other,' Anne-Marie shouted, darting around them and trying her best not to get too near, as if they might contaminate her.

Ed pulled Jimmy and Lee apart and Lily grabbed Emily. Finally, they all became quiet and stood, looking ashamed.

'Enough,' Ed said. 'I should never have left them alone.' He was no longer amused, but actually worried about his wife's health. She was teetering on the edge of desperation.

'Your behaviour is totally unacceptable in my resort,' Anne-Marie started. 'I have done my best with you but you have proved yourselves unworthy of my hospitality and now I find out that one couple even lied to me.'

'Two couples, actually,' Ed explained, having overheard them.

'You are kidding? Who?'

'Carla and Lee.'

'Why did you enter my competition for new love if you weren't even in love? It just seems unbelievable.'

'We—' Thea began.

'Stop.' Anne-Marie held up her hand to silence them. 'I don't care any more. We spent all day trying to get you on a flight home, but unfortunately they are all full. There's nothing we can do until next week, but I can't have you behaving like this until then. I just don't know what to do.'

'Maybe we should discuss this,' Ed suggested. He hadn't had time to think about what they would do next, apart from the fact that they certainly couldn't send the couples back to their original rooms.

'There is no need,' Lily said. 'Anne-Marie?'

'I'm afraid that I can't run the risk of having you running riot around my resort. Too many people are upset. Mr and Mrs Greyton have left and we had to give them a full refund. By the way, Tim, I am still considering suing you.'

'Well, I don't actually have any money,' Tim explained.

'Then I'll just take a pound of flesh.' Her eyes were ablaze with anger. 'So, here is what I am going to do. Carla, you will share a room with Thea. Tim, you will share with Jimmy. Emily and Lee, you will have to share. I don't have any spare rooms, so you will all accept my decision on the matter.'

'Fine by me,' Emily said, defiantly staring at Carla.

'What about keeping an eye on them?'

'Oh, Ed, darling, I am so glad you brought that up. You will all agree to my terms, or I shall throw you out of the resort with nowhere to stay and no way of getting home. Why am I being so accommodating to you? I don't know, but I am a kind person. So, the terms are that you stay in your rooms until it's time for dinner. You will all dine together, under the watchful eye of Lily, who will be your evening chaperone. Tomorrow, we will work something out. I feel that I owe it to Carla and Jimmy not to have to spend time with Lee and Emily, so please don't worry, I shall ensure that after tonight that doesn't happen. However, apart from Jimmy, no one is blameless in all this.'

'I think that's a marvellous solution,' Ed said.

'Hang on. Can I just clarify?' Tim asked.

Anne-Marie sighed. 'If you must.'

'We have to stay in our rooms until you say otherwise?'

'Yes.'

'And we have to have a babysitter?'

'Correct.'

'We're adults, Anne-Marie, and we're on holiday. This isn't fair.'

'Tim, what's not fair,' Anne-Marie bared her teeth, causing him to take a step backwards, 'is that you owe me over ten thousand dollars. That you lied to get here and then you all created havoc. Why I even have to explain myself, I have no idea. You are doing your best to ruin my resort and I will not have that. Now. For the last time. HAVE I MADE MYSELF CLEAR?'

Everyone was too scared to respond.

'I thought we'd have an early supper. What would you like?' Katie asked.

'Um, I don't mind. Maybe some fish?' Todd answered distractedly.

'Leave it to me.' Katie picked up the phone and ordered dinner. Todd heard her say that it had to be served at seven o'clock sharp before telling him she was going to get ready. He had no idea what she was getting ready for, but the predatory look in her eyes unnerved him.

After he relayed the day's events over the telephone to his very amused brother, he showered in the second bathroom and pulled on a pair of shorts and a T-shirt. When he went outside, he saw her, wearing what seemed at first to be a negligee, but on closer inspection was just a slutty dress. It was black and sheer. She was wearing knickers, but no bra. As he tried to avert his eyes from her nipples, he noticed that she was wearing full make-up and a pair of diamante high-heeled shoes. Gulping at the thought of what was in store for him, he sat down as she pulled out a bottle of champagne from the ice bucket and insisted that it was time to celebrate. He took the glass from her, still unable to speak and then he realised that he was in for a very long and torturous evening.

For someone who never ate, Katie was making a huge fuss about food. She had ordered all their meals for them and then made an enthusiastic display over every dish served up, before taking a mouthful and discarding it. Todd was almost more disappointed by the fact that his wife was a Hollywood cliché than he was by the fact that he had a wife.

'This is so perfect, Todd,' Katie said, as they sat in the lazy chairs, sipping champagne.

'It's a great setting. A bit over the top, but breathtaking.'

'Romantic, though – it really is romantic.' She bit her lip and looked at him.

'It is.' It was romantic, the setting, just not the couple in it.

'Todd?'

'Yes?'

'Do you realise that this is our one week anniversary here?'

'Huh?'

'We've been here on honeymoon for a week today, and I think that it's time we—' As the plates clattered down on the table behind them, she looked round. 'Marcus, did you have to be so clumsy? I was in the middle of talking to my husband,' she snapped.

'Sorry.' He didn't sound sorry. He looked at Todd, and then at Katie. Todd noticed Marcus looking Katie up and down, and his face said that he knew she was trying to seduce her husband. In her tiny designer dress – was it Valentino? Her killer heels – Blahniks? The G-string that was just hinting at its presence, La Perla? As Todd felt he was reading Marcus's mind, he refused to meet his eyes. He couldn't bear to meet his eyes.

'We should sit down to eat,' Todd suggested, grateful for the interruption but also uncomfortable at its instigator.

As they sat, Todd felt Marcus push something into his hand. Still unable to meet his gaze, he put it in his pocket. He knew that over dinner he would be thinking of the note, desperately wanting to read it.

'Marcus, you can go,' Katie snapped.

'Katie . . .' Todd started, as soon as they were alone. He was unsure where he was going to go with the conversation, but he knew he had to have it. He also knew that he should have had it a long time ago. He had to take some of the blame.

'Todd, I have never been as happy as I am now.'

'What?'

'You know I love you. I have loved you from the moment I saw you. I wanted to marry you. This whole studio thing, that didn't matter to me. I wanted you.'

'But, Katie, you have to understand—'

'No, Todd, I don't. Because I know, I know that deep down you feel exactly the same way.'

Momentarily dumbstruck, Todd knew he was in big trouble. He took a deep breath, 'Katie, I'm gay.' Could he be any more succinct?

'Well, yes, you say that, but a lot of men are bisexual, and I don't mind that. I'm quite happy for us to be together, knowing that you've slept with men. I mean, a lot of women are bisexual as well. I might even be. You never know, because I've never slept with a woman.'

'So we have something in common then.' He laughed; she didn't.

'We have so much in common, Todd.' Katie edged closer.

Todd was at a loss. It seemed that reason didn't work with his new wife. But he had to do something.

'Katie, I'm gay.' He looked at her, begging her to understand.

'Why?' she pouted.

'I just am.' He felt he was banging his head against a brick wall.

'But you might—'

'No, Katie, no. We will never be more than friends. I like men.' He was shouting and he felt awful. She seemed so hurt. He felt guilty and mean, but what could he do? Over the last few days he thought he understood her, but now she'd come back with this whole seduction routine. He met her eye apologetically, but she didn't say anything. She just started crying.

'Katie, I'm sorry, I didn't mean to make you cry.' He felt terrible; his emotions were murdering him.

'Todd, no one has rejected me for years. I don't understand it. Why don't you like me?'

'It's not that I don't like you.' He reached over and took her hand. Wondering if that was a smart move or not, he squeezed it briefly then dropped it. 'I do like you. Although, if we're being honest, I don't always like the way you treat people. Like Mary.' It was time to try to get her to understand; time for honesty.

'Oh.'

'Yes, and the hairdresser and everyone that works for you.'

'Mary was really sweet to me.'

'And maybe you should be sweet to her, at all times, not just when you need something from her.' David would have a field day when he told him how he actually felt sorry for his wife.

'So, if I was nicer to people, which I can be, then you'd fall in love with me?' Her eyes sparkled with hope; Todd put his head in his hands in despair. 'I'll go and call Mary right now. I'll apologise and explain everything. I'll do whatever it takes to get her forgiveness.'

'That's great, Katie, but it doesn't change things.' What could he do? She was determined to interpret things in her own way. He couldn't win.

'Not right now, Todd. I understand you're angry with me for being so horrible, but once I've put things right, then you'll feel differently.' She trotted off on her heels.

As soon as she'd gone, he pulled the piece of paper out of his pocket. There was no harm in reading it; he didn't have to act on it. As he read the note, confusion swept over him.

'I can't wait to see you again,' it said. 'Please meet me tonight by the north entrance to the beach. There's a shack there used for storing equipment. We can be alone. Be there at nine thirty. Please. Marcus.'

Harriet's words about being careful flooded his mind. But then Katie's determination to seduce him knocked them away. The shack would be deserted. Marcus probably had keys so he could lock it. If anyone saw him he would say he was taking a walk. He'd check around that no one was there. He would be careful. Being careful didn't mean he couldn't go.

Making a decision, Todd stood up. He had to be gone by the time Katie came off the phone. That way, there was nothing to stop him.

Todd stood nervously at the shack. He knocked on the door and was relieved when Marcus opened it and pulled him inside. He was sure no one had seen them; he'd been extra vigilant. He kissed Marcus, long and hard.

'I was afraid you weren't going to turn up,' Marcus said.

'So was I,' Todd replied, kissing him again.

Tim paced the room he was now sharing with Jimmy.

'Tim, what's the story with you and Thea?'

'What do you mean?'

'Well, I just found out today that you're not even a couple, so I just wondered, really.'

'Hmm. If I say that I never think about Thea and me does that make it clear?'

'As mud.'

'What I mean is, well, I don't think about us because we just are. She's always been there, like a twin really, and I love her but not in that way, and I think she feels the same.'

'So there's nothing sexual in it at all?' Jimmy was having a job processing the revelations of the day that had just passed, and he wasn't sure he ever would. It was more bizarre than anything he could have imagined.

'God, no, it'd be like incest, and I believe that's still illegal. You know I really didn't want to come here. When she told me she'd won a competition, I said that if I had to act like her boyfriend for two weeks I'd mess things up.'

'Well, you did.'

'Anyway, Jimmy, let's just put aside the whole awful incident for the moment.'

'How can I?'

'For the greater good, man, for the greater good.'

'Huh?'

'Look, we cannot stay cooped up in this room together, only being allowed out for dinner. It isn't on.'

'I don't see what choice we have.' Jimmy didn't care where he was. He just wanted to crawl into bed and wake up when the nightmare was over and he was back inspecting the underside of a car.

'Look, Thea hates me; you hate Emily and Lee, as does Carla, blah blah. But we still have to be here for another week or something like that.' He stopped and started counting on his fingers. 'Anyway, the point is that we are on holiday, not in prison.'

'That's true.'

'And, Jimmy, did we or did we not travel a very long way to get here?'

'We did.'

'Therefore, do we not want to have some fun before we go back, despite everything?'

'Well, I suppose so.' At this point in his life, fun had never been further away.

'Right then, we call a truce. For now, we must all stick together. We can hate each other later.'

'Well . . .'

'Now, what's the number of your room? We need to come up with a plan.'

★

Thea and Carla had painted each other's nails and pampered themselves in a vain effort to cheer themselves up, both refusing to talk about what was really happening. Then they'd received the phone call.

'I really don't think it's a good idea to listen to Tim,' Thea said.

'No, although Jimmy seemed quite keen, and he's usually the sensible one.'

'Who has just been dumped by his fiancée. No, he's not in his right mind. We can't listen to him either.'

'But then what about us? We're both really hurt by this. God, I even had a fight with Emily, and I haven't had one of those since primary school.'

'You mean maybe we're not in our right minds and we should listen to Tim?'

'Well, the thing is, he does have a point. I know we won these holidays on false pretences, and I know that we have caused problems for the resort – well, some of us have – but it's still our holiday. And although this is probably the maddest, worst holiday we'll ever have in our lives, maybe, just maybe, we should do something. I mean, well, either we sit in here and get bored, or we have some fun. We can't get into more trouble than we're already in. Can we?'

'We probably can, but I'm not sure I care any more.'

'So, we're all in,' Tim said.

'I'm not sure I can face Lee and Emily.'

'I know, mate, but I couldn't not ask them. Anyway, when we make our escapes we can go separate ways. I'm not sure Thea wants to be near me, to be honest.'

'So what did Lee say?' Despite his feelings, Jimmy couldn't help but be curious.

'He said they'd come only because Emily didn't want to. I

heard him tell her that he wasn't going to be told what to do all the time.'

'I should have done that.'

'Um, you probably should.'

'Tim, are you giving me relationship advice?'

'Shit, I hope not. If I was, I didn't mean it.'

Ed opened the office door and walked in carrying a bottle of brandy.

'I think we deserve this, after the day we've had.' He poured three glasses. Anne-Marie smiled. There was an uneasy truce between the three of them.

'The shoot went really well, which is the most important thing.'

'Lily, you're right. And those little upstarts can be dealt with.'

'What are we planning for during the day?'

'I thought we'd send them on excursions for the rest of their stay. They come back, and then they change, go to dinner and then to bed. I can't think of anything else for it,' said Anne-Marie.

'As long as I don't have to go.'

'Oh, Ed, I think you've done enough babysitting. No, we have sufficient staff here; we'll sort it out.'

'So, what shall we do about dinner?' he asked.

'Well, I'm dining with Abigail, so perhaps you could help Lily with our little problem children? God, I know they're *not* children but it makes me glad we never had any, eh, Ed?'

Ed smiled weakly, desperately trying not to think about what the offspring of him and Anne-Marie would be like. He was glad his wife was dining with Abigail, although he was a little worried about her. She was highly strung at the best of times, without the drama that had occurred. However, Abigail was the better comforter, and he would rather be with Lily.

★

Anne-Marie opened the door to Abigail and fell into her arms. Abigail stumbled backwards before tentatively putting her arms around her and trying for a comforting pat.

'Oh, Abigail, it's all so, so terrible,' Anne-Marie said, pulling her publisher inside and giving her a drink before she recounted the goings-on to her.

'Jesus,' Abigail whistled as Anne-Marie brought her up to date.

'Quite.'

'What are you going to do?'

'Well, apart from keeping a close, close eye on the horrible young people, I don't know.'

'What about the book?' Abigail's eyes bulged.

Anne-Marie looked at her, shocked. 'How can I write when these people are intent on destroying me?' She took another drink and looked at her publisher again. How could she think of the book at a time like this?

'Of course you can't, darling, of course,' Abigail comforted. Anne-Marie's face was covered in relief, but then she began to cry.

'Is everything else all right?' Abigail asked awkwardly.

'Abigail, I'm a writer, I live for my work, but this resort . . . well, I'm beginning to think I made a mistake.'

'You know, it's a lot of responsibility. I always wondered why you didn't just buy a beautiful house here.'

'Looking back, I wish I had.'

'It's not too late,' Abigail started.

'I think it might be. My book, the one that I was so excited about, has been tainted and I don't know if it's irrevocable.'

'Oh, darling, I'm sure it isn't. Now, how about we order some supper to soak up some of this champagne?'

'So, we get to babysit tonight,' Ed said, as he stood in Lily's bungalow, getting dressed.

'At least we'll be together. Ed, you know despite the fact I can't stand her, I did feel a bit sorry for Anne-Marie over all this.'

'That's why I love you; you're so compassionate.'

'But they have caused destruction ever since they've been here, though that hasn't been very long. Do you think she's going to be all right?'

'I thought it was quite funny at first, but now we have to keep them out of harm's way, it's not, is it? And I am worried about her too, she seems a bit unhinged. But I'm not sure that we're to blame for not stopping Emily and Lee last night.'

'That would still have left Tim. Anyway, what can we do?'

'She only wants Abigail, my darling. We can't do anything.'

'No . . . Ed, why did you and Anne-Marie never have children?'

'She didn't want them. She wanted to be the centre of attention at all times. Anyway, I realised early on that she'd be a terrible mother.'

'But you would be a great father.'

'I know and I do want children.'

'Well, so do I.' Lily reached over and began unbuttoning his shirt again.

He looked at her and grinned. 'We'll be late for the baby-sitting.'

'They can wait. This can't.'

The six of them stood behind a bush like fugitives. Tim was dramatising the situation and enjoying it.

'Do we all have money?' Tim asked.

'Yes,' they answered in unison.

'Right, so what we do is we get to the front of the resort, and get the security guard to order us a taxi, and we go and find a local bar.'

'Sounds really daring,' Thea said sarcastically.

'We'll have broken free of our chains, Thea, remember that,' Tim retorted. They looked out from the bush and saw that the resort was deserted. 'Now, Lily said she'd pick us up at eight thirty, so that gives us half an hour to be clear. Jimmy?' He spoke with the authority of a man commanding an army. Clara giggled despite herself.

'All clear,' he whispered.

'Right, troops, go, go, go.' Tim took off and ran across the grounds with five people hot on his heels.

They managed to get the guard to hail them a taxi, and they all squashed in. There had been protests for separate cabs, but Tim, who was their commander, said there was too much risk involved in that. Instead, they were all to go into town together, then go their separate ways, to avoid arguments. The truce was on very shaky ground.

They got out of the cab and readjusted themselves, standing awkwardly on the pavement by the main stretch of bars. Thea took Carla's arm protectively. Emily did the same to Lee, and the pairs glared at each other.

'Right, let's go,' Tim said. 'Meet back here at midnight. Synchronise watches.'

'Tim, you don't even have a fucking watch,' Thea retorted before she and Carla walked away. They went in one direction, Emily and Lee went in another.

'Well, it's just you and me,' Tim said cheerfully before leading Jimmy to the nearest bar.

'There's no answer,' Lily said, as she tried Tim and Jimmy's room again. Ed looked at her, and then they rushed to the next room.

'No one's answering.'

'And I can't hear anything in there.'

'You don't think . . . ?'

'We are a bit late.'

'Right, you take the Coral Restaurant and I'll go to the Lovers' Bistro. Meet at the main bar.' They both rushed off.

Twenty minutes later they stood at the entrance of the bar.

'Nothing.' Ed said.

'Nothing.'

'We'll have to get keys and check the rooms. They could just be playing silly beggars with us.'

'Let's hope so.'

They went to the main desk and got a set of keys. Ed and Lily opened each room and found them empty.

'Oh shit!' Lily exclaimed. They looked at each other. 'We are in so much trouble now.'

They rushed to the main gate, and approached the security guard.

'Did six young Brits leave here by any chance?' Ed asked.

'They asked me to get a taxi and they all got in. I didn't know that wasn't allowed.'

'Of course you didn't,' Ed soothed. 'Listen, please let me know the minute that they come back, and then don't let them out of your sight.'

'What now?' Lily asked.

'Let's have a stiff drink, and then we're going to have to tell her.'

'You realise she'll kill us?'

'Of course, darling, but at least we'll die together.'

'I almost feel sorry for him,' Thea mused, over a cocktail with Carla. The bar was dark and half empty; music played quietly in the background. It wasn't the best bar they could have chosen, although their choice was limited.

'Tim?'

'Yes, he says that I suffocate him. Do you think I do?'

'Thea, I don't know, but do you think so?'

'We've been together for so long – obviously not that kind of "together". I think of him as part of me, but the thing is, neither of us has had a relationship for ages, and I'm not sure why.'

'It sounds as if you two depend on each other.'

'What, you mean that I need him as much as he needs me?'

'Yup.'

'God, that's fucked up.'

'It is.'

'Are you sure you studied English, not psychology?'

'Quite sure. Otherwise, I wouldn't have made such a fool of myself with Lee.'

'Why did you?'

'The thousand-million-dollar question. I thought I was in love with him. He was my first, and you know, I kind of got it into my head that he was the one I was supposed to be with. Leading me to waste almost three years of my life on that quest. How could I be so stupid?'

'No idea. But you don't come across as some mad obsessive woman.'

'Thanks. I hope I'm not, but I sound it. Shit, you know what, I think I hid behind it.'

'Behind what?'

'Behind this thing for Lee. Other men did ask me out occasionally, but I always turned them down because they weren't Lee. But maybe I used him, and the non-relationship we were having, as a security blanket because I was scared.'

'Bloody hell, this is getting too deep for me. Maybe I did the same with Tim.'

'That means we're both probably certifiable.'

'In that case, let's leave this dangerous ground and get another drink.'

The waiter approached them. 'Ladies, two men at the bar would like to give you these drinks and ask you to join them.'

Thea looked at Carla; they both giggled. Looking at the bar, they saw two men who were portly and obviously over forty. They giggled again and shook their heads.

'Tell them thank you, but we're lesbians.' Thea smiled.

'Christ, with the way we behave with men, maybe we should be.'

Carla went to the bar and came back with some cigarettes. She pulled one out and offered the packet to Thea.

'I didn't think you smoked,' Thea said, grabbing one. She didn't smoke either but she felt that she needed one.

Carla lit her cigarette. 'Lee hated smoking.' She took a long drag and smiled.

Thea went back to thinking about why she was like she was with Tim. They used to be so cool together, best friends, and they always had fun. Throughout school, they'd played pranks and she'd been as much to blame for the mischief as he was. At university, they'd always held the best parties. People loved being around them; they wanted to be part of their group of friends. Thea had been fun. She was always laughing and joking and teasing. So when had she stopped? She knew exactly when. When they'd moved to London together, both full of ideas about their futures, but she'd started working and he hadn't. She'd lost herself somewhere in the growing-up process. Perhaps Tim had noticed that too, and maybe, maybe that had contributed to his drinking, and messing around.

'What do you think will happen to us when we get back?' Carla asked.

'Well, Anne-Marie can't kill us. Can she?'

'Wouldn't put it past her. She's like this little demonic pink thing. She'll probably put a curse on us.'

'You don't think she'll throw us out without anywhere to go or any way of getting home, do you?'

'If she does we'll go to the magazine and tell them how horrible she was to us.'

'Of course, she won't do anything that would give her any bad publicity, would she?'

'You know what, I don't care,' Carla started. 'I've been such a fool. When I think back to university and the way that I devoted my life to Lee, I feel so stupid. Totally insane. I mean, I'm an intelligent, fairly attractive woman, who should be having the time of my life. But instead I became obsessed with him and now I can't even remember why. Is that because I'm drunk?' She lit another cigarette and burst out laughing, neither of them was sure why.

'What do you think the others are doing?' Carla asked.

'Well, I suspect Tim is getting very drunk somewhere, Jimmy will be despairing, and Lee and Emily are probably boring the pants off each other. Although not literally.'

'You think he's boring?'

'No, not really. I'm just trying to make you feel better.'

'Well, I do.'

'Tim, please get down,' Jimmy said, frantically holding on to one of Tim's legs. He had climbed into a DJ booth that sat above a dance floor, because there was no one in there and no music playing.

'I'm fine; I was ever so good at climbing as a child.'

Jimmy wrangled but finally managed to get him back down – luckily, as the barmen were glaring.

'Let's get another drink and forget about the music.'

Tim looked at him, appeared to think for a second, then agreed.

'Nice place we found here,' Tim said as they went to sit at a corner table, where, Jimmy hoped, they couldn't cause any trouble.

'Tim, do you always behave like this?'

'Like what?'

'Like now. You know, getting behind the bar, stealing drinks, hitting on women and climbing up into booths.' Tim was exhausting; Jimmy wasn't sure how Thea coped.

'Um, I don't think so, but I couldn't be sure. You'd have to ask Thea.'

'If you do, then you can't blame her for being annoyed with you.'

'Annoyed? That's the understatement of the century. She hates me.'

'Anyone can see she doesn't.'

'Well, she should. Do you think that perhaps I should make an effort to be better behaved?'

'Um, yes.'

'OK, well, I will. Here's a toast to the new improved Tim.'

Jimmy wasn't sure whether to laugh or cry as Tim charged his drink and downed it.

'Mind you, I'm not sure that I'm the one that should be called insane here. What on earth were you thinking of with that girl? She walked all over you.'

'Yeah and I still have the scars to prove it. What an idiot. Mind you, she's gorgeous.'

'I suppose so, but really bossy.'

'I think the worst thing is that I feel such a wimp for letting her treat me like dirt.'

'But if it's any consolation, at least you and Emily were genuine, and you're the only one Anne-Marie doesn't want to kill.'

'It's not, but thanks.'

'Oh look, the DJ's started up. Let's dance.'

'Tim, are you mad? Me and you on the dance floor?'

'Come on, Jimmy, do something that you wouldn't normally do, for once.' Madonna's 'Holiday' blared through the bar.

'Well, OK, but I'm not much of a dancer.'

'Can't be any worse than your limbo.' As Tim, arms swinging, jumped on to the dance floor, Jimmy shook his head and followed him.

Anne-Marie poured two large glasses of brandy and sat down next to Abigail. 'So, I've had papers drawn up. They have to agree not to speak to anyone about their time here, now that they've done their interview. I'll make them sign it by threatening to sue them all, and we'll be all right.'

'Good thinking, darling. You seem to have everything under control.'

'Oh, but it's been hard. The hardest few days of my life. Could you imagine if Todd and Katie found out? Or if the press found out?'

'They won't, I promise. You have been more than kind to them.'

'I know. They don't deserve it. Any of it.' Anne-Marie sighed. 'I just don't know . . . Abigail, are you listening?'

Abigail was looking at her watch.

'Sorry, yes, I was just thinking about things, and my head.'

Anne-Marie gave her publisher a funny look. 'Dear Abigail, I wish you'd let me get you a doctor—' She was interrupted by an insistent knock on the door. She opened it and a distraught Katie, followed by Mary, her maid, walked in.

'Katie, darling, what is it?' Anne-Marie asked, gesturing furiously at Abigail to come and help.

'This note.' She handed her a piece of paper. Mary had hold of Katie's hand.

'What are you doing here?' Anne-Marie demanded of Mary.

'I need her, I need her,' Katie wailed.

Anne-Marie and Abigail read the note and exchanged glances.

'Marcus wanted to meet you by the shack. You've seen him before? You're having an affair with Marcus?' Anne-Marie's eyes were wide with horror.

'And you're married to Todd Cortes,' Abigail added, looking equally shocked.

'The note is not for her,' Mary explained, as Katie carried on sobbing.

'Well then, who is it for?' Anne-Marie asked.

'It's for Todd.'

'Todd Cortes is gay?' Abigail was wide-eyed.

For a moment the world spun and Anne-Marie thought she might faint. She took a deep breath and pulled herself together.

'Right, let's go.' She grabbed her cloak. 'Abigail, I need you with me.' The four women marched determinedly out of the house and down the path.

'Katie, did you know Todd liked men when you married him?' Abigail asked.

'I thought once we were married, I'd be enough.'

'Of course you did, darling,' Anne-Marie said. 'What a cheating bastard. Imagine, on your honeymoon.'

'It wasn't exactly like that,' Mary cut in.

'What do you mean?' Anne-Marie rounded on her; she didn't like having a maid trailing them, especially when she had pride of place by Katie's side.

'She means that he was gay when we started dating and gay when we married. The Studio arranged it all so no one would think he was gay and also to boost my popularity.'

'This is a fucking joke, right?' Anne-Marie stopped dead.

'No.'

'So, you two weren't for real?'

'Well, I hoped we would be.'

'Fucking hell, my resort. *My resort*. Even you have tainted it.' She looked at Abigail, and shook her head angrily.

'Darling, let's just get Todd first and then we'll sort this out,' Abigail soothed.

'Strange . . .' Ed said. He found the door to his house open but no one there. He and Lily had geared themselves up for the confrontation, but there was no one to confront.

'Maybe she went out with the competition winners,' Lily suggested, giggling then hiccuping.

Or maybe she's been abducted by aliens,' he suggested, a little tipsy. They'd had a few large brandies: Dutch courage.

'Hang on, there's a note.' Lily picked the note up off the floor.

'Who could this be for?' Ed asked.

'Oh my God, your wife is having an affair with Marcus!' Lily exclaimed as she read it.

'Really?'

'And if we go and catch them at it, you can just divorce her,' she added.

'What are we waiting for?'

23

The Staff

The Love Resort's staff are specially trained to be discreet and non-invasive. Whatever their role, they are all highly professional. They cater for your every need but also know that this is your time and they will not encroach on that. Anne-Marie Langdale takes personal pride in her staff. If you have any comments to make on this matter, please direct them to her.
Guest Handbook

Todd lay naked in Marcus's arms. 'Can I see you again?' he asked, all rational thought forgotten.

'You're seeing me now,' Marcus replied.

'I know, but we can't stay here for ever.'

'Sure,' Marcus answered vaguely. 'Kiss me,' he demanded, and as Todd obliged a flashbulb went off and the door of the hut swung open.

'What the hell . . . ?'

'What on earth . . . ?'

'Oh my God.'

Anne-Marie stood in the doorway, her arms folded. Todd jumped up and grabbed his clothes. Marcus looked ashen, as did another man, who emerged from behind a pile of diving equipment in the corner, clutching a camera.

'Well, what do we have here?' Anne-Marie asked, unaware where to start. Katie burst into noisy sobs. Mary held on to her and Abigail stopped dead.

'Who are you?' Todd asked, pointing at the man with the camera. His heart was thumping; he thought it might jump out of his chest.

'Yes, who are you?' Anne-Marie seconded.

'Marcus's boyfriend,' he answered, looking terrified.

'Marcus, how could you?' Todd asked, feeling like an utter fool.

'Todd, how could you?' Katie demanded.

'Marcus and Todd, and you . . .' Anne-Marie rounded on the stranger, '. . . how could you?'

They all looked at each other, frozen in horror.

'Right, I think someone needs to take control,' Abigail said finally. 'Marcus, Todd, put some clothes on.' They obliged her. 'That's better,' she stated, when the men were fully clothed.

'Abigail?' Anne-Marie looked near collapse.

'It's all right, darling; let me handle this for now.' She moved forward. 'Now, let's start with you, Marcus's boyfriend. Do you have a name?'

'Adam.'

'Adam. Would you like to start by telling me why you have a camera and why you were hiding?'

'It was . . .' he faltered.

'You see . . .' Marcus began.

'Blackmail,' Todd finished.

'So, let me get this straight. You had no idea Todd was gay until you started serving him. Then you got a vibe that he might be, and told Adam.'

'Yes.'

'You must have thought this was a gift from God. A famous movie star, you're his personal butler, he's on his honeymoon and you think he's gay. When you put it to the test, you discover that you're right and you two hatch this plan.'

'Yes.'

'So you were going to blackmail him and you chose tonight.'

'Yes.'

'Let's just skip the bit about Adam watching you do whatever it was you were doing – and I'm guessing you were doing more than swapping recipes – so you get your photo and then you both confront Todd and offer him your silence for how much?'

'A hundred thousand dollars.'

'A hundred thousand dollars? Are you insane? This man is worth about twenty million. Christ, that's a ridiculously low amount.'

'Aren't you getting off the subject a bit, Abigail?' Anne-Marie squeaked.

'Oh, yes, sorry. Right, well, first things first. Let's have the camera.' She moved towards Adam. Adam looked at Marcus, who looked at Adam, just as Abigail grabbed hold of him; he threw the camera to Marcus, who made a run for it.

'This is going to be fun,' Ed said, rubbing his hands together gleefully.

'And there I was feeling sorry for her. But now, you get a hassle-free divorce and we can skip off into the sunset.'

'Yes, my darling, yes.' The shack was in sight, and they just reached the entrance when they were knocked into by a man holding a camera. Ed grabbed hold of him. 'Marcus, is that you?'

'Keep hold of that man,' a voice shouted from inside the shed, and despite Marcus's struggles, Ed did exactly that.

Lily nearly fell over in surprise. It wasn't what they'd been expecting, that much was clear.

'Oh, Ed, thank goodness,' Anne-Marie said.

'Nice stop,' Abigail added.

'What's going on?' Lily asked, surveying the scene. Mary was holding on to Katie, who was crying. Abigail had her arms clamped around a man who Lily had never seen before. Anne-Marie was rooted to a certain spot, and Todd looked as if he was going to join Katie in her crying.

'Is this some sort of orgy?' Ed asked.

Abigail began to explain.

The six competition winners met at the appointed time. Although they had all had fun that evening, as soon as they saw each other again, they lapsed into silence.

'Here's the plan,' Tim started, savouring his role of leader once more. 'We get two taxis back. Emily, Lee and Thea go in one, we'll go in another. When we get to the entrance we'll sneak back in the way we came. We'll all go straight to our rooms. When they ask us what we did, we'll just say that we wanted to go out but we didn't do anything to upset any of the guests, so they can't be too unreasonable.'

'Good plan,' Lee said, slapping Tim on the back, as they went to find some taxis.

'Yes, well, I seem to be good at being a fugitive,' Tim replied.

'Why do I have to go back with them?' Thea asked, as she and Emily glared at each other.

'I thought you didn't want to be near me.'

'Christ. It's like a choice between two evils,' Thea stated.

Thea purposefully sat in between Lee and Emily in the back of their taxi.

'So, did you two have a good first date?' she asked, her voice full of disapproval.

'Oh God, it was our first date, wasn't it?' Emily replied, leaning forward to look at Lee.

'Yup, babes, it was.'

Thea sighed. 'So, did you have fun?' she pushed.

'It was wonderful,' Emily replied dreamily.

'Yeah, Em, it was really good. Thank you,' Lee said. Thea could barely believe her ears.

'Glad to see you're not feeling guilty,' she spat.

'Actually, Thea, that's not true,' Lee replied.

'Really?' She folded her arms.

'We talked about nothing else all evening. How it seems wrong for us to be so happy when we hurt people. But you have to know that we didn't mean to. I didn't set out to hurt Carla, I know I'm at fault, but I am sorry. I know what you think but I do care about her. She's my friend.'

'You should be telling her this.' Thea wasn't in the mood to forgive.

'Like she'd believe him. I feel wretched about Jimmy, really I do. But, Thea, our relationship wasn't working. They say you can't help who you fall in love with . . .' Emily trailed off.

'Are you saying you're in love?' Thea's eyes were wide.

'Yes,' they replied in unison.

'Oh, for fuck's sake.' She sat back in the taxi and gave up.

'Lily, can you get my mobile?' Ed asked. He needed both hands to restrain Marcus. Lily reached into his pocket and pulled out his ringing phone.

'Hello?'

'It's security. Is that Lily?'

'Yes. Are they back?'

'They're here.'

'Right. Well, put them in the welcome room with some of your guys. Don't let them out of your sight.'

'Is who back?' Anne-Marie demanded.

'The winners.' Lily cringed.

'You mean they got out?'

'They escaped before we were due to pick them up for dinner.'

'For fuck's sake, can't you do anything right?' she shouted. Everyone in the shack jumped.

'Look, just a suggestion,' Ed started. 'But this display would be better held somewhere a bit more discreet.'

'My bungalow is nearest,' Lily suggested, and led the way.

*

'They can't actually do anything to us, can they?' Emily asked.

'Emily, shut up. You keep saying that,' Jimmy snapped.

'Sorry, but I'm worried.'

'We're all worried, but for now all we can do is wait.' Thea sounded calm.

'It's not like they can do anything illegal anyway. I don't think they'd want to kill us or anything like that, would they?' Lee looked nervous.

'Don't be so stupid. All they're going to do is tell us off and probably put us under total surveillance for the rest of the trip.' Tim appeared convinced, but Carla wasn't so sure. She didn't relish the idea of sleeping rough on a Caribbean island. There were probably snakes and stuff around. She looked at Thea, who took her hand and squeezed it for reassurance. 'Thank you,' she whispered, and then sat down to continue to wait.

'Why are we still here? This is torture,' Lee said, stomping around the room; they were all trying to avoid the dodgy look that the security man at the door was giving them.

'This is probably part of our punishment. You know, they're making us sweat.'

'I would give anything for a drink,' Tim said. Thea looked at him sharply. 'Sorry.' He put his head in his hands.

'What are we going to do?' Emily asked, but no one answered her.

At her bungalow Lily had taken charge. She needed to get this mess sorted out so they could go and sort out the other mess awaiting them in the meeting room.

'Firstly, Ed, take the camera and destroy the film.'

'It's digital,' Adam boasted.

'Great, well then, Ed, destroy the camera.' Ed grabbed the camera, let go of Marcus and threw it down hard on the stone floor. He repeated the action.

'I think it's broken now,' Abigail said, looking at the shattered pieces.

'I'll dispose of it, just in case,' Ed replied.

'We need to keep this quiet, so we won't be able to press charges. Anne-Marie, you remember those confidentiality agreements that I drew up for the others?' Anne-Marie nodded. 'Well, I propose that Adam and Marcus sign them.'

'What if we refuse?' Adam said.

'Then we'll tear you apart,' Lily threatened. Adam recoiled as if he'd been struck. She went over to her table and picked two papers up from it. 'Now, please sign, and if you speak of any of this again, I'll sue you.'

'My job?' Marcus said.

'You're damned lucky I don't kill you,' Todd said. He was shaking with anger.

'And you're lucky Katie doesn't kill you,' Mary stormed. 'You like boys, so that's fine, but you didn't just put yourself at risk with your doings, you also put my Katie at risk. She could have been humiliated, a laughing stock. Did you think of that?' Everyone looked surprised by Mary's outburst.

'No.' Todd's shoulders fell.

'Neither had I,' Katie added, before finding a fresh batch of tears.

'Back to the original question of your job,' Lily began. 'You are, of course, fired, but if you sign that agreement we'll give you a glowing reference so you will get another job. If you don't sign, then you'll never work again. And as your crazy blackmail plot failed, I guess you need the money.'

She stood over the men as they both signed the papers. Then she picked up the phone and summoned security.

'They will escort you off the premises, and I trust that we will never see you again.'

★

'Right,' Lily said to the film stars after the two blackmailers had been led away, 'you two can probably use some time alone.'

'But they lied to us,' Anne-Marie protested. 'We have to do something.'

'What? Look, we need to keep this quiet, Anne-Marie, which means that they go back to their bungalow having made a promise to us to keep up the pretence for the rest of their honeymoon.'

'I guess.' But Anne-Marie wanted them to pay. She wanted the competition winners to pay. She wanted Ed and Lily to pay. She wanted everyone to pay for what they'd put her through.

'I think that's best, darling,' Abigail said. She put a consoling arm on Anne-Marie.

'I'll stay with her,' Mary told her employers. 'I am not leaving you,' she reassured Katie, folding her arms determinedly.

'Thank you, Mary.' Katie had genuine gratitude in her voice.

'Yes, Mary, I trust you will keep them out of trouble tonight,' Anne-Marie agreed.

'I am sorry—' Todd began.

'Uh, save it. Save it for your wife,' Anne-Marie spat.

'Darling, I'm going to leave you to it. You know where I am if you need me.' Abigail kissed Anne-Marie and followed the departing honeymooners out.

'So, now . . .' Anne-Marie began.

'Now we have to go and deal with the others,' Ed said, sounding weary as they too left the bungalow.

'Right, this is ridiculous,' Thea said angrily. Just then the door opened and they all stopped dead.

'Well, here we are again.' Anne-Marie had spent the short walk from Lily's to here berating her husband and PR manager for their failure in such a simple task. 'So, once more, do you have anything to say for yourselves?'

'We're sorry?' Tim suggested.

'You are getting on my fucking nerves, you smug bastard. Now, here's what I'm going to say. You've had your fun, and I hope it was worth it. From now on you are under room arrest and you will only come out of your rooms when someone comes to get you. You will be watched at all times and you will not, I repeat not, get the chance to escape again.'

Realising that she was tired and almost running out of steam, she looked at her husband and Lily. 'You two, escort them to their rooms. Find some way of locking them in. I am going to bed.'

'I'm not sure whether to be disappointed by the night's events; I mean, we thought we were going to catch your wife, not the famous Todd Cortes.'

Lily and Ed were walking back from escorting the six back to their rooms, after getting security to lock them in.

'Oh God, it's all such a mess, and Anne-Marie looks close to breaking point.'

'Yes, I suppose you ought to go and take care of her.'

'Darling. I'd rather be with you but she seemed so wired.'

'She did.' Lily tried to bite back her disappointment.

'The last few days have been weird: partner swapping, finding out those couples weren't couples, Tim and Mrs Greyton, the magazine and now gay sex and blackmail.'

'Putting it like that, it has been eventful. God, she's so angry with us.'

'At the moment she doesn't have the energy to be angry. Or not her usual anger, anyway. With luck, by the time I get back she'll already be asleep.'

'That wasn't as bad as I thought,' Tim said to Jimmy as they got into bed.

'It feels really strange, sleeping with a man.'

'Well, we're not going to do anything. Are we?' Tim looked a bit scared.

'No, and if you so much as come near me I'll go and get Anne-Marie.'

'I promise, even if I did want to come near you, which I don't, that's enough of a threat to keep me away.'

'I wonder what the rest of the holiday has in store.'

'From Anne-Marie's reaction, I'm guessing our holiday is well and truly over.'

'Carla, are you all right?' Thea asked, as she climbed into bed.

'Funnily enough, I am. I feel like a weight has been lifted.'

'Lee?'

'Yeah, what was I thinking?'

'Don't know. But he's quite good-looking.'

'Oh, he is, but he's no movie star.'

'No, that he isn't.'

They looked at each other and giggled.

'This is like a girly sleepover,' Carla said.

'Yes. I wonder how the boys are doing.'

'Tim?'

'I miss him. It's weird because I know, I'm one hundred per cent sure, that we're not in love or anything, but I almost feel as if he should still be by my side.'

'Thea, remember that stuff about Tim being your security blanket?'

Thea nodded. 'I know, but you'd think that if I needed one, I'd have chosen one who didn't cause so much trouble, wouldn't you?'

Anne-Marie tossed and turned, wondering where she'd gone wrong. She had done nothing to deserve the hardship that she was suffering. She'd only tried to bring romance into people's lives – romance, love and happiness. Was that it? She was being punished for being so nice? She sighed as she tried to sleep, tried to conjure up the romantic images that usually bade her good night. The book was ruined now. Todd wasn't the hero she wanted, nor could even use. The whole thing was perverse; wrong. Even Katie had lied. They'd all lied. And Ed couldn't be relied on. Again, she was back to the same thing. The circle met at its usual point. Abigail was the only person she had; apart from her she was totally alone.

She heard Ed climb into bed and she made for the far side. There was no way she wanted to be near him.

'I'm sorry,' Todd said again.

'It doesn't help. I feel humiliated; oh, I can't even begin to tell you how I feel, actually.'

'Sorry.'

'Oh, shut up. You're like this pathetic stuck record. Todd, I thought you were the man I was going to spend the rest of my life with.'

'But you knew.'

'Maybe I did, but I didn't really, did I? Not until tonight. I loved you. I hate you right now, but I really loved you, Todd, and I really wanted our marriage to work.' Katie's eyes swam with tears and Todd, again, felt desperate that he'd caused it. When they'd started dating, she'd seen it as a business arrangement, as he had, but now it seemed he didn't take her feelings into account; he actually didn't give her any credit for having any.

'I told you. I told you that we could never really be together.'

'Well, I don't remember that.'

Just as he felt sorry for her, and vowed to try to make it up to her, she went back to arguing. One thing was for sure: Katie somehow brought out the worst in him. 'You only hear what you want to hear.'

'You only care about yourself.'

'You're a fine one to talk.'

'Actually I am.'

'Katie . . .'

'Todd . . .' They stared at each other defiantly.

Mary stepped in. 'Enough. Now, Todd, you sleep here tonight, on the sofa. I will sleep with Katie in the bed.'

'And first thing tomorrow I'm calling Bernie. And I'm telling him everything.'

With that, Katie stormed off, leaving Todd feeling very, very sick.

24

A Day In The Life Of The Resort
— By Anne-Marie Langdale

The Love Resort offers so much to you that I decided to put in my own words how I think you should spend a typical day.

You rise early in the arms of your loved one. You get ready and breakfast in one of our wonderful restaurants. After breakfast you take some time to relax by one of the pools or on the beach, read one of my books!

Before lunch you might want to freshen up, and after lunch you could swim, or take a walk round the beautiful gardens. Later on you could engage in a fun water-sport activity. Finally, end the day with a nice relaxing bath (with your loved one), before dressing for dinner.

After dinner you can either take part in our wonderful entertainment or spend some private time on one of our love seats, or in a hammock. Watch the day end in the most perfect setting, with the one you love.

Guest Handbook

Anne-Marie was wide awake, having slept fitfully at best. She looked at the pink clock beside her bed; it was only half past six. She glanced disdainfully over at her husband, who was snoring; fast asleep. As with her last thought, her first thought was one of solitude. Only Abigail, one person. Not a lot to show for her life.

She dragged herself out of bed and padded gently to her upstairs terrace where she opened the door and banged it closed, hoping to wake up Ed. It would serve the oaf right for making her life so difficult, she thought, as she looked at the early morning view.

It always took her breath away. The sun was just finding its momentum. The waves were lapping softly, introducing themselves to the sand. The Caribbean birds were chirping merrily away. The resort was empty; all activity at that time was behind closed doors. She breathed in the heady scent of the sun, the sea and the garden. It was all so intoxicating. She loved her resort now, when it was just waiting to come to life, although she rarely saw it this early.

The kitchens would be busy; waiting staff setting up the breakfast in the main restaurant. The chambermaids would be at their early briefing; the entertainment staff getting the day's events set up; the gym would be just opening – the spa not for another three hours. In half an hour, her couples would begin to spill out from their rooms. Going to breakfast, some to the gym before breakfast, and then the resort would change.

Instead of standing, seeing, hearing and smelling such beauty, there would be ruination. Gaudy colours clouding her soft focus; low-class noise invading the tranquillity; activities that created fools of everyone, detracting from the romance; unattractive people making the most beautiful place in the world look ugly. She gulped back a sob as she realised how far from her dream she was; how the promise of the resort had become the lie. And that was before she dared let herself think about the previous day. There was only one thing for it: she would go and see the sole person who she could rely on. And then she'd ask for help.

Anne-Marie put on a pale blue sundress, and tied her hair back. She didn't apply her make-up; too impatient to get out. She closed the door with a bang, and started making her way towards Abigail's bungalow. She felt lighter as she walked, with the knowledge that she would soon see Abigail comforting her.

After all, Abigail had been her saviour last night. If it wasn't for her, she'd never have coped. She shuddered again at the memory.

She reached the front door and knocked. Then she waited. There was no answer. Damn, Abigail must still be asleep. She tried the door handle; the door was open. She decided to go and wake her; after all, dear Abigail wouldn't mind. She surveyed the mess of clothes, tossed around in the living room with some surprise. Even more so when she realised that draped over the back of the honey-coloured sofa were a pair of men's shorts. Horror rushed around her head as, terrified, she moved towards the bedroom. She raised her knuckles to knock, but then she thought better of it. This was her resort, her publisher, hers, hers, hers. She opened the door, and as her eyes adjusted to the dark she saw her greatest fear realised.

'Ahhhhhhhhhh!' she screamed.

'Anne-Marie?' Abigail sat up quickly.

'What on earth . . . ?' André said.

'How could you?' Anne-Marie spat. 'How could you?'

'Anne-Marie, can you go on to the terrace and let me get dressed, and then I'll explain?' Abigail asked reasonably.

'And him?' Her eyes bore into André, the butler, who wasn't quite as calm as her publisher.

'André, will go and get to work?'

'Yes,' he mumbled.

'That's assuming he still has a job,' Anne-Marie pointed out.

'Of course, but don't do anything until we've had a chance to talk. Please, darling.' Abigail gave her a beseeching look.

Anne-Marie stood, arms folded looking at them. Her publisher had picked up a gigolo at her resort; in fact, Anne-Marie had given him to her. She was supposed to be here for *her*, not for sex. Like some cheap slut, she was having an affair. And now the headaches and the absences all became clear. How could she do this to her? Oh God, all the things that went

against her beliefs were happening here. She felt her chest
constrict. She had to concentrate on breathing. What would
happen if she lost Abigail?

'I'll wait. But don't keep me waiting too long.'

'Come inside?' Abigail asked, as André slunk out, almost
melting under Anne-Marie's glare.

She shrugged her shoulders, pouting, then did so.

'I've put some coffee on, would you like some?'

Like a petulant child, Anne-Marie shrugged again. Abigail
went to the coffee pot and poured two cups. She put them
down on the counter.

'Will you say something?' she asked.

'How could you?'

'How could I what? How could I fall for a gorgeous, charming, intelligent young man?'

'You're married.'

'Yes, and you know that Philip is dull as dishwater. It's a
loveless marriage. He's also become boring in bed – not that we
ever have sex these days. All he cares about is the business,
nothing else. I found something magical in André. You have to
understand, you write about this sort of magic.'

'You're married.'

'Are you telling me that you would stay married to Ed if you
fell in love with someone else?'

'How dare you? I am in love with my husband.'

'That's a joke.'

'Abigail, how could you? I love Ed and I would never, ever
cheat on him. No one in my books cheats. No one.'

'Of course they don't.'

'And you, you did. In my resort. Are you going to tell
Philip?'

'I'm leaving Philip.'

'You're what?' Anne-Marie let out a pained wail.

'I'm going to ask him for a divorce.' Abigail looked aghast as

Anne-Marie collapsed on the floor and started sobbing. 'Anne-Marie? I didn't realise that you were that fond of Philip.'

'I'm not,' she sobbed.

'So why?'

'Because of the DIVORCE. No one in my novels ever, ever utters the word. It's a terrible word, a nasty word, a word used by evil people,' she spat.

'Can I point out that this isn't one of your novels? André and I are in love, really in love, and I'm leaving my husband for him.'

'It's The Love Resort, don't you see? This *is* one of my novels. Living here was supposed to be like living in my novels. That's *exactly* what it was supposed to be.' Anne-Marie knew she was shouting but she didn't care. How could the one person she could rely on not understand her at all? This was her novel. Her world was her books, and she was living in one. Until they ruined it.

First the old, fat people with the bad dress sense. Then when she tried to do something about that, the competition winners with their drunken behaviour, their lying, and their cheating. Then Todd and Katie – oh, she would never have gay people in her novels, they weren't even allowed in the resort. It was against her rules. They had all ruined it for her, just as they obviously set out to do. Now Abigail with her talk of divorce. Everyone was trying to destroy her. She was utterly alone; her against the world.

'Anne-Marie, this is nothing like living in one of your novels. You talk about how no one cheats in your books, how no one gets divorced, how no one is gay, but how about swearing? You say no one swears in your books, but you sometimes have a mouth like a sewer. And then your women barely drink. Well, you drink copious amounts all the time. You can't have it all ways, you know. You're not the perfect heroine you claim to be, just as this place can't live up to your expectations.'

'You're a liar. A cheat and a foul-mouthed liar.' Tears streamed down the novelist's face.

'Anne-Marie, I want to help you, but I don't know how.'

'Give him up.'

'I can't. I love him.'

Anne-Marie looked defiantly at her publisher, who showed no signs of backing down. Confusion enveloped her, as did despair. It wasn't meant to be like this.

'Give him up.'

'No, Anne-Marie, no. I would do most things for you, but not this.'

'Then you can no longer help me. I shall have to help myself.'

Lily rested her head on Ed's chest. When he'd called to offer her breakfast in bed, she'd forgotten all about the trouble and let herself think only of him. It felt like a rare luxury.

'I wonder where she went this early?'

'No idea, although my guess would be that she went to Abigail. Where else would she go?'

'Abigail seems to be more on our side, don't you think?'

'Yes. I hate her for introducing me to Anne-Marie and I blame her for how Anne-Marie turned out; Philip and Abigail kept pushing her to be this romance person, the whole package, and she did. Then when people loved her, she also became a complete bitch.'

'But maybe she realises that now? Abigail, I mean.'

'Maybe. Because there is no way she's getting a book out of Anne-Marie. She used to write for eight or so hours every day – you couldn't get her away from her keyboard. But since we moved here, which, by the way, was to help her writing, she hasn't written a thing.'

'What will happen?'

'I don't know and I'm a little frightened. Lily, this is all I care about, you and me. Anne-Marie and Abigail can shove their book and this resort up their arses.'

'You don't mean that. You're worried about her.'

'You're right, darling. That's the truth. I don't love her but I am worried.'

'Edward,' Anne-Marie shouted as she opened the door. There was a note on the table saying that he was waiting for the competition winners to take them to breakfast. She looked at her perfect house, and she knew that Abigail was lying. The one person she trusted was a liar. Now she had no one.

The phone rang insistently, but she ignored it. If she was alone then she would have to deal with things alone. She had to decontaminate the resort. She had to get the pests out. She had to control things herself. She needed to fight the enemy. The answer dawned on her, and as soon as it did, she swept out of the house once more.

She dialled Ed's mobile.

'Hello?' he answered.

'Ed, it's me. Listen, I'm going to breakfast with the competition winners myself. You can go and man the office and make sure that Lily does all we need her to do.'

'If you're sure . . .'

'I am.'

'Darling, are you all right?' he asked.

'I'm absolutely fine,' she said, before hanging up and wiping away her tears.

'So?' Lily asked, as she got out of bed and pulled on her robe.

'She wants to handle them herself. We're to go to the office as usual.'

'That doesn't sound right.' Lily knew her boss well enough to know that she wouldn't normally do that.

'That's what I thought.' Ed sighed. 'OK, let's get showered, dressed and go and find her then.'

At least now she had a plan, Anne-Marie found her resolve. There was a bungalow above the resort that was going to be restored. About a week ago, the police had told her security that it had been broken into – local kids they thought. Ed himself had spoken to the owners, who were overseas, and assured them that they would secure it. Her own security had done the job. It was a safe place and one that wasn't part of her resort.

She got hold of a guard in the security office and asked for the keys. He was unsure but gave them to her anyway, after she reminded him that she was the boss. Then she scribbled a list and told him to deliver everything himself to outside the bungalow straight away.

'What for?' he asked.

'It doesn't concern you. Now if you do as I ask, and keep this quiet, then I'll make it worth your while.' She pulled a thousand dollars out of her pink handbag and gave it to him.

He looked at Anne-Marie and nodded. She smiled and told him to call her when he was done.

'Oh, and you'd better give me the keys to the rooms you padlocked last night.' She smiled in satisfaction as he did what she said.

Anne-Marie strode with renewed purpose to the hotel, where she went to the first door and opened it.

'Uh.' Jimmy jumped as he found himself facing Anne-Marie. Tim was in the bathroom. Jimmy told himself to stop shaking.

'Jimmy, good morning,' she said pleasantly, unnerving him further. 'I need you to get dressed and meet me on the landing. Chop chop. There's a surprise for you and I need you in ten minutes.'

After delivering the same message to the others she waited
for them. It was so simple, so beautiful. Once she had got them
there safely she would go back for Todd and Katie. She
debated putting Abigail there too, but she realised that she
couldn't do that to her, no matter how much she deserved it.
No, this would be her solution, as she knew that she was the
only person she could rely on in the whole wide world. She
would tell no one else.

As her six competition winners emerged from their rooms,
looking sheepish, she tried to hide the contempt that she felt
so keenly. Their good looks had faded for her the minute they
behaved badly. Well, they would get their punishment, she
was sure of it, just like everyone else. But first, she would
make sure that they didn't cause any more problems for her
resort.

'Come along, this way,' Anne-Marie chirped as she led them
up the hill to the edge of the resort. She kept looking furtively
around her, but it seemed that her route was attracting no
attention. Good.

'Where exactly are we going?' Tim asked, huffing and
puffing.

'Ah, well, that's the surprise. Now, I am going to give you a
challenge for the day.'

'A challenge?' Thea eyed Anne-Marie suspiciously.

Anne-Marie kept walking fast. So much for young people –
they were all huffing and sweating in the heat, although they
should have been far fitter than she was. Instead they all looked
like messes. She had definitely made the right decision.

'Well, you know that we can't have you running around the
resort? And I thought I'd spare you another of Ed's dreary day
trips.'

'It was a bit dreary,' Tim agreed.

'Quite. So, I thought that I would set you a challenge.
Something exciting.'

'Sounds great,' Lee said, holding on to Emily's arm and helping her up the steep hill.

They reached the edge of the resort, and Anne-Marie led them through a gate. The small bungalow was hidden by trees and bushes; it couldn't be seen from the resort. It was rundown; ramshackle. Its paint was peeling, and the window frames were visibly cracked; it looked tired. As did the six guests by the time they reached the door.

Anne-Marie saw that the baskets were stacked up outside the front door, just as she requested. She took the keys out of her pocket and undid the padlock. She opened the second lock and the third, satisfied that it was secure enough.

'Now,' she turned to face her charges, 'you will go in with all these baskets of goodics, and then I shall send up instructions for your challenge. It's going to be very, very exciting; I can assure you of that.'

'Really?' Thea asked.

'Thea, dear, believe me, it's this or Ed.' She looked at her, her head tilted sideways.

'I'll take this,' Lee enthuscd, grabbing a basket and going inside. Jimmy followed suit, as did Emily and Carla.

'Go on, Thea. Within the next few minutes you will receive your instructions and also a wonderful surprise.' Anne-Marie gave her a little push. She reluctantly went in.

'Tim, is there anything I can do for you?' Anne-Marie asked, noticing him shuffling about outside.

'I was just wondering, there wouldn't be anything to drink in those baskets, would there?'

She smiled at him sympathetically. 'Well, there's only one way to find out.'

She shut the door behind him and relocked it. She had one more delivery to make to them before she could relax. Praising herself for her genius, she made her way to her next stop.

★

Thea led the way around the bungalow they were in. The entrance they'd been shown into led on to a large living room. There was no furniture, but there were a few empty wooden crates. The paint was peeling off the walls, as on the outside, and the filth made it almost impossible to see out of the heavily secured windows. Off the first room was a kitchen, grey where it had once been white, with a rusty old cooker, and a few empty cupboards. She turned the taps on at the cracked ceramic sink; water reluctantly spluttered forth. She then walked through the living room again, to a bedroom with a bathroom leading off it. Again, there was no furniture, but there was at least some loo roll. On the other side of the bedroom there was a dressing room, big enough to be a bedroom, but with built-in wardrobes and a full-length mirror, which was broken. As Thea shuddered, thinking about the sumptuous bed in the rooms, the crisp white sheets, the marble bathroom, and the decked terrace, she felt miserable. She walked back to the living room, her five companions hot on her heels.

'What are we doing here?' Carla asked.

'She said it's a challenge,' Lee reminded her.

'I don't like it,' Emily said. 'It's too hot.'

'Open a window then,' Jimmy suggested, and he went to do just that. 'Oh, they seem to be locked.'

'And they have bars on them. Why would they have bars on them?'

'Unpack the baskets,' Thea ordered, filling up with dread. They surveyed the food and the water, looking at each other suspiciously.

'Well, she said she'd be back with our instructions soon,' Tim pointed out.

'There's enough food here to last us a few days,' Thea said, her mind whirring.

'Yeah, but we won't be here for more than today,' Lee said. 'What the hell is she playing at?'

No one answered.

★

Anne-Marie knocked on the door. Mary opened it.

'Ah, Mary, I need to speak to Todd and Katie. Now, can you go and organise breakfast to be brought up in half an hour, please?'

'I don't like to leave Katie,' Mary said.

'Mary, may I remind you who pays your wages? Now, I promise I won't leave them alone until you come back.'

Mary huffed but did as she was told.

'Hello, Todd,' Anne-Marie said, trying hard to be friendly.

'Anne-Marie.' His voice was grim.

'Where's your wife?' she enquired sunnily, as if nothing was wrong. Just then Katie appeared from the bedroom, wearing a pretty top and slim skirt, and no shoes.

'Hello.' Her face was red and puffy; devoid of make-up she looked ordinary. The famous film star *was* pretty ordinary, Anne-Marie decided.

'Right, now, I don't want to go over last night again, but I do need you to come with me.'

'Where?' Todd asked.

'Well, it's a surprise.'

'What sort of surprise?' He narrowed his eyes.

'After last night, you're lucky I don't throw you both out. So please do not question me, just follow me. Chop chop.' Anne-Marie waited on the terrace for them to get their shoes. When they came out, she smiled, and gestured for them to follow her.

'Where's Mary?' Katie asked.

'She'll be joining you soon,' Anne-Marie promised. 'Now, please just do as I say, and I won't ask for anything again. I won't go to the press; I won't ruin your lives, which I think is very generous of me under the circumstances.' They nodded and followed her.

The sun was beating down as they made their way up to the

top of the resort. It was a twenty-minute walk, and Katie was dripping with sweat. When they reached the bungalow, Anne-Marie stopped.

'What are we doing here?' Todd asked. He still looked so handsome, she couldn't believe what a terrible waste of a man he was.

'There's a surprise for you in there. What I have decided, being the woman I am, is that you should spend some time alone, to talk. Now, I think that that is the best solution. To be honest with each other.'

'We could have done that in our place,' Katie pointed out.

'No, not without interruption. Now, in there is everything you need. I shall come back for you in a few hours and hopefully you will both be feeling much better.' She smiled widely.

'It's not a bad idea,' Katie conceded.

'Are you sure?' Todd asked.

'Yes, Todd, I think it's time we sorted this out once and for all.' Anne-Marie opened the door and ushered them in. Then she closed it behind them and locked each and every lock.

'Oh, hi, Abigail,' Lily said. She had just pulled on her work uniform before the knock on the door.

'Lily, I need to see Ed.'

'Ed? But why would he be here?'

André appeared from behind Abigail, looking grim.

'She knows; I told her,' he said simply.

Lily wondered if all the staff knew about them as she led them inside.

'Ed,' she called, 'it's Abigail.'

Seconds later, Ed appeared, dressed in his chinos and a white shirt. His face was red.

'We were just going to find her. Did she send you?' he asked.

'No. Ed, I think you'd better listen.'

Abigail and André sat side by side on Lily's cream sofa. Lily sat down on a wooden chair and Ed stood beside her as Abigail told him the story.

'So, you mean you two have been together all this time?' Ed asked; he found the idea of the iron lady and André incredible.

'Well, I didn't seduce him the minute I met him, if that's what you mean?'

'When did you then?'

'Ed, don't you think this is a bit off the point?' Lily asked.

'I'm just asking.'

'I seduced her,' André said. 'After three days of her being here, I thought she was hot.'

Ed tried not to look surprised. He wasn't sure how anyone could find Abigail hot.

'No one has thought that about me in a long time. Anyway, I told your wife that we're in love. She didn't seem very happy for us,' Abigail said tightly.

'What do you think she's going to do?'

'Or what has she done?' André pointed out.

'Ed, she was crazed.'

'Have you tried the house?'

'I called there, but there was no answer.'

'Look, I'll go there. Lily, can you go and check on Todd and Katie? Can you two go and check on the competition winners?'

'Sure.' They went off in separate directions, unsure of what they were looking for, but knowing that whatever it was, they were dealing with a mad woman.

'What on earth . . . ?' Todd asked, as he and Katie stepped into the living room. They turned back towards the door as they heard the locks being turned. Then they turned round and looked at the six people perched on wooden crates in front of them.

'Is this our challenge?' Lee asked uneasily.

'What challenge?' Katie replied, looking at him as if he were mad.

'Are you?' Thea stopped in her tracks.

'Do you know what's going on?' Todd asked.

'We were rather hoping you'd tell us.'

Todd sighed. Everything was getting weirder. 'I'm Todd Cortes, and this is Katie Ray.'

'Katie Ray-Cortes,' she reminded him.

'The film stars,' Thea said, staring at them shamelessly.

'Oh my God, but you normally look so glamorous,' Emily said gawping. Katie scowled at her.

'Did Anne-Marie send you here for us?' Lee asked.

'I'm not drunk, am I?' Tim asked. 'Or am I dreaming? I mean, this might be one of those really unusual dreams I have where I'm locked away with you guys and two famous people. Really, my imagination—'

'Why are you here?' Jimmy cut Tim off.

'We don't know. We thought it was to talk,' Katie said, sounding confused.

'To us?' Tim asked.

'No, each other. We have no idea who you are,' Todd pointed out.

'Then we have a head start. Let me introduce everyone to you.'

'My God, that's some story,' Todd said. Sitting down on the floor, he pulled a crate next to him and gestured to Katie to sit with him. She was hesitant but as she was terrified she obliged.

'Do you think we've been kidnapped?' Thea asked.

'Isn't that a bit overdramatic?' Katie said; Todd hoped it was.

'We are talking about Anne-Marie Langdale. They invented the word "overdramatic" for that woman.'

'If she has kidnapped us, then we could sue her,' Tim said.

'If we ever get out,' Todd pointed out.

'Todd, do you mind if I call you Todd?' Todd shook his head at Tim. 'We told you all about us, but, well, why are you here, exactly?'

Todd sighed. How on earth would he explain things to these strangers? He looked at Katie, who was looking resolutely away from him.

'There's no sign of Todd and Katie. Mary is hysterical. She's told Erik that they're missing so I had to pacify him and make sure he doesn't go round blabbing. She said that Anne-Marie arrived, sent her to get breakfast, and when she got back there was no sign of them,' Lily said. Panic was spreading; something was very wrong.

'The competition winners didn't answer their phones. I went to the rooms to find them open and empty,' Abigail stated, as André nodded.

'OK, did they take their stuff?'

'Didn't seem to have, although it was quite messy.'

'Todd and Katie?'

'No, nothing appeared to be missing there.'

'Anne-Marie is not at home. No one has seen her either.'

'What should we do?'

Ed stood up and walked in front of his desk. 'Lily, call their publicist and see if she's heard anything. Abigail, you and André go and wait at the house. I'm going to get security, to see if they know anything.'

Lily almost buckled. He was so sexy when he was in command.

Anne-Marie hid behind a bush. She had a pair of binoculars on her, trained on the bungalow. If they did manage to escape, she'd be the first to know. She would stay here for as long as it took, because she wasn't going to let them out until their flights arrived. She thought about letting Todd and Katie go because they could order their private jet any time, but decided against it. She didn't feel that that would punish them adequately. But this would, she thought, looking for any movement. All the awful, nasty people, shut away together. That would teach them to mess with her and her resort. She laughed manically as she congratulated herself once more.

25

Complaints

We do not anticipate that you will have any complaints* about your stay at The Love Resort, but in the rare cases that you do, then please put them in writing to Lily Bailey, PR manager.

Your stay has to be perfect for us to be happy, and if you feel that it isn't, we will put it right for you straight away.
Guest Handbook

* All complaints will be evaluated. However, please ensure that they are of a reasonable nature.

Ed, Lily and Abigail sat in the office.

'We've searched everywhere we can think of.'

'Are we going to alert anyone?'

'It's too risky. Obviously I have to call Harriet, but apart from that, we need to keep it between us at the moment.'

'What about Mary?' Abigail asked.

'We'll have to keep an eye on her. We're moving her to the house, where we'll be based. If Anne-Marie shows up, it'll be there,' Lily explained.

It had been a hellish morning. She picked up the phone, and dialled.

'Harriet.'

'Hi, Harriet, it's Lily.' Lily braced herself; Ed shot her a reassuring look.

'What can I do for you?'

'Well, we sort of have a problem . . .'

'Ed, I need to ask you something,' Abigail beckoned Ed to the other side of the room, while Lily continued her conversation.

'Go on,' Ed said.

'I want to leave. It's been, well, it's been interesting, but I know I'm not getting my book anytime soon, so I have to go and deal with the fallout from that. I also need to tell Philip about André. Actually, I'm taking him with me.'

'But all the flights are full – we checked,' Ed said, suddenly wanting Abigail to stay.

'Darling, you obviously only checked economy. I have two first-class tickets to London this afternoon.'

'Of course I did – old habits die hard,' Ed laughed. 'But I don't know how we would have coped without you,' he added graciously.

'I think I owed you. Ed, I am sorry. Sorry I thought it would be a good idea for you to marry her; sorry that I treated you like you were, well, the hired help. I was such a bitch.'

'I think you're forgiven, and actually I now think I owe you.'

'Well, I have my reward. I have André.'

'What's going on?' Lily asked, as she made her way over to them.

'Abigail's leaving us.'

'Yes, Anne-Marie's novel isn't everything. My stay here, and meeting André, has shown me that. Besides, I have another idea up my sleeve. By the way, how did the phone call go?'

'Just as expected. Harriet called me "fucking incompetent", and told me that if I didn't find her film stars I would be hung, drawn and quartered.'

'Nice,' Abigail said sympathetically.

'Yeah, well, I knew that she'd respond like that; when she tells her boss he'll say the same to her. Anyway, after all the swearing and shouting and threats, she told me she's coming over and she said she was going to bring Todd's brother. I asked her not to, but she hung up on me.'

'Ouch.' Ed took her hand.

'Can you imagine? He'll blame us too. Maybe we should leave with Abigail.'

'Don't tempt me.' But they knew they weren't going anywhere.

Later, Ed, Lily and Mary sat at the house; all calls from the office had been diverted there. Senior management had been made aware that there was something wrong, even if details had been kept deliberately vague.

'I should have been with her. I could have stopped whatever it was she's done.'

'She went out.'

'I know, but I should have followed her. We knew that she wasn't coping.'

'And you were with me.'

'Which is where I wanted to be, sweetheart, it's just that I can't help feeling that I could have prevented this, somehow.'

'You two as well?' Mary asked, wide-eyed. 'There is just too much loving going on in this Love Resort.'

Anne-Marie was pleased with herself. Her plan had worked, it seemed. Half an hour and no sign of anyone breaking out. Of course they couldn't get out; she had them just where she wanted them. She smiled at the warm sun, as she congratulated herself, once again, on her genius. She didn't need anyone else. She could completely rely on herself. It was time she took control. She'd let Abigail control her for so long, Abigail told her what to do and she did it. Well, Abigail could go to hell. In fact, she was sure that that was exactly where the treacherous, adulterous, bitch would be going.

She sat down for a moment. It was hot and she was tired

from her nearly sleepless night. Then she lay down, and before she knew it, binoculars clutched to her chest, she fell asleep.

'We don't know why we're here. We were just on our honeymoon, that's all,' Todd lied.

'You've been staying here all this time? And we didn't know.' Thea looked incredulous.

'We had a secluded villa. The only day we went to the main resort was when we had a magazine shoot. I don't know where you guys were.'

'Oh, that must have been the day we did the island tour,' Jimmy said, realising that that was the reason they'd been kept out of the way.

'It's incredible,' Thea started, 'that you are locked in here with us. I can't believe she'd do that to you.'

'That's if you believe Todd,' Katie stormed.

'Katie . . .' Todd warned.

'What, Todd? What? Do you think we'll keep this quiet? When the Studio finds out what's happened they'll be after your blood. And I am going to be the one who ends up humiliated.'

'You'll end up humiliated? Well, I'll be the villain.' Todd looked at her, and then at the six faces that were watching them with interest.

'And you are! Todd, you slept with another man while we were on our honeymoon.'

'Katie, please don't.' That was all hope of keeping it between them out of the barred and locked window.

'Huh?' Tim leant forward.

'What? Don't tell these people how my husband is gay?'

A gasp rang round the room.

'I was gay before I was your husband. Christ, Katie, you knew that, you knew I was gay and the wedding was a studio stunt to keep everyone fooled. You agreed. You married me because they told you to. They offered you a lead role in my next movie on the basis. That's why you married me.'

'No, Todd. No, I married you because I love you.'

'How could you love me? You don't even know me. Even when we were fake dating we had people with us at all times. We never even had a conversation until after the wedding. And then it was you trying to convert me to heterosexualism and me telling you that it couldn't be done.'

'I loved you.'

'Katie, the only person you've ever loved is yourself.'

Katie got up off her crate, Todd stood up too. 'You are a fucking bastard. A fucking gay bastard.' She pulled her hand back and slapped him.

'And you knew all that before you married me,' he spat, rubbing his cheek.

'Is this for real,' Lee asked, 'or is this part of our challenge?'

'Will you stop going on about the fucking challenge? There is no challenge. We're locked up here because we've all upset the owner. Now, while all this is entertaining, I, for one, intend to find a way out.' Tim stood up and began to try the door.

Todd, glaring at Katie, went to help him.

'Are you all right?' Thea asked, approaching Katie.

'It's such a mess. Look at us. Big movie stars locked in a dirty house with you.' She looked disdainful.

'Well, at least people will probably be looking for you. Won't they?'

'Oh God, I hope so, I really do. Will we starve to death?'

'She left us food.'

Thea, Carla and Katie went to the kitchen and surveyed what they had. The dusty white counter housed enough food for a couple of days, but nothing beyond that. Resigning themselves to their fate, they began to put things away.

'Jimmy, you're a mechanic, aren't you?' Tim asked, his door examination proving fruitless.

'Yes.' He went to join them.

'Well, you must know something about all this stuff.'

'I know about cars, Tim.'

'Well, cars have doors, don't they?'

'Not normally with big deadlocks attached.'

'What about the windows?'

'I checked them earlier; they've got heavy-duty locks on them too.'

'Shit. Todd, was all that for real?' Tim asked.

'I'm afraid so. Katie, and Anne-Marie and her entourage caught me with another man in the beach shack.'

'You're kidding?'

'No. And you all know now so it'll only be a matter of time before the press finds out.'

'Oh, I shouldn't think we'd sell the story. Although you never know. It's a good one and must be worth a fortune.'

'Thanks, Tim.' Todd smiled despite himself. The press would love this. If he was ever going to come out, then that would be coming out with a bang.

'Lee, are we going to be all right?' Emily asked, snuggling into him.

'I don't know, but my guess is that if Thea is right and we're kidnapped, then we'll be let out in time to get our flight.'

'But that's not for days.'

'Well, that is the worst-case scenario. Look, I'm going to help the guys to see if we can escape. Why don't you go and help the girls?'

'Because they hate me.'

'Emily, if we are really stuck here, now is a good time to try to make friends. I'm going to do that with Jimmy.'

'I guess so.'

'Don't start being petulant. For once there are more important things at stake.'

Emily kissed him and went to the kitchen.

'This isn't going to last us very long,' Carla was saying, as they stood back and stared at the food on the counter.

'It's all going to go off in a few days,' Thea pointed out.

'That could be a good thing. It could mean that we're not going to be here long,' Emily chipped in as she approached them. Carla glared at her, and then relented.

'Let's hope you're right.'

'What do you suggest?' Katie asked.

'We don't even have a fridge.' They looked at each other in defeat.

'That's some story, Katie, you know – you and Todd,' Thea said. She had stopped being star struck. After all, they were all locked up together, and to be in awe seemed stupid, especially after what they'd heard. It was so surreal: Thea wanted to be an actress and here she was with Hollywood royalty, in a dirty house in the Caribbean. She could barely believe it; she wasn't sure that she did.

'I know.' Katie sounded sad.

'You really loved him?'

'He's right, I didn't really know him. But I loved Todd Cortes.'

'Oh my God, who doesn't?' Thea laughed, and then added, 'You're not the only one who is disappointed that he's gay. Not by a long shot.'

'No, women all over the world will be weeping when they find out.' Katie managed an uneasy laugh.

'Which you think they will?' Carla asked.

'We can't live a lie. It's just a case of how much this will finish us. The Studio will drop us both, and the public will hate us for lying.'

Thea couldn't think of anything reassuring to say.

★

'I – and these men can vouch for it – am very good at escaping,' Tim announced, puffing his chest out proudly.

'Really?' Todd was amused by this funny blond British guy. In fact, he thought they made a really odd group. After the stories they told, he wondered why they hadn't killed each other, although according to Tim they had tried. Jimmy was stiff, he moved a bit like a robot, but Todd guessed he was still a bit shocked by losing his woman to Lee. Lee had that sort of confidence that was attractive, almost cocky, but not quite. He was more composed than Jimmy, who Todd really felt sorry for. He looked as if he was holding all his emotions in, and would burst at any minute. Tim was just completely mad, and he guessed that Tim's devil-may-care attitude had brought about their all being here.

'Oh, yes. You see this isn't the first time that Anne-Marie Langdale tried to incarcerate us.'

'It isn't?'

'No, and last time we escaped.'

'How?' Todd thought maybe Tim was some sort of expert and he began to hope.

'The last time we escaped, Tim, the doors were unlocked,' Jimmy pointed out.

'Oh, that's just a detail. Now, let's think. We definitely can't get out of the door or the windows. So, I think that maybe we need to look at other ways.'

'Hell, Tim, you're a genius,' Lee snapped. 'Have you got any idea what these other ways are?'

Todd looked around him. There was no way out.

'I need time to think. Jimmy, are you sure you can't break these locks?' Tim asked.

'Do we have any tools?' Jimmy asked.

'Good point, search the place for tools. There might be something lying around.' Tim sounded hopeful.

★

'So we have a nail – which technically, Lee, I don't think is a tool – a very small screwdriver and some sort of grippy thing,' said Tim. He, Lee, Jimmy and Todd stood staring at their bounty as if it would suddenly become useful.

'That's a spanner,' Jimmy pointed out.

'So, can we do anything with this?' Todd asked.

'We could put up a picture, unscrew the bathroom cabinet and take some bolts off,' Jimmy said grimly. 'We can't use these on the locks, it'd be hopeless.'

'I hate to be defeatist, but I don't think escape is an option,' Lee said.

'Then what do we do? Just accept things?' Jimmy was getting slightly hysterical; Lee resisted the urge to take hold of him.

'Jimmy, I think we have to. All we can do is hope that she comes back to let us out soon.'

'We can't stay here.' Tim had a demonic look in his eyes. 'We have to get out.' Then he stopped, thought and smiled. 'I mean, there's only one bedroom, no bed, where on earth are we expected to sleep?'

'This water isn't going to last us very long,' Katie said.

'There's sixteen bottles. Eight of us. Two bottles each.'

'That's only enough for one day.'

'You drink two bottles of water a day?' Emily was shocked.

'Yes, of course. For my skin.' She glared at Emily. 'So she can't be planning on leaving us for longer than that. Anne-Marie Langdale is the sort of woman who knows the value of water for the complexion.' Katie smiled smugly. She snatched one of the bottles, opened it and drank thirstily.

'Don't you think we should conserve it, just in case?' Emily asked unsurely.

Katie shot her her best withering look. 'Do what you want. I really don't care.' She took the bottle into the living room, and with all the grace she could muster, she sat herself on a wooden crate and tried to look like the star she was.

Thea looked at her watch, it was eleven a.m. It felt later, as if they had been there all day, not just a few hours. She looked at Tim. He was humming contentedly; she was frightened, she acknowledged, not just for herself but for him too. Anne-Marie couldn't keep them there too long, could she?

Todd looked at his watch. It was midday. It felt later. The time was passing so slowly, especially as resignation had settled in to the group. Katie, perched on her crate, was refusing to talk to, or look at, anyone. He tried to catch her eye but she was deliberately ignoring him. He owed her and he needed to try to take care of her; he had to make some sort of peace with her. However, she was intent on ignoring him. And he couldn't really blame her. He sighed. He couldn't bear it.

Todd stared at Katie again. She was clutching an empty bottle of water. He saw her look at her diamond-encrusted Rolex; he could tell that she was really fed up. He wanted to speak to her, apologise, to offer her some comfort. But how could he? After all they'd gone through he didn't know what to say.

'Food, anyone?' Lee stood up, as did Emily. The other six just looked at him as if he was insane; no one spoke.

Jimmy seethed silently. His watch told him it was four in the afternoon, and Emily and Lee hadn't returned from the kitchen. He heard the old giggle coming from them, which irritated him beyond belief. He was hungry himself, but there was no way he was going in there; no way he wanted to face them. It was bad enough that he'd lost his girlfriend – his brand-new fiancée to Lee, whilst on holiday – but then to be locked away with them . . . It was more than rubbing salt into the wounds; it was worse than anything. He felt tears prick his eyes. How easy it seemed to call Tim's truce. It hurt, yes, although he was beginning to see that Emily wasn't worthy of him. Or was he? He put his head in his hands. Who was he kidding? What he really felt was that still, despite everything, he wasn't worthy of her.

Carla looked at Jimmy, then at her watch. It was five, and as she looked out of the dirty window she saw the sun was dimming. She was so hungry, but Lee and Emily hadn't emerged from the kitchen and it had gone quiet. God knows what they were up to. Carla shuddered. She wasn't ready to deal with the reality of Lee with Emily, even if she had accepted it in theory. She still felt like a fool, but she couldn't just forget how much she'd adored him for the past three years. Her feelings couldn't be eradicated just like that.

Her stomach rumbled. She looked at Thea; begging her to understand.

'I think we should eat.' Her fears were apparent.

Thea nodded, gestured for her to wait there and went into the kitchen. Carla waited and saw her emerge five minutes later with Emily and Lee. Carla stood up and followed Thea back to the kitchen, as did Jimmy.

Thea saw a tiny glimpse of what might have been the sunset through the window as she emerged from the kitchen with a plate of sandwiches. Tim shook his head, as she offered him one.

'Tim.'

'Yes?'

'Are you all right?' It wasn't what she wanted to say, but she couldn't find the right words.

'Oh yes. For a kidnap victim I'd say I was very well.' He smiled.

'Are you sure?'

'Thea, please stop worrying about me.'

Would she ever stop worrying about him? She doubted it. She didn't know anything else. She couldn't remember a time when she didn't worry about him; there probably had never been one.

Katie looked at the sandwich being offered to her and shook her head. Todd took one and bit into it.

'Todd, a word in private, please.' Katie stalked into the kitchen with Todd right behind her.

'This,' she pointed at him in case he was under any illusions, 'is all your fault.'

'I know.' He put his sandwich down on the counter and sighed. He wasn't in the mood for another row. There had been too many recently.

'I can't stay here,' she stated simply.

'I don't see what choice we have.'

'I am Katie Ray. I'm a famous film star. I'm locked up with a bunch of nobodies and I am not staying here.'

'Katie, those are people out there. And they're not exactly thrilled at being locked up either.' He wondered if she was being a bitch just to get a reaction out of him. He wasn't going to rise to the bait.

'Oh, I'm sure they love it. Being locked up with us, famous people, who they could only dream of meeting. I have no hair-brush, no change of clothes, and no make-up. I simply can't be expected to survive,' she trilled.

'But you will. This isn't the worst thing that's ever happened.' He picked up his sandwich.

'Oh, really? You think? Well, I disagree. Todd, I want to get out of here and I want out now.' She poked him, taking him by surprise. He dropped his sandwich on the floor.

'Well, there's nothing I can do.' He took a deep breath and told himself to stay calm.

'I hate you, Todd Cortes, I really hate you.' She pounded on his chest with her fists, and he let her.

★

'This is all your fault,' Carla stormed as Lee tried to pass her another sandwich. She knocked it out of his hand with all the force she could muster. 'You and her. If you'd just kept your grubby hands to yourselves, then we would have been all right.'

'Not this again,' Lee said, putting his head in his hands.

'Well, face it, it's not going away. We're stuck here with these crappy sandwiches and it's all your fault.' She felt like screaming.

'I know, I know, but what can I do?'

Carla looked at him with vehemence in her eyes, then she kicked the crate she'd been sitting on. Pathetic, she told herself, she was pathetic. 'Look, Carla, I really do care about you and I am sorry, you've got to believe me.'

'You wanker.'

'Carla, what do you want me to say? I thought we were mates. I might have ignored that you felt more, but we were friends, housemates.'

'And now we're neither. You are a selfish bastard.'

'Leave him alone,' Emily begged tearfully.

'Oh, this is as much your fault as his,' Jimmy spat. He'd been going round in circles, but now he was tired, longed for a bed and a proper meal, and was frustrated with his inability to know what to do.

'I know it is, but please . . .' she begged.

'Oh, for fuck's sake, there's just no point in arguing with you. You just fucking cry.' All the times that she was mean to him, or critical, and he had taken it without a word, came flooding back. It was too late, he knew that, but standing up to her now definitely made him feel better. Less of a wimp; more of a man.

'Steady on, mate,' Lee started.

'Don't you tell him to steady on,' Carla responded.

'Hey, enough,' Tim shouted. 'We should really try to make the most of it.'

'Of what?' Thea stormed. 'There is nothing here to make the most of, and it's all your fault.'

'What did I do?' Tim asked.

'Do I have to remind you that you slept with someone else's wife?' Perhaps it was everyone else's anger that was feeding hers, but once again, she felt frustrated with him, and she couldn't keep it under control.

'You know I don't think that I did. I was drunk; I probably couldn't have done anything anyway.'

'You're always drunk, Tim, that's the problem.' Everyone else was quiet.

'And you nag like an old fishwife. You drive me to drink,' Tim shouted back.

They stared at each other before Tim turned and stalked off.

26

Meeting Anne-Marie Langdale

As you know, when you booked your holiday you are automatically given the chance to meet the famous author, and you
will also be given the chance to dine with her one night of your
stay.*

'l o Anne-Marie her guests are incredibly important, and
therefore you will see her frequently around the resort,
checking on your wellbeing and that you are enjoying your
stay.

She feels that you are her own personal guests, and your
holiday will reflect this. She will take it upon herself to ensure
that this holiday is the holiday of your dreams.

Guest Handbook

* Please note that dinner with the author is a group activity.

Lily sent the resort's limousine to pick Harriet and David up.
It was dusk by the time they arrived, and herself, Mary and Ed
were more than a bit frayed. It had been a very long, trying
day.

There was still no sign of Anne-Marie; Mary was refusing to
leave until she knew that 'her Katie' was safe. Ed was finding it
hard to think rationally, and Lily blamed herself. At the back of
her mind, nagging at her, was the fact that if she hadn't made
Ed stay in bed with her longer that morning, they probably
could have got to the winners before Anne-Marie. And then

they could have stopped her doing anything. Because, it became clear to Lily, she definitely had done something. She just couldn't figure out what.

At first they thought maybe she'd taken them out. After all, the previous evening she'd been huffing and puffing about having to do everything herself. But there were no buses gone, no drivers, and no cars missing. Same with the boats. It was as if the guests had disappeared into thin air, taking her with them.

More than a little scared, Lily held on to Ed's hand, despite the disapproving looks that Mary was giving them. Her boss had done something stupid, she knew. And her publisher knew it too, which is why she'd skipped off rather than staying to help. Abigail knew that there was no book in Anne-Marie and she wasn't there to look after an author who didn't write. Ed might have forgiven Abigail, but Lily hadn't. The woman had created a beast and then run off with her toy boy when the beast got out of control.

Ed felt responsible. Despite her faults, Anne-Marie was vulnerable, which was why she acted like such a bitch at times. She treated people like dirt because she had to feel worthy. He knew it wasn't a justification for such behaviour, but at the same time he did feel slightly sorry for her. Especially as he could have prevented it, whatever it was. He should have seen that she wasn't coping, especially after the Todd/Marcus débâcle, and he should have stepped in and offered his help and support. But instead he had taken her preoccupation as an opportunity for him to be with Lily and he'd left his wife to her dementia.

He couldn't think what she had done. Todd, Katie and the competition couples were gone, and so was she. That was all he knew. They weren't in the resort. He'd stationed a security guard at Todd and Katie's bungalow, and another by the rooms of the competition winners. If they came back, he would know. He just wished they would come back right now.

★

Lily left Ed at the house and went to meet Harriet and David's car.

'Hi.' She welcomed them and arranged for a porter to deal with their luggage.

'Wow, this place is something else,' David said. Harriet was silent.

'I know,' Lily agreed.

'It's like a queen's paradise,' David uttered, looking around in wonderment.

'Well, he *is* a queen.' Lily clamped her hand over her mouth as Harriet gave her a filthy look. 'Sorry.' She led them up to the house.

'Right, first of all we need to know what you're doing about this situation,' Harriet demanded as soon as they were through the door.

'We've done everything we can: searched the resort, checked with security that no one has left, or any transportation's been taken . . .'

'Can I just stop you there? You haven't found them?'

'No.'

'But they can't have disappeared into thin air?'

'No.'

'Right, well then, I don't understand.'

'Harriet, neither do we.'

'The Studio wants them back in one piece.'

'So do we.' Lily couldn't believe this woman's rudeness. She was worse than Abigail on the frosty thermometer.

'So again, what are you going to do?'

'Harriet, I think you need to stop blaming these guys,' David said.

'Oh, do you?'

Lily sighed as a row threatened to erupt. Silencing them, Lily organised drinks, forcing Mary to have a glass of wine; her glare, along with Harriet's, was going to turn them all to stone. Lily distracted herself by ordering food to be delivered.

'So, you are Harriet. I know about you,' Mary said.

'Good.' Harriet looked surprised. 'You have an advantage on me.'

'I looked after Katie. At first I was her maid, but then I became her friend. She talks to me a lot and I know about you.'

'Right . . .' Harriet now seemed nervous.

'You were always mean to her. You bullied her. You made her do things she didn't want to do.'

'Well, that's a bit harsh,' Harriet protested.

Lily noticed that David smiled and she felt the urge to giggle.

'The thing is, Mary,' Harriet started, 'Katie could be quite difficult. She was very hard to work with and I was only ever doing my job.'

'That's nothing.' Mary dismissed her. 'She was once mean to me, but then she explained. She had a very bad life, and she's very insecure and people always use her. No one takes enough time to get to know the real Katie, and they should because if they did, then they would know how wonderful she is.'

Harriet obviously had no idea how to respond. Lily went to the kitchen to get more drinks; Harriet looked like she needed it.

'Let's get back on the subject, shall we?' Ed suggested. 'What do you want to do? I know you must be tired, but I'm guessing you want to wait for news.'

'Have we called the police?' David asked.

'No way,' Lily answered quickly.

'David, if we call the police the media will be all over this story, and until we know what's happened, I'd rather keep it quiet. Especially in view of his stupid actions,' Ed explained.

'He was an idiot, wasn't he?'

'The Studio are very angry—' Harriet began.

'Harriet, for once can you shut the fuck up about the Studio?'

'So, Ed, Anne-Marie is missing as well?' Harriet was red-faced as she turned her back on David.

'Yes. No sign of her, and we've looked everywhere.'

'Mary, before she took Todd and Katie, you saw Anne-Marie. You might have been the last person to see her today, apart from them. How was she?' David asked.

'She was crazy. She had this look in her eyes.' Mary tried to show them, but it wasn't quite right. David raised an eyebrow. 'She ordered me to go and organise breakfast, kept saying "chop chop". So I went, but she promised she would look after my Katie until I got back. I shall never forgive myself for leaving.'

'Mary, you did what your boss told you to do, that's all,' Ed said reasonably.

'Look, I know we don't want the publicity, but we might have to speak to the police,' Lily said. 'It's dark now and there's no sign of anyone. Maybe we could have a discreet word with a police chief; we have good relations with them here.'

'I don't know,' Harriet said. 'I guess we don't have a choice. I need to call the Studio to see what they want us to do.'

'I'm not comfortable waiting until morning,' David said.

'No, David, neither am I,' Ed agreed.

'Shall I?' Lily felt nervous. What was she reporting? A missing author, eight missing guests, two of whom were famous film stars. It was all too crazy. Ed nodded, and Lily made her way to the phone.

Just then the door burst open and Anne-Marie, wearing what could only be described as half a bush, walked in.

Anne-Marie woke up without knowing where she was or why she was there. She felt something on her chest and, picking up the binoculars that lay on top of her, she wondered what they were for. She stood up uncertainly and thought it was time to go home. She wasn't sure where home was but she thought it might be down towards the lights. After taking some wrong turns, she opened the door of a bungalow.

'Hello!' she trilled. A half-naked man came out and looked at her. 'Do I live here?' she asked. Stunned, he shook his head as his wife came to join him.

'Oh, Anne-Marie, how wonderful,' she gushed, rushing up to her favourite author.

'Wonderful, wonderful, wonderful,' Annc-Marie repeated before she smiled and walked out.

She had known that this was her house because the front door was pink and that made sense. She had found her way home, and as she opened the door and walked in, she wondered why she didn't know she was having a party.

'Where are they?' David shouted. Anne-Marie looked startled, then scared, and she jumped.

'David, no,' Lily commanded. 'Let Ed handle this.'

'Darling?' Ed said.

'Yes. I am quite darling,' Anne-Marie said, as she put her hand to her head and pulled off a twig.

'Why are you wearing binoculars and camouflage?' he asked. Anne-Marie looked at him as if he were mad.

'Why not?' she replied, pulling more leaves from her dress. Ed sighed, this wasn't right. This wasn't his wife. Even when she was drunk she was more together than this. Fear of what she'd done and what had happened to her was very real. Fear for her and fear for himself.

'Anne-Marie, we've been worried about you.'

'Why?'

'Because you've been missing all day. And Todd and Katie, Tim, Thea, Jimmy, Carla, Emily and Lee are also missing.'

'Well, what a coincidence. But who on earth are they?'

'Darling, you know who they are.'

'No idea. By the way, who are you?'

'She needs a doctor,' Mary intervened.

'What's wrong with her?' Lily asked.

David and Ed half carried, half dragged Anne-Marie to the sofa and lay her down. She was delirious or something.

'You people would say she's lost the plot, but it's serious, some sort of breakdown,' said Mary.

'You're kidding?'

'No, I've seen it before. I was a nurse once. You must get her a doctor.'

'I'll call one now.'

'So, we can guess that she knows where they are, but she's not in her right mind, which means that they could be in danger.' David clenched his fists.

'It'll be all right,' Lily tried to reassure him.

'She's an idiot. OK, so she's ill, but ill people do stupid things. What if she has done something to them, my brother, my little brother?' David's fear was justified, Ed thought. Anne-Marie was mad – that much he knew – and she could have done anything. If they had little time, then she was going to be no help.

'Look, the doctor's on her way. She might be able to help.'

'Anne-Marie needs sectioning.'

'Oh God, if she's . . .' There was no bright side.

'Exactly, Harriet, exactly.'

Hazel Cottingham was an American doctor who worked on the island. She was retained as the doctor for the resort, looking after both staff and guests, and she came immediately when called.

'We need to keep this quiet for now,' Lily explained, leading her to the bedroom where Anne-Marie had been taken. Ed sat by her side, looking worried, and, despite herself, Lily felt a stab of jealousy.

'Right, now you say she's been acting strange.'

'She doesn't remember who I am – or anyone else, it would seem.'

'Can you leave us for a moment?' Hazel asked. They nodded and left.

'Anne-Marie, do you know who I am?'

'Haven't the foggiest. Nice blouse, though. I do like pink.'

'Thank you. You are at home.'

'Oh, I know that.'

'You do? Good. Now the man who just left is your husband.'

'I don't think so.'

'You don't?'

'No, I don't have a husband. I'm far too young. You see, my first book's just been published and it was a huge success. I know that I don't look like your traditional romance writer, with my big glasses and my tracksuit and, well, my complexion is a bit off and I don't know how to wear make-up, but I love romance and I love writing about it.'

'Anne-Marie? When did your first book get published?'

'Oh, last month.'

'What year is it?'

'You don't know what year it is? Why, it's nineteen eighty-five. I don't know about the whole eighties thing because I think I feel more comfortable the way I am. And I don't have a husband; I don't even have a boyfriend. I dated a piano tuner once, which is so funny because I don't even have a piano.'

'What's the verdict?' Ed asked as Hazel appeared. She looked around the room. 'It's OK; you can talk in front of them.'

'Well, I've given her a sedative but she needs round-the-clock care. I can arrange for psychiatric nurses. I'll get one here tonight. There is every possibility she will snap out of it on her own, but I am also going to send a psychiatrist to see her tomorrow.'

'Maybe electric shock treatment?' David suggested.

'We don't do that any more.' Hazel shot David a withering

look. 'Ed, she doesn't think she's married; she doesn't know who you are. She thinks it's nineteen eighty-five, when her first book came out.'

'Why would she think that?'

'In my experience, breakdowns are caused by a build-up of trauma. It might have been triggered by one event, or just the culmination. I think she's chosen a time when she was happy.'

'Before me,' Ed said sadly.

'Before the resort,' Lily added.

'Before the creation of Anne-Marie Langdale,' he finished.

27

Our Policy

As well as everything we promise you on your holiday with us, it's our policy that you will be with like-minded people. As this is an exclusive resort we can promise you that there will be a certain standard of guest staying here. Here we take away the worry of mixing with people you'd rather not mix with.

It's our policy that guests are all considerate to each other, respecting each other's privacy and peace. However, we know that you will make life-long friends at The Love Resort, and we are delighted to be able to make such friendships happen.

Guest Handbook

Thea couldn't believe it. So they'd been kidnapped, they'd all been rowing, it had been a nightmare, but was that really such a huge price to pay for what was happening? She and Todd were in the kitchen, clearing away the food and talking about acting. She was really having a discussion with the great Todd Cortes! She had to pinch herself before she was convinced it was for real.

'I suppose I haven't really thought about exactly what I want to do. I know I hate working as an extra but I need the money.'

'It's a hard life, and you're right, what your passion is, be it stage, or TV or film, has to take a back seat to earning a living. But once you do find success, that will come back to you again.'

'Does it? Or does it become about what pays the most?'

'For some people, I'm sure it does. Thea, we get paid obscene amounts in Hollywood, but really, I only do films I believe in.'

'That sounds so corny.'

'I know, but it's true. Why do you think I married Katie?'

'I'm not sure. Why did you?'

Thea hoisted herself up on the kitchen counter and listened to Todd telling her all about the film he was set to direct. He was so passionate about it that she couldn't help believing him when he said he did only what he believed in. He believed in this enough to get married for it.

'It's funny that we're in the twenty-first century, and most people consider themselves open-minded, yet you have to lie about your sexuality.'

'Because I'm sold as a heart-throb. If I was openly gay, they would never give me a straight role again in my life.'

'Would that bother you?'

'It would annoy me having to play the gay part all the time. I'm an actor and I want to act, not play myself all the time. Although maybe I should get used to the idea that I'm going to have to give up being an actor.'

'Understood. But what now?'

'What do you mean?'

'Todd, Katie caught you with another man. Even if you persuade her to keep her mouth shut about that, you've been kidnapped and there might be police looking for us. This story, the one you're hiding behind, is trying to tell you something, don't you think?'

'That it's time to come clean?'

'Yup. Set Katie free and yourself. There's always ways of doing it that will make you look OK.'

'What do you mean?'

'Oh hell, I'm no spin doctor, but you know, you love Katie but you've been battling with your sexuality for a while, the love you have for her is more sisterly than anything. You are ashamed that you have hurt her and you hate yourself for it, but Katie is the true innocent. You know the kind of thing.'

'Thea, I think you might be a genius.' She glowed with pride. Her idol was calling her a genius. 'But what about the film?'

'You mean if, despite sounding so nice, they won't let you direct?'

'They probably won't.'

'I guess. But there must be a way.'

'I'll have to beg the Studio to give me a chance.'

'Of course, that's it. You give up the lead. You just direct. You keep Katie in the female lead and get her an actor to work with. Shit, maybe she can marry him next.'

Todd smiled, then leant over and kissed Thea on the forehead. 'You know when I said you were a genius? Well, I didn't give you enough praise.'

'I just thought I'd tell you that I think you've all behaved badly,' Katie started.

'We know that,' Tim said defiantly.

'And if you hadn't done, then maybe we wouldn't be here,' Katie continued.

Carla looked at her. She wasn't nearly as glamorous as she was on screen, but she was indisputably beautiful. It was weird enough, having two such famous people there in such a bizarre situation, without one of them telling everyone off. Carla couldn't help but find it amusing, although she accepted that that might be due to hysteria.

'How can you blame us? Your husband is gay. Anne-Marie doesn't let gay people in the resort,' Tim argued.

'How do you know?'

'I read the brochure. It's against the rules to have same sex couples here.'

'Surely that's discrimination?' Jimmy pointed out.

'I don't think Anne-Marie cares about things like that,' Tim finished.

'You two are quiet,' Katie sneered, as she rounded on Lee and Emily.

'We're just trying to get through this,' Lee mumbled.

'What about Jimmy and Carla? Having to watch you pawing each other?'

'But we're not!' Emily objected.

'Oh, really? Well, you should show some respect. How can you live with yourselves?'

'We are sorry, we didn't mean it, but no one will believe us,' Lee tried to explain.

'Oh yeah, your libido got the better of you. Of course no one will believe you,' Katie spat.

'Why are you doing this to us? Why are you picking on us?' Emily burst into her customary tears.

'Because you hurt people and I've been hurt and I know how much it sucks.' Katie burst into tears as well.

Jimmy looked at his shoes.

Carla kept very quiet. The scene was unbelievable. Lee, the object of her obsession for the past three years; Emily, her love rival, who had won; Jimmy, dejected; Katie also feeling rejected; and finally Tim, who was looking horrified. All feelings of amusement deserted her. She was tired, she was scared, and she was unsure why she was there. She burst into tears.

'Holy shit, three crying girls. What have we done to deserve this?' Tim asked, looking unsettled.

Jimmy hugged Carla, Lee hugged Emily and Katie sobbed on her own.

In the kitchen Todd asked Thea, 'Can you hear them?'

'We'd better go back. You have to make it up to Katie.'

'I know.'

'Not only because it's the right thing to do but because you need her.'

'I know. And you know what? Despite her front, I do like her; I thought I was beginning to understand her before I fucked it all up.'

'Good.' Thea smiled.

'Katie, honey, it will be all right.' Todd came through, sat down and took her in his arms. And she let him.

Thea looked around. She went to sit by Tim; again, wondering what they were all doing there. It was like a bad joke.

'Thea,' Tim said calmly.

'Yes?'

'Is there anything to drink?' His voice was quiet, almost a whisper.

'Water, although Katie seems to be drinking so much of that we might run out.' She felt her panic growing, and she told herself to keep calm. She couldn't look at him. If she looked at him, then she'd lose it.

'You know I didn't mean water.'

'Tim, there's nothing else.' She saw the desperation in his eyes and felt frightened all over again.

'That just can't be true,' he announced, and dramatically stood up. The others stared after him as he left and went to the kitchen.

'What's with him?' Todd asked, but Thea, in the grip of fear, merely shrugged and followed him.

She watched Tim open every cupboard. When he found nothing, he slammed the doors with all his strength. He ransacked the entire kitchen, hopelessly. He swore, loudly, then again and again before returning to the other room and banging on the front door.

'Let me out of here,' he shouted. 'Let me the fuck out.' He pounded with his fists.

'Oh shit,' Thea said.

'What's wrong with him?'

'He was looking for something to drink. He didn't find anything.'

'There's water . . .' Katie started then stopped. 'You didn't mean that.'

'I'd better stop him.' Thea took a deep breath, walked up to Tim and tried to grab him. He turned round, but broke free of her grip.

'Tim, Tim, honey, we'll be gone soon, and then it'll be all right.' Her voice was soft but the crazed look in his eyes told her that she'd said the wrong thing.

'This is your fault. You made me come here and now look what's happened. You're supposed to be my friend but you don't care about me. You just want to hurt me.' Tim was advancing on Thea, prodding her in the chest. She had never seen him this angry before; certainly not with her.

'Tim, don't,' she begged. He was scaring her; she didn't recognise him. Tears welled up in her eyes.

'You fucking selfish bitch. All you think about is yourself, never about me. I didn't want to come here, I don't even like the sun, and now I'm locked up and I might die and it'll all be your fault.' She had never seen him look so manic. He pulled his hand back and she really thought he was going to hit her. Tears sprung out.

'No, Tim, don't,' she shouted, as Jimmy ran up to them. He stood between Tim and Thea, looking at each in turn.

'What am I doing?' Tim asked. He put his head in his hands.

'It's all right,' Thea said.

'Thea, it's not all right, he was going to hit you,' Jimmy pointed out. He folded his arms.

'No he wasn't.' Thea moved between Jimmy and Tim. She wouldn't let Jimmy think badly of him; she had to protect him. That was her role, and she would never stop doing it. Tears cascaded down her cheeks as she mulled it all over. It was her fault; she had brought him on this stupid holiday because he'd been spending all his time in their flat, not writing and drinking his dole money. She was at the end of her tether: tired beyond belief, miserable in her job, and constantly worrying about Tim. She needed to sort her life out but she didn't have any time left to think about herself. It was all threatening to come crashing down.

'He was,' Jimmy argued, but backed away.

'Thea, what am I doing?' Tim asked. As he sank to the floor and she sat down to comfort him.

'We have nothing to sleep on,' Lee observed.

It was late, although it felt later to most of them. By now they had all accepted that they had been kidnapped. No one had any idea what to do about it.

'Well, we'll have to lie on the floor,' Thea replied.

'No blankets, no cushions – we'll never sleep,' Carla said.

'I'm not sure we would anyway, not tonight.'

'Oh hell, this is just madness. Can't we try to escape again?' Lee insisted.

'It's hopeless, we tried. Sorry, but there's nothing we can do.'

They all looked and felt despondent as the night closed in and they were still unsure exactly why they were there or for how long.

Ed's living room resembled a dormitory by the time they'd finished. There were five extra beds; Ed had to sleep there as well. The sofa and chairs had been pushed to one side, and the beds were all lined up in a row. Mary had already crawled into hers and seemed to be praying. Harriet and Lily were in the kitchen. David sat on the edge of his bed, dangling his legs over the edge and looking worried, and Ed was more confused and confounded than ever.

He couldn't help but feel responsible, although what he'd done exactly he was unsure of. Could Anne-Marie have found out about him and Lily? Was that what had tipped her over the edge? No, the Anne-Marie he knew would have been more upset about Abigail and André than him and Lily. He was pretty sure that it wasn't that. It was the competition winners, Todd and Katie, and Abigail. Nothing to do with him. Although, now that his wife was a gibbering wreck, he couldn't help but feel sorry for her. How could he leave her now? That was the real problem; he couldn't leave her when she was like this. Where did that leave him and Lily? None of it was funny.

He should have seen it coming. Should have known that she wasn't just being a drama queen. She was upset. Her resort, the dream of the resort, wasn't right from the start. He remembered back to when she'd first suggested it.

She told him that England was stifling her creativity. She couldn't write any more because the weather was horrible and her environment wasn't romantic. It wasn't, he agreed. They lived in a large house in London, all decorated to her taste, and he hated it. She said that she needed to choose the decoration so her house would be condusive to her work. He should have realised that Anne-Marie had been sucked into her books and wanted – no, needed – to live that way.

When she had the idea of moving to somewhere more beautiful, Ed envisaged a house on the beach, in the Caribbean, and thought that maybe, despite his wife's constant criticism, her demands and her contempt of him, perhaps they could be happy there. He never thought about leaving her because he'd tied his life up with hers. He worked for her, he lived with her, and without her he had no idea who he was. He was unhappy but safe, and until he fell in love with Lily, that was enough. But then Anne-Marie showed him her plans. The Love Resort, her brainchild, her chance to live in her own idea of romance. At first he was horrified, but then when he looked into it he saw it from a business point of view. It was a new challenge for him, something that he could work on, and something he could make a success out of. It would take away his boredom.

Finding an old resort that was in need of renovation was easy. Then drawing up plans, getting the work done, hiring staff, kept them both so busy that they didn't have time to worry about the state of their marriage. He felt a sense of purpose and a sense of self. It was all about her, as it had always been, but Ed had more of a role to play, and he threw himself into it.

When the work was finished and they opened with a blaze of publicity, he felt heady with success. The money rolled in and gave him a sense of achievement. It was only with the arrival of Lily that he realised there was more out there, and for him. Lily finally made him see how unhappy he really was, and how happy he could be. And now, as his wife lay upstairs with a nurse watching over her, and he had the missing guests to worry about, he was in danger of losing that happiness and he saw that he was to blame. If not for all of it, then definitely for some.

Lily kept herself busy. She didn't want to think about the consequences of everything, of Anne-Marie. She didn't want to think where it left her. Ed was, of course, going to feel responsible; after all, he was a kind person, a loving man. He had a heart. She just hoped that she hadn't lost him. She couldn't bear to lose him. Had Anne-Marie, by going mad, somehow managed to save her marriage?

Lily was desperate to talk to Ed about it, but he was deep in thought. She wouldn't lose Ed, no matter what, and if she had to find the guests alone, and fix Anne-Marie herself, she would. She would do anything for him. Tears welled up as she realised how frightened she was.

When she first came to the resort she was getting over a bad break-up. She wasn't heartbroken; she was just relieved to be out of what was a tiring relationship. She was drained and the idea of a job, in the sun, in a holiday resort with a famous author appealed to her. As soon as she met Ed, it all made sense – why she was there, why she'd applied. She put up with Anne-Marie treating her like dirt so she could be close to Ed. Lily would never have stayed otherwise. She wouldn't have let her boss shout and scream and swear at her on a daily basis had it not been for him. And when she discovered he felt the same way about her, she vowed she would do anything to be with him.

That vow still stood. They were made for each other. Life without him wasn't worth contemplating.

'Who are you?' Anne-Marie asked, sitting up and seeing someone in a white uniform at the end of her bed.

'I'm here to look after you.'

'Oh, good. That's nice. Did Abigail send you? Dear, dear Abigail.'

The nurse nodded.

'I'm very tired. You know it's really hard work writing books. Have you ever written one?'

'No, I never have, but I hear yours are fantastic.'

'Oh, I've only written one, but my next one will be finished soon. I plan to write loads and loads. You know, I always thought of myself as ordinary, but now I'm not, I'm a writer. I'll never be ordinary again.'

With a smile across her lips, she lay back and went to sleep.

28

'Please, please, please get me something to drink,' Tim asked, looking at Thea with fear in his eyes.

'Have some water.' She put the bottle to his lips. He pushed it away.

'I need a fucking drink.'

'Tim.'

'My head is buzzing, it won't stop buzzing.'

'Tim, there is nothing.' She felt sweat on his head, and wondered how he could be so desperate. God, how could she have not known? Or did she know?

'Please, please, please.' Everyone looked at him.

'Is he all right?' Emily asked, looking uncertain. 'It's just that, well, with growing up in a pub you see this a lot . . .'

'He'll be fine,' Thea snapped, her overwhelming desire to shield him kicking in. She wanted to protect him at all costs. Was that the problem?

'If I could only have a drink.' Tim reiterated. 'My mouth is dry.' He clicked his tongue to demonstrate. 'And I feel sick, and hot. Thea, please.'

'He's an alcoholic, isn't he?' Katie asked.

'Don't be silly. He likes a drink, that's all. He's fine,' Lee said.

'Lee, he's not. Katie's right,' Emily said gently. Emily and Katie looked at each other in understanding.

'Emily, Tim's the funniest person we know, he's not got a drink problem,' Jimmy defended him.

'Thea?' Katie said.

'They're right. Tim likes a drink but he's fine.'

'And who are you trying to kid?' Katie said harshly.

'He's *fine*. He just needs to sleep,' Thea snapped back. Tim started shaking in her arms.

'Listen to me,' Katie started. She looked at Todd. 'God knows when he had his last drink but he's definitely suffering from withdrawal.'

'That just isn't true,' Thea flew at her.

'Thea,' Todd said gently, 'I think you know that it is.' He looked at Katie with a new respect, then at Thea with compassion.

'Please shut up, just shut up,' Tim begged before he vomited.

'Emily, can you get a cloth?' Katie asked as she went to Tim's side. She knelt down beside him and put her arms around him. 'I need your clothes,' she said to Lee, Jimmy and Todd, 'your shirts.'

'Why?' Thea wasn't happy about being sidelined; she wouldn't let these people interfere with Tim.

'He's cold, Thea. We're all hot and he's cold. He's got the sweats. It's important that we keep him warm.'

'Maybe he's got a bug,' Carla offered lamely, wanting to help Thea.

'He's an alcoholic,' Katie retorted.

'He's not, he's not,' Thea stormed, although she knew he was. She knew, had known for ages, but she'd been in denial. She was so far in denial that she'd managed to convince herself that his drinking was a temporary phase. He drank too much, she had accepted that, and she had even told her friends that, but despite the fact that she knew he had a problem, she had always refused to face it properly. A holiday wasn't the solution – he needed something far more serious – but he was her Tim, her best friend, her family. He needed her; she needed him.

Carla went to Thea and put her arms around her.

'Thea, you must have known.' Thea looked at her. Of course she knew; she just didn't want to. He was all she had.

'Of course I did, and it's all my fault,' Thea replied before bursting into desperate tears.

'I need a cloth for his forehead,' Katie said, once the mess had been cleared up. 'I think we should take him to the other room. Todd, Jimmy, can you help me?'

The moans coming from Tim were getting louder as they moved him. Thea started to go after them.

'Stay here,' Katie ordered. 'Thea, I'm not being horrible, but this is not going to be pretty and I think you should stay out here. I'll take care of him.'

'He needs me!' Thea cried. 'I can't leave him.'

'Thea, you're not leaving him, you're just letting me take care of him for a while.' Tears glistened in Katie's eyes; she was so gentle. Todd felt it almost knock him over; this woman whom he'd mocked, married, humiliated, almost despised, was human after all, more than human.

'I'll help,' Emily offered.

'Let's see if we can get some sort of bowl or bucket as well, Emily,' Katie said, before she and the boys carried Tim into the bedroom.

Thea sat in the living room with Jimmy and Carla on either side of her. Lee had gone to help Emily. Todd had his head in his hands.

'Is he going to be all right?' Thea asked.

Todd nodded but he had no idea. What was happening to them? In the last few days he'd been with a man, been the victim of attempted blackmail, had argument after argument with his wife and now this: kidnapped with a bunch of strangers, one of whom just happened to be an alcoholic. And Katie had been the biggest surprise with her actions. This just served to make him feel guiltier. How could he ever make it up to her? He stood up and went into the bedroom. Tim was lying on the floor; Katie had put a rolled-up T-shirt under his head. She'd tried to make a blanket out of the other shirts to cover him with.

'He doesn't look good,' Todd observed, feeling stupid for stating the obvious but at the same time feeling the need to tell Katie that he admired her.

'He must have a serious drink problem, probably drinks nearly all the time. He probably gets up in the night, and drinks when Thea is asleep, or something. For him to suffer withdrawal this quickly, he must, I think.'

'You seem to know . . .' he trailed off. What business was it of his?

'My father,' Katie said, just as Tim threw up again.

Emily came in with fresh cloths. 'I'm rinsing them all as fast as I can, but there's only three in the entire place.'

Katie nodded encouragement. Then, she took off her thousand-dollar top and handed it to her. 'Soak this in water, needs must.'

Todd looked at her in surprise. The famous Katie Ray had taken her top off, and was sitting, nursing an alcoholic in only her bra. He felt something for her that he'd never fully acknowledged before: genuine affection.

'Katie, I really need to apologise.'

'You're not the only one. But this puts things into perspective, doesn't it?' She sounded sad and far away.

'Would you like to tell me about your father?' Todd asked, sounding a bit like a psychiatrist, and sitting down next to her.

'I loved him. I think perhaps he's the only man I've ever loved. But it was all so depressing. My mother constantly shouting because the farm was going down the tubes. I hated her then. I still can't talk to her because I thought she was the meanest woman in the world for shouting at my daddy.' Katie shook her head. 'What was I thinking? Trying to make you straight, shouting and screaming about being in love with you. You were right. I barely knew you. I'm an utter fool, a tired, scared fool. Todd, I feel like the girl from the farm once again.'

He put his arm around her. She was so different, so vulnerable.

'But your mother, she was trying to take care of things?'

'Yup. She didn't have time for anything else. Trying to keep enough food on the table. It's not a new story.'

'But it happened to you.'

'Yes. I left home when he died.'

'He died?'

'His liver failed. The drink killed him. I couldn't repair the relationship with my mom. There was nothing left between us. So I went to Hollywood and slept my way to the top. That's the edited version.' She smiled tearfully.

'Katie, I am sorry. I thought—'

'That I was a shallow airhead, with no feelings, no compassion. But really, I buried myself because I didn't want to be hurt again. And I forgot. You know, maybe not forgot totally, but I didn't remember. Not until I saw Tim.'

Tim shivered, and turned over. Katie, still with tears in her eyes, rubbed his back. As soon as Tim was settled again, Todd took her in his arms and he let her sob and sob for ages.

'Thea,' Emily started uncertainly, 'Katie knows what she's doing. We're lucky she's here.'

'But I don't know what to do,' Thea said, looking at Emily for answers.

'Oh, you know this isn't your fault. I grew up in pubs, and we saw loads of people with proper drink problems. They never do anything about it until either they're ready to, or they're forced to.'

'I could have forced him.'

'No. He'd have run a mile from you. Now this mad woman has locked us up, he has to face it. But you couldn't have made him and I don't think you should blame yourself. I know you're going to, but you shouldn't.'

'What next?'

'Depending on when we get out of here, or if we get out of here, then he needs help and you need support. We'll all help.'

'Really?' Thea looked at Emily with new respect, as did Carla and Jimmy.

'Oh, guys, I'm not the selfish princess that I make out. Well, not all the time. Thea, we've been put in the weirdest situation ever, and I have no idea how to make sense of it all, but if this means that Tim gets better . . .'

'Then we'll have Anne-Marie to thank?' Carla asked.

'My God, I suppose we will.'

They heard another moan coming from the bedroom.

'I should go,' Thea said, feeling desperate.

'Thea, Emily's right: Katie knows what she's doing. You stay here and let us take care of you. I bet you never usually have anyone do that,' Carla said.

'Not often,' she admitted.

'I think he might be asleep,' Katie whispered. Tim was still shaking, but not quite so vigorously.

'I'm going to stay here with you.'

'Thanks, Todd. I need to stay awake, just in case.'

'Katie, what did you really do? I mean, I've heard the rumours, but, well, it's none of my business, but . . .'

'How did I get to be so famous? The unedited version?' She raised an eyebrow.

'Only if you want to tell me.' Todd felt an overwhelming desire to learn everything about her.

'Well, I pulled myself up from nothing to be a star. I always thought I was proud of that, but to be honest there's nothing to be proud of. I slept with the most awful men, I groomed myself, learnt how to look good, walk, talk and act like I should be a star. I turned into a bitch, I hurt people who were in my way, and I lost myself.'

'It's not an unusual story, Katie.' Todd felt sorry for her. He knew how the system worked, and he knew that underneath the exterior, there was a human being. Something he would never have thought two weeks ago.

'No, not unusual, but it worked for me and although I know I have a bad reputation for being a diva, I really made myself believe that I deserved to act like that. After all the blow-jobs, the hand jobs, the perverse sex that I had to endure.' She shuddered.

'We could talk about what we're going to do when we get out of here.'

'Don't you mean "if"?'

'No, I mean when. We have to face the Studio.'

'Well, we'll just have to tell them the truth. Or we just say we made a mistake. Plenty of people get quickie divorces in Hollywood. No one will be at all surprised.'

'I think I should come clean.'

'What about the movie?'

'I could beg them to let me direct it still, but with a different leading man. If I'm a director no one will care if I like men or not.'

'Women everywhere will still weep.'

'They'll get over it.'

'So, you think Bernie and co. will go for it?'

'Probably not, but it's worth a try. After all, I'm looking forward to directing you.'

'Really?'

'Katie, there's a great actress inside of you, there really is. I think I can get it out.'

'You sound so utterly pretentious, Todd Cortes.'

'I do, don't I?'

'Which is why you'll probably make a brilliant director.' She winked at him.

29

Anne-Marie Langdale – A Bright Shining Star

It seems only fitting to provide you with information on your host, the kind that, as a guest of The Love Resort, you receive as a mark of the privileged position you are in. As a gift there is a glossy brochure with a full biography in, and also a list of her books.* From *Only Where the Sun Shines*, her first book, to *Find Me at the End of the Rainbow*, her latest offering, her career has been one of the great success stories of recent times.

Of course, this is all shared knowledge, but what you, as guests, receive is a special insight into the lady herself. She's a small person with a big personality. Her vibrancy, her lust for life, is infectious, and you will see that by staying here. She radiates warmth, compassion and she loves nothing more than laughter.

Guest Handbook

* This biography is exclusive to The Love Resort and cannot be obtained anywhere else.

'Anything?' Lily asked.

Ed shook his head.

Harriet, David and Mary were sitting around the breakfast table outside. The sun was shining, they'd been served a fine breakfast but they all felt frazzled by their near-sleepless night.

'The nurse who left said she was still stuck in the past. She slept for hours, but, again, that's apparently normal under the circumstances. She's awake but has still no idea who I am. We asked about the guests but she looked at me as if I was mad. She thought I might be a policeman, then she got scared and the nurse had to ask me to leave. The doctor is due in an hour; hopefully she might be able to tell us something.'

Ed knew that his wife had lost it, properly; he didn't need a doctor to tell him that. The problem he faced was deciding what to do about it. First, Anne-Marie needed help, and who knew how long it would take before they got any sense out of her? Then there was the matter of the missing guests to tackle, and he knew that David would probably demand proper police involvement today. So that made the press a problem. Then there was Lily. How could they leave now, with things like they were? He didn't like his wife, would go so far as to say that he hated her most of the time, but he couldn't just walk out. His life was all spinning out of his control, and it wasn't just for his wife that he was worried.

'Oh God. They could be anywhere by now. There's nothing we can do. Nothing.' David put his head in his hands.

'Come on, David, what can she have done?'

'That's what I'd like to know. She's mad.'

'She's not mad, she's ill.'

'Whatever. Ill people can harm other people.'

'My Katie is all right,' Mary announced.

'I'm glad you think so. What about the others?' David snapped. He was looking agitated and Ed thought that he would blow a fuse any minute.

'They'll be all right too. I know it in my heart.'

David rolled his eyes. 'I'm going for a swim, I need to cool off.'

The doctor arrived and went straight to Anne-Marie. Ed paced the living room, waiting for her to return. Lily and Harriet went outside.

'You'd think he still loves her, the way he's behaving,' Lily said. She felt like crying; like she'd lost him.

'What?'

'You know, as soon as Todd and Katie left we were going to leave too. We were going to start our new life together and, you know what, we'd have been guilt free. The way she's treated us, we wouldn't have had one moment of worry about her. But now she's turned into a dribbling idiot, we will be guilty, and I bet you that Ed won't leave her.'

'Right.'

'Oh, what am I going to do?'

Lily looked at Harriet imploringly; Harriet looked a little scared.

'Mr Smith?'

'Please, call me Ed.'

'OK, well, your wife's condition is unchanged, although it's still early days. The psychiatrist will be along later, for an evaluation. To be frank, I am expecting him to want to section your wife.'

'Well, if that's for the best . . .' Ed felt sick at the enormity of what he was hearing.

'She's very sick, and in these cases, the patient either snaps out of it quickly, or it takes a long healing process. You have to face the possibility that your wife might not ever fully recover.'

'Jesus.' Ed thought of her, her vibrancy, her demands, her shouting and swearing and terrorising everyone. He couldn't help but feel sad for her, despite everything. However, he did need to know what this meant for him and Lily. He hated himself for his selfishness but just because Anne-Marie was ill, didn't mean he had to stay with her. Did it? He felt as if he was being weighed down with boulders.

'You have control, Ed. I think it's important that you know that. If she's sectioned, then you will have to sign a consent form, otherwise we might have to forcefully do so.'

'Look, if that's the conclusion you come to, then I won't stand in your way. I want what's best for my wife.' He had a feeling that whatever that was, wasn't going to be best for him.

'Of course you do.' The doctor smiled sympathetically, and Ed felt pathetically grateful that she didn't know the full extent of what was going on.

'He told us not to see her, to leave her alone for now,' Ed said, once the psychiatrist had gone. He had also told Ed that the next twenty-four hours were crucial. After that, the next course of action would be taken.

'Did you tell him we're missing eight people?' Harriet asked, slightly hysterically.

'Yes, and he said that the only thing we could do was to call the police, who wouldn't be able to get anything out of her. If you want the police involved, then I will call them. Oh God . . .' Ed put his head in his hands; Lily felt sorry for him. She shot Harriet a sharp look.

'Sorry,' Harriet said.

'It's OK. I just feel responsible. We were leaving.' He had no idea why he was telling her that.

'Lily said.'

'I still want to, but you know, I can't walk out on her with this going on. And, the thing is, that although I know it's not rational, I blame myself.'

'Which is perfectly normal, although wrong,' Lily said.

'Maybe.'

'It's not your fault.'

'I agree,' Harriet added, looking surprised at herself. 'Look, I need to call my boss. Wish me luck. I've never heard of anyone being murdered over the phone, but there's always a first time.' Ed and Lily were both shocked when Harriet actually laughed.

*

Katie walked into the living room. Thea and Carla were huddled together, Jimmy was next to them. Lee had his arms around Emily and was whispering to her.

'Did you sleep at all?' she asked. They all shook their heads. Jimmy couldn't believe that Katie Ray stood before him in her bra. She was tired, and stressed. Everything was more than freakish; he couldn't even begin to process what was going on, what had been going on, or what would happen to them next.

'Katie, how is Tim?'

'He slept some, but he's not good. Really he needs a doctor; they have pills for this sort of thing, to make it easier.'

'Oh God, what are we going to do?'

'I'm going to check for a way out again. There must be something,' Jimmy said, jumping up. He was used to feeling useless but never more so than now.

'I'll help.' Carla joined him. Jimmy didn't hold out much hope but needed to feel they were doing something.

'Can I see him?' Thea asked, and Katie nodded.

'I don't suppose she left us any coffee?' she asked hopefully.

'If she did there's no kettle,' Emily answered apologetically.

'Thea?' Tim asked as Thea approached him.

'Hi,' she whispered. He looked awful. Grey and gaunt. Bags hanging under his eyes. He was still shaking, she noticed, as the pain of it ripped through her. He needed her help but she was useless. His hair was stuck to his head where he'd been sweating. He was really sick and she should have prevented it.

'I don't feel good.' He tried to smile but coughed instead.

'You've looked better too,' Thea replied, kneeling down, and kissing his head. As her heart broke for him, she felt utterly responsible.

'I'm really sick, aren't I?' His tone was that of a child.

'Yes, Tim, you are.' Thea said a silent prayer.

'But now I can get better.' His eyes glistened with hope.

'You will get better,' she answered, and then lay down next to him and held him. She couldn't fix him. In acknowledging that, she felt she had at last admitted her problem.

She told him stories from their childhood. How they used to play hide-and-seek and how whenever they were playing and their mothers called them in for tea they would hide in their best place and time how long it took for them to be found. How they would go on holiday together, always – either to Wales, with Thea's mother, or to France, Normandy, with Tim's. How there were so many good times: they'd learnt to ride bicycles together although Thea was much better than Tim; how they went to horse riding lessons for a while until Tim deemed it mean to the horses and refused to go. How when Thea joined the drama group, Tim, who couldn't act and didn't like to act, joined too to keep her company.

There were bad times too, she told him. When his mother moved in with Steve and Steve hit her, and tried to hit Tim once, so Tim ran away. Thea's mother sorted his mother out, and she sorted Tim out. Then there was the time when her grandfather died and she told Tim that she would die too, because she loved him more than anyone (apart from Tim). Tim stayed talking to her and made her realise that her grandfather would hate it if she did that.

There were so many memories linking them, she told him, so many stories. And as she stroked his head, she finally knew that when she complained about her lack of family, she had one – she had one right there.

'Thea, I'm sorry,' he said, when she stopped.

'It's OK.'

'No, it's not, it's not OK. I don't know what it is at the moment, but when I'm better I will.' She nodded.

*

'If we get out of here, I'm going to help him,' Katie decided.

'How?' Todd asked.

'I'm paying for him to go to the best rehab place. There's that one back home. I know it's full of screwed-up famous people but then I could visit him. Todd, I couldn't help my father. This won't make up for that, but it might help me to come to terms with it.'

'And it'll help Tim. What about Thea?'

'She's an actress. Todd; we must be able to do something for her.'

'Maybe we could give her an audition. If we have any clout, that is.'

'If Thea turned out to be a rubbish actress, even with the best director directing her, then that's that. But you can at least give her a break.'

'If I still have a career.' Todd shuddered as he thought about how much he'd done for his precious career.

'Oh, you will. We both will. After getting through this, persuading the Studio will be easy. I bet we could do it, especially now we're friends.'

'We are friends, aren't we?' He laughed as he thought about it.

'Yes, and every girl needs a gay best friend.'

'And every gay man needs a diva with great dress sense as their best friend.'

'It's hopeless, Jimmy, hopeless.' Carla tried each window in turn, while Jimmy concentrated on the door.

'She's got us secured all right.'

'But she can't leave us here for ever. When is our flight?'

'I don't know. I've lost track of the days. I mean, we've only been in here for one but it feels like more.'

'I know what you mean. Are you all right?'

'About Emily?' he asked; Carla nodded. 'Surprisingly I am. I was angry but now I'm too tired, and Lee and her – well, they seem more natural together than we did.'

'I hate to say it but you're right. I thought he was the only man I could ever love.'

'Shit, you sound like one of Anne-Marie's novels.'

'You're funny, Jimmy, really.'

'I think that's a compliment.'

'You seem more confident without her.'

'I hope so. As do you, without him.'

'I suppose I am. Now all we need to do is fall in love and then there's a perfect ending.'

'Carla . . .'

'I'm joking. The only thing I care about right now is getting out of here.'

'It's not that I don't find you attractive.'

'Jimmy, I don't need you to reject me, I was joking.'

'And so am I.' His eyes twinkled and although their task was proving fruitless, they both laughed.

'I know we've only been together for a few days, although it seems like more,' Lee began.

He was in the kitchen with Emily and Todd. Todd looked at them, amused. It was as if they were confessing to him.

'I know, but then we didn't really get together under normal circumstances. In fact, we've only been on one date,' Emily added.

'Really?' Todd asked. He wasn't sure if he approved of what they did, but then he wasn't really in a position to sit in judgment.

'Yes, but what happens when we get out of here?' Lee asked.

Todd wasn't sure if he was addressing him or Emily. 'What do you mean?' he asked.

'I'm going to London to study and Emily lives in Devon.'

'In a pub,' Emily added.

'Oh, yeah, maybe I'll come and live with you. Sorry, bad joke.'

'Oh, for God's sake, just because Tim has a problem with drink doesn't mean you can't mention the pub.'

Again, Todd wasn't sure if they were talking to him or each other.

'I guess not. Anyway, how are we going to do this?'

'I suppose that I could visit you. I mean, I work in the pub but I'm on great terms with the boss.'

'And if it works out then maybe you could move to London,' Todd suggested.

'With you, Lee?' Her eyes sparkled with excitement, and Todd melted. There was something so endearing about a couple newly in love.

'Well, I'm not sure, but I think so.'

'In that case, I'm not sure either, but I think so too.'

'Glad we've got that sorted,' Todd finished.

Thea looked at Tim in horror; he was deteriorating fast. She had dozed off, after all the talking she'd done, and when she'd woken, she'd found Katie and Todd watching them, and Tim like this. The shakes were getting worse and although he drank some water, he kept vomiting it up. She rubbed her eyes.

'What can we do?'

'Todd,' Katie said calmly, 'can you take her to the other room?'

Thea looked at her, ready to object.

'Believe me, you should go with Todd. I'll take care of him. Ask Emily to come and help.'

Todd pulled Thea to her feet and led her out. She let him; she had no strength to argue.

'Hi,' Emily walked in and sat down; Carla was with her.

'Emily,' said Katie, 'can you keep trying to get water down

him? He's dehydrating and I think he might pass out.'

'Oh God. Of course.' Emily tipped Tim's head up and started feeding him water.

'Is there anything I can do?' Carla asked. Katie shook her head; Carla thought she looked as if she might burst into tears.

'To be honest, I have no idea what to do. I'm out of my depth. He needs proper care. Actually, could you resoak the cloths?' Katie handed them to Carla, who went to the bathroom, grateful for something to do. She knew that the situation was serious with Tim, so much so that she hadn't even thought about her own situation. She returned to the room and gave the cloths back to Katie.

'Thanks.'

'He seems to have kept some down,' Emily said, giving him more water.

'Thank God. I can't think of anything else to do.'

Prayer seemed fruitless.

'So what's the story with you and Tim?' Todd asked.

He and Thea were in the kitchen away from the others. Todd had renamed it the Confessional.

'I've known him all my life. Our mothers were friends. My father walked out when I was a baby and his left when he was ten. We've stuck together ever since. Like brother and sister really.'

'You're not in love?'

'No, don't be silly. Tim and I could never be together. It would be like incest.' She managed a weak laugh. 'I really mean that. We bathed together naked as children, I know everything there is to know about him. Well, not everything.'

'Why does he drink?'

'That's what I don't know. It started to get bad when we left university. I guess he lost his structure and couldn't cope. I worked, doing crappy extra work to pay the bills, going to auditions, classes – you name it – so I didn't really spend much time with him. I guess that's why I didn't notice; I was focusing on my career, which wasn't, isn't, going anywhere.' Her guilt was nudging her.

'Hey, we've all been there,' Todd said kindly.

'Really, even you?'

'Have you seen many B-movies?'

'No.'

'Good, because otherwise you will have seen my worst acting. There are quite a few of them as well.'

'But you made it.'

'I was lucky. Then, I did work for it; I even married Katie for my career. I would have done anything. But now, it doesn't seem as important.'

'Nope. It doesn't.'

'But that doesn't mean you should give up. You're young and you just happened to be kidnapped with two people who can help you.'

'Really? You'll help me?'

'And Tim as well. Katie wants him to go to this very good rehab place in LA.'

'But it's so far away, and I don't have any money.'

'She's going to pay. She wants to, Thea. This is personal for her, but I'll let her tell you. Anyway, if Tim is there, then you can be too.'

'How do you mean?'

'Well, we can give you a chance. If you're good, then there must be something we can help you with. Even if my career is over, I'm fairly well connected.' He raised his eyebrows like a lecherous old man. 'You scratch my back and I'll scratch yours.'

'Not sure I'm your type,' she quipped.

'No, Tim is more my type than you'll ever be.' Enjoying the honesty of the exchange he reached over and hugged her.

*

'Can I help?' Lee asked awkwardly, as Carla went back to the living room.

'Not really,' she replied.

'Tim's bad, isn't he?' Lee looked really worried. 'Am I to blame? I mean, I encouraged him to drink, and I drank as much as him, or I thought I did. Oh God . . .'

'Lee, he's sick. But we'll get through this,' Carla said sensibly. She wasn't sure if she should be hugging him or hitting him, but she knew that this wasn't the time to have another confrontation.

'I've missed you.' Even with Jimmy there, slumped on a crate, having given up as hopeless any attempt to find a way of breaking out, Lee was feeling confessional and contrite.

'Lee . . .'

'No, Carla, I have. We've been friends for three years, and I always thought of you as one of my best mates. I know the sleeping together thing wasn't right and it also wasn't right that I somehow led you on—'

'You didn't know,' she cut in. She wasn't sure where her anger had gone, but it definitely had.

'I should have done.'

'Yes, you should,' Jimmy stated protectively. Carla was glad he was there. Thea had Tim to worry about, but Jimmy and Carla had a bond as a result of their cuckolded status and their broken hearts.

'I know but I do care about you and now I feel as if there's this barrier between us.'

'My ex-fiancée.'

'Yes, Jimmy, we'll come to that. But, Carla, I do still want us to be friends. I'll understand if you can't.'

'How big of you,' Jimmy snapped.

'Jimmy, it's all right. Lee, I am mad at you but more so at myself. But I do miss you, your friendship. Perhaps we can salvage that.' She was surprised by how easy it was to say that, although she wasn't sure if friendship was going to happen again. Their relationship had been built on deception. She hadn't told him how she felt, and he hadn't acknowledged her obvious adoration of him. She didn't know where their friendship was now, or if it even existed. But this wasn't the time to analyse it.

'Jimmy?'

'We were never friends.'

'True, but we were getting there, before all this happened. I thought.' Lee looked at Carla, his eyes looking for mercy.

'Jimmy, you should forgive them,' she said simply.

'Why?' He folded his arms stubbornly.

'Because right now we've only got each other. And Tim needs us.'

'Oh, what the hell?' Jimmy held out his hand and Lee shook it. 'Anyway, you're better with her than I ever was.'

'Thank you.'

'But if you ever hurt her—'

'I won't.'

'Well, if you ever do, just let me know and I'll thank you.'

'Jimmy!' Carla said, looking at him and then at Lee's puzzled face.

'Joke. Christ, I should stick to being serious; no one ever gets me when I'm trying to be funny.'

'There's a reason for that,' Lee said, with a smile on his face.

'That was nice of you,' Carla said, as Lee left them.

'He'll never be a friend, though, and as Emily wasn't my friend before she was my girlfriend I don't see why she should be either.'

'That's fine.'

'I know, but you're right. It feels better to not be bitter. I'm even looking forward to going back home, to my garage.'

'See, Jimmy, I told you. Now, shall we start digging a tunnel?'

'I'll go and get a spoon.'

'Will he be OK tonight?' Todd asked Katie, as they saw the light begin to fade outside.

'I don't know. He's had some water, which is a good sign, and the shaking seems to have settled a bit, but it might not last.'

Todd had never been this tired. Even when he was filming and working eighteen hours a day (which happened regularly), he had felt better than this.

'How are you feeling?' he asked.

'Like a train wreck. I don't know how I am going to get through this, but he needs me.'

'How about I go and see if we can get some food together?' He felt so useless, never more so than now. Katie nodded.

'Who wants to help me make dinner?' Todd asked, trying to sound cheerful.

'How's Tim?' Thea asked. She was huddled up against Jimmy, and had clearly been crying.

'He's settled at the moment,' Todd explained. He looked around. Carla was asleep, and Emily was talking to Thea, as Jimmy held on to her. 'Lee, come and give me a hand.' Lee did as he was told.

'This is like *Ready, Steady, Cook*,' Lee observed as they stared at the food on the counter. There were two apples, a banana, a chunk of cheese, some stale bread, and two tins of some sort of meat.

'What's that?' Todd asked.

'Oh, some UK game show. Todd, does the oven work?' Todd tried it.

'It all seems to work. We could toast the bread, pan fry the meat, to make it a bit less nasty and then melt the cheese on top.'

'Sounds good.'

'Well, it doesn't, but it sounds better than eating it all like this.'

'You're really normal, you know.'

Todd laughed. 'Normal? And by that you mean for a gay man or for an actor?'

'I meant for an actor. It's weird that we're all here, and you and Katie are really famous.'

'The whole situation is outlandish. We've been kidnapped. Without everything else, that is weird enough.'

'It is. You must think I'm really bad.'

Todd laughed, they were back in the Confessional after all. 'Yup. But then I also think I am. I shouldn't have slept with that guy. I had no idea he'd turn out to be a blackmailer but that's irrelevant. We've all done something wrong, which is why Anne-Marie felt the need to punish us.'

'But I broke up an engagement.'

'Lee, sounds to me like you want everyone to hate you.'

'I'm a bloke's bloke. You know – football, pints, and mates before sex.'

'No, I don't know.' Todd rolled his eyes. 'Do tell me.'

'Well, I would never take another bloke's woman. It's against my principles.'

'Right, so why did you?'

'I couldn't help myself. I think I love her. Todd, I've never said that word to any woman, and I've never thought it and I've never said it about a woman to another man. Don't you see, something really bad has happened?'

'Or really good.'

'Yeah, or really good. But I wish I hadn't caused so much trouble.'

'Carla will forgive you.'

'Are you sure?'

'She's a smart girl, and we've had a chat about it.' Todd was beginning to feel like a camp counsellor among the British kids, who weren't really kids although they were a few years younger than him. 'She's ready to get on with her life. And no offence, Lee, but she thinks she can do a lot better.'

'And if he hurts her – this "a lot better" – I'll kill him.'

The nurse came down the stairs.

'Should you leave her?'

'She's asleep. I came to ask you to bring up some water and also to give you these.' She handed Ed a set of keys.

'What are these for?'

'I have no idea. She said it was her fairy castle. I'm guessing she doesn't actually have a fairy castle.' The nurse turned and made her way back upstairs.

'They are safe,' Ed announced, joining the others and brandishing the keys.

'Where are they?' David asked, jumping up.

'That I don't know. But we have keys, and my guess is that when we find out what they're for, we will find our missing guests.'

'I've never seen these before,' Lily said, examining them.

'Nor have I. I'm going to see Security now. If anyone knows anything about these keys, they will.' He smiled, and desperately tried to convey some hope. They were close now, he knew that, really close. They would get the guests back and then that part of the nightmare would be over.

Lined up in front of Ed in his office were six security men. They were like an army unit, albeit a small one, with the head of security at the front. Their uniforms were immaculate and their faces sombre. He expected them to start marching and saluting any minute.

'Thank you for coming. Now, I have found some keys, and I desperately need to find out what they're for. So, if you could have a good look at them, and see if you recognise them, then I'd be really grateful.' Ed handed the keys over.

The men examined the keys, very carefully, taking their time, before passing them on. Each shook his head.

'Nothing?'

'Mr Smith, I've never seen them before. They don't belong to any buildings in the resort. I'm sure of that.'

'Right. So, what now?' Ed's heart sank; the police would soon be his only option. Then the media would be involved. The scandal would be enormous. He shook his head; he couldn't think about that.

'There are four guards off today. They'll be in tomorrow, shall I call them?' asked the man in charge.

'It's unlikely that they'll know anything. But give me their numbers, please, just in case.' He didn't hold out hope. He wanted to, but he felt despondent.

He didn't want to go back to the house empty-handed. He could imagine Harriet's icy glare and David's hot-headedness, and he couldn't yet face that. He dialled the four numbers. The first three men he spoke to didn't know anything, and on the last call there was no answer. He left a message, asking the guard to call in urgently. Then he put his head on the desk and decided to have a bit of a rest before he faced them again. He wasn't sure how long it would be before it all fell apart on him. Or had it done so already?

'Bernie, Bernie, calm down a minute.'

'Harriet, give me one good reason. They're missing, he nearly got blackmailed and there are quite a few people who know they're not for real. More than should know. This is not a situation that makes me feel calm.'

'Or me. Listen, one of the people who knows is bonkers. The others will keep quiet, but we do have a very real problem. Firstly, we don't know where they are; secondly, if we call the police the media are going to get wind of it. Thirdly, I'm not sure about the state of the marriage after the incident, on either side. But I think they're safe, thankfully, because we found keys. We just don't know what they're for.'

'Are you on drugs? Is that what this is all about?'

'No, Bernie, I'm not on drugs.'

'What do you suggest?' he growled.

Lily raised an eyebrow; she could only hear half the conversation and actually felt sorry for Harriet. She remembered what it was like dealing with these power-crazed bullies, only too well.

'OK. Keep the police out of it for the next twenty-four hours. If we haven't found them within that time, we get the police and you send over a team of top private detectives. We release the story to the press before they get it, putting our own spin on it. Owner of The Love Resort goes mad, kidnaps guests and locks them up somewhere. Todd realises that although he loves Katie, he's actually gay. Katie helped him come to terms with his sexuality despite the fact that she loves him, because she wants him to be happy. They get an annulment but are still going to work together on the film, but Todd will just direct and some other hunk will star.'

'You're a genius. But why should I give Todd his directing job after this?'

'The press attention surrounding it will ensure it's a monster hit.'

'Harriet, no police and no press. Not until they're back here and we can mastermind it.'

'Sure, Bernie.'

'And keep me informed.'

As Harriet hung up, Lily smiled; she was impressed.

'I'm sorry.' Returning to the house, Ed felt personally responsible for the fact that they still didn't know where the keys were for. Just why, he wasn't sure.

'Fucking hell. This is ridiculous. There must be something on this resort that uses those keys.' David clenched his fists; Ed willed him to keep calm.

'No. Not that I know of.'

'It could be a shed or something.'

'It could be. But we have had the grounds searched.'

'Ed, let's go ourselves, just to be sure, and we'll take the keys.' David stood up looking likc hc meant business, and Ed meekly followed him outside.

'Someone knows something,' Mary said suddenly, startling Harriet and Lily, as she laid the table for supper.

'Really?'

'She didn't do this herself. Well, even if she did it herself, someone else must have known about the keys or the place where they are. They might not know much but they know something.' Mary was speaking with authority, as if this were fact, not just her opinion.

'But who?'

'I don't know. But I know someone else knows.'

'Maybe that security man Ed was talking about.'

'Let's hope so.'

'So what's the story with you and David?' Lily asked Harriet, as they tried to eat supper. Mary was staring at them both suspiciously, as if they would find Katie and not tell her. Lily still thought she was amazing, but she was also a little scary.

'No story. He's Todd's brother, and therefore, by default, had to be here. They're really close, and I thought Todd could use the support when we find him.'

'He's pretty cute.'

'What?'

'And he's straight.'

'Yes, Lily, he's straight. But I'm working.'

'I am glad there is one person here who has that attitude,' Mary cut in, glaring at Lily.

'Yeah, but you wouldn't kick him out of bed, right?' Lily teased, enjoying her theme.

Harriet blushed scarlet. 'I told you, I haven't had time to think about anyone like that.'

'So what's the story with you and Harriet?' Ed asked, trying to keep David's mind occupied as they admitted defeat with the search.

'She's my brother's publicist.'

'And?'

'And she doesn't seem to have a personality. She's married to her job and seems to be willing to die for the Studio.'

'She's very attractive.'

David looked at Ed and smiled. 'Yeah, I guess in a corporate-bitch-from-hell kind of way.'

Ed laughed. 'Do you like women?'

'Yes, Ed, I like women. I'm not gay.'

'So, what's stopping you?'

'If you don't mind I'd rather you concentrate on finding my brother than finding me a girlfriend.'

'Understood.'

'Anyway, this place is all about relationships but they cause nothing but trouble, it seems,' Mary said, warming to her theme.

'What do you mean?'

Lily and Harriet were on the receiving end of a lecture. 'You and Ed, there you are running around like a couple of teenagers while his wife becomes a loony.'

'Mary, that's a bit unfair.'

'No, it's true. And then her publisher, Abigail, is running around with a boy young enough to be her son, which tips

Anne-Marie over the loony edge. Then there's your Todd, who sleeps with a man and nearly gets blackmailed. Not to mention the competition winners. So, really, my Katie is the only blameless one here.'

'Christ, it's pretty unbelievable, but I think she might actually be right,' Harriet concurred.

'Well, Mary, if I promise that Ed and I won't run around like teenagers any more, would that make you happy?'

'No, because I know that it won't work. I know you can't help it. And don't get me wrong, Lily, I think that you deserve each other. Anne-Marie was a bad woman to him, and I don't think you are.'

'Does that mean we have your blessing?'

'I suppose so. But I still think there is too much trouble here.'

Dinner had been pretty awful but they'd eaten, because they were all hungry. Apart from Tim, who was still only drinking water.

'There's no more food,' Todd pointed out.

'Then we have to get out of here,' Jimmy said.

'Maybe she was planning on letting us out tomorrow anyway, you know. She might feel sorry for us by then.'

'She might think we've learnt our lessons.'

'Christ, listen to us. I know we behaved badly but this is ridiculous.'

'Let's hope she lets us out – let's really hope so.'

Katie and Todd were sleeping in with Tim again. The others were confined to the living room. Lee was holding Emily as they slept; Thea, Jimmy and Carla huddled together. It wasn't cold but they all felt cold, or they just wanted the comfort that without a blanket or a sheet, they lacked. Jimmy made a pillow with his trousers and Thea's shorts, and Carla rested her head on his chest. They weren't very comfortable but they soon fell asleep, tiredness getting the better of them.

*

'Get the fuck away from me. Oh my God, get them off me, get them off me!' Tim's screams rang out and woke everyone. Immediately Thea rushed to the bedroom, with Jimmy and Carla on her heels. Emily shoved Lee to get him up, and followed.

Tears streamed down Thea's face. Tim stood there, wearing nothing but a pair of boxer shorts, highlighting his too-thin frame, his eyes wide with fright. How had she let this happen? Todd and Katie were trying to get to him, but he was manically waving his arms around.

'Get them off me; they're crawling all over me. Please, please, please. Get them off.'

'What off? Get what off?' Todd asked as gently as he could.

'The spiders, they're everywhere.' Tim fell to his knees. He was trying to brush the imaginary spiders off his body, and he was sobbing.

'Let me, Tim, let me get them.' Katie stepped forward gently. 'Todd, get me the bucket so we can put them in and make sure they never come back.' Todd did as she asked. 'Stay still, Tim, please stay still, and I'll get them off you,' she promised. He finally obeyed and Katie pretended to pick them off, putting them in the bucket that Todd held. 'Tim, honey, I think they're all gone now. Do you want to check?' Tim looked at her, and at his body, and at Todd, who was covering the top of the bucket. He nodded, and slumped back down.

'Thea, I never liked spiders, did I?'

'No, Tim, you didn't. But they're gone now. Todd has taken them away and they won't come back.'

'Will you stay with me, just in case?'

'Of course I will. And Katie will too.'

'Good. I don't like them.' He sounded so much like a child, as he drifted off to sleep.

'Katie, we have to get him out of here,' Thea whispered.

'I know. Thea, it's going to be all right,' Katie said.

Thea hoped she was right, but she had to admit it didn't look good. She was worried, really worried.

'How can you be so sure?'

'I'm going to pay for him to have rehab when we get out of here. I know the best place.'

'Todd said you would. It's really kind but—'

'No buts, no objections. It's what's best for him.'

'I know, it's just that I think I should be doing it.'

'Look, Thea, you will always be his friend, but this I can do easily, and you can't. I can make the decision based on what I've seen. He might beg us not to send him, and what happens then?'

'I give in to him.'

'Exactly. Thea, let me help. I'm not shutting you out or anything like that. He's going to need you so much, but let me help you, please.'

'I need to ask for help as much as he does.'

'Yes, and you know if you're going to help him you have to let go a bit.'

'That's what my friends say.'

'Well then, they sound very wise to me.'

'Katie, you're so nice, all that stuff they say . . .'

'Is all true. But somehow, I managed to find my nice side. It was always there, just a bit buried underneath Hollywood crap. Thea, if you get an audition in LA, and you get a part – which, by the way is no guarantee even with Todd on your side – then never lose yourself, never believe what people tell you about yourself. It's awful, really bad.'

'I'll remember. Katie, I'm glad that you're you now.'

'So am I. I really am.'

30

Security

For your peace of mind, we would like to assure you that The
Love Resort is the safest place that you could ever visit.* Not
only do we have the best security people working here, but this
is also a very low-crime island.

Our security guards are always on patrol and they are the
most alert, highly trained individuals that you could hope to
find.

So please, enjoy your stay with us, knowing that you, your
loved one and your belongings are totally safe.

Guest Handbook

* If a crime occurs when you are outside the resort, on the island,
The Love Resort is not liable.

Ed woke up in a tiny bed with Lily to hear banging on the door.
He got up, still fully clothed, as the others stirred. He opened
the door, to find a terrified-looking security man standing the
other side.

'Hello, you got my message?' Ed asked, as the rest of the
group got up and made their way over.

'Where's Anne-Marie?' The security man looked as if he was
expecting to be questioned by the Gestapo.

Ed knew that he knew something about the guests' dis-
appearance. The guilt was written all over his face.

'Please come in. My wife is ill, and she doesn't remember

anything. Not even me. So you see my problem.' He looked at the others and gestured for them to stay where they were, while he led the security guard to the kitchen so he could find out what he knew in private.

'I don't know anything.'

'I think you do.'

'Well, I do, but I don't know why she wanted the keys.'

'But you gave them to her?'

'Yes.'

'But they're not for anywhere in the resort.'

'No.'

'Can you tell me what they're for?'

'Am I in trouble?'

'No. Not if you tell me. Look, I'm sure that my wife demanded the keys and you gave them to her and that's all.'

'That's right.'

Ed thought the man looked a bit shifty but he didn't have time to deal with that. 'So, where is the place the keys belong to?'

'At the top of the resort.'

'Oh my God. The Americans' bungalow that we secured?'

The security guard nodded.

'I forgot all about that.' Ed felt terrible; it hadn't even crossed his mind.

Lily dived on the phone, as soon as it rang. 'Hello,' she said breathlessly.

'Lily, it's Security. We have a problem.'

Lily felt her heart sink as she looked around at the others. 'What is it?'

'We have about a hundred journalists here. They're all at the main gate and they're demanding to be let in.'

'What do they know?'

'I spoke to them; they say they know that the famous film stars are there.'

'Are you sure that that's it?'

'Yes, that's all they said. But we need some help, Lily.'

'Don't worry; I'll call you back in a minute.'

'Holy shit. What do we do?' David asked when Lily had explained.

'I'm going to have to call the police. The resort is private property, but although we have all our men at the front gate, some might get in. And they're going to be trying to find other ways in too. Hold on, I'm going to get Ed.'

'What for?' Ed asked as he appeared from the kitchen.

Lily explained the situation again; he in turn told her what he'd recently discovered.

'OK,' Ed shouted, looking at the panic in everyone's faces. 'We know where they are. Mary, David and I will go to get them. If we see any press we'll hide.'

He was asserting himself wonderfully, Lily thought proudly.

'You deal with the press. Get the police here, and then get them to stand at the gate, while the rest of the security men sweep the grounds. I think you should also tell the guests to stay in the resort today. You realise that we'll probably end up having to refund these guests, the problems that they've incurred.'

'Ed, does that really matter?' Lily asked, shocked.

'No, I guess not.' Ed found old habits hard to let go of.

'Anyway, Harriet, maybe you should go and give a statement to the media,' suggested Lily. 'Tell them that Todd and Katie are honeymooning here but they need their privacy.'

'It might be too late for that,' Harriet replied. She turned to Ed. 'Look, you go to the house, and I'll call the Studio. I need to speak to them before I speak to the press.'

The sun was just warming up as Ed drove David and Mary in the golf buggy.

'I can't believe she did this,' David snapped, after being given all the information.

'David, at least we know where they are, and we'll be there in a second.'

'She could go to jail.'

'She's mad, David,' Mary pointed out. 'They don't put mad people in jail.'

'I'm sure she's suffering enough,' Ed said sadly. Although maybe the world she was in now made her happy.

'Yes, Bernie, they're all here. We have called the police, but only about the journalists. What do we do?'

'Release a press statement. Dictate it to one of the secretaries, and you read it to the mob there, while we send it out here.'

'Do you want me to make sure they're safe first?'

'No. Just say that they are here on their honeymoon and ask for the press to respect their privacy. Then as soon as Todd and Katie are safe, fly them back with you. We'll deal with the rest when they're in LA.'

'Shouldn't we check with Katie and Todd first?'

'No. Do it now. I want it out within the next half-hour. If you get news of them in the meantime, then let me know, but stick to the plan.'

Lily got all the managers together to make an announcement. She hoped that the guests would find the press invasion exciting, and that they wouldn't make too much fuss. Although, thinking about it, it was the least of her problems.

The doctor came and went straight to Anne-Marie. She wondered what they should do about that. They would have to release a statement about her at some point. She had had a number of telephone conversations with Abigail (who seemed quite delighted about all the developments, which Lily felt was a little callous of her), and they'd come to the conclusion that if she was sectioned they wouldn't be able to keep it quiet. She would be glad when this whole episode was over – when she and Ed could be together properly. If they could be together, properly.

'My God, they're in there?' Mary asked, pointing at the little bungalow, which had prison-like locks.

'I don't know, but this is what the keys are for.' Ed rushed to the door and began undoing the locks. David stood beside him, fidgeting nervously. Finally he opened the door and the three of them burst in.

'Oh, thank God,' Emily cried.

'What did she do to you?' Mary asked. Ed stood rooted to the spot. They were all half dressed and dirty; dust and dirt clung to them. And there was a mass panic going on.

'It's not me,' Emily cried. 'It's Tim. We can't wake him. Please help us. We need an ambulance.' Ed immediately radioed to security, giving them orders. At the same time he rushed, superhero-like, to the bedroom.

Tim was lying on the floor, under a lot of clothes, which explained the nakedness of the others. He was breathing, but also sweating profusely. Ed, who knew first aid, checked his pulse, and his breathing, and finally his pupils.

'He's unconscious but his breathing is steady. I've called an ambulance. Is everyone else all right?' They all nodded.

'Oh my Katie, my Katie . . .' Mary rushed to her and took her in her arms.

'It's been so awful, Mary. Tim is so sick and she didn't care. She locked us up here. Anything could have happened to him.'

'Thank God for Katie,' Todd said. He was holding on to Thea, who was shaking. Mary looked from Todd to Katie and she smiled.

'Todd,' David said, rushing up to embrace him. 'Are you all right?'

'I'm fine. Dirty, tired and hungry, but fine. What are you doing here?' Todd asked.

'And how did it take so long to find us?' Jimmy asked.

'She's gone mad. Oh God, it's a long story.' Just then the ambulance arrived and the paramedics rushed in.

'Are you going with him?' Katie asked Thea.

'Yes, but would you come? I mean, you might not want to, but I'd like it.'

'Of course.' Katie put on Todd's T-shirt, took Thea's hand and followed her into the ambulance.

'We're only allowed to take one person with the patient,' the ambulance man said.

'Do you know who I am?' Katie shrilled, but as she did so she gave Thea a massive wink.

Ed left the buggy there and led them down to the bungalow that Abigail had been staying in. He was leading them in a way Tim would have been proud of, Lee noted, as he ensured that they didn't come across any members of the press. Once in there, after Ed had left, Mary got on the phone and ordered clean towels, lots of soap, and clothes from their rooms to be brought. She then ordered them a feast for breakfast.

'So, you're telling us that Anne-Marie has flipped?' Carla said, as they all sat around eating.

'Yes, they are deciding today if she's going to be sectioned. She didn't know her own husband.'

'I hope Tim's going to be all right,' Emily said. Lee stroked her arm.

'They'll call us as soon as they know. But he will be,' Mary tried to assure them.

'And Mary was right about you lot, so you should listen to her,' David pointed out.

'At least we're free,' Todd said. 'My God, I can't believe it.

Three days holed up there and I'm acting like it's been ages.'

'It felt like ages,' Carla added.

'Oh, and the food left a little to be desired,' Lee laughed.

'You know, I think that somehow I'm going to remember this holiday for as long as I live,' Emily giggled. They raised their coffee cups to that.

'So, you know where you are?' Dr Jonas asked.

'Of course. I'm in London.'

'You're in the Caribbean, Anne-Marie.'

'Don't be ridiculous. I'm in London, the book is called *Love Me, Doctor*. You're Dr Dirk Davidson, and I'm Ella, and I am so in love with you but you feel torn between your professional interest in me and the brain transplant you are going to perform, and your romantic feelings towards me.'

'That is not the case.'

'Oh, you doctors, you always are so very difficult.'

Ed signed the papers confining Anne-Marie to a psychiatric hospital. Lily stood behind him.

'We need to make a press statement.'

'Ed, I'll draft one, we'll read it at the same time as Harriet, and I'll fax it to Abigail for her to deal with the UK press.'

'We have no choice, do we?'

'No, honey. They gave her the most time they could. She needs professional care.'

'That leaves us in charge, you know that. I feel so guilty, but then I feel so angry. My wife didn't even give me the chance of leaving her.' He knew that even if Anne-Marie recovered she wouldn't want to be with him. She never really had. And he wanted to be with Lily. He wasn't going to deny himself the chance of happiness now.

'She'll get better.'

'You think?'

'Yes, in time, and in the meantime we will do whatever is best for all of us.'

'I love you, Lily, and as of now we are officially a couple.'

He gave the papers back to the doctor who was looking at them oddly.

'He's going to be fine,' the doctor declared after tests had been conducted.

'It's just normal withdrawal?' Katie asked.

'Yes, his system went into shock without alcohol. Now, we're going to give him something which should stop the shaking and the vomiting, but in the long run he needs to go to AA.'

'We're putting him in a rehab unit; I'm going to book him in as soon as we leave,' Katie said.

'He's very dehydrated, so he's on a drip and we'll keep him overnight. I suggest you go back and change.'

'I don't want to leave him,' Thea said. She was relieved but also thought if she left Tim then something bad might happen.

'Look, he's sleeping, Thea,' Katie pointed out. 'Let's go back, shower, change and eat and then you'll be far more use to him anyway.'

They sat in the back of the taxi, ignoring the odd looks the taxi driver was shooting them through his mirror. It was only when they pulled up at the resort they saw the press.

'Oh shit, they found us.'

'Great timing.'

'How come we didn't see them when we went in the ambulance?'

'We came out of a different entrance, remember?'

Thea barely remembered anything; she'd been so worried about Tim.

'Don't worry, I'll get you through.' The taxi driver hit down on his horn, causing some of the journalists to jump and the photographers to pick up their cameras.

'Katie, put your head in my lap.' Thea pulled her head down.

The policemen waved the crowd back, and one of the security guards with the actions of an expert lifted the barrier but slammed it down the minute the car was through.

31

And Finally – Returning To Us

Of course we hope that you enjoyed your stay so much you will return again. Not only do we offer you attractive discounts if you do decide to come back, but we also have an exclusive loyalty club which you will gain membership to if you return.

All the benefits of return visits are available to you by asking Guest Services. Register with them now.

We hope you enjoyed your stay and look forward to seeing you again.

Guest Handbook

Harriet and Lily stood side by side. The press looked at them expectantly. Harriet, who was due to go first, smiled, but Lily felt nervous about her forthcoming performance.

'As you know, Todd and Katie Cortes are honeymooning here. It isn't a secret, as you'll have read it in *Movie World*. The honeymoon has been a time for them to be together in peace and they would like you to respect their privacy over this period. As soon as the honeymoon is over, I will call a press conference and you can talk to them yourselves.'

Lily prayed they knew nothing about the fact that they'd been missing, and, as per Ed's call, that they'd been found safe.

Harriet nodded as a hand shot up.

'I just want to know if the person in the taxi that came in was Katie. It sure looked like her.'

'I cannot confirm that at this time.'

'Is there anything else you can give us? Can we have a photograph of the happy couple?'

'No, not at the moment. As I said, they are together, in the resort, but they're on honeymoon and want to be left alone. That's all I have for you right now.'

Lily couldn't hear because questions were being flung at Harriet from all directions, so she just smiled and kept quiet.

'I, however, do have something to say,' she shouted finally, causing the crowd to quieten. 'I am Anne-Marie Langdale's publicity manager and it's my duty to inform you that she's very unwell. She will shortly be taken to hospital, and we will keep you informed of her progress.'

'What's wrong with her?'

'She's, I am sad to say, being sectioned. She's suffering from a breakdown of some sort. Again, I would like you to respect her privacy at this time.' Lily and Harriet looked at each other, and with the questions starting again, they walked away.

'When they get the full story they'll have kittens,' Harriet said.

'They'll be having tigers – big, fat, tigers.'

That evening there was a rare sight at The Love Resort. Katie Ray and Todd Cortes walked into the dining room, going up to guests and greeting them. It had been Mary's idea, as a way to keep the guests pacified. She was turning out to be some sort of genius, Ed reflected. He watched as his wife's resort came to life with their presence. Everyone was so excited to meet them, and they seemed to be excited as well. He smiled. It was kind of like the magic that she had always talked to him about creating.

His five competition winners were also dining there, Thea having been parted from Tim's bedside by the doctor, who insisted that he needed rest. He was much better, she reported, and an unlikely friendship seemed to exist between them and Todd and Katie. He would never have thought it possible.

Anne-Marie was in a private hospital, receiving the best care available. The early verdict was that it would be a long, slow road to recovery for her, and in the meantime Ed had power of attorney over all her affairs, although most were in joint names.

Abigail had told him of her plans and he'd given her his blessing. After all, they now shared an understanding, he thought, as he looked at Lily.

David and Harriet sat with Lily at the bar; the stress of the last few days seemed to be slowly lifting as they began to relax. Ed felt relaxed, even though he felt guilty about that, with his wife locked up in hospital. He had to admit he felt as if the large boulder had been lifted from him. He went to join them.

'I got you a brandy, honey,' Lily said tenderly.

He kissed her on the cheek and took the drink from her.

'Maybe a toast is in order.' He raised his glass. 'To those who are absent.' He thought of Anne-Marie and Tim. 'And to those who are here. To a mad week and the inevitable madness ahead.'

'To the fact that they're safe,' David added, raising his glass.

Ed looked at the kidnap victims. It really wasn't much of a kidnapping, even he had to admit that as he saw them all looking happy and healthy – apart from poor Tim, of course. He shuddered as he thought about what could have happened there.

'To Katie, for surprising me more than anyone has.' Harriet raised her glass.

'To The Love Resort,' Lily charged. 'And to Love,' she added. She looked at Ed, she looked at Emily and Lee, and she knew that even though the others weren't in love, they had shown love by the bucketload.

'So, are you two going to run this place now?' David asked, after glasses had been clinked.

'You're kidding?' Lily replied.

'First thing in the morning, it's going on the market,' Ed finished with a smile.

32

Questionnaire

Please take a few minutes to fill in this questionnaire before you leave. Your comments are very important to us.

Would you say your stay here fulfilled your romantic expectations?

How would you describe the level of service?

Was the food all you imagined from a five-star resort?

Were the staff attentive to your needs?

Would you return to the resort at a later date?

How did you find the owner and brainchild behind the resort, Anne-Marie Langdale?

Thank you for your time, and Goodbye. The Love Resort misses you already.

Guest Handbook

'Welcome back to *The Morning Show*. I'm your host, Margaret Harding, and right now I am joined by Abigail and André, of *The Love Resort* fame. That's some story, Abigail.'

'Oh, I know, it's amazing. And you wouldn't believe it if it hadn't been all over the press,' Abigail replied, smiling, as she and André held hands.

'Well, yes, did you think the press dampened the revelations at all, as everyone knew most of what was going on already?'

'No, because, of course, the book is about a lot more than just that. The whole incident happens to feature in it, but there's so much more, isn't there, André?'

'The book, which spans twenty-odd years tells a story which I think is both moving and touching, and funny and romantic,' André added.

'Yes, and it has been massively in demand, although it's not out until next week!' Margaret clapped her hands excitedly. 'Pre-sales have exceeded all our expectations.'

'And I wanted to ask you, how did your husband, the publisher of the book, react when you told him that you were leaving him, in one breath, and writing a book, in another?'

'Well, he understood that our marriage had run its course, and naturally he was delighted with the idea for the book. Can we change the subject?'

'Did you think you were exploiting people in the book? Anne-Marie, for instance?'

'Although there was no way I could get her approval, as she didn't recognise me, I know in my heart she will be grateful for the sensitive way we handled her story. And I did seek the approval of everyone else that I wrote about, and I got it.'

'Can you believe her?' Ed asked as they watched the interview. 'We didn't get any money from her; she almost tortured my agreement out of me.'

'She did not. She just said that if she told the story we'd be protected.'

'I'm not sure we should have believed her, are you?'

'She seems to have come out of the whole thing pretty well,' Lily replied.

'As did I. I managed to sell that awful resort and I got you. Poor Anne-Marie.'

'Will get better and when she does she's got a pot of money waiting for her.'

'Her career is over.'

'No way. Imagine, everyone will want to interview her. There will be self-help books . . .'

'Lily, you sound like Abigail.'

'Bugger off, although, like her, I quite like London.'

'A bit colder than the Caribbean.'

'Actually, honey, I think it's so much warmer.'

'Todd, Todd, are you there?' Thea stood in front of him, smiling madly at the sight of him in his director's chair.

'Sorry, Thea. I was just thinking about that scene . . .'

'Of course. Listen, Carla just called me from London. Abigail and the book are all over the press. She's sending me the clippings.'

'Why we let her do this I'll never know.'

'Someone was going to. Anyway, we got paid.'

'I didn't, but at least I got the film rights for free.'

'Are you going to make it?'

'I kind of feel really tempted. Hey, if you do a good job on this film you might get to play yourself.'

'I'd rather be Anne-Marie.' They laughed.

'How is Carla?'

'Dating everyone in London, by the sound of it. And her journalism course seems to be good.'

'I'm glad it's working out for her. Does she see Lee?'

'No, thank God. She said she wanted to be friends but I don't think she really did.'

'Right, I'm done for the day. Where's my leading lady?'

'Ah, haven't you heard? She's holed up in her trailer with your leading man.'

'Jesus, it didn't take her long to get over me. Do you want a lift?'

'I'm going to see Tim.'

'Come on, I'll take you. He's so much better.'

'Yeah, I know, but when he finally gets out of rehab he'll be mad that Abigail wrote the book before he could.'

'Hi, Carla,' Jimmy said, after pulling himself out from under the classic Mercedes he was working on to answer the phone.

'How are you?'

'Fine. I just bought another classic car. It's a beauty.'

'With Abigail's money?'

'Yup.'

'Good, because she's on television again. Her and André. Love's young dream. My God, it's so funny.'

'So how's your love life?'

'Jimmy, you never used to be this forward. But it's fine, thank you, and I'm loving the course that I have Abigail to thank for.'

'Believe me, I have a feeling she's going to make more money out of this than we are.'

'Sure, and I spoke to Thea yesterday and she sends her love.'

'Enjoying being a big movie star, is she?'

'Apparently she has only ten lines, but anyway, it's still exciting. Hey, she said Tim was doing well.'

'I wrote to him. It felt weird but I thought it might cheer him up.'

'You're so sweet.'

'I guess I am. Carla, I had a breakthrough. I went to the pub.'

'Emily's pub?'

'Her parents' pub. Anyway, they told me that she's moved to London.'

'With Lee?'

'Yes. They looked really embarrassed, but it was cool.'

'Abigail's on television now, that's what prompted me to call. She just said she didn't believe that they'd last.' They both laughed.

'I can imagine that Emily will be hopping mad. But anyway, I have a date.'

'My God, spill.'

'Oh, a customer just turned up. I'll have to call you back.'

'You rotter.' Carla grinned into the phone as she heard him hang up.

'Thank you so much, Abigail, André. Margaret turned to face the camera and picked up the hardback book. 'Just to remind you, the book is called *The Love Resort – The Demise of Anne-Marie Langdale*, it's out next week, on the fifteenth, and is priced at eighteen pounds ninety-nine.'

'Thank you,' Abigail said, beaming with pride.

'Just finally, your story is in there as well, Abigail, your falling in love with the gorgeous André here.'

'Thank you,' André said.

'You're welcome.' She laughed. 'So, any final words from you about love?'

'Of course. The thing about love is that it can't be made. It has to happen, naturally, organically, magically. It's different from romance, very, very different.' She paused, looked at Margaret, then at André, and finally into the camera. 'Romance can be created, but love, true love never can.'